THE NIGHTMARE BEGINS...

Machen looked up to discern a stunningly attractive raven-haired young lady glaring out of the second-floor window of an ordinary terraced house. The setting sun shone into the whites of her eyes to turn them red with anger and hatred. It was as though there was behind those eyes a tortured soul screaming out of Hell. At the next instant, she threw some object out of the window and cried out: 'God damn you, Dr Black, I will have no part in your devilry!'

The object fell into the street. It bounced once and hurtled up towards Machen. He caught it and discerned a stone, a black pearl embedded in the loop of an ankh and marked with curious lines and incisions . . .

About the author

Gerald Suster was born and raised in London and educated at the University of Cambridge. His first published novel was the cult classic *The Devil's Maze* and he has several other notable novels of supernatural terror to his credit. He has also written nonfiction books on such varied subjects as the Tarot, boxing, military history, the occult roots of Nazism, the Hell-Fire Club and Aleister Crowley. He lives in North London with his wife.

The God Game

Gerald Suster

NEW ENGLISH LIBRARY
Hodder and Stoughton

KINGSTANDING

Copyright © 1997 by Gerald Suster

First published in 1997 by Hodder and Stoughton
A division of Hodder Headline PLC

A New English Library paperback

The right of Gerald Suster to be identified as the Author of
the Work has been asserted by him in accordance with the
Copyright, Designs and Patents Act 1988.

10 9 8 7 6 5 4 3 2 1

All rights reserved. No part of this publication may be
reproduced, stored in a retrieval system, or transmitted,
in any form or by any means without the prior written
permission of the publisher, nor be otherwise circulated
in any form of binding or cover other than that in which
it is published and without a similar condition being
imposed on the subsequent purchaser.

All characters in this publication are fictitious
and any resemblance to real persons, living or dead,
is purely coincidental.

British Library Cataloguing in Publication Data

A CIP catalogue record for this title is available
from the British Library.

ISBN 0 340 66648 X

Typeset by Avon Dataset Ltd, Bidford-on-Avon, Warks

Printed and bound in Great Britain by
Mackays of Chatham PLC

Hodder and Stoughton
A division of Hodder Headline PLC
338 Euston Road
London NW1 3BH

For Michaela

CONTENTS

1: STRANGE OCCURRENCE IN 1899   2

2: STRANGE OCCURRENCE IN 1997   15
(*PUNCH & JUDY*)

3: THE PERPLEXITIES OF A   37
PRIVATE DETECTIVE (*SPOOKS*)

4: AN ADVENTURE IN   61
CLERKENWELL (*PRETTY LITTLE
ANGEL EYES*)

5: THE ADVENTURE OF THE   91
FLAGRANT IMPOSTURE (*IT*)

6: A CRISIS AT THE CONNAUGHT   117
(*BACK TO BASICS*)

7: PECULIARITIES IN   141
PENTONVILLE (*PLAYING DOUBLES*)

8: PROGRESSIVE PECULIARITIES   165
IN ENTONVILLE (*THE HERMIT*)

9: THE ESSAYING OF EVIL (*THE   193
BOY FROM BRAZIL*)

10: BEWILDERMENT IN 221
BARNSBURY (*OUI AND JA*)

11: INCIDENTS OF LIES AND TRUTH 249
(*THE BORE*)

12: THE ADVENTURE OF THE 273
TALKING HEADS (*HEADS OR TAILS*)

13: A VIXEN IN VERULAM

14: THE DANGERS OF 291
DISORIENTATION (*THE PURSUIT
OF POWER*)

15: A WOLVERINE OF THE WORLD 303
(*THE WICKED WOOD*)

16: VISIONS OF VENGEANCE 327
(*BEYOND THE GRAVE*)

17: IMPS IN INFINITY 363

18: CARE IN THE COMMUNITY 369

CHAPTER ONE

STRANGE OCCURRENCE IN 1899

It was dusk one evening in the autumn of 1899 when Arthur Machen learned for certain that books can come back to haunt their authors. He was about to be drawn into a series of extraordinary incidents, laced with unique horror, that his rational mind could not explain in any of the ordinary ways.

There was a dull red glow in the sky, as if great celestial furnace doors had opened, when Machen left his chambers at Verulam Buildings, just off the Gray's Inn Road, in order to walk towards Clerkenwell in search of a good pub that sold good ale that had not been adulterated. He was a slim, clean-shaven man in his early forties whose beloved wife had died recently and he still nursed an aching grief at the loss. His eyes were nevertheless as blue and clear as the rivers and streams of his native Wales still were at that time. He wore a bottle-green suit of velvet and around it had wrapped a black cloak. He was wearing also a broad-brimmed hat, for he always liked to dress with a certain style whenever he ventured forth into the streets of the London that he loved. He carried a walking-stick of stout oak. This was partly because he enjoyed swinging it as he paced the pavements and also in case he ventured into dangerous districts, which he often did for he loved to explore London. But he nonetheless thought it best to navigate its more lawless areas while speaking softly and carrying a big stick.

Machen always liked to go by the unexpected highways and byways of the metropolis and close to Farringdon

Underground Railway Station he discerned a road by an open viaduct that he had never explored before. Having ventured along it, he discerned little of note, just drab and dreary dwellings. Yet, since he was a serious literary artist, he looked at them with some interest, believing that literature could be extracted from matters glimpsed from within the weariest walls; and that every house contains a story, if only one can find it. He honestly thought, having studied the Alchemists, that by the Magick of Literature one can encounter the basest and transmute it into the finest. He was thinking again that every house in every street contains a fund of stories within it, and that he must extract these for his future work, when he heard a woman scream.

'No!' she shrieked and added some obscenity. Machen looked up to discern a stunningly attractive raven-haired young lady glaring out of the second-floor window of an ordinary terraced house. The setting sun shone into the whites of her eyes to turn them red with anger and hatred. It was as though there was behind those eyes a tortured soul screaming out of Hell. At the next instant, she threw some object out of the window and cried out: 'God damn you, Dr Black, I will have no part in your devilry!'

The object fell into the street. It bounced once and hurtled up towards Machen. He caught it and discerned a stone, a black pearl embedded in the loop of an ankh and marked with curious lines and incisions. For some reason this disturbed Machen even more than it would have disturbed any other sane man. His temporary state of shock was probably what prevented him from taking immediate action when the front door opened and the woman he had seen at the window dashed past him. She was followed an instant later by a big, burly man in a tight, ill-fitting though expensive suit. His facial features were distinguished, if that could be the word, by a pair of bulbous chin whiskers, an unpleasant ginger in colour.

THE GOD GAME

The sole action Machen had taken was to pick up the ankh-set stone with curious etchings and engravings upon it and to slip it inside his left trouser pocket.

Machen watched with growing amazement as the woman ran past him, her skirts swishing and terror manifest in her facial features and bodily motions. The burly man who pursued her had a florid fury upon his face, twisting it into an ugly, demonic grimace such as to make the soul shiver. Machen, a Welshman who was never lacking in courage, now strode forward boldly, fully prepared to defend a lady against a monster with his life, if need be. He was nevertheless relieved to see that at the corner of the street there was a hansom cab that had just halted and the lady sprang within as the previous passenger stepped out. Machen breathed a sigh of relief as the cab drew away with its familiar clip-clopping of horse's hooves before the ugly, rampant pursuer could lay a finger upon his prey.

The passenger who had alighted from the cab the young lady had so speedily taken only vouchsafed Machen a brief glimpse of his person. He was a well-dressed, clean-shaven fellow whose high silk hat, long dark coat and ebony walking cane proclaimed him to be a gentleman – but he vanished swiftly into the autumn mist.

Meanwhile, the burly man with the deplorable ginger chin whiskers now proceeded to yell for a cab. But he yelled in vain. Then he began to dance with rage upon the public pavement, the brass knuckles upon his fists glittering in the moonlight. Machen was relieved when he too vanished into the evening haze.

When he finally arrived at the Old Red Lion on Essex Road, Machen sank his first pint of bitter within a minute and ordered another, after which he sat down in a quiet corner of this alehouse that had existed since the fifteenth century to ponder the perplexities of all that he had seen. He felt that this was all too much for a sane man to stomach.

The slow and agonizing death of his beloved wife Amelia by cancer had caused him pain virtually beyond endurance. The greatest shocks, he reflected on her dying day, are generally sustainable upon immediate impact, but afterwards there had come a numb and aching desolation of the spirit. He was beside himself with despair and torment. During the day he fell asleep and during the night he awoke and cried. His writing no longer mattered to him and everything appeared to be utterly devoid of interest.

And then a certain semi-secret Process had occurred to him. The translator of the *Memoirs of Casanova* and the execrated author of *The Anatomy of Tobacco*, *The Great God Pan*, *The Inmost Light*, *The Red Hand* and, above all, *The Three Impostors*, books termed 'gruesome and unmanly', was also a keen student of Alchemy. He did not think that alchemists such as Nicholas Flamel, Roger Bacon, Cornelius Agrippa, Dr John Dee and others were fools wasting their time in fatuous chemical experiments for the purpose of turning garbage into gold. Although he acknowledged that these men had laid the foundations of the modern science of Chemistry, he held that these obscure, symbolic works supplied the reader with keys to the spirit that would unlock the doors of perception. He believed with all his heart that this could be done through a change of consciousness and that the difference between Literature and mere literature could be summarized in one word: *Ecstasy*.

Admittedly knowing little enough of the matter, he had essayed his experiment – and the results were far beyond his expectations. His grief was swept away entirely and he found his every day to be rather like floating in a sea of bliss. When his feet landed on the pavement of his dear old Rosebery Avenue or Gray's Inn Road, he felt as though he were literally walking upon air. A jump of joy in a flower-strewn public square in Barnsbury or Pentonville gave him the same sensation as a leap on a trampoline.

THE GOD GAME

Here and now, though, sitting with his pint in a pub, he felt his rapture to be fading and being replaced by something novel, disturbing, troubling and sensational. For some months he had felt as though he had been invited to the City of Syon. Now it looked more like the city of Baghdad, straight out of *The Arabian Nights* or perhaps the *New Arabian Nights* of Robert Louis Stevenson that had inspired his own *The Three Impostors*.

He took another pint and pondered his situation. The novel he intended to be his masterpiece, *The Hill of Dreams*, had today suffered its tenth rejection from a publisher. Even his friends praised him as being merely a good minor writer. He had a comfortable flat at Verulam Buildings but even at his present modest rate of spending, his money would run out within the year. Then his hand fondled the curious object flung from a window by the raven-haired, beautiful young lady which had led to an obscene chase.

He pulled this *objet trouvé* out of his trouser pocket and looked at it again. Yes, it was an ankh of brass in the hole of which reposed a curiously-marked black pearl. He recalled the conversation he had once enjoyed in a Pentonville pub with a maker of metals when he had been asking how brass was cast. 'Brass is cast,' the good man had replied, 'in the same way it was done in the time of King Solomon, when it furnished the Temple built by the design of Hiram the Architect.'

'Ah, Hiram al Abif,' Machen had replied. 'I think I know what happened to him.'

'Are you on the square?' the man had responded. Machen had assured him that he was not in fact one of the Widow's Sons. The symbolism of Freemasonry fascinated him but its practice did not.

Now he looked at the black pearl embedded within the ankh. Yes, although he claimed to be no expert upon these matters, he could see at a glance that the pearl was genuine. The curious incisions upon it came as no surprise to this student of

Hermetical and Alchemical Mysteries since they all symbolized the sexual union of the male and the female.

Machen decided to put the object back into his pocket since there were further mysteries to ponder too. 'All things end in Mystery' was one of his favourite and frequently quoted sayings of the Mystics before him. He would contemplate it and meditate upon its meaning and significance later, when he went home. Meanwhile, his brain whirled as he tried to understand what had transpired earlier, bringing this precious or semi-precious jewel into his hands.

It was all most perplexing. Five years before, he had written a short story called 'The Inmost Light'. Here his hero, the languid and scholarly Mr Dyson, a charming dilettante, takes a walk in the red, raw suburb of Harlesden and is horrified by the sight of a demon-woman staring out of a suburban window with a light in her eyes reflecting a lust so savage that not even fire, water, air or earth can quench it. Dyson is drawn into a curious chain of incidents which leads to his coming into possession of a stone and of a manuscript. The latter explains that the woman's husband, a Dr Black, a practitioner of Magick and Alchemy, had essayed an experiment by which his wife's soul entered into a certain sacred stone and the daemon of the stone entered into his wife's body. The daemon was what Mr Dyson had seen in Harlesden: something human remaining in the wife's central nervous system compels her to kill herself.

The raven-haired young lady had shouted, 'God damn you, Dr Black, I will have no part in your devilry!'

Arthur Machen scratched his head bemusedly and took another pint. Although his friends rightly esteemed his excellent taste in wine, he often felt that good English ale is the emperor of all alcoholic beverages. Now he contemplated the fact that, in certain circles in London, he was renowned as an expert on the Holy Grail or Sangraal, having studied the matter for years in the Reading Room of the British Museum and having authored a number of articles on the matter for reputable publications such as *The Pall Mall Gazette*. In these he had argued skilfully that in the best authorities, most notably the *Parzival* of Wolfram von Eschenbach, *the Grail is a stone*.

Realizing suddenly that he had not yet had any dinner, Machen returned to the bar and ordered a ham sandwich, the meat carved from the Wiltshire bone, on white bread and with lashings of English mustard. He followed this with a further order for a Cheddar cheese sandwich on brown bread with lettuce, tomato, onion and pickle. Having received his order, he was just about to embark upon devouring this welcome prospect when he was startled by the sudden appearance of a man whom he had never seen before – save within his imagination. He was a portly, middle-aged individual, impeccably dressed in a grey three-piece suit who, to all outward appearances, radiated benevolence and serenity from his bald crown to his short, plump legs. Two features, however, detracted from his pleasing impression. One was the tight, compressed mouth, the lips of which were moist. The other was the eyes: small, yellow, beady, and hooded by fleshy eyelids. He ordered a large malt whisky in a dry and cultured voice.

Machen was startled by the fact that this man bore such a stunning resemblance to the villain of his novel *The Three Impostors*. As Machen munched his sandwich slowly, the portly gentleman took his glass and approached the table.

'Excuse me, sir,' he said to Machen, 'is this seat taken?' He gestured to the chair opposite and Machen shook his head in pleasant but uneasy invitation. 'Thank you, my dear sir.' He sat down and appeared to savour the joys of his malt whisky. 'Pardon my asking,' he continued courteously, 'but are you not, by any chance, Arthur Machen the author?'

Machen put down his half-eaten ham sandwich and hastily gulped from his pint of beer. He was unaccustomed to being greeted as an author by complete strangers and so he nodded a hesitant assent.

'Splendid, sir!' The other extended a chubby hand. 'And what a pleasure it is to meet you. Your exquisite novel *The Three Impostors* must rank among the finest ever written in the Gothic genre of Literature.' He pronounced the latter word with a deliberate capital 'L'. Machen shook his hand, noting that the grip was surprisingly strong, and wondered what would happen next. It seemed as though the characters he had created were coming to life, a feat which perhaps, he reflected wryly, they had failed to perform before. 'Allow me to introduce myself, my dear sir, and I do apologize for this no doubt unwarranted and unexpected intrusion upon your quiet contemplation. My name is Black, Sebastian Black, and I am at your service, sir. May I add only that I am a Doctor of Medicine?'

'The pleasure of meeting you, sir,' Machen responded with the customary courtesy of his native Wales, 'is entirely mine. I also thank you for your kind words.' Inwardly, he was wholly astonished.

'Sir,' Dr Black addressed him politely, 'allow me to request your advice, if you would be so good as to give it.'

'I shall do all I can,' Machen responded with equal politeness, 'though I cannot imagine why you might want it.'

'Ha! Ha! Excellent!' Dr Black chortled. 'I can see, sir, that you are a gentleman and I do not wish to waste your time. Tell me, sir, and tell me true, does Life imitate Art or does Art imitate Life? Eh? Hm?'

'Both,' Machen responded calmly, 'since they both come from the same original source.'

'Which is . . . ?'

'God,' said Machen.

'Ah, philosopher, sir, and theologian with it, eh? Hm?' Dr Black produced a silver case from his inside breast pocket, snapped it open to reveal a plentitude of cigarettes and proffered

THE GOD GAME

it to Machen. 'Take your pick, sir,' he said. 'Virginia, Turkish, Egyptian, Russian and/or Havana!' Machen explained that, much as he appreciated this offer of cigarettes, he preferred to smoke a pipe. For some minutes they discussed tobacco and Dr Black listened intently to Machen expounding the virtues of old shag and American Cavendish. 'I can see that you are a man of discernment, Mr Machen,' he remarked. 'Now, kindly allow me to explain the nature of my question. I seem to have been caught up entirely in your novel *The Three Impostors*. Do I not look like your villain, Dr Lipsius?' Machen nodded bemusedly and gulped more beer.

'It's extraordinary,' Dr Black continued. 'The instant that I read your book, I found myself catapulted into a set of improbable and outlandish circumstances. I am, as it happens, and in common with your character Dr Lipsius, a patron of the arts and a collector of curious and unusual anthropological and ethnological items. My collection is extremely valuable and that is why I employ a man called Sandeman to protect it. He is a somewhat bulky, bovine individual with a thick ginger moustache that flows into a pair of bulbous chin-whiskers. The cultured, I suppose, might call him an uncultured brute but he is very good at his job and he bears a most uncanny resemblance to your character Richmond. Now, naturally I do not indulge in the foul perversions your work attributes to the fictitious Dr Lipsius and nor, of course, do any of my associates.'

'I'm sure not . . .' Machen scratched his head and accepted Dr Black's offer of another drink. He wondered if perhaps he might have stepped into another Universe.

'In my fervent pursuit of Art and artefacts,' the engaging Dr Black resumed his tale, 'I employ agents, connoisseurs of the matter to aid and abet me. One is a tall, smooth, smiling, clean-shaven man who usually wears a high silk hat. In your book, he appears as Davies. You have not seen him, by any chance . . . ?' Machen recalled the passenger who had stepped out of the hansom cab that the raven-haired young lady had caught before he'd vanished into the mist. He thought it wise to shake his head. 'Extraordinary coincidence, eh? Hm?' Dr Black exclaimed. 'For *his* name is Davies, too.' Machen swallowed uneasily. 'And you have, sir, in your book, sir, a most enchanting portrayal of a she-bitch and vixen called Helen who always tells lies. She has a "quaint and piquant rather than a beautiful face, with eyes that were of shining hazel."'

'Well,' Dr Black sipped some more whisky appreciatively, 'it just so happens that my agent Davies has a somewhat wayward sister called Helen, whom I agreed to employ and who bears more than a passing resemblance to your character, sir. You have not seen her by any chance, eh? Hm?'

'Dr Black,' said Arthur Machen, 'I have. Kindly do not play games with me for I do not take kindly to them. And kindly explain to me why, this evening, I saw a beautiful, raven-haired young lady fleeing from a house nearby in abject terror whilst pursued by your man of murderous aspect. If I do not have the truth here and now, sir, I shall go straight to the police.'

'Ha! ha! ha! Excellent, my dear sir!' Dr Black was laughing so hard that casual observers might have feared he would injure himself internally. 'Capital!' He laughed again in Arthur Machen's face. 'And what would you be exposing to the Metropolitan Police, sir? A game of charades? But I shall tell you the truth, in spite of your threats. Helen is a somewhat wayward young lady whom I have done my best to assist. Tonight she has abused her benefactor. She has betrayed, robbed and insulted me. Not for nothing sir, is Helen the name of your bitch-goddess in your excellent story *The Great God Pan*. For she has stolen the Holy Grail!'

'The Sangraal . . . ?' Machen faltered.

'Indeed, sir.' Dr Black clicked his tongue twice. 'We are speaking of the sacred object that passed through many hands before the birth of Christ, though the Christians later misappropriated the tale for their own nefarious purposes. However, through divers sources it came into my hands. I made the mistake of trusting Helen. In a hot fit of temper, she smashed the glass case containing the Grail and ran away. Given the outrage, it is hardly surprising that my good Sandeman pursued her with such vigour. Obviously, you saw him do so. And then I cannot resist remarking on yet another surprising coincidence. In your novel, Mr Dyson and the scientific and sceptical Mr Phillips are drawn into an imbroglio of intrigue that by the end comes to resemble an inferno.' Black's tone suddenly hardened. 'Come, sir, give it to me.'

Arthur Machen pondered the matter for a time, drank some beer and then stared into the beady eyes of Dr Black.

'I do not know, sir,' he replied evenly, 'what on Earth you are talking about.'

'Oh, you *do* know what I'm talking about,' Dr Black returned with an evil leer. 'And please don't try to look so innocent.'

'Please don't try to look so guilty,' Machen murmured back.

'After Helen insulted me, smashed the glass case and ran away,' Black looked thoughtful, 'the Stone that is the Holy Grail vanished. That leaves two possibilities. One is that she is still carrying it about her person. The other is that you have it about *your* person.'

'Sorry?'

'She threw it out of the window,' said Dr Black, 'and you picked it up.'

'There is a third possibility, Dr Black,' said Machen. 'It is in your front vegetable garden, where she threw it!' He was utterly bewildered by the complexity of events. He had recently been working on another novel, *The Secret Glory*, in which a man at odds with the society around him unexpectedly becomes the Guardian of the Grail. He did not honestly know whether the curious object in his trouser pocket was the Holy Grail or not, but he had no intention either of using it for personal profit or of handing it over to the sinister Dr Black.

'Mr Machen,' Dr Black smiled ingratiatingly, 'I don't think that you quite realize my point. Eh? Hm? In your book, your scholarly heroes are drawn into matters which do not concern them by finding the Gold Tiberius coin. Is that not so?' Machen nodded assent. 'This coin, in your tale,' Dr Black continued, 'has been stolen from Dr Lipsius by the Young Man with Spectacles – eh? Hm? The agents of Dr Lipsius proceed both to hunt for the Gold Tiberius and to tell lies – as the three impostors of the title – and add to the matter by telling exquisite tales of horror and the supernatural. Now, sir, the Sangraal came into *my* possession. It will return into *my* possession. It is possible that I have been most shamefully betrayed not only by Helen but possibly even by her brother, Davies. Presently,' he licked his thin lips, 'I cannot trust anyone.'

'I know the feeling,' Machen muttered back.

'Now, sir, one last chance,' Dr Black declared. '*If* you have the Sacred Stone, the Holy Grail about your person, *do* please hand it over to its rightful and legal owner, eh? Hm? For the consequences of not so doing are severe. Do you recall, Mr Machen, the eventual fate of the Young Man with Spectacles when eventually seized by the agents, the three impostors, of Dr Lipsius as witnessed by your two heroes? In any event, allow me to remind you, sir. The artistic Mr Dyson and the scientific Mr Phillips come upon a deserted residence and, on exploring, discover the Young Man with Spectacles chained to a stone slab with live red coals upon his dead genitalia and the smoke of his torment ascending.'

CHAPTER TWO

STRANGE OCCURRENCE IN 1997
(PUNCH & JUDY)

It was dusk one evening in the autumn of 1997 and the sky glowed with a dull red over the rooftops of London as Adam Stride, private detective, prepared himself to see his final client of the day, a Miss Alison Featherstonehaugh.

'Another cup of tea, Mr Stride?' his personal assistant Ms Rosa Scarlett enquired. As he nodded assent, Stride reflected on the irony that the name 'Rosa Scarlett' was reminiscent of the heroine in a Harold Robbins or Jeffrey Archer novel. In fact, Ms Scarlett was a stout and extremely capable lady of mature years with grey hair and glasses. Stride himself was a man in his forties, tall and slim still, whose greying beard and moustache had led some wits to compare him to Mephistopheles.

'Ah, thank you, Ms Scarlett,' he murmured as he received his cup of tea. 'Just what I need right now.' Ms Rosa Scarlett gave him a kind smile and left the room. Stride gazed out of the window and wondered what the next case might bring. He took a genuine pride in his work even though much of it consisted of dull drudgery. He did not actively enjoy the cases which consisted merely of obtaining evidence for an outraged wife concerning the adultery of her husband so that she could sue him for divorce and, with the evidence provided from Stride's snooping, obtain by court order a substantial part of her spouse's hard-earned fortune, though these mundane commissions provided the bulk of his income of £25,000 a year.

He felt tired and gazed dreamily out of his window at the rising moon, hoping that his next client would not present him with yet another dreary and uninspiring case. He much preferred cases involving the curious and unusual, the solutions of which had earned him the respect of the Metropolitan Police, with whom he enjoyed friendly relations.

His office was ordinary enough and situated in Clerkenwell, a stone's throw from Farringdon Underground Station. The nature of the neighbourhood had been described well by one of Stride's favourite authors, G.K. Chesterton: 'The passer-by is only looking for his own melancholy destination, the Montenegro Shipping Agency or the London office of *The Rutland Sentinel*, and passes through the twilight passages as one passes through the twilight corridors of a dream. If the Thugs set up a Strangers' Assassination Company in one of the great buildings . . . and sent a mild man in spectacles to answer enquiries, no enquiries would be made.'

However, there *was* an enquiry with which Adam Stride had to deal on this particular autumn evening. This was when Ms Rosa Scarlett ushered in one of the most beautiful women that Stride had ever seen. The beauty did not reside entirely in her slender face, which was quaint and piquant and adorned by eyes of shining hazel. She wore a fussy and frilly white blouse, although it seemed as though her breasts were threatening to split it, and a knee-length skirt, pleated in navy blue, which swished as he greeted her. He judged her to be a woman of thirty as he noticed her black seamed stockings and high-heeled court shoes of shining black leather.

'Good day, Ms Featherstonehaugh,' Stride said, arising to greet her. His education at public school and Cambridge University had given him manners that were superficially formal and courteous. 'May I offer you some refreshment? Tea or coffee?' In fact, Stride was dying for a pint of beer or a stiff whisky after a hard day.

'Good day, Mr Stride,' the lady replied in a high, delicate, cultured and slightly lisping voice. 'I would prefer refreshments after rather than before our forthcoming discussion, though I thank you for the kindness of your offer. And my name is, in fact, pronounced "Fanshawe".'

'Very well, Ms Fanshawe.'

'Please, Mr Stride, not "Ms". It is "Miss", if you don't mind.'

'Of course, Miss Fanshawe,' Stride replied genially, even though he felt like spanking her. 'Now, how can I assist you?'

'I understand,' said this irritating bitch, 'that you, as a private detective, have managed to solve a number of most unusual cases that have baffled the police.' Stride nodded modestly. 'I also understand that you are considered in other circles to be an expert on the life and work of the author Arthur Machen.'

'Too kind, Madam, too kind . . .' Stride sighed, since this was in fact the case. He had had many essays on aspects of Machen's writing published in specialist journals. His one and only novel hitherto, *The Labyrinth of Satan*, inspired by Arthur Machen's *The Three Impostors*, had been published to modest acclaim and even more modest commercial success. Presently he was devoting much of his leisure time to his attempt at writing a definitive biography of Arthur Machen, his major difficulty being the difficulty of discovering just what had happened to the man in the period 1899–1900 for, clearly, here was something quite out of the ordinary.

'Allow me, Mr Stride, to explain the nature of my predicament,' said Miss Alison Featherstonehaugh. Stride admired her long, glossy, wavy hair that was raven-black in colour. He wanted to say: 'Are you not getting fucked enough?' but that move, however instinctively truthful, would hardly be professional. 'My dear father has just died and left me a few million pounds.' Stride remained impassive. 'Of course,' the lady continued, 'I realize, as you do, that a few million pounds is just chicken-feed nowadays. I might have, say, twenty-three million but the Sultan of Brunei has twenty-three *billion*. So I am just a humble millionairess. However, I am prepared to spend a small sum, let us say a hundred thousand, on ascertaining certain matters. Part of his estate,' she added, as she whipped out an object from her black leather bag, 'is this.' She passed over an object that looked like a brass ankh containing a black pearl upon which various incisions had been made. 'I know absolutely nothing about these matters but my daddy's Will declares that the fabled Holy Grail of the King Arthur legends is a stone, and that this stone reposes here, this black pearl within this brass ankh. Now: the first thing I would like you to find out, Mr Stride, is whether there is any truth in my father's allegations. For, if there is, he charges me with the duty of being this jewel's "holy guardian", whatever that may mean. I just want to know everything about the history of the Holy Grail and the people who have held it in their hands. Naturally, I shall give you all the data I have concerning my father. I simply want to know the truth here.'

'Madam, I gladly proffer you my best endeavours,' Stride replied, although inwardly his head was whirling. 'This is the most interesting problem I have been set in a long time. But where does Arthur Machen, for whose work I have an unashamed passion, come into the matter?'

'Shortly before he died,' said Alison Featherstonehaugh, 'my father told me that Arthur Machen had at one time been "the Guardian of the Grail", whatever that means. My first request, therefore, is that you trace its history, with particular attention to the past hundred years.'

'Miss Fanshawe,' said Stride, 'the Holy Grail and the object I am presently holding in my hand may not be identical. Do you want the history of the Holy Grail which, frankly, can be researched in any library or do you want the history of this particular object?'

THE GOD GAME

'Both,' Alison answered. 'If you can do that to my satisfaction, that will be your first hundred thousand. Now to your second.' She looked within her bag and out of it pulled, not the devastating item of evidence that Stride was expecting, but a packet of Dunhill cigarettes, which she offered. Stride promptly accepted and lit her cigarette with his own chunky lighter. Alison inhaled deeply and blew out two jets of smoke from her snobbish nostrils. These jets of smoke curled in the air as if they were serpents. 'You must see this, Mr Stride.' She passed him a fax which read: 'WE WANT THE HOLY GRAIL FROM YOU' and which had apparently been sent from some Indo-Pak grocery store. Stride thought momentarily of *The Moonstone* by Wilkie Collins.

'Worse is to come,' Alison said, her front teeth protruding slightly. 'I have received threatening phonecalls from call boxes, which I have duly reported to the police, although unfortunately they have not yet been swift enough to catch the criminal. Even so, there is always the same flat, hard voice declaring: "Hand over the Holy Grail or we string you up." Can you not understand my distress, Mr Stride?'

'Of course, Miss Fanshawe,' Stride replied. 'This is quite shocking. But has the caller not made any suggestion for the time and place of the demanded handover? You see, I am thinking of setting a trap. Are there any further clues that might enable me to set it?'

'Yes,' the lady lisped, producing a brown paper envelope from her bag. 'I received this this morning.' Stride opened the package to extract a typed letter and a handwritten manuscript. The letter read:

Dear Lady Alison,
You have absolutely no right to the Holy Grail whatsoever.
The reason is because you do not have the first notion of
how things really are in the Universe. You do not appear

to understand the noble words of Arthur Machen:

'I believe there is a perichoresis, an interpenetration . . . It is possible indeed, that we three are now sitting among desolate rocks, by bitter streams.

'And with what companions?'

'What on Earth do these words mean?' Alison demanded shrilly.

'The writer,' Stride said, 'is telling us that there might be dimensions in the Universe as there are pages in a dictionary. The surprise that he is adding is the possibility that words on page 156 might possibly jump to page 666. This comes as no surprise to anyone who studies quantum physics, for that is how electrons, protons, neutrons and even smaller particles such as quarks habitually behave. It is perfectly conceivable, theoretically, that as we are sitting here we are interacting with another invisible and intangible alien dimension. Although,' he blew out a perfect smoke ring, 'we could merely be dealing with criminal fraudsters, in which case, Madam, you have come to the right place, and I assure you both of my protection and of my best scholarly endeavours.'

'That is all very well, Mr Stride,' said Miss Alison Featherstonehaugh, 'and I thank you for your explanation; but what do you make of the matter that follows?'

Stride noticed a handwritten inscription at the head of the manuscript stating:

'I may be Punch but don't you be Judy!' Then he read on:

PUNCH & JUDY

by

Septimus Keen

Truth certainly is stranger than fiction. I saw yet another illustration of this paradox one night in a Maida Vale bar opposite a council estate. I had gone there for its good beer and also because I had desired to write a good tale about my favourite sport, boxing. As I chased the phrase, searched for words, looked for plot and sketched out dialogue and characterization, I was conscious of another man who was playing darts in the centre of this pub.

'You!' he shouted suddenly at a younger and much bigger man. 'You! You just fuck off out of here and don't come back while I'm around!' The younger, heftier man slunk out of the door looking like a wet poodle. The darts player promptly threw one that hit the bull's-eye.

I carried on writing but unfortunately it did not go well. Both my plot and my prose seemed lifeless. I stared around the pub in the faint hope of inspiration, noticing that a young couple had taken the seat next to mine. They obviously wanted to be left alone so they could just kiss and cuddle but the darts man strode up to them with a pint in his hand and took the seat opposite them. He was in his mid-thirties, with a skinhead haircut, a hard, bruised face, a lean, lithe and muscular body and an aura of aggression. He wore a tight denim shirt with even tighter denim jeans, Doc Marten bovver boots and tattoos. Beneath the knuckles of his left fist there was the word 'Cocksucker': 'Motherfucker' adorned his right. I thought that I might have seen him somewhere before, possibly in a photograph in *Boxing News*. Boxing, at any rate, was the subject with which he was regaling the unwilling ears of the loving couple, who seemed too intimidated to do anything other than listen politely. Since my writing was going nowhere that evening and I always like to meet boxers, I decided to come to their rescue.

'Boxer, are you?' I said, adding, 'Sorry, couldn't help overhearing your conversation.' He gave me a straight look with icy blue eyes. 'Excuse my interruption. It's just that I love boxing.'

'Love boxing, do you?' He grinned, showing me strong, white and undamaged teeth. 'Well, so do I. Mind if I join you for a moment?'

'Please do,' I said and he moved to face me across the table. The loving couple looked visibly relieved and returned to their cuddling. 'Professional, I imagine.'

'You imagine right,' he returned. 'Very professional. Ever heard of Jim Martin?'

'Of course I have!' I exclaimed as his name and face clicked into place. 'You were the British Super-Welterweight Champion around 1987.'

'Dead right, mate.' He smiled and a glow of pleasure came off him. 'Ever seen me fight?'

'Only once,' I said, 'and that was on television. You knocked out the French champion, Marcel Routis, in a magnificent piece of skill, swiftness and savagery. I was hoping that you were going to be a world-beater.'

'Could've been. That was one of my best performances.' He relished the memory and its recognition with joy, then his face became very sad and mournful. 'Could've been,' he added. 'See, it all went wrong.'

'Why's that?' I asked. But at that moment, the final bell rang.

'You a journalist?' he enquired.

'Sometimes. Freelance.'

'Look, mate,' he said, 'I live just over the road. Why don't you come back to my place, meet the wife and I'll give you a taste of some Cockney hospitality. I've eaten. Hope you have?'

I nodded. 'Well, there's loadsa booze. And then I'll tell you the true story.'

'Great,' I said. We drank up, left the pub and crossed the road to the council estate. It was an ugly place where the buildings looked like a set of giant up-ended Kleenex boxes that had been painted puke-green. The lift wasn't working so we climbed several flights of stairs, taking care to step over the dogshit. Graffiti greeted us on every floor. 'NIGGERS GO HOME' was not an inspiring start on the first but the second was better with 'EVEN THEY CAN'T STOP SPRING'. On the third, some bright spark had scrawled:

'HE WHO WRITES UPON THESE WALLS
ROLLS HIS SHIT IN LITTLE BALLS.
HE WHO READS THESE LINES OF WRIT
EATS THE LITTLE BALLS OF SHIT.'

'This way,' said Jim Martin, former British Super-Welterweight Champion as he led me down a urine-stained corridor, turned a key in a lock and admitted me to his home. Some council flats are graced with fine interiors, but this one was not. The kitchen and bathroom were barely adequate and there was only one living room, filled by a big bed. A young woman with long, unwashed hair and a careworn face lay upon that bed, cradling a baby in her arms. She nodded tiredly as we entered.

'My wife and kid,' said Jim Martin.

'Pleased to meet you, Madam,' I said to her and shook the pale, clammy hand she extended. 'I hope I'm not intruding.'

'Nah, don't worry about 'er,' said Jim Martin. 'If she were rude to a guest of mine, I'd belt her.' The wife, who still hadn't been named, returned to the suckling of their baby. 'Beer?' he asked me, then opened two pint cans of Abbot Ale. We went and sat on the end of the bed. There was nowhere else to sit, apart from the floor. 'This bloody country,' said Jim Martin. 'I mean, I know I've been inside – for something I didn't do, incidentally – but they could give us something better than this.' I swigged at my can and nodded. 'Know what I mean about this country?' he continued. 'It's like the bloody Nazis. Can't say what you like. Got no freedom of action. I mean, don't you agree with me?' We swigged at our cans. 'Got plenty of those,' he added.

'It's not *quite* like the Nazis,' I demurred. 'Yes, this country has its faults but there's more freedom here than in most.'

'Give over,' he retorted. 'Don't make me laugh. I mean, you can't bugger any boy unless he's over eighteen, can you? Against the Law, ennit? And since you're gay, that must bug you.'

'What're you talking about?' I demanded testily. 'I'm not gay.'

'You are,' he answered. 'You don't fool me. Come off it.'

'No.'

'You sure?'

'Yes.'

'You're not gay?'

'No.'

'So what the fuck are you doing talking to a bloke like me?' he demanded as his wife suckled their baby.

'I told you. I love boxing. And you're Jim Martin.'

'Well,' he smiled sourly, 'what would your reaction be if I were to tell you that *I* am gay?'

'I'd say it's your affair.'

'No prejudice?'

'I'm not a man of prejudice,' I replied: though I'd never met a gay professional boxer before. 'But your ring career interests me much more.'

'Oh, yeah . . . ?' He lit an Old Holborn roll-up and looked momentarily thoughtful. 'All right,' he sighed at last. 'I reckon I can tell you the truth. I've never told this to anybody before.

THE GOD GAME

I just want you to swear to me on your word of honour that you'll write it down exactly as I've told it to you.'

'I swear on my word of honour.'

'Good man.' He extended his hand and I shook it. Boxers and surgeons have very soft handshakes for their hands are the tools of their trades. 'See, the thing that worries me is that I don't reckon that any bugger will believe me.'

'I might,' I said.

'Okay,' he said. 'Remember a boxer called Hogan Goka?'

'Certainly do. Terrific fighter. British Champion. Came out of Ghana, originally. Always wondered about the truth behind your fights with him.'

'That's what you're going to hear,' said Jim Martin. 'See, when I was young and up-and-coming, Hogan Goka was my main rival. What a fighter he was! Mind you, I was among the best, even if I say so myself. *Boxing News* certainly did. I had a snappy left jab and a left hook that could knock a man off his feet if I hit him right. As for my right, well, I never could master that straight-from-the-shoulder right cross but it was a short and devastating punch. I broke noses, jaws and ribs with that. I was also a wicked body puncher. Head shots look good on TV but you really slow a man down when you whack him to the liver, the heart and the solar plexus. I could move a fair bit and I was good at slipping punches. If somebody did catch me with a good shot, well, if it was a really good shot, I admit I didn't like it – I mean nobody *likes* a really good shot – but I could always take it. In twenty fights I'd never been off my feet before I met Hogan Goka. I reckoned I had everything it took to become not just British Champion but Champion of the World at my weight.

'I trained so hard. Ten miles of roadwork a day. Then I just brushed away my first twenty opponents. Fifteen of them never beat the ten count. Then I got my chance to challenge Hogan Goka for the British title.

'Oh, what a man and what a fighter he was! Remember him? All right, I know he was a nigger – but I'm not prejudiced same as you might be. A man's a man. And wasn't he a flash nigger? Remember how he used to come into the ring sporting that cloak of purple, all decked out in golden stars? Then he used to vault over the ropes and pose arrogantly in front of the crowd. That night he really laid into me during the first round.

'I remember sitting in my corner at the end of that one. My nose was broken and there was blood gushing all over my chest. They were sponging down my face and chest and giving me the water bottle. Your throat's so fucking parched at the end of a round yet they tell you that it'll ruin your body if you drink. You're just supposed to gargle, rinse and spit into the sawdust bowl they put in front of you. Then they gabble advice and instructions and it all seems so meaningless at the time.

' "Which round was I knocked out in?" I asked.

' "Fool!" my manager screamed at me. "Yer still in there!"

'Hogan must've thought that he had me for he came out showboating, shuffling his feet and jutting out his jaw. Fighters dream of a bloke leading with his jaw and I smacked it with a right peach of a punch. I could feel the force travel all the way down to the soles of my feet as he went down and out for the first time ever.

'So there I was, British Champion. It didn't bring me that much fame 'cos who really cares about the Super-Welterweight division? It didn't bring me that much money either since the match hadn't been televised and we were just fighting at some converted swimming baths in the East End. After my manager had taken his thirty per cent cut plus deductions for training expenses, all I had left was a few bob for a few beers.

'There was a prospect of more money, though, via a return match. My manager and Goka's wanted to build the gate. He knocked over a couple of has-beens and never-wases in spectacular fashion and so did I. That includes Marcel Routis, the French champion, who was good in his time but way past it when I met him, to be fair. Hogan Goka also developed a new gimmick. Before his every fight, during the referee's instructions, he'd eyeball his opponent, tap gloves and state solemnly: "May the best man win". This won him many fans.

'Now, during this build-up, I got to know Hogan personally. I tell you straight, there couldn't've been a finer fella who ever laced on a glove. Then, and I know this may sound weird to you, we liked each other so much, we went to bed together, 'cos he was gay too, same as me. I buggered him and I loved every second of it. Afterwards he said that when he'd beaten me and won back his title, he would bugger me. I agreed.

'Don't get me wrong. We were only ninety per cent gay, not a hundred per cent. Both of us had girlfriends. Mine didn't matter to me very much as long as she kept the place clean. He obviously did like his. She was a stunning true Cockney and she was called Judy. She hated me. I reckon she suspected what was going on between Hogan and me. Whenever she'd had a few, which was often, this bint used to scream at me: "I hope Hogan beats the fucking shit out of you! And he will!"

'Obviously I didn't see much of Hogan during the final build-up to our fight. We posed for Press photographs and pretended to hate one another. Usually boxers don't. It's the fight game and we'll pose to sell a few more tickets and earn a quid or two extra. The night came and it was at the Royal Albert Hall in front of the TV cameras. You don't know what "ring-nerves" are if you've never been in the ring yourself. Let's just say that you feel like puking, pissing and shitting all at once. It's just that your bravery consists of conquering your fear.

'It was a great moment to be introduced to the crowd that night as Champion of Great Britain. They roared. Then a very fit Hogan Goka came walking towards me, stared me in the face with his deep, dark eyes and tapped my glove as we listened to the referee's instructions. "May the best man win," he said. His supporters read his lips and cheered. "And now I've got you, chump," he added; "*Chump!*"

'I went back to my corner remembering my word of honour to him: that if he beat me, this nig-nog could bugger me. Well, I didn't want that. The first round was difficult, though. He'd obviously done a lot of work in the gym and had greatly improved his already good boxing. I couldn't get to him at all. He won the second too, picking me off with a snake-like left. The third saw him open a cut over my left eye, after which the bastard kept circling to my left, grinning at me, then adding insult to injury by grinning at the crowd. I couldn't land solidly at all. He was just too slippery and evasive.

'After peppering me with combinations during the fourth, he left me gob-smacked by openly inviting me to do what I'd been dying to do all evening. Standing in the centre of the ring, he waved me in to come and trade with him. We slugged it out toe-to-toe as the crowd roared yet he took all my best shots with – how can I put it? – yes, a joyous abandon. Then he stuck me with one to the liver, just neatly placed below the right ribcage and I dropped like a stone and fell flat on my face.

'My body was paralysed as the referee started counting. Nobody had ever hit me like that before. I just knew that I wasn't going to make it before the ten count – but the bell rang. Somehow I crawled back to my corner. I ignored all the yabbering there. They didn't have anything to tell me I didn't already know. Yes, he was beating the shit out of me and taking away my British Championship. What they didn't know was that, after the fight, he was going to bugger me too.

'I retreated to the ropes as he came for me in the fifth, covering my liver with my elbow. He popped me a few times to the head and I faked it as though I was seriously hurt. As he came in closer to finish me, the referee never saw the thumb that gouged his eye. It was easy, in the clinch, to whip around and into the ropes, though I wasn't expecting the ropes to get twisted and his arm to be trapped there. At that point, I leapt at him and threw everything I had.

'I don't know how many punches I threw at that bobbing head. The papers said forty though it was probably less. Anyhow, I had very fast hands and a lot of power in each. All I remember is this red mist and a head waving very softly up and down before the referee hauled me away.

'You probably read the rest in the papers. Hogan Goka went to hospital in a coma and died three days later. I tell you, I was truly in grief. No man wants to *kill* another man in the boxing ring. I sat for days outside his ward: because his Judy hated me so much, she wouldn't have me in the same room, by the bedside where she was sitting. I just sat in a chair outside and waited, hoping that he'd recover. I reckon I would've given my arse for his recovery.

'Doctors and nurses came and went. Suddenly I saw Judy coming out and staring at me with a chilling and murderous hatred.

' "You fucking bastard!" she spat at me. "You killed him just because you're half the man that he was! Well, let me tell you, Hogan knew the Juju magic of West Africa and he taught it to me and, you fuck-faced sucker, from now on, you're *hexed*."

'There wasn't much I could do generally except express my regrets and carry on boxing. After all, I had to earn a living. Though to tell you the truth, I hid in a hotel that night and cried my eyes out for Hogan. I tell you truly, I loved that man.

'My manager wisely decided to get me an easy opponent for my next title defence. It was Tom Todd and he was a joke. Remember him? All blond hair and poncey features, not like my ugly mug. You know, he just wore fancy togs well and knew how to talk to the media. They built him up as he knocked out has-beens and never-wases, old men who'd do anything to get a meal for the wife and kids. Makes you sick. I mean, my kid sister could beat Tom Todd. He couldn't punch his way out of a wet paper bag. He couldn't break an egg. He's possibly the most useless fighter in Britain.

'Still, I took no chances and trained as hard as ever. When I got into the ring, though, I noticed that Judy Hogan was in a front-row seat and sneering at me. That worry went when I took a good look at Tom Todd. He looked as though he was shitting himself. Now, I didn't have any desire to kill him. I never want to do that to another man again. I just wanted to teach him a lesson, bust up his pretty little face and send him home to his girlfriends.

'He was even easier than I thought as I felt him out during the opening minute. My first left jab broke his nose. He backed away, then countered with two-handed powder-puff punching. I dug one into the heart and his body writhed as he gasped. I started wondering whether I should make it last and give the crowd a show or else perhaps I should make the knockout quick and merciful. It wouldn't take much for him to lie down. He just wanted to get out of the ring and spend his paycheck.

'That's when it happened. I was looking over his shoulder at Judy. *She spat at me.* And suddenly I wasn't fighting Tom Todd any longer, I was fighting Hogan Goka. He came off the ropes with a stunning combination, drove me to the centre of the ring and dropped me with the worst body shots I've ever taken. I puked on the canvas, pissed myself and shat myself as the referee counted ten with all those people watching.

'I'd lost my Championship on a first round K.O. to some poncey little clown. But I tell you the truth, it wasn't ruddy Tommy Todd who knocked me out, it was the ghost of my lover Hogan Goka and the *hex* his wife Judy put on me.

'"How d'you feel now?" she screamed at me as they carried

me out of the ring, all covered in puke, piss and shit.

'"I've knocked out loads of guys," I said and passed out.

'Well, that's the story,' Jim Martin said. 'I was never the same fighter after that – and Tom Todd went out in his first defence against some poofter I could've done with one hand. Life hasn't treated me too well since then, I must admit.' He sighed heavily and drank some more beer.

Shortly afterwards, I made my excuses, said goodnight to Jim, to his wife and to their baby, and left. I needed some sane fresh air.

'You're a good man,' he said, as he accompanied me down the stairs to the entrance. 'Come down my manor any time. Oh, but one thing I haven't told you. That Juju hex taught to Judy by Hogan Goka really did work. I'm stuck with AIDS, mate. And with Judy as my fucking wife.'

'A most intriguing tale,' Stride said as he passed it back to the lady. 'In fact, I am exceedingly surprised, since "Septimus Keen" is an anti-hero in my one and only novel hitherto, *The Labyrinth of Satan*. You don't know anything about this character, do you? I had thought that he was purely an invention of my imagination!'

'Alas, no,' the lady replied, whisking her pleated skirt as Stride inwardly sighed for a whisky after work. 'All I ask is that you investigate it for me and give me the results that justify my payment. I presume you would want some advance?'

'Yes,' Stride answered, 'that is how it is usually done. A cheque with a card would be okay, though, of course, we take American Express and other credit cards.'

'Very well, Mr Stride.' Alison Featherstonehaugh produced a manila envelope from her handbag and placed it delicately upon his desk. 'Here is ten thousand pounds in cash. We shall meet again in one month's time, and I shall not pay you one penny more unless you have satisfactory results for me. If you do, then obviously our agreement stands. It has been a pleasure meeting you, Mr Stride. If you do a good job, I shall gladly pay you every pound promised. If you do a bad job . . .'

'Yes . . . ?' Stride stared into her cold, incurious eyes.

'I shall have your balls cut off and shall personally stick them in your mouth.'

CHAPTER THREE

THE PERPLEXITIES OF A PRIVATE DETECTIVE

(SPOOKS)

Before Stride could recover his composure the infernal woman had departed, leaving ten thousand pounds upon his desk. Stride checked the notes to ensure that they had not been forged and pondered the matter. He disliked being threatened with violence, though that misfortune had been visited upon him on too many occasions. Since he was skilled at martial arts, he had always coped well enough with the *actuality* of physical attack. No man who had ever assaulted him wanted to try his moves again. No man likes going to hospital.

Adam Stride reflected that a sane man might well be tempted to return the ten thousand pounds to Miss Alison Featherstonehaugh. Yet his being fed on challenge. He asked himself how it was possible that this intriguing and exceptionally sexy young lady could have come to see him over a matter so dear to his heart, the matter of Arthur Machen. He also reflected that he was being offered the welcome possibility of a hundred thousand pounds to research matters that he was only too willing to investigate without pay anyway. Even so, how was it possible for Miss Alison Featherstonehaugh to bring him a tale by 'Septimus Keen', a character of his own invention, a decadent transvestite writer and magician of the 1890s? He had invented Keen for the purposes of his own novel, *The Labyrinth of Satan*. It was disturbing to discover that this character was, in some mysterious way, coming to life again.

The remains of his tea had gone cold. Stride pulled a bottle of Scotch out of his desk and poured himself a generous glass as he lit a Senior Service, a taste he had cultivated during his time in the SBS where he had achieved the rank of Captain. This matter was all the more alarming in view of the file in his left-hand bottom drawer labelled 'crank mail'. *The Labyrinth of Satan* had drawn some very odd letters from the reading public, but none so odd as this:

> P.O. Box 666
> London BCM (-)
>
> Dear Mr Stride,
> I very much enjoyed reading your novel *The Labyrinth of Satan*, based as it was upon *The Three Impostors* by Arthur Machen, for whose work I share an equal love. Septimus Keen was, in fact, my uncle.
> Would you be interested in discussing this matter further?
> Yours in anticipation,
> Jacob L. Keen.

Stride had written back, demanding documentary evidence that a creature of his fiction could have mortal existence and in response had received the following:

> P.O. Box 666
> London BCM (-)
>
> Dear Mr Stride,
> Thank you for writing to me again so quickly. Your letter greatly surprised me since I find it most incredible that you claim to have invented a man who goes by the name of Septimus Keen, after my great-uncle. It really is a most remarkable coincidence – you must be familiar with the work of H.P. Lovecraft, maybe something similar is going on here? Perhaps you are, or have been, 'tuning

in' to the vibrations set off by Uncle Septimus in his life, that is the only explanation I can think of. You said in your third numbered point that I have yet to supply you with proof. Yet I sent you one of the few photographs remaining of Septimus (the best one, as it happens). Unfortunately, when it was returned it got slightly damaged in the post and so this time I will be sending you only photocopies instead of originals. Spurred on by your words, I have been rooting around in the loft looking for more 'documentary evidence' to satisfy you so I can claim my royalties. That is why I have not been able to reply to your letter sooner. So far I have only managed to come across two certificates for infant and junior school – I know there are some others. Will this do for now?

How about if you were to come over and look through Septimus's bits and pieces in person? I could show you my loft and we could have a look round in it. Do you like whisky at all? If so we could make an evening of it and celebrate our partnership. Please let me know when you would be able to call around and I will try to arrange a convenient time.

Yours in anticipation,
Jacob L. Keen

He had responded in September but had received no reply as September passed into October. He drank whisky and mused that, given the case of Miss Alison Featherstonehaugh, his projected biography of Arthur Machen and these peculiar documents, it was possible that he might find himself hurled into books that both he and Arthur Machen had created. Further, that which Machen and he had done in their separate fictions could conceivably be done in fact. Then he dismissed the thought as being too preposterous and pressed the buzzer to summon Ms Rosa Scarlett.

'Is everything all right, Mr Stride?'

'As right as rain,' Stride murmured as the autumn rain itself bespattered the window panes which rattled with the howling of the wild wind. 'A small whisky, Ms Scarlett?'

'Well, just a small one, Mr Stride.' Stride had never asked her why she had never married nor had she ever mentioned any matters to do with her personal life. As far as he was aware, she owned a flat in Archway, did not wish to discuss her personal details and performed her job impeccably as she had done for five years. She never asked about a case unless he informed her of the matter, and here he had found her intelligence to be invaluable. He therefore proceeded to inform her of every detail concerning the curious case of Alison Featherstonehaugh. 'Difficult,' she muttered, 'yet also interesting.'

'Indeed so, Ms Scarlett,' said Stride; then he noticed that her glass was empty. 'It is quite a problem. Another whisky?'

'Only a small one, Mr Stride. Ah! Thank you.'

'My pleasure. Now, tomorrow, don't come to the office until you have checked out these documents.' Stride passed her the papers he had received from Jacob Keen. There was no need for him to add any extra instructions since Ms Scarlett had repeatedly demonstrated her abilities in ascertaining by thorough research whether documents were true or false. 'Furthermore, you should know me by now, Ms Scarlett: here is a bonus of a thousand pounds. As I always say, if I do well, you do well.'

'Thank you, Mr Stride.' His clear blue eyes stared into hers, which were the colour of warm, dark chestnuts, as he wondered whether she adored him or despised him for this unexpected act of generosity. 'Thank you very much.'

'You deserve it, Ms Scarlett.' He lit another Senior Service. 'And there'll be more for both of us if we can solve this case. Well, I think we've worked hard enough for today . . .'

Ms Scarlett bade Stride a warm goodnight and, as she left

the office, Stride reflected that she was always adorned in wool. She invariably came to the office in a dress made of wool, her coat was of wool and she wore woollen stockings. In cold weather, she wore a woolly hat upon her head. Stride wondered if, when she went home, she wore woolly slippers. In fact, he thought, the only thing that was not woolly about her was her brain. Stride had never had any patience with those who scorned the intelligence of black ladies.

Lightning flashed and thunder crackled as Ms Scarlett made her departure. At that instant, a police car siren screeched out its news of yet another emergency on the Farringdon Road. Inner-city dwelling had its advantages though it did numb the nerves and so Stride paid that sound only passing attention. The front door was slammed tight by Ms Scarlett, indicating a satisfied female employee who liked her boss and who wished to keep the place secure. Yet, moments later, there was the clicking of a letter box flap. Stride dashed downstairs and found an envelope addressed to A. STRIDE ESQ. Upon opening it, he found the following:

To: Adam Stride Esq
From: You Know Who
Dear Mr Stride,
Re: THE LABYRINTH OF SATAN
Thank you for giving a reader so much pleasure by writing a good novel. The short stories by 'Septimus Keen' it contained were for me an especial joy. I share your love of Arthur Machen's writings since he was a good friend of mine.

If I may say so, you have made some serious errors in your otherwise laudable work. You pass off the Septimus Keen matter as though it was a literary joke on your part. You attribute your own short tales to Septimus Keen, a character whom you claim to have invented, at least you so claimed in the course of a correspondence with me in which I pretended to be my own nephew, Jacob Keen.

For, you see, I am not dead. I am very much alive, having studied and practised the Arts and Sciences of Alchemy and Vampirism so as to discover the Elixir of Life. Without your knowing it, I inspired you to write the tales you attributed to Septimus Keen.

You obviously thought the whole book to be proof of your own imaginative ingenuity. Allow me to assure you, my dear sir, that it is nothing of the kind. You thought that Septimus Keen was merely an invention of your own teeming brain and that *The Three Impostors* were but an invention of Arthur Machen upon which you proceeded to capitalize. Did you not realize that you were actually describing *realities*?

I can show you things such as you have never seen before. I am going to take you by the scruff of your stiff neck and give your life a shaking. If you do not believe me, I dare you to go to the Three Tuns in Clerkenwell, just around the corner from you, where you can be given more information about Septimus Keen – assuming, of course, that you have the courage to face realities that you have so far denied. Be there at 8:00 p.m. this coming Thursday, the day after tomorrow, should you wish to improve your understanding.

Yours sincerely,
Septimus Keen.

PS: I enclose the real thing.

SPOOKS

by

Septimus Keen

The rain hissed upon the pavements on the evening following Alan's funeral. It was a foul night and the afternoon in Hertfordshire had been dank and abominable. I had never known his family and I only knew one of his friends. Edward kindly offered me a lift back to London and then suggested a drink in Hampstead. I needed one.

As we left the car and walked to the pub, I noticed an ageing moon that had all the appeal of molten tallow. The pub itself was warm and friendly enough, one of the last outposts of bohemia in an area that had embraced the tawdry values of yuppiedom and thus had lost all its original character. Edward bought a couple of pints from the barrel on the bar. It had been Alan who had introduced us. He'd been at school with Edward and then at university with me. Subsequently he'd pursued a highly successful career in television. Edward and I had both endeavoured to write books. Mine had been published and his had not. He had responded to that by studying Law and had been called to the Bar two years before, where he now made a far better living than I did. Meanwhile, Alan had been earning more in two months than both of us in one year combined. As a star reporter and later as a star producer, he had gone to investigate the trouble spots of the world. Unfortunately, in the Sudan his jeep had run over a landmine and he'd been blown sky-high. Edward and I had just witnessed the burial of the pieces that had been left and after the funeral we had refrained from talking about Alan on the car journey back to London. We waited until the pub.

'Going back to Alan . . .' Edward said as he presented me with beer and sat down opposite me.

'Yes, going back to Alan . . .' And we proceeded to reminisce about his undeniable achievements. Edward recalled his splendid captaincy of the Second XI Cricket Team at school. I recalled his equally impressive captaincy of the College Second XI at football, also the skills he had had in academic matters – he secured a First at Cambridge – and his willingness to participate in amateur dramatics. We both agreed that in later years he had achieved his ambition to create, in his own words, 'absolutely first-class television'. His investigations of Northern Ireland and the Lebanon had been particularly notable. His death had been a grave loss. We were sorrowful and we tried to talk about something else, only we had run out of beer.

'Going back to Alan . . .' I said as I presented Edward with another pint.

'Yes, going back to Alan . . .' he responded; and we reminisced about the excellence of his intellect, the sharpness of his wit and his fierce determination to succeed.

'Do you remember that time,' I said at one point, 'when the three of us went walking on Hampstead Heath together and he said that he could never, ever commit suicide, because if one holds on for just one week, there is every chance that it will get better?'

'Yes,' Edward said, 'but if I recall it rightly, you were very depressed that day and he even refused to give you a lift down the road. Another beer?'

Over that one, we started to remember just how awful Alan could be. We discussed all the times he'd made a fool of himself with women, the times he'd refused to help Edward and the times he'd refused to help me. Over a fourth pint, we joked about how awful he could be socially. As the final bell rang, Edward said: 'Let's face it. He was a shit.'

At the time I was living in Kilburn and I used to go to a rather plain, rough 'n' ready pub in the High Road. I'd come into this harsh, simple place for a Guinness after work, as usual. I'd taken my seat and was contemplating all that I had written that day, and then, just as Barleycorn's 'Fields of Atheney' came on the jukebox, I thought I saw a familiar face.

He was sitting alone at a table and drinking a pint of lager. He hadn't changed at all since I had last seen him. There was the thick, well-combed and neatly parted brown hair, the 'intellectual' glasses and the supercilious smile. There was a blazer, the quiet pale blue shirt, the royal blue scarf and the beige cavalry twill trousers. He was still wearing chukka boots on his feet. This could not possibly be an hallucination: though perhaps there *was* someone in London who looked exactly like Alan. I went and sat opposite him.

'Hello,' he said. 'How nice to see you after all this time.'

'Alan . . . ?' I choked on my Guinness.

'The same.' He smiled his familiar supercilious smile.

'But I thought you were . . .'

'Dead?' He finished my sentence. 'Well, don't tell anybody,' his eyes flicked around the pub, 'but I am, actually. And, frankly, it's not very interesting.'

'I don't know what to say . . .'

'Hardly surprising,' he murmured, 'but perhaps you'd like another Guinness?'

I sat there dazedly as he bought another round.

'One can't really recommend death,' he remarked easily as he came back from the bar with the beers. 'Thanks a lot for coming to my funeral, by the way. Much appreciated. Cheers!' He lit a Marlboro, always his favourite brand. 'You're probably wondering why I've come back.'

'Yes.' I nodded. There wasn't much else I could do or say.

'Do you remember our discussions about life after death?'

'Yes.'

'And if I recall it rightly,' he licked his lips which was a habit of his, 'you always declared your belief that there is life after death . . . ?'

'Yes . . .' I swallowed hard.

'And I didn't think so.' That was true. 'But the fact is that there *is* life after death. I know that. I died. Got blown up in a jeep that ran over a landmine in the Sudan. Dead, dead, dead. But I've come back to tell you that there's life after death. I don't care if you don't believe me. Here it is.' He smirked quite infuriatingly. 'What I'd like you to do,' he continued, and I was very glad that he continued since I was utterly lost for words, 'is bring Edward here to meet me at this time of the evening precisely one month from this date. And for proof,' he smiled, 'here are two marbles from the dead. 'Scuse me, just have to go to the loo.'

I stared dumbly at the two marbles in my hand as Alan departed from the bar and went to the loo. They were plain, ordinary marbles, the sort that a relative might give to a child when short of money. Meanwhile, twenty minutes passed and Alan did not come back. I went to the loo. There was nobody there, though the window was open.

'This is the most preposterous story I've ever heard,' Edward said when I met him in a Fleet Street pub a few days later. Here the beer was awful and the place was packed with besuited men who brayed loudly about nothing. 'Surely you're not seriously saying that Alan's come back from the dead?'

'I'm telling you what he told me. Look: here are the marbles he gave me.'

'Well, I can't possibly accept this nonsense,' Edward said as he handed the marbles back to me. 'People don't come back from the dead and act like that.'

'Then how do they act?'

'Not like that.'

'Expert, are you?' I enquired. 'Look, are you prepared to come and see him on the date he suggested?'

'Yes, I am,' he replied, 'for one's got to keep an open mind after all. But I don't believe in ghosts at all. I find it quite impossible to believe that somebody who's dead could come back to life and drink beer and smoke cigarettes with you. There're two rather more plausible explanations. One is that Alan was doing work for the Secret Service. This would square with his TV work in Northern Ireland and the Lebanon. It's not impossible that the Secret Service could've faked his death. What's he doing in Kilburn? Obviously he's investigating the IRA in what the cab drivers call "Little Dublin". You say that he vanished suddenly but that the lavatory window was open. Rather obvious, isn't it? Of course I'll be there to see him on the date he suggested. Be an absolute delight to see the old bugger again.' Edward grinned. 'And he gave you two marbles? Don't lose your marbles.'

I was there at the Kilburn High Road pub on the night Alan had dictated and there he was, sitting comfortably in a corner. I hadn't been there since the last time I'd seen him.

'Awfully good to see you,' he smirked smugly. 'Is Edward coming?'

'Should be here shortly,' I said.

'And you've still got your marbles?' I nodded. They felt rock-solid in my right trouser pocket. 'Good,' said Alan. 'You see, the trouble with a chap like Edward is that he's all right in his way, but he simply doesn't see reality. I want him to see it for just one moment in his life. Here,' he passed over an Instamatic camera from a canvas bag beside him. 'Take a photo.' I noticed a flashlight attachment. 'Take two,' he added. He then posed genially and I shot two photographs. 'Keep the camera and the film,' said Alan, 'they're not much use to me now that I'm dead – but the proof could be very amusing. Anyway, do stop being such a bore, since it's your round. Mine's a Tennant's Extra.'

I walked to the bar and bought the drinks. When I turned

around, I saw that Alan had gone, presumably to the loo. Edward was sitting in his seat. I greeted him and bought him a pint.

'Alan should be out in a moment,' I said. 'He's just gone to the loo. Presumably you saw him as you came in.'

'No,' Edward replied.

'Well, he was here a moment ago . . .' I coughed. 'Excuse me a moment.' I headed straight for the door marked 'GENTLEMEN'. Someone had puked into the urinal and it stank to high heaven. All the windows were closed from the inside.

Alan did not return that evening and I had to endure ribbing from Edward. It was obvious that he didn't believe me.

'How much are you drinking these days?' he asked me at one point.

'The marbles!' I shouted. 'He gave me the marbles!' Then I put my hand inside my right trouser pocket only to discover that the marbles had gone.

'You were saying . . .' Edward murmured.

It was not a successful evening. Edward clearly disliked the pub and made no secret of the matter. He spoke about a £20,000 brief he'd just received for something at the Old Bailey, involving a mere five days of work. Meanwhile I was contemplating the prospect of signing on the dole. He made his excuses and left as soon as he decently could. I took another Guinness.

'All right?' the barmaid asked as she poured it for me.

'Sure,' I said.

'Nothing wrong with a man talking to himself in a pub, that's what I always say,' she declared. 'Writer or artist, are ye?'

'Tell me,' I enquired, 'have you ever seen a friend of mine in this pub who's got thick, brown, well-combed hair, "intellectual" glasses and who dresses quite conservatively?'

'No, never seen him,' she replied, 'never seen the fella. But if you want to talk to yeself, that's all right in this establishment just so long as ye don't harm the other customers.'

I drank up and went home quietly that night. When I arrived back at my Kilburn bedsit I noticed that I'd forgotten to throw away a Christmas card from Alan that was standing in a dusty corner atop my bookshelves. It had been signed with the message: 'See you again soon', just a couple of months before he died. I also found the marbles that he'd given me underneath my pillow, but when I told my girlfriend the story she said that I'd merely been careless. Whenever I pointed out the facts that Alan had given me a camera and that I'd taken two photographs of him at his request, she replied that the camera no longer worked and that the photographs had not come out.

Adam Stride pondered the matters before him with a growing mixture of suspicion and bewilderment, feelings that Ms Rosa Scarlett had not evinced upon her own face. There seemed to be absolutely nothing in the world that could trouble Ms Scarlett. Stride felt that if a hideously mutilated corpse were shown to her, she might have no comment to make other than: 'Strange that the liver is missing.' He decided there and then to give the imperturbable Ms Scarlett greater involvement on this most perplexing case.

He stared moodily around his very ordinary office as he poured himself another whisky. Miss Alison Featherstonehaugh had vanished so swiftly after making her threat that he had for once lost his presence of mind, and so did not have the slightest idea where she might be living. All he had as proofs of her existence were nine thousand pounds in cash and the brass ankh which contained a black pearl within its loop. He had been given a month to come up with some information useful to his client and the promise of a further ninety thousand pounds if he succeeded in the matter. He had also received a most unpleasant threat of even more unpleasant punishment were he to fail.

The initial, material stages of the case appeared to be relatively easy: he would give Miss Alison Featherstonehaugh a digest of all research upon the Holy Grail to be found in the British Library. He would also track the legend of a stone purporting to be the Grail or related to it, a stone which, apparently, he now held in his hand. He would alert all his contacts, on both sides of the law, to the fact that some criminal or occult grouping was threatening a lady who allegedly held some precious gem in her possession. (Although, he mused, this responsibility appeared at present to have passed temporarily to him.)

Then there was the matter of protection for his client. Given the sum offered, Stride would happily have subcontracted this matter to reliable men. Yet she had not specifically asked for protection and, since he did not know where she lived, it would not be possible to protect her anyway. She had complained about threats; yet she had also threatened him. It was a problem made all the more perplexing by the matter of Septimus Keen. Alison had handed him a story by 'Septimus Keen', a character he had believed himself to have invented in his own novel, *The Labyrinth of Satan*; and yet here was another Septimus Keen tale dropped through his doorway. 'O, by whom?' Shakespeare had written in *Macbeth*. The intriguing Alison had meanwhile departed leaving no address nor a precise date for another appointment. However, Stride thought, she could hardly have casually left him holding the Holy Grail. Perhaps this was merely a sick joke in bad taste, in the same vein as Alison's parting words. Stride was used to the curious ill humours of some of his clients, especially those who had money to splurge upon whims and self-indulgence.

'*Who shall roll away the stone?*' he mused – and then came the abrupt ring of the doorbell. Springing down the stairs with an athleticism unusual in a man of his years, Stride opened the door to admit a strikingly beautiful young woman. 'Antonina!' he exclaimed with pleasure. 'What an unexpected pleasure!'

'A pleasure to see *you*, Adam,' said this tall buxom blonde, who was dressed entirely in gleaming black leather and whose skirt clung to her voluptuous hips and slender thighs as though it was a second skin. Stride was only too happy to offer her a whisky and Antonina was only too pleased to accept.

Antonina was one of the strangest women whom Stride had ever met. He had done so whilst sitting next to her at a blackjack table in the Palm Beach Casino Club of the Mayfair Hotel. Both of them were winning by playing the same system: the table states clearly 'Dealer must draw on 16 and stand on 17'. He and Antonina had proceeded to play by precisely that rule, which also included a stand-off if the dealer and the punter had precisely the same score. Stride believed that if one played by the House system this would narrow the House percentage, after which all depended on the cards dealt to one by Lady Luck. As it happened, they had both been favoured by the cards that night and so had departed from the table several hundred pounds the richer, after which she had accepted his invitation to go back to the one-bedroom flat above his office. Whereupon they had enjoyed a sensational sexual session.

Subsequently he had developed a most satisfying relationship with Antonina and learned more of her life. By day, she earned her living as a computer expert, specializing in solving virus problems that can plague information technology and working as a freelance principally employed by the Inland Revenue and the Department of Social Security. In the evening she went to the gym to practise aerobics and martial arts. By night she enjoyed visiting sadomasochistic clubs where she took much joy in whipping men who had visited the premises for precisely that purpose. This was not to the sexual taste of Adam Stride but he found the whole matter to be highly amusing. On this particular evening, Stride fucked her upon the floor of his office in a rather brusque though friendly fashion.

'That was good,' she said as she smoothed down her leather skirt. Then she glanced at the carpet. 'What *will* the cleaners say, though?'

'They'll turn to Ms Scarlett and wonder aloud what on Earth I have been up to.'

'Have you never been told,' she answered, 'that you should not end a sentence with a preposition?'

'I concur with Winston Churchill,' Stride replied. 'This is

the sort of English up with which we will not put. Look, that was a good quickie, darling . . .' He stared into her eyes, which were a curious mixture, no, a *compound* of blue and gold. 'Will you help me? Are you on for an adventure?'

'Darling Adam.' She fluttered her heavily blue-shadowed eye-lids. 'I am *always* on for an adventure. Tell me more.' Stride gave her a warm smile since he genuinely liked her. Ever since his divorce of ten years before, he had enjoyed seducing women and presently he was happy with his relationship. From Friday night to Monday morning, they stayed together, either at his flat upstairs or else at her flat in Maida Vale. Once a week they had dinner and made love together at whichever place was more convenient upon leaving the restaurant. Stride proceeded to tell her over another whisky an edited version of all that had happened.

'You know from my *Labyrinth of Satan* how I told the lie about Septimus Keen so convincingly,' he said, 'that for years I have received letters from earnest young students asking for more information to assist their proposed A-level, BA, MA or even PhD theses on the intriguing minor writer of the 1890s, Septimus Keen? It has always pained me to inform them regretfully that he is purely a creature of my own imagination.'

'This is nuttso,' said Antonina. 'The whole thing is loopy. And now you want to go to some lunatic meeting?'

'Probably,' Stride replied, 'but I never can resist a challenge. You know me by now. I'm always on for an adventure. Let's go to this pub, the Three Tuns and see what happens. We shall enter separately and you can cover me. If he turns out to be a psycho, I can take care of him. Can I get a witness?'

'Okay,' she said. A woman who has in the past dared the Hell's Angels of Berkeley, California to play chicken by lying down on the rails in front of an oncoming freight train, thereby becoming a Mother to their Chapter, was, Stride thought, likely to be a first-class partner in a potentially tight situation. 'Can

I take a look at this stone you mentioned?' Stride passed it to her and watched eagerly as she stared at it. 'If this *is* the Holy Grail,' Antonina murmured, 'what the fuck is this bitch doing loaning it to you? Have you checked your wall-safe? Horseshit! This is weird . . . I keep seeing pictures inside this black pearl. Aargh! What *is* this fucking thing? Oh, for fuck's sake, Adam, I'm tired tonight and I don't need this. I'll look at it over the weekend, okay? Take a look for yourself.'

'All right.' Stride took the ankh containing the black pearl from her hand, noticing meanwhile her long, scarlet talons. 'I hope you'll be able to stay the night . . . ?'

'I was going to a club to whip some wankers,' Antonina answered, 'an activity which I so enjoy that I do it free, gratis and for nothing. What I saw in that stone has so disturbed me that I would honestly prefer to stay here with you, if that is what you would like. My sole condition is: can we have a takeaway pizza?'

'Yes, of course, darling,' Stride murmured absent-mindedly as he gazed at the black pearl within the brass ankh. 'Just dial them from the card on my desk. The Elephant Crispy Pizza is especially good, though you might prefer the Sea Lion or the Meaty Bull. Porky Pig might be fine too, or else . . .' His voice trailed away as he held the ankh in his hand and stared at the stone. At first it was simply a black pearl with crude incisions that signified the union between a man and a woman. He was vaguely conscious that in the background Antonina was ordering a pizza; then he fell into a curious reverie in which his vision blurred. For an instant, he felt as though he were watching some weird sort of television: for there was his favourite writer, Arthur Machen, whose visage he knew from photographs he'd seen. Machen was frowning with a manic intensity of concentration, then appeared to be suddenly startled before vanishing suddenly. It was as though a TV programme had been cut off abruptly.

'This is all too much,' Stride murmured. 'Too much for one day. Excuse me a moment...' He dashed to his lavatory for a genuine call of Nature but also because his safe had been installed there by a professional safe-cracker, an ex-SAS man and old buddy of his, and it was hidden beneath the floorboards and the linoleum. He stashed the gem in this hiding place. 'Study it tomorrow,' he muttered through gritted incisors as he returned to his office to find Antonina helping herself to another Scotch. 'Well, Antonina,' he declared with a genial grin, 'as Shakespeare has it, "There are more things in heaven and earth, Horatio, Than are dreamt of in your philosophy..." How true, huh? Antonina...' The phone rang.

'Always at the wrong time,' Stride groaned. 'Will you get it?' he asked Antonina and added grumpily: 'Find out who it is and tell him I'm in – unless it's some useless bore.' Antonina took the call and looked distinctly disturbed as she replaced the receiver. 'Well?'

'I do not know whether it was a male or a female,' she informed him. 'Whoever it was announced the name of *Septimus Keen*, declared that *Stride's life is on the line* – and hung up.'

'All the more reason to meet a maniac on Thursday,' Stride replied. 'Anyway, let's have our pizza, whenever it eventually arrives, and then let's go to bed for the best moment of the day.' His deepest desire at that moment was simply to hold her naked body within his strong arms and to feel her warmth, her heart beating against his.

'I'd like that,' she answered, 'to hell with going to clubs. To hell with diamonds. To hell with the spades that bury the dead. I prefer hearts.' Yet she failed to hide the unease of her tone.

'Oh, nothing to worry about if it's just some crank,' he retorted breezily – and the doorbell rang. 'Ah! Pizza! Not cardboard here, I can tell you! The base is *the real thing*: crisp and crunchy. My honey, I think you'll see what I mean. Excellent, firm... be with you in a moment.'

Stride had expected to open his door to a pizza courier. Instead he saw that something else had just come through his letter box. Initially he thought it was a red parcel such as he often received from his old Aunt Agatha acting in conformity with the slogan 'Post Early for Christmas'. So he expected to pick up a boring red box of socks.

Then he thought of Arthur Machen's story 'The Red Hand' as he saw that a severed, bloodied hand had been dropped right on his doormat.

CHAPTER FOUR

AN ADVENTURE IN CLERKENWELL
(PRETTY LITTLE ANGEL EYES)

Stride called the police instantly but the incident turned out to be exceedingly embarrassing. As Antonina and he had ascertained before the cops' arrival, the 'Red Hand' dropped through his letter box was, in fact, a plastic hand garnished with red ink.

'Now, let me get this straight, sir,' said the crew-cut PC Woodhams, who was accompanied by a yawning WPC Brown. He consulted his notes with the manner of a man who feels that his time is being wasted but who is too polite to say so. 'You have written a book,' this stolid, thickset man continued, 'called – er – *The Labyrinth of Satan*,' he swallowed uneasily, 'in which you have invented a character called Septimus Keen.' Stride nodded assent. 'You have since received a letter and a phone call from somebody claiming to be this – um – Septimus Keen of yours, inviting you to join him for a drink at the Three Tuns in Clerkenwell, just off the Farringdon Road by here, this coming Thursday. Is that right?' Stride again nodded his assent.

'Meanwhile,' WPC Brown interposed, ' a plastic hand bought from some joke shop and covered in red ink has been dropped through your door.' Stride nodded once more. WPC Brown was a slim young woman with blond hair, a pert face and hard, sceptical, ice-blue eyes, and whose voice came out of the top of her snub nose. 'Do you feel threatened?' Stride felt as if she was a primary schoolteacher asking if he was worried because some boy in the playground had said 'Boo!' to him. He shook his head. 'With all respect, sir,' she smiled condescendingly, 'it's not a crime to throw a plastic hand through a letter box even if the item concerned is covered in red ink. It's children, probably, what with it being close to Hallowe'en. I mean, it's hardly Malicious Damage.'

'Oh, I don't want to waste your time, officer,' Stride replied, biting his tongue to restrain him from telling them that Arthur Machen's story 'The Red Hand' was, among other things, about an occult group that commits the foulest of sacrificial murders. 'I just thought it best to have the matter reported and logged. After all, one can't be too careful these days. So many nutters around . . .'

'Quite right, sir,' the two police constables agreed, regarding Stride as if he was a nutter himself.

'But the matter should be recorded,' Antonina insisted anxiously.

'It will be, Madam,' PC Woodhams answered wearily as he contemplated the unpleasant prospect of at least twenty forms of paperwork. He looked as though he had spent the past week being pelted with stones by violent thugs on some lawless council estate, opening up the boots of cars to discover chopped-up, bloodied bodies, and entering flats to contemplate the corpse of a raped old age pensioner, tortured to death for the 93p in her purse. 'You see, we can't do much unless something against the law that's *serious* has actually been done. Now, if I were you, sir,' he turned to Stride, 'I would leave this proposed meeting at – er – the Three Tuns well alone. Does no good to mix with cranks, you take my word.'

WPC Brown gave Stride a disdainful glance that stated her own views concerning this case.

On the following morning, Stride went to the British Library to pursue essential research. Walking inside that beautifully built Dome of the Reading Room never failed to stimulate him. One could sense the presence of ghosts such as the conservative Thomas Carlyle or the communist Marx – and, indeed, Arthur Machen. There were men who looked as though they had been living there for thirty-five years. One saw a scholar open a dusty tome and was abruptly seized by the desire to grab a dustpan and brush so as to dust not only the book but also the scholar.

Only a cretin, Stride thought, could argue for the proposed transfer of books from this wondrous Reading Room to a concrete monstrosity so incompetently designed and constructed on the Euston Road: his friends in the building trade had told him that it would crack at the seams and collapse within five years. Stride felt that little more could be expected from a government that had so obviously embraced ignorance and barbarism.

'It is not at all Tory in the sense of traditional,' he had indignantly exclaimed to Antonina on the previous night; 'it is only Tory in the sense of tyrannical. It claims to be Conservative, but it is impossible to discern any aspect of the national heritage which this squalid bunch of mercenary sleazebags is bent upon conserving.'

The three matters that now preoccupied him were the compiling of a report on the Holy Grail for his client Miss Alison Featherstonehaugh, and here he found the essays on the matter by Arthur Machen himself to be an invaluable guide; further research on Machen for his own purposes of a biography; and an investigation of the curious black pearl embedded in the brass ankh, which presently reposed within his cavalry twill trouser pocket, lying within a zipped slit. His initial scrutiny of this stone had shaken him more than somewhat. He had not yet dared to look at it closely again.

Even so, it was a pleasure for Stride to receive and read books and to enter into the pleasures of a warmer and, it appeared, more civilized era. As he wrote the first draft of his report on the Holy Grail for Alison Featherstonehaugh, his concentration was occasionally distracted by memories of her quaint and piquant rather than beautiful face, with its eyes of shining hazel. That was how Arthur Machen had described 'Helen' in his *The Three Impostors*, she who was also 'Miss Lally' and 'Miss Leicester': and that was how Stride had described her in his sequel, *The Labyrinth of Satan*.

As he waited for more books he had ordered, he pondered the words of the second volume of Machen's autobiography, *Things Near and Far*. Here Machen related that a great sorrow came upon him towards the end of the 1890s. Obviously he was referring to the death of his first wife, Amelia Hogg, by cancer. He then described how, when alone and a widower and dwelling in Verulam Chambers, just off the Gray's Inn Road, 'a horror of soul' had come over him whereby 'I could not endure my own being'.

At this point in his acute state of nervous depression, a mysterious 'Process' had occurred to him. He declared that he knew very little of its nature and had many doubts about its efficacy but nevertheless undertook this experiment: and the results were way beyond his expectations. He recorded that the initial result produced within him so violent an ecstasy that he felt there was no vessel strong enough to hold this joy. As he paced the pavements of the London he loved, he felt as though he were walking on air to the sacred place he called 'Syon'.

This merged into a second state, which he called 'Baghdad', for his life began to resemble events taken from *The Thousand Nights and a Night* of Arabia as translated by Sir Richard Burton. Above all, the characters and events of his novel *The Three Impostors* came to life and in consequence he was accosted in the streets and in taverns with preposterous tales of the improbable, of horror and of the supernatural.

During this period he joined the Hermetic Order of the Golden Dawn, allegedly a grouping of 'Rosicrucians', a secret society dedicated to the enlightenment of humanity and an organization whose very existence remains a matter for conjecture. This grouping of the Golden Dawn practised Ceremonial Magick, to which so many of the age's leading luminaries had been drawn: the leader was S.L. Mathers, translator of *The Kabbalah Unveiled*, *The Greater Key of Solomon* and *The Book of the Sacred Magic of Abra-Melin the Mage*; his wife Moina was a talented artist and daughter of the renowned evolutionist philosopher, Henri Bergson. Other members included W.B. Yeats, poet and Nobel Prize-winner; Maud Gonne, the beautiful Irish revolutionary whom Yeats loved in vain; Allan Bennett, who brought traditional Theravada Buddhism to Great Britain; Florence Farr, dramatist, actress and lover of Yeats, Bernard Shaw and Aleister Crowley. Crowley would later be excoriated in the tabloids of the time as 'the wickedest man in the World' yet he was another Golden Dawn member and a master of poetry, chess and mountaineering. The roll-call continued: Annie Horniman, who subsidized the excellent Horniman Museum of Ethnology in South London and did English repertory a fine favour by founding the Gaiety Theatre; Peck, the Astronomer Royal for Scotland; J.W. Brodie-Innes, author of *The Devil's Mistress*; A.E. Waite, a life-long friend of Machen and author and editor of many occult tomes; Bram Stoker, author of *Dracula*; Arthur Starsfield Ward, aka 'Sax Rohmer', author of *Brood of the Witch Queen* and the 'Fu Manchu' stories; Algernon Blackwood, an adept of supernatural tales – and Arthur Machen.

Stride filled in forms to order more books about the Golden Dawn and the allegedly ancient fraternity of the Rosicrucians, meanwhile noting that Machen had let his membership lapse around 1902, writing subsequently that the Golden Dawn 'shed no ray of light upon my path'. Machen thence described the third stage he underwent, following from his mysterious 'Process'. He called it the stage of the 'Silly Fool'. All his illusions and delusions dropped by the wayside. There was certainly some transformation, though: Machen had subtitled his *The Three Impostors* 'The Transformations'. Machen, this intense introvert, had metamorphosed into a garrulous extrovert, had married another actress, had gone on the stage with Sir Frank Benson's Shakespeare Company and had become a star reporter for the London *Evening News*: an unusual turnabout for a man who had hitherto been a shrinking violet.

Stride took 'a smart turn in brisk air', as recommended by one of Machen's more hostile critics, while he walked towards Hatton Garden for a luncheon appointment. He was trying to comprehend the nature of Machen's mysterious 'Process'. What on Earth was it, in Heaven's name or in Hell's teeth? So far, the only clue he could find lay in a 1935 letter to an American correspondent, one Munson Havens, in which Machen stated that it was akin to Hypnotism but that 'it would be of no use to me now'. He implied that these methods were inappropriate to the life of a man married contentedly.

What had actually taken place here after this bizarre action of 'The Process'? There had been ecstasy; then weird scenes, some of them of an arguably hallucinatory nature; then a sensation of 'silly fool'; and then a more satisfying and integrated marital and material life. Stride thought of LSD. This could have had a similar effect but they did not have that substance in the 1890s. Machen had observed in his writings that stronger effects could possibly be felt by taking mescaline – the active ingredient of the peyote cactus which Aleister Crowley had introduced into Europe around 1910 in its smoking form of anhalonium – but he insisted that his experience was not a drug-induced phenomenon. Yet he had written about drugs most poignantly in *The Novel of the White Powder*, possibly the finest tale in *The Three Impostors*; and

THE GOD GAME

also in his exquisite novel *The Hill of Dreams*.

On that day, Stride remained unable to solve the puzzle of Arthur Machen's 'Process'. It was clear, at least, that whatever it was, it had given him the ecstatic, mystical and magical experiences after which he had always hungered and of which he had always written and would continue to write. It was more difficult to understand how the characters of his novel *The Three Impostors* could have come to life in order to invade his; just as something similar seemed to be happening to Adam Stride. Stride hoped that there might be some light thrown on matters during his lunchtime meeting with his old schoolfriend, Moses Cohen.

'So what would you like, my dears?' asked the stout, motherly waitress at The Nosherie, Hatton Garden. 'The chopped liver is lovely today and I can also recommend the lokshen pudding. Why, sir,' she looked at Stride, 'you look as though you could do with a bit of feeding up.'

Stride and Cohen ordered chicken soup with dumplings, chopped liver, hot salt beef and the glowingly recommended lokshen pudding, all of which proved to be excellent, as they chatted pleasantly about old times.

Moses Cohen was now a fat, prosperous, balding man with a wife and four children: he was also renowned as one of the finest experts on jewels in Hatton Garden and had frequently assisted Stride in the past. It was over coffee that Stride showed Cohen the stone within the ankh. Cohen regarded it with curiosity and then turned very pale, handing it swiftly back to Stride.

'I don't vant to know,' he said.

'How d'you mean?'

'I just don't vant to know.'

'There's not a word of advice you can give me?'

'No,' said Moses Cohen, 'apart from get rid of it or else

you will undoubtedly be robbed with violence if anyone else finds out you have it. I don't vant to talk about it, okay? Anyway, put zat avay.' Stride did. 'A pleasure seeing you, as always.' He paid the bill for both of them and left with an almost indecent haste.

Stride felt cheered by the meal but annoyed by his friend's behaviour, as well as puzzled. He took the stone to Levi & Son where it was examined in a back room by... Levi and Son.

'Brilliant,' said young Mr Levi.

'Iss not brilliant at all,' said old Mr Levi. 'Iz vorthless.'

'But Dad, it's a genuine black pearl...'

'I don't vant to know,' said old Mr Levi, handing the object back to Stride. 'Please to leave.'

Stride eventually found a jewellery dealer in Hatton Garden who was not Jewish. This shop was called simply *Smith*.

'Where there's muck, there's brass,' said Mr Smith as he surveyed the object. He was a tall, thin man with waves of thick hair and glasses. 'Might be worth a bob or two. May I ask you, sir, how it came into your possession?'

'I'm simply enquiring on behalf of a friend.'

'Oh yeah...?' Mr Smith looked as though he were thinking: *they always say that*. 'I might be interested in dealing with this, sir, provided that you can show me a certificate of sale.'

'I simply wanted a valuation.' Stride smiled. 'And I'm prepared to pay for it.'

'I am not insinuating anything,' Mr Smith answered him, 'but I want nothing to do with this matter until you can show me a certificate of sale. That's the way in which I do business, sir.' He coughed and then lit a Player's Medium Navy Cut with a Bryant & May safety match. 'Bring me what I need and I'll take another look. Meanwhile, sir, I really wouldn't flash that thing around if I were you. Might draw the attention of the wrong sort of people.'

*

THE GOD GAME

Arthur Machen had always loved Clerkenwell. In his *The London Adventure* he had written: 'I am sure that they are all secret people who live there, to the east of the Gray's Inn Road; secret and severed people who have fallen out of the great noisy march of the high road for one reason or another, and so dwell apart in these misty streets and squares of 1850, wondering when it will be 1851.'

When Stride entered the Three Tuns there, he doubted if the decor had changed since 1850. When he looked at the customers, he doubted if *they* had changed since 1950 and perhaps they were wondering when it might be 1951. These middle-aged and elderly skilled craftsmen, some of whom were sitting pleasantly with their wives, spoke of working in marble, concrete and brick; of watches, jewellery, boxing and football as Stride bought his pint; and also of the virtues of sausages and fresh fruit and vegetables. There were windows of frosted glass; and walls and tables of oak; and the beer was certainly good and reasonably priced. Machen would have liked it, Stride thought; even now.

'Don't share your opinion with all respect, Mr Simpson,' he heard one old man saying in between puffs on his gnarled briar pipe. 'These new fancy sausages of yours are all very well for the folks who've got the dosh and more of it than they have sense, but I tell you straight that you can't beat good pork sausages with sage.' Stride took a comfortable seat which gave him a good view of every entrance and exit as he quietly enjoyed a pint of excellent ale.

'Too old fashioned, Mr Dawson, that's your trouble, with all respect,' his stout, florid-faced friend replied as Antonina entered the pub, wearing her Hell's Angels leather jacket. 'What's wrong, I ask you, with sausages of beef and Guinness?' Antonina took a pint of Snakebite with blackcurrant juice, then walked to a table diagonally opposite Stride's, as previously arranged, without arousing any comment. Stride brushed some dust away from his navy blue blazer and grey flannel trousers. The man entered just as Stride was adjusting his cravat.

'Gobsmacked' is a better word then 'astonished' to describe Stride's reaction to this man. He stood six feet five and must have weighed around 280 pounds. His complexion, the colour of molten wax, was not noticeably improved by a thick ginger moustache which merged into a pair of bulbous chin-whiskers. His eyes were small and muddy brown, his teeth large, broken at the front, uneven and discoloured; and his cheeks looked heavy and swollen. His hair looked like thick and curly ginger wire wool. At the bar, he asked in a Canadian accent for a pint of their strongest lager. When they gave it to him, the mug disappeared within his paw; he drank it down in five seconds flat and ordered another. As soon as the barman gave it to him, he strode over to Stride's table.

'You're Adam Stride, author of *The Labyrinth of Satan*, right?' he enquired.

'Sure,' Stride responded as he arose to shake the proffered paw, all the while wondering how on Earth this unprepossessing individual could know that. They sat down together and Stride was faced with the dubious pleasure of meeting the spitting image of a character from fiction in the flesh: Richmond, conjured into print by Arthur Machen in 1895 and by Adam Stride in 1995.

'Allow me to inter-dooce myself,' he said, taking off his baseball cap and flinging it upon the table. He was wearing a thick check shirt, the armpits of which were stained with sweat, and jeans which could accommodate three buttocks. 'Butcher's the name,' he said, 'Ron Butcher. And pleased to meet ya!'

'Pleased to meet you too, Ron,' Stride answered. 'But with all respect, who sent you?'

'Ha! ha! ha!' Ron Butcher laughed so hard that Stride feared he might be injuring himself internally. 'Ha! ha! ha! Why, it's

Septimus Keen, of course. Ha! ha! ha! He'll be glad you showed up.'

'Well, I have,' Stride replied. 'But what's this all about?'

'Ya dunno, do ya!' Ron Butcher answered. 'Listen, pal. Ya been a miner? Ya been in de US Marines? You been in jail in Detroit? You fought the toughest guys in prairie town bars? Hell, I went fighting in your Finsbury Park bars last Saturday night. I fought the Heavyweight karate Champ of Great Britain and – uh – heh heh! – he broke my nose but I am still going. Don't ask me about him. Know anything about that?'

'No,' said Stride.

'And ya still wonder what this is all about?' Ron Butcher laughed wickedly. 'I'll tell you what this is all about, pal. I'll tell ya what this is all about. But first lemme tell ya a joke, huh?' Stride could see that Antonina was looking concerned but he signalled to her that nothing bad had happened . . . yet. 'See,' Ron Butcher continued, 'Al Capone gets kinda tired of running all the rackets and decides he wants some kinda culture. So he calls his gang togedder and he tells 'em to get him a book. They go to the Chicago Civic Library and they say: "Hey! Ya gotta book on Dick de Shit?" The librarian, he sez: "Sorry . . . ?" They sez: "Hey, dere was dis guy Dick, right? He was a shit, okay? We want a book on Dick de Shit." The librarian sez: "Sorry, I can't help you there." So they kill him. Then they go into the Library saying: "Is dis a book on Dick de Shit? Nah! Is dat a book on Dick de Shit? Nah!" A few people turn around and go: "Sssshhh!" So they kill them. Then there are witnesses, so they kill them. They kill everybody in the Chicago Civic Library. Then they still can't find a book on Dick de Shit so they lose all their patience, get in the kerosene, throw the books on the floor, pour all the kerosene on the books – then they strike matches and torch the place. The entire civic pride of Chicago goes up in flames. Then they go back to Al Capone and they tell him what they've done. "Gee, we're really sorry, Al, we couldn't find no book on Dick de Shit." And Al Capone goes crazy. "Ya stupid bunch of stinking crummy bums!" he yells. "I didn't want no book on Dick de Shit. I wanted a book on RICHARD DA TOID!"' Stride smiled as Mr Butcher collapsed laughing.

'Good, huh?!' Mr Butcher exclaimed.

'Good,' Stride responded mildly. 'Another pint?' Butcher nodded and Stride bought him a pint of strong lager. Antonina still looked worried. Stride took Ron Butcher's strong lager and his own strong ale back to their table. 'A good joke, Ron,' he said, 'but you promised to tell me what this is all about.'

'Okay.' He shrugged his massive shoulders then drank half of his pint, treating his throat as a drain. 'Ok-ay.' He fixed Stride with his mud-brown eyes. 'I gotta message for ya.' He produced a crumpled pile of paper from the back pocket of his dreadful jeans and tossed it over the table to Stride. 'Read it now, pal.' Stride read:

PRETTY LITTLE ANGEL EYES

by

Septimus Keen

It was in a small art gallery, hidden away in the drab streets of Lewisham, South London, that I first encountered Dwight Wright. A poster on a brick wall by a railway bridge in Brixton had encouraged me to go there, for it was all to do with vampires. A remarkably well drawn and effectively coloured image of a man and a woman biting one another's throats as blood trickled from their necks promised the prospect of interesting art.

One was welcomed at this small and obscure gallery with a glass of good red wine, served by a hatchet-faced bitch with a stunning slim figure and bright emerald green eyes. She was dressed in tight, gleaming leather. She told me that her work was on display.

'Whereabouts?' I asked.

'That,' she replied, 'is something you must see for yourself. Here,' she had a hard New York accent, 'why don'tcha just take a look?' I did: and saw that the Vampire was indeed the theme of every painting. Some were executed in traditional Gothic style; there were renditions of post-Impressionist vampires in the style of Redon; there were Symboliste paintings of vampires in the manner of Gustav Klimt; Expressionist portrayals in the manner of Edvard Munch; endeavours to present the subject in an abstract manner; use of Surrealist techniques in the style of Salvador Dali; startling explosions of line and colour as might have been done by Austin Osman Spare. There was also one painting that was utterly original. Although the standard of craft had been refreshingly high in everything I had hitherto seen, *this* was quite exceptional.

One's initial, superficial reaction was indifference since the picture simply showed a man I judged to be in his thirties sitting behind a big white desk. It had been titled 'The Chairman of the Board' and painted in the same sort of manner that, in my view, disgraces the Royal Academy Summer Exhibition with its timid and sycophantic conservatism. The figure in the portrait had a chunky build and was smiling slightly at the computers and fax machines and other tools of communication that were dotted about his desk. His suit was grey, immaculately tailored and straight out of Brooks Brothers, New York City; his silk tie was Ivy League; his shirt was probably Turnbull & Asser in just the right shade of pale blue; and his black, shiny leather shoes, which one could see in the gap between desk and floor, were obviously handmade, probably in Jermyn Street. So far, so conventional: it was just that where there should have been eyeballs there were blank, black holes with small, sharp white teeth around the empty sockets' rims.

'Enjoying the exhibition?' came a soft American voice. I turned to see a copy of the man in the painting, exact save in that he was wearing dark glasses, clearly purchased from some leading designer, that made it quite impossible to discern the exact nature of his eyes.

'Very much,' I replied, noticing that he was carrying a copy of *The Outsider* by Colin Wilson under his left arm, upon which fact I commented.

'Oh, I am so glad that you too like this book,' he responded in his cultured East Coast accent. Then he introduced himself as Dwight Wright, the patron of this particular exhibition, who had hired the gallery and financed the posters and other advertising for artists to display their works. 'You know, every time I go out carrying this book, I meet *so* many interesting people. Strange, perhaps,' he laughed mirthlessly, 'but then life *is* strange, m'friend. What is your opinion of this portrait of me before you now?'

'It is very fine,' I answered truthfully, 'and somewhat disturbing and unusual.'

'Oh, indeed,' he returned easily, 'and it was painted by my dear friend Durga, who no doubt welcomed you to the gallery and gave you a glass of wine . . . but I see that your glass is now empty. Allow me, sir.' He snapped his fingers and a stunning blonde appeared out of nowhere to replenish my glass. I nodded my thanks as he continued with his discourse. 'I feel very sorry for most visual artists. However good they are, they can barely scratch a living. An artist spends, say, three months on a painting and has to charge at least six hundred pounds. Who can afford to pay that? The public will only buy if firstly, there is that money to spare; and secondly, if some art critic sanctions the choice as a matter of good and fashionable taste. I have therefore gathered a collection of some of the finest, hitherto unknown artists of our time, until now quite unjustly neglected, and I have ensured that there will be favourable notices in the newspapers and journals by critics who are friends of mine. What is the result? These artists are at last selling their paintings.'

'Laudable,' I said. At this moment our conversation was interrupted since Dwight Wright was surrounded by male and female artists who heaped praises upon his head, thanking him effusively for opportunities. He responded quietly and modestly. I saw slim men in leather and fat men in battered corduroys thank him. I saw fat women in smocks and slender girls in rubber thank him. I also saw him surrounded by strong men and lascivious women, his entourage, and these were obviously not artists such as the gallery exhibited.

'Septimus, I have to go now,' said Dwight Wright. 'But I am giving a party at one of my places next Friday. Would you like to come?' He lit a very long cigarette with a chunky gold Dunhill lighter, then glanced quickly at his gold Rolex. 'Or why don't we meet at one of my offices and have a glass of champagne beforehand?'

*

I accepted his invitation. His office was in South Audley Street, Mayfair and I was shown into the Chairman's sanctum within thirty seconds. The business was evidently something to do with banking and investment broking, conducted principally via computer. His colleagues were courteous and evidently dedicated to their work. We went to enjoy the promised glasses of champagne at a nearby wine bar.

'I am very proud of my financial team,' he told me. 'They were all unemployed before I gave them an opportunity to put it all back together again. I hate to see talent going to waste.' Then we took a cab to 'one of my places' in Chelsea, just off the King's Road, at a Victorian mansion block near World's End. During our journey, he told me that he was 'a people collector' because it was 'such a relief from staring at my computer screen. In my leisure time, I find such satisfaction from giving opportunities to those whose talents have been neglected. We have to make use of potential, assuredly.'

We arrived at his luxurious apartment, which was just like any other 'international' luxury apartment and so is barely worth description. An ageing maid had laid out the canapés and finger rolls: Dwight Wright treated her with a patrician disdain and dismissed her. To drink, there was an acidic Mumm Cordon Rouge to be served throughout the evening. Myself, I always find that the first glass of champagne is the best; a second can be good; and a third gives me heartburn. But there was no alternative.

'Wait till you see the guests,' he said. I did. I also took a look inside his bedroom on my way out of the loo and saw glass cages of bird-eating spiders.

The guests arrived and music was played. I doubt if I have ever heard worse music, since good music plays upon the heartbeat and this did not. Being bad pop at its most moronic and insulting to the intelligence, it also fuddled the brain. The men were either the artists I had seen before or else young, slim and handsome and wearing tight leather trousers. The women were a curious mixture of the artists I had seen before, naive debutantes and common prostitutes; at least three told me that they had artistic aspirations and that Dwight had picked them up in Leicester Square. Now, I only know whores socially – they can often be most charming company – and if I had not struck up a friendly conversation with a red-headed bitch, who told me that her name was Samantha and, fancying that I was a rich man, gave me her phone number, I might remain even more puzzled by ensuing events than I am. I did not enjoy the party particularly, since there seemed to be no life and soul to it; it seemed to be going nowhere other than a subsequent bad hangover. Since the increasingly acidic taste of the champagne was afflicting me, I took my leave in friendly fashion and welcomed the long walk from Mayfair to my bedsit in Kilburn. At least I could see the stars in the sky.

A couple of days later, I called Samantha since I am a keen student of human nature. The conversation went as follows:

'Hallo, Samantha. Septimus here.'

'Oh, hallo, Septimus. Look, I'm in a bit of a rush. Enjoy the party?'

'Yes. Well, sort of. Where're you rushing off to?'

'Somewhere. Ha! ha!'

'More jolly parties with Dwight Wright, Samantha?'

'Never again. Look, Septimus, I must go. All I can tell you . . . two things. Look at the newspapers. And remember that some people are short-sighted and want to see better. Good luck. Bye.' I never saw her again. A few moments later, the phone rang and it was Dwight Wright. I assured him that I had greatly enjoyed his party.

'Well, that's great, Septimus, I'm glad.' He then invited me for 'a quiet little supper, just the two of us', at his home today week. I accepted the kind invitation. 'Oh, and by the way,' he said, 'my dear lady friends say that you have the most beautiful eyes. "Angel Eyes", some of them call you, even "Pretty Little Angel Eyes" like in the pop song by good ole Curtis Lee.' I laughed and assured him that I was honoured by the compliment.

'You seemed to be getting on well with Samantha,' he remarked.

'Charming girl altogether,' I replied. There was an undefinable *something* about his tone of voice that made my scalp crawl and my eyelashes flicker.

'Seen her lately?'

'No,' I answered truthfully, 'I have not seen her.'

'Well, it will be a pleasure to see you, Septimus. The phone is all very well but there's nothing like eyeball-to-eyeball, as we like to say in America. Of course, we do things differently there.'

During the following week, I did in fact go through the newspapers as Samantha had advised me and I was not entirely happy with the data that I discovered. Murders are so vulgar and common that they rarely make the front-page headlines these days but since at that period I had time on my hands, my attention *was* attracted by certain items. I think it was H.P. Lovecraft who said: 'The most merciful thing about the human mind is its inability to correlate all its contents,' or words to that effect.

I discerned that there had been a number of murders of both men and women up and down the country. Study of the provincial papers gave me information on suicides. There was nothing unusual about these events until I read in the *Yorkshire Post* that in a bedsit in the city of York one Carol Brown, a prostitute and junkie known to the police, had apparently committed suicide by an overdose of heroin which she had injected into her right eyeball, an unpleasant practice used by prostitutes, striptease artistes and dancers who don't want the needle-marks to show. Apparently her name on the game was 'Samantha' and she had red hair.

In the week before I saw Dwight Wright for 'a quiet little supper', I read of five suicides: one prostitute, two unemployed actresses, one male artist and one male stockbroker. These had taken place in London, Portsmouth, Newcastle-upon-Tyne, Manchester and Birmingham. I also read of six murders: these had taken place in Liverpool, Leeds, London, Plymouth, Reading and Swindon. The victims were one prostitute, one female artist, one male artist, one ex-stockbroker, one writer and one ex-teacher, all registered unemployed. There was precious little to link these cases since one killing had been done by poison, another by a pump-action shotgun fired into the belly, a third by a knife slash across the throat, a fourth by strangulation with a rope, a fifth by beheading with an axe and the sixth by a crushing blow to the skull with a wooden club. Nothing connected these hideous killings apart from one grotesque theme. In each case, the eyeballs had been removed from their sockets.

I decided that it was time to see an old friend, Bill, an ex-member of the SAS presently earing his living at private security work since it struck me, purely on a hunch, that I might be in need of some protection. Bill, who was tall, lean and dapper, would not strike one on first inspection as being an SAS man, but then they never do. He loved adventure and gladly agreed to accompany me to dinner with Dwight Wright, our cover story being the moderately truthful one that an old friend I had not seen in years had dropped by unexpectedly so I hoped that our host would not mind.

In fact, Dwight did mind. I have rarely seen such fury cloud a human face as when he turned his head away just after shaking hands with Bill. Nor was he pleased about the fact that both of us were wearing dark glasses, though he himself was, and although he had promised 'just the two of us', there were three other guests *he* had unexpectedly invited. Durga the artist I had met before. She was the only one without dark glasses and I shall never forget her pretty little angel eyes, so bright in their emerald green. Dwight Wright's two other guests in the room were dead ringers for the kind of Mafia and IRA killers I had met before. They moved in perfect synchronicity, like a pair of trained Dobermanns. Whenever one put his glass down, the other one picked his up. Apparently they were called Franco and Loco and came from Yugoslavia and it was very hard to tell the difference between them.

Dinner was served by Durga, and though I had no objection to her cream of mushroom soup, spare ribs with coleslaw and a baked potato covered with sour cream and chives, followed by blackcurrant cheesecake, I did take exception to the way in which she kept trying to stare me out. I stared back, taking off my dark glasses at one point on some pretext and focusing upon a place in between her eyebrows. This usually brings a puzzled frown to the face of one's antagonist and a turn of their head and Durga was no exception. Franco and Loco appeared to be looking hard at me as Durga brought in a further sizzling dish.

'Got eyeball trouble or something?' I enquired. Bill remained calm.

'I hope *you* don't have eyeball trouble or something, Septimus,' Dwight Wright chuckled uneasily, 'for these are sheep's eyeballs, a great Arabian delicacy.'

'Pass, thanks,' Bill said. 'No offence intended.'

'Very kind, Dwight,' I said, 'but I'm just not quite in the mood for them tonight. I'd rather eat the other delicious dishes that Durga has graciously prepared for us.'

'Oh, that's okay.' Dwight Wright scrunched an eyeball between his teeth and chewed it with evident enjoyment. Franco and Loco followed suit. Dwight proceeded to open and pour vintage claret, a Chateau Mouton Rothschild 1955 as I recall, and then he drank it as if it was Coca-Cola. 'One thing that is required in the modern world,' he declared, 'is intelligent terrorism. Interested, Septimus?'

'No,' I replied, 'by no means and not at all.'

'But,' Dwight smiled sweetly, 'you are an idealist. Don't you want to help change the world?'

'Not like that,' I answered. 'Seen any good bits of babies' bodies flying by on account of "intelligent terrorism" lately?' As the tension escalated, Bill appeared to be blithely oblivious. 'All that will happen is that terrorism will give governments further excuses to implement fascism.'

'Oh, Septimus . . .' Dwight's smile was by now so sweet that I feared he might contract diabetes. His tones positively caressed me. 'I figure that you just don't really understand what is really going on.'

'You may be right there,' I responded. 'What is?'

'You'll see soon enough,' Durga observed wearily, then again eyeballed me with her green emerald stare. I responded with a glance from my own blue eyes and another move I knew, which is to put the heels of your feet together and suck your thumb whilst looking thoughtful but thinking of nothing. Durga obviously knew that move for she could not help but laugh and look away. I wondered how, when, where and by whom she had been trained.

'There is no such thing as "intelligent terrorism",' I said. 'The whole matter is stupid and disgusting. Of course, terrorism is often used by the CIA and suchlike outfits to repress people. They provoke disaffected individuals into committing dreadful actions which they would not do otherwise. These awful acts then provoke people to demand a government which curtails their civil liberties.'

'Who cares about civil liberties?' Dwight asked easily.

'I do,' Bill answered. I could have hugged him for that.

'Don't you *see*?' Dwight demanded as he served more wine.

'No, I don't see, I'm afraid,' I answered. 'In fact, I'm all at sea here.'

'Then I'd give your perceptions C minus,' said Dwight. 'With all respect, it strikes me that you are being just a little bit blind.'

'I see the blinds on the window,' said Bill. I noticed that there was no natural light coming into the room.

'Oh, fuck this,' Durga muttered under her breath – though I could hear her.

'Enough of all this effing and blinding,' I said, arising from the table. 'Bill and I have an urgent appointment. Forgive us. Thank you for the excellence of your hospitality, Dwight. I fear that we must take our leave, though I see that all of this has dazzled me with its blinding light . . .'

At a signal from Dwight, Franco and Loco overturned the table and sprang at us.

'Watch the spoon!' I heard Bill yell. It was only later that I realized that Loco had intended to use it on my eyes. Violence is usually nasty, brutish and short and this occasion constituted no exception. I simply crouched with my face and my vulnerable parts covered, as I had learned from Tai Chi, and seconds later Loco, Franco and Durga were all on the floor and unconscious. It was fortunate that Bill had previously ascertained the layout of the building. Figuring that it would be hard to escape through the thick front door, locked as it undoubtedly was, he smashed through another with one kick, burst through the window of the room thus reached and dropped easily on to the pavement. It was simple to follow suit.

There are a number of sequels to this story.

Bill and I went straight to the police who raided the house and found nobody there. Further investigations revealed that the flat had been rented by one Pasquale Motta of Brazil, a self-employed businessman about whom nothing more was known. Still further enquiries disclosed that the office in South Audley Street had been vacated and that the company had gone into liquidation. The name 'Dwight Wright' was not found in any of the somewhat slender company records.

Some weeks later, I received a postcard from Rio de Janeiro. It was signed 'Dwight', it showed a picture of Jesus Christ and he had written simply 'HEAVEN!'

A week later, I received a clipping from a newspaper of Rio de Janeiro informing me that a terrorist had killed twenty-three people with a bomb placed in a church. Upon the scrap of newsprint, what looked like a female hand had scrawled the words: 'DWIGHT IS DEAD. I HATE INCOMPETENCE. DURGA.'

I do hope that he *is* dead for I do not wish to see him again: on reception of this communication, I was hardly howling with grief or even pondering the wisdom of an eye for an eye. It struck me that anyone who could not see the situation had to be blind.

Bill, who is a down-to-earth sort of chap if ever there was one, tells me that he was horrified as we tore through the door and the room: although he cannot swear to it, he believes he saw rows of jars of pickled human eyeballs.

I too cannot swear to this, since I did not see the jars at all: I was blind to everything other than my need to escape at that moment. What I shall never forget, however, is what I had seen when Dwight Wright's dark glasses fell off his face during the fighting, as did those of Franco and Loco.

I saw blank, black sockets with white teeth around their rims.

I still wonder from where Durga obtained her pretty little angel eyes.

'*Dis*-gusting!' Mr Butcher exclaimed as Stride drank some beer very slowly, holding the mug in his right hand as he handed the manuscript back to his unusual companion with his left. 'Is it not your considered opinion that this tale that you have read is truly disgusting?'

'No, not really,' Stride murmured mildly. 'I found it very interesting.'

'Exactly,' Butcher replied with an ugly grin. 'Oh, you'll see that, pal, you'll see that – and I hope you won't be blind to it, heh! heh! PAL!' Mr Butcher shouted, then quoted a TV commercial from Stride's childhood: 'PAL meat for dogs! P-A-L. Prolongs Active Life . . . Enriched with nourishing marrow-bone jelly!' Stride was starting to feel increasingly uneasy as the men at the bar and the tables around them continued to chat pleasantly and Antonina continued to look concerned.

'Innovation, Mr Dawson,' Mr Simpson was saying, 'intelligent innovation, building on the past; that's the method of the future. Take my venison and wine sausages, for example, though whether you grind the meat coarse or smooth is of course a matter that can be debated . . .'

'I'm not sure, Mr Butcher,' Stride said, 'if I see what this is all about. What does all this lead to? Is there some sort of coded message in this story?'

'Oh, boy . . .' Mr Butcher responded with an evil chuckle. 'When you started writing about Septimus Keen, you had no idea of what you were getting into, right? Waal, it's about time you found out.' Extracting a large and dirty white handkerchief from his pocket, he blew his nose so loudly that it might have been a bad audition for Purcell's 'Trumpet Voluntary'. 'I gotta go. Now.' He stood up.

THE GOD GAME

'Hey, one moment,' Stride interposed sharply. 'I thought that you were going to tell me what this is all about. "About time you found out"? Found out *what*?'

'That's your problem, pal,' said Mr Butcher. 'Are you gonna stop me from going?' Stride pondered the possibility and intuited the impossibility. Mr Butcher extended his hand, Stride responded and, though his own was a fair size, it virtually vanished within Ron Butcher's enormous paw. 'Think about it, pal. Just think about it.' Butcher turned his broad back, shrugged his muscular shoulders and strode swiftly out of the pub.

Stride briefly entertained the idea of following him but seconds later realized that he could not do so without being spotted. Antonina darted across the bar and to his table.

'You okay?' she asked. Stride nodded. 'What happened?'

'I would to high heaven that I knew,' Stride answered. 'I just can't grasp the point of it.'

'It's the grinding of the meat that's vital, Mr Simpson,' Mr Dawson was saying. 'Never forget the importance of the *grinding*.'

CHAPTER FIVE

THE ADVENTURE OF THE FLAGRANT IMPOSTURE

(IT)

Arthur Machen sat in his chambers at Verulam Buildings and pondered his situation with growing perplexity. The midday sun blazed in a sky of azure blue and he rejoiced in the sight as he regarded the dusty, dead leaves of October littering the gardens without; yet still he desired to make sense of all that had happened to him. Clearly the world was being presented to him at a new angle. There had come to be a strangeness in the proportion of things, both exterior and interior. 'And it is in these latter,' he had declared to his friend Arthur Edward Waite on the previous night, 'that I held and still hold that the true wonder, the true mystery, the true miracle reside.'

He was still bewildered by the 'Process' he had obtained by his study of the alchemists and which he had tried ere having any precise knowledge of it or of its likely results. He had done it without any more exalted motives than those which urge a man with raging toothache to get laudanum and take it with all convenient speed. He had suffered from a more raging pain than that of any toothache and he had wanted that pain to be dulled: that was all.

'"Here in this world he changed his life" is far too high in its associations . . .' Machen murmured to himself. He could make nothing much of the great gusts of incense that had been blown into his nostrils, of the odours of rare gums that seemed to fume before invisible altars in Holborn, in Claremont Square, in the grey streets of Clerkenwell, of the savours of the sanctuary that he had perceived in all manner of grim London wastes and wanderings. He thought of the Knights of the Grail who were aware of 'the odour of all the rarest spiceries in the World' before the Vision was given unto them; then reflected that he could hardly consider himself worthy to be a Knight of the Grail.

He recalled a bright, keen morning only the other day, when he had been walking along Rosebery Avenue. He had suddenly become aware of a strange sensation and as suddenly recollected the old saying 'walking on air'.

He remembered thinking at the time: 'This is incredible'; and yet it was a fact. The pavement of that drab street had suddenly become, not air, certainly, but resilient; the impact of his feet upon it was buoyant; the sensation was delicious. Then he recalled the occasion when he had been sitting in his room at 4 Verulam Buildings, Gray's Inn Road. The walls had trembled and the pictures on the wall had shaken and shivered before his eyes, as if a sudden wind had blown into the room. He had noticed that there was no actual physical wind and had in consequence become a little alarmed, not knowing what would happen next. The pictures on the wall opposite to the garden on which his window looked out first shook and shivered, then trembled, dilated, became misty in their outlines; seemed on the point of disappearing altogether, and then shuddered and contracted back again into their proper form and solidity. Machen had witnessed this with a shaking heart and with a sense that something, he knew not what, was also being shaken to its foundations. The shivering pictures had seemed on the point of dissolution and return into chaos, and there was a sensible thrill of delight that accompanied this strange manifestation.

'What exactly *was* your "Process"?' his friend Waite had asked him.

'I am not allowed to describe it,' Machen had replied, 'save to state that I discovered it in the alchemical texts of Nicholas Flamel, Cornelius Agrippa, Paracelsus and Dr John Dee in the Reading Room of the British Museum. Silence is a condition of using this Spell. If you are puzzled, I am doubly so. I couldn't have hypnotized or "magnetized" or mesmerized or autosuggested or in any way bedevilled myself into the condition obtained for the very good reason that I had never hitherto heard of it, had not the faintest notion of it, and was, in fact, not a little alarmed by it: half-thinking, if the truth be told, that I was very near to death.'

Were the incense clouds that had come to his nostrils in places where, assuredly, no material incense burned, of consequence? Were the pictures that shivered and wavered on the wall of consequence? He did not know; but he was sure that the state that followed this last experience *was* of high consequence. For when he arose, afraid, and broke off the Process in which he had been engaged, he found to his utter amazement that everything within had been changed.

Amazement; for the utmost that he had hoped from his experiment was a temporary dulling of the pain occasioned by the prolonged illness and death of his beloved wife from cancer during an agonizing six years, a brief opium-oblivion of his troubles. And what he had received was not a mere dull lack of painful sensation, but a peace of the spirit that was quite ineffable, a knowledge that all hurts and dolours and wounds were healed, that that which was broken was reunited.

Everything, of body and mind, had been resolved into an infinite and an exquisite delight; into a joy so great that it had become almost intolerable in its ecstasy. Machen remembered thinking at that time: 'There is wine so strong that no earthly vessels can hold it.' Joy threatened to become an agony that must shatter all. For that day and for many days afterwards, he was dissolved into bliss, into a rapture of life that had no parallel of which he could think, no analogies by which it might be made more plain. He thought of his chambers in Verulam Buildings and the traffic of Theobald's Road was distinct enough, distinct often enough, to be an annoyance. But on one night, the *Ping! Ping!* of the omnibus bell, the grind of the many wheels upon the cobblestones, had sounded to him as marvellous and tremendous chords reverberating from some mighty organ; filling the air, filling the soul and the whole being with rapture immeasurable.

During these strange days, the sense of touch had become to him an exquisite and conscious pleasure. He could not so much as place his hand on the table before him without experiencing a thrill of delight that was not merely sensuous but carried with it, mysteriously and wonderfully, the message of a secret and interior joy. This had fallen out to him in dim Bloomsbury squares, in noisy, clattering Gray's Inn Road; in a train on the Underground, amongst hustling crowds in common streets. He had received joys and known wonders as the trams clanged along the Clerkenwell Road in the grey winter afternoon. This experience of ecstasy, of which he had written and would again write, an experience he called 'Syon', was now fading into a new mode of being, that which he internally termed 'Baghdad' since it seemed to him as though the streets of London had been transformed into those of a magical city in which something exquisitely strange might happen at any moment.

What *was* he to make of the adventure of the other day in which a vicious chase and the persons involved had recalled his own novel, *The Three Impostors: or The Transformations*? What was he to make of the Dr Black who had threatened him? Seizing a pencil and paper, Machen wrote the following:

1 – I saw a woman with fire and light in her eyes run from a house in Clerkenwell. She had raven hair and I heard her shriek out that she would have no part of the devilry of a Dr Black.

2 – I saw her pursued with apparently murderous intent by a big, burly man with a pair of bulbous chin-whiskers, an unpleasant ginger in colour.

3 – This pursuer resembled the Richmond I had imagined in my novel *The Three Impostors*.

4 – The woman threw an ankh of brass with a black pearl set within it into the street and this is now in my possession. This episode is uncomfortably similar to one I included in *The Three Impostors* in which, in the course of a sinister and unusual chase, my Mr Dyson finds flung before him the rare Gold Tiberius.

5 – I saw the raven-haired lady take a hansom cab out of which a well-dressed, clean-shaven man had stepped. I hope he is not the Mr Davies of my *The Three Impostors*.

6 – I then encountered a Dr Black, who had the same name of the evil man of experiment in my story 'The Inmost Light': and who looked just like the evil Dr Lipsius whom I described in my *The Three Impostors*. Dr Black stated that he felt caught up in my *The Three Impostors*, which novel he professed to admire, and admitted that the furious man of the bulbous ginger chin-whiskers was one Sandeman, an employee. He claimed also that the well-dressed gentleman I saw stepping out of a cab may well have been another employee of his called Davies, just as in my *The Three Impostors* and that if so, he is the brother of Helen, whose 'quaint and piquant, rather than beautiful face, with eyes that were of shining hazel', I again portrayed in my novel. 'Helen' also happens to be the name of the she-bitch I portrayed in my *The Great God Pan*. Dr Black has accused this particular Helen of stealing a valuable object from him.

7 – He alleges that what I accidentally have in my possession is the secret and sacred stone of the Sangraal.

8 – He has threatened me with the torture given to the Young Man with Spectacles in my novel *The Three Impostors* if he

discovers that I have it and do not return it to him.

Arthur Machen stared at what he had just written and scratched his head in bemused bewilderment. He had always claimed to be rational; yet he had equally claimed that all things end in mystery. Now here he was, faced with a mystery which his rationality could not explain. He sighed and looked at his dog, a bulldog he had named Juggernaut.

'What do you think of it all, Jug?' he asked. His dog responded by wagging its tail, jumping up and placing its paws upon Machen's thigh. 'Yes, yes, very good,' Machen murmured as he stroked the dog. 'Ah, I suppose you are like Sancho Panza in *Don Quixote*: "I come from my own vineyard; I know nothing." Eh, Jug?' The dog licked his fingers. Only a creature of this nature, Machen mused, was capable of giving absolute affection. Some time before, a man had bored him to the verge of insanity. This was a young man who had approached him in the Café de l'Europe, just off Leicester Square, professing an admiration for *The Great God Pan*, 'The Inmost Light' and *The Three Impostors*. Machen had warmly invited him back to his chambers only to discover that this young man wished to speak exclusively about his own particular psychological problems. He had subsequently wearied Machen on a number of other occasions and furthermore had had a most peculiar habit. Whenever he left at one or half-past one in the morning, he appeared ignorant of the fact that the Raymond Buildings Gate and the Holborn Gate had watchers by them who would open the portals all the long night. So when he left Machen, he would climb the spiked wall that separated Verulam Buildings from Gray's Inn Road and make off into the gaslight. On the last occasion, Machen had found it hard to disguise his boredom in the company of one who so clearly found monologue to be a substitute for conversation. English bulldogs are not usually especially active creatures, but suddenly Juggernaut had arisen, sprung across the room and sunk his teeth into the young man's trousers. The young bore had yelped, Machen had apologized profusely and once again this young man had left by the spiked wall, never to be seen again. On the following morning, Machen had gone out to the butcher and bought his dog a pound of prime steak.

'What *do* we make of it, Jug?' Machen wondered aloud. He poured himself a glass of Vouvray from his favourite part of France, Touraine. 'I have seen a lousy, lazy tramp drinking from a roadside stream that drips cold and pure water from the rock in burning weather. Then the wastrel passes on his ill way, refreshed indeed, but as lousy and lazy as ever. But what's your opinion?' Juggernaut licked his hands and wagged his tail. 'I know,' said Machen, 'you want to go for a walk, don't you?' The dog licked his ear. 'All right.' He flung a black velvet cloak around his shoulders, clipped a lead around Juggernaut's collar and ventured out into a windy day that hurled dust into the eyes, though Machen was lost in thought as he walked his dog along Southampton Row. As he stopped to allow Juggernaut to answer a call of Nature by a lamp-post, he was suddenly accosted, very politely, by a smooth, smiling, clean-shaven gentleman, well dressed, who spoke with the merest suspicion of an Irish accent.

'A fine dog you've got, sir,' this gentleman declared. 'I should be very glad if you'd come up with me and show it to a lady I know who lives in the flats opposite.' Machen assented to his proposition and displayed the dog Juggernaut to the strange lady, who had a quaint and piquant rather than beautiful face, with eyes of shining hazel, her head being surmounted by a mass of flaming red hair. As Machen accepted a glass of dry sherry, he noticed that she appeared to be on terms of polite acquaintanceship with the gentleman. Jug was duly admired and the gentlemen and Machen went down into the street again. The lady had not evinced the faintest astonishment at the introduction of a total stranger with a bulldog into her flat.

Machen felt bemused and bewildered. The flat had been a quiet and unostentatious one. There had been no drugs dropped in the sherry. The mysterious young lady of the flaming red hair had not invited him to look in again some evening for a quiet game of cards with a few congenial friends... and here was his curious companion presenting him with a visiting card that read:

MR CHARLES O'MALLEY,
Castle O'Malley, Co.Galway.

This card increased the credibility of the smooth, smiling, clean-shaven gentleman by his side. Machen invited Mr Charles O'Malley to join him for a drink at the nearby Princess Louise pub. As they walked there, Machen mused that presently in his life, there was a lack of purpose, a certain fantastic confusion, a sense that something without reason might happen at any moment. Nothing began, nothing ended: strange people were apt to separate themselves from the crowd, to engage in queer discourse without intelligible motive or meaning, and then to sink back again, leaving no trace behind. For instance, Mr Charles O'Malley bore a resemblance to the smooth, smiling, clean-shaven Mr Davies, an evil man created by Machen in 'The Inmost Light' and *The Three Impostors*: but there were plenty of smooth, smiling, clean-shaven men in London. Upon arrival at the pub, Mr Charles O'Malley asked for a pint of dark ale. Machen applauded his choice inwardly and had the same himself, since he firmly believed that dark beer is the best for autumn and winter weather.

'A fine dog you have sir, indeed,' said Mr O'Malley.

'Oh, certainly, and thank you,' Machen responded. 'A noble dog of a noble breed. I hope that he will eventually become, after his life has ended, a gargoyle on the parapet of some great Gothic church of the skies.'

'You are clearly a man of wisdom, sir,' said Mr O'Malley, 'and clearly a man of discernment. May I request your opinion upon a matter of Literature?'

'You certain may, sir,' Machen answered warmly, since few matters held greater interest for him. 'Literature and literature: ah, now there's a question. What distinguishes Keats from a political pamphlet? What distinguishes 'Kublai Khan' by Coleridge from *The Dunciad* by Pope? I tell you, sir, the word is *ecstasy*. That is my test as to whether a book or poem is Literature or literature.'

'Jane Austen?' Mr O'Malley raised an eyebrow.

'She builds a neat Georgian house,' Machen replied, 'but where is the cathedral? If you really want to know why the grocer bowed his head an extra inch when he saw the bishop, read Jane Austen. It is all very well executed, but I cannot discern the slightest notion of *ecstasy*.'

'And can you define it?' Mr O'Malley enquired gently.

'Rapture. Awe. Wonder. Call it what you will. All these words describe the same phenomenon.'

'And have you experienced this particular phenomenon?'

'Yes,' said Arthur Machen. He was speaking as truthfully as he knew whilst inwardly growing increasingly uneasy. Only the previous day, ten total strangers had addressed him without any manifest reason and to no discernible end. The mysterious messages were as incomprehensible as if they had been in cipher. He had begun to wonder whether he was constantly being mistaken for someone else, this Someone Else being evidently a prominent member of a secret society who would be aware of the signs and passwords of the Order.

'You have a fine dog, sir,' said Mr O'Malley again, contemplating Jug who was slumbering contentedly.

'Yes, he is a fine dog,' Arthur Machen replied, 'but green

bulldogs with blue spots are finer.' If he was hoping that the meeting would become coherent and tend to some end, with Mr O'Malley leading him back to the mysterious young lady in the flat, pressing a secret panel to disclose ... he did not know what – but *some* sort of solution to this mystery, he was sorely disappointed.

'I enjoy your delightful humour, sir,' Mr O'Malley replied smoothly. 'But would you do me the courtesy of reading the astonishing tale I have here and of giving me your opinion?'

'Yes,' said Machen as he took the proffered manuscript and proceeded with growing astonishment to read the following:

IT

IT made me think that Bob had gone mad, that first conversation that I had had with him over the matter. He had asked me to come and visit him in Harlesden, where he lived with his parents, in order to assist him with a difficulty, to be explained. I was at that time teaching classes at the Workers' Educational Institute which is how I had come to know this younger man.

I do not know quite why Harlesden fills me with horror. I suppose it is the curious fact that one sees red, raw suburbs which then melt into sweet and gentle countryside . . . but no, it is not quite like that. It is almost as though these red, raw suburbs have been built upon a site that exudes evil, though I do not know why. Morale seemed distinctly low as I entered a tavern and asked for a pint of beer. The barman appeared to despise me simply for entering a place fit only for drunkards and infidels. My beer was given to me sullenly and begrudgingly and as I took my seat, I felt virtually suffocated by an atmosphere of sulking hostility. I wondered why Bob had chosen it as our place of meeting.

Like most students, he was late, but when he finally appeared I was pleased enough to see him. He was a tall young man with thick brown hair and soulful dark eyes. He had told me that he liked my books and thought of me as some sort of adept at esoteric studies.

Initially, his account was quite astonishingly incoherent. Eventually, my rigorous questioning managed to elicit some sort of sense. Apparently he had wandered into the ambit of an alleged witch called Sara Szozymi. Her husband, Carlo, ran an Italian restaurant, bar, night-club and bordello. They had a red, raw villa in Harlesden. She owned a bookshop in Willesden Green, staffed by students whom she called 'my slaves'. She was also most hospitable and at her home gave wine and sandwiches freely to workers and students who professed an interest in the occult.

According to Bob, in his account of Sara's story, she had given birth to a boy roughly ten years ago. It had looked as though the infant would die. Sara, apparently a professed witch, undertook a ritual to ensure the survival of that child and in consequence she sincerely believed that she had summoned a supernatural entity which she called IT, and with IT she had made a pact, signed in her own blood. The terms of this pact were that her infant son would live and that her elder, healthy son would always have sexual congress with women whenever he needed it on condition that he brought each female to whom he made love back to his parents' home, which IT inhabited. Moreover, there would be health and wealth for Sara and her family. The whole matter had apparently been done via the 'automatic writing' of Sara, who would also acquire magical powers as part of the pact.

IT seemed, according to Bob, to have kept to the terms of the pact, and in a most devastating fashion. The child had indeed lived, although it was a physical and mental cripple. Sara was widely reputed to have formidable powers of sorcery and she always attributed them to IT, 'the honoured guest' within her home, a fine redbrick villa built in the early 1890s. Sara's husband Carlo was making a small fortune from his various schemes of business. Hospitality was freely dispensed to idealistic young students. As for Vince, he was never lacking for an attractive girlfriend. He always invited them back to his mother's house and the relationships never lasted long after that. All his girls committed suicide, entered mental asylums or had nervous breakdowns. Apparently he had no conscience about these matters at all and merely laughed about the matter.

'Can I learn anything there?' Bob asked me.

'You can learn *some*thing from a streetsweeper,' I replied as

I tried to make sense of all this nonsense. 'When can I go and see the place?'

'Later tonight?' Bob suggested. 'Meanwhile, come and have supper with my folks and, after we have seen Sara, spend the night with us.' I acceded to his suggestion and we walked through a howling wind to a small flat. Here his parents were most welcoming and gave us a hearty supper of mutton chops with mustard and fried potatoes followed by suet pudding and custard. His father, a market-stall trader, was openly sceptical about his son's educational aspirations though he showed respect to his guest and teacher of his son. Bob's mother was kind and indulgent.

'Do be careful of that Sara Szozymi, Bobby,' she warned him. Bob's father seemed initially to be a man of few words.

'You're so bloody conservative,' his son said to him at one point.

'How do you know what I am?' his father replied. 'When do you ever listen to me?'

'When do you ever talk to me?' Bob replied.

'Oh, stop it, the pair of you,' his mother said; and they did.

That evening we went out to see Sara Szozymi. Her villa was furnished lavishly and in execrable taste. There is little to be said for gilt-plated door handles, and the reproductions of portraits by Sir Joshua Reynolds did not inspire one either. However, she welcomed us warmly and made free with acceptable red wine and ham sandwiches as many young students from the Workers' Educational Association sat at her feet. She was a fat woman in a floppy dress whose protuberant brown eyes suggested an overactive thyroid gland. She proceeded to make an announcement to a somewhat overawed audience. She declared that she had had enough of IT, which she had now banished from her home. She also passed me a book of writings 'received' from IT. Although the students she had gathered beneath her roof appeared to be in awe of the matter,

I could make no sense at all of what struck me as being a series of random, haphazard and rather crazy jottings. The lines:

> 'Growl through Aethyrs for wisdom half-spent
> For knowledge grasped in truest fundament,'

did not strike me as possessing any especial virtue, and were typical of the content generally. I asked Sara what benefit this had been to her and she replied that she did not know.

'It is just there, it is not?' she demanded.

'Possibly,' I replied uneasily, but further conversation was interrupted by the entry of her son Vince accompanied by a frail, waiflike girl. She appeared to be thin to the point of ill health, yet refused all refreshment as Vince devoured two plates of sandwiches and guzzled several glasses of red wine. She said that she was tired and asked if she could just lie down for a moment. Sara said that she was only too welcome to stay; and why did she not enjoy a rest in one of the spare bedrooms upstairs? Vince gently escorted her there, doubtless put her to bed, and came downstairs to gorge another plate of his mother's sandwiches and another goblet of wine. Then, with a casual nod to his mother, he left, muttering something about coming back with another friend on the following evening. No one seemed to care about knowing the name of the waif abed upstairs.

I could make very little sense of Sara's conversation with her young guests but since I was only a guest present for the first time, I had to be polite. Essentially, she informed us that there are powers and dominions and thrones way beyond mortal ken and that she was in direct touch with them. I grew increasingly weary for I did not find the energies she generated via these platitudes and banalities to be inspiring at all. I had heard similar nonsense from so-called 'mediums' subsequently exposed as fraudulent.

I was really rather relieved when Sara's husband Carlo entered and took sandwiches and wine with us for he seemed to have no interest in these matters whatsoever and it was good to engage him in an enlivening conversation about sport. He was a jovial, fat man, wearing a tailored suit of grey who appeared to like his wife, to whom he was most attentive; and he was affable to the guests. He listened with most attentive approval to the discourse of his wife but I was hearing no sense and was finding the atmosphere oppressive. Just before Bob and I took our leave, I entered the kitchen to have a glass of water.

A small, malfunctioning, hideous and gibbering idiot was sitting in a chair, slobbering at the mouth.

I said hallo and goodbye.

On our return to Bob's home, we found his father dressed in a smart brown suit, wearing gleaming black shoes of cheap leather, and straightening his maroon silk tie. He wore also a very clean white shirt.

'Now,' he declared proudly, 'now I go to *work*.' He straightened his back. 'A man must work,' he added, with a pointed glance at his unemployed son; then he strode out of the house with an immaculate dignity.

There were twin beds for Bob and myself. I had brought some brandy and so we did not fall asleep until dawn and did not arise until four in the afternoon. After a few cups of tea with his mother, it was time to eat again with his father, who had worked, come home, slept and was looking forward to going to work again. There was certainly nothing wrong with the chicken pie and beans with mash followed by treacle sponge and custard.

'How about . . .' I suggested to Bob, 'how about you introduce me to some of the better pubs around here tonight and we have some good fourpenny ale and chat about things in general?'

'That's a very good idea, Bobby,' his mother said. 'Here, I

can give you the money...' Bob had told me that she worked as a cleaner in a local shoe-polish factory. Her husband snorted disgustedly but was silenced by one fierce look from his wife. 'It's education that's all-important, Joseph,' she said to her husband. 'We *want* our children to be better than us.'

'So do I,' her husband replied, 'but presently I do not see how that may be.' He coughed. 'Where is the *work*?' He laughed coarsely. 'All this education nonsense and my son is without employment.'

'Joseph,' his wife pleaded, 'Bobby is working with his *brain*.'

'Oh?' her husband grunted and growled. 'So that's what they call it nowadays.'

'Bobby,' said his mother, 'here's a few coppers for your pints. Teach him well,' she added to me, 'for he's a good boy. A good boy, aren't you, Bobby?' Bobby smiled uneasily as his father farted. 'But Bobby, just stay away from that Sara Szozymi,' She turned to me. 'Don't you think that she's terrible?'

'Yes,' I said, 'and that's why I would rather see some good pubs around here, Mrs Brown.' She laughed; and it was the first time I had heard that sound in the house.

We left and I was hoping to talk some sense into Bob whilst drinking in better pubs than those in which I had suffered hitherto. After we had relaxed, I was going to tell him that he was wasting his time with Sara Szozymi, for there was no wisdom to be gained there. Bob did indeed show me to a friendly pub near the cemetery of Kensal Green; we came out in order to explore the area for another congenial hostelry and just as I was beginning to enjoy the bracing evening air, a hansom cab drew up very fast. Out of it crept a young man I vaguely recognized from the previous evening. He was cadaverous and skinny with a hunched bodily posture. I think that Georgio was his name.

'Sara wants to see you,' he told Bob.

'Very well,' Bob responded and stepped into the cab. Since

I was a guest, there was no alternative except to follow him.

'IT has come back...' These were the words with which Sara greeted us as we entered her home, 'and at my specific invitation.' The scene was much the same as before, for the wine flowed and there were plenty of sandwiches and half-starving students from the Workers' Educational Association, all of them thirsting for further knowledge. However, the atmosphere appeared to be a little hostile to Bob and also to me.

'Do you,' Georgio asked Bob, 'perform any magical or mystical practices?'

'Perform...?' Bob faltered. 'Well, in line with what Sara has been saying, I essay Astral Travel.'

'How much does a Season Ticket cost?' I asked: and I noticed that Sara was twitching with an inner fury. 'Are you telling me that your spirit can leave your body at will and proceed to weird and wonderful places? Or do you merely engage in pointless mental drifting?'

'Who is this man?' Georgio enquired of me. I looked at him and thought that he might be the inspiration for an evil servant in *Dracula* by Bram Stoker. Sara, lying upon a sofa, twisted her body and cracked her knuckles. 'Stop annoying Bob,' Georgio added.

'I am not being annoyed, Georgio,' Bob responded with dignity. 'As far as I am concerned, anyone is entitled to question me.'

'Splendid, sir!' I cried out. 'Allow me to serve you another glass of this good wine!'

At the instant that my hand touched the large half-full bottle of Valpolicella, Sara Szozymi sprang to her feet with her unappealing, flabby facial features twisted into the lineaments of rage.

'Get out!' she screamed at me. 'Just get out! GET OUT OF HERE!'

'With the greatest of pleasure,' I replied, adding in an undertone: 'Extraordinary notions of hospitality...' Bob looked at the glass in his hand and then, in a rejection of which his father would have approved, he threw it hard into the open fire. The glass shattered. 'Let's go,' I said.

It was only two miles on foot to his home and I needed a good walk in the cold, crisp and clean air. We had gone about one mile when suddenly a brougham pulled up and Carlo and Georgio jumped out, neither of them looking especially friendly.

'You!' Carlo shouted, pointing his finger at Bob. 'You! You have insulted my wife. You have thrown a glass at her! And in my house!' Behind him, Georgio did his best to look menacing. This was not a particularly convincing act and it was easy to stare him down.

'I did not throw a glass at your wife, Carlo,' Bob responded quietly. 'I threw my glass into the fire.'

'Something hit her!' Carlo shouted. 'She is bleeding.'

'You will be soon,' Georgio mumbled feebly.

'There is no point in this,' I said. 'Why don't we all just go home quietly? Isn't that the best for all of us?' I stared hard at Carlo and I could see that he would not welcome any further problems. His ghastly wife had forced him into putting on this undignified display of bad manners; and I had no quarrel of any personal nature with him.

'You do not come to my house again,' Carlo said to Bob, then he waved to Georgio and they both climbed back inside the brougham as the driver scratched his head. There was a third party in that carriage.

For an instant I thought that it was a *skeleton*: but it was probably that skinny waif brought back to Sara's home by her son Vince in consequence of her pact with IT.

When we reached Bob's home, his mother had gone to bed and his father was polishing his shoes.

'To *work*,' he declared proudly. 'A man is not a man without work.' Then he stood up straight, adjusted his tie, which was perfectly knotted, marched into the cold late-autumn night and went on his way.

'Thank you,' Bob said as I caught a hansom just outside his home. 'I reckon that you have saved my sanity.' He coughed awkwardly. 'See you again.'

'A pleasure, Bob, always a pleasure,' I replied. 'Anyway, bloody vampires, that's the long and short of IT, eh?' I mounted the hansom feeling as though I had done something good. During the course of my journey, I tried to put together the words I would tell to my lover, Perpetua. Sloane Square, where I sometimes lived with her, was a far cry from a small flat in Harlesden.

The visual images of Sara's face, twisted with black, inhuman rage, and that of Sara's youngest son, the gibbering, idiot, drooling dwarf, reverberated within my mind. There was also the memory of the skeleton.

I had promised Mr and Mrs Brown that I would do all I could for their unemployed son via my connections in addition to my teaching of him but what on Earth would I tell Perpetua?

'Darling!' she cried out as I entered her town mansion, 'you're just in time for a glass of fizz. Oh, and Julian and Dominique are coming round later for a spot of *foie gras*. How was your time in Harlesden?' she asked, as though I had visited Tierra del Fuego.

'Very ordinary,' I said. 'Just trying to help a student.'

The goodly Mr and Mrs Brown need no longer have any fears about their son, whom I have rescued from the frightful clutches of Sara Szozymi. IT certainly showed him something, especially the fact that Sara had no class. Bob is now a bonded manservant of Perpetua and does a fine job in keeping the house immaculately clean and tidy for her. After all, and as his father rightly says of this vampirized slave, 'a man is not a man without work.'

NOTE ON THE AUTHOR

Arthur Machen was born in 1863 in Gwent. His career began in London where he tutored in classics, cataloguing also for antiquarian booksellers, especially in the field of esoteric literature. He was also employed as a translator: his twelve volumes of *The Memoirs of Jacques Casanova* is the definitive edition in English.

His nonfiction work, *The Anatomy of Tobacco*, and his pastiche of Rabelais, *The Chronicle of Clemendy*, launched him upon his career as an independent writer. His *The Great God Pan* and 'The Inmost Light' caused quite a sensation when published in 1894, bringing forth both adverse criticism and praise.

His finest published work hitherto, however, is considered by connoisseurs to be *The Three Impostors*, published in 1895 but severely criticized by contemporary reviewers as being 'decadent' due to the hostile atmosphere at the time, occasioned by the disgrace of Oscar Wilde.

It is to be hoped that 'IT', the latest tale from his haunting pen, will restore a rightful reputation to an unjustly neglected author.

'This is a most absorbing and provoking tale,' said Arthur Machen as he folded it slowly and returned it to the smooth, smiling, clean-shaven gentleman very quickly. 'There is only one problem, Mr O'Malley,' he added with some indignation and righteous asperity. '*I* am Arthur Machen and although the facts stated about me are true, for the most part, I did *not* write this story called "IT". Although it has many merits, it has not been done in my manner at all; it is not even a good pastiche of my manner.' He drank deeply of his beer as Mr O'Malley produced a silver case and calmly flicked it open so that he could select a Turkish cigarette. 'Who is this impostor who purports to write tales of horror and the supernatural whilst usurping my name?'

'Why, sir...' Mr O'Malley looked utterly astonished, even more amazed than Arthur Machen, 'you really do surprise me. Wonders will never cease, it seems. Arthur Machen is a very good friend of mine and I encouraged him during all the early struggles that most fine writers must endure. I was delighted when his work at last began to receive the acclaim it so richly deserves. In my opinion, his *The Three Impostors* is a masterpiece of Literature by the standards of which we spoke earlier. Now, sir, given this and the excellence of his tale "IT", which, as you rightly remark, forms a new and, I think, productive stylistic departure, well... your claims leave me breathless. How can you possibly pretend to impersonate my excellent friend, a most kindly soul, incidentally; and how can you possibly purport to be this exquisite artist in literature? Forgive me, sir, but I think that this is something of an insult to my esteemed friend.'

'I *am* Arthur Machen!' Machen expostulated. 'I *am*, for

better or for worse, the author of *The Three Impostors* . . .' He paused; for Mr O'Malley was regarding him as though he was an escaped lunatic.

'It pains me to say it, sir,' Mr O'Malley responded, 'but I have scant patience with impostors.'

'I demand,' said Arthur Machen, 'to meet this man who claims to be "Arthur Machen".'

'I think that we had best discuss this matter over another beer,' said Mr O'Malley as if he was humouring a madman. Machen noticed that his glass was empty and assented to this proposition, absolutely determined not to let go of this matter until he had made sense of all this nonsense that was causing his head to whirl. He looked at Jug and decided that he would be as determined as his bulldog. He certainly required another beer. And then he noticed that Mr O'Malley was not standing at the bar. Machen assumed that he was answering a call of Nature. Ten minutes passed without sight of Mr O'Malley. Machen entered the door marked GENTLEMEN himself but still there was no sign of his erstwhile companion. He made a subsequent enquiry at the bar, only to be informed that the smooth, smiling, clean-shaven gentleman after whom he asked had departed swiftly and without explanation. When Machen returned to his seat, he found the tale entitled 'IT'.

Machen's subsequent research and enquiries disclosed that there was no Castle O'Malley in County Galway.

All matters before him were melting into a Scotch mist or, in this case, an Irish mist – elusive, intangible and yet sinister.

CHAPTER SIX

A CRISIS AT THE CONNAUGHT
(BACK TO BASICS)

'Miss Fanshawe,' Adam Stride said to Miss Alison Featherstonehaugh over dinner in the restaurant of the Connaught Hotel, Mayfair, to which she had peremptorily invited him, 'if you would be so kind, I would like you to make yourself clear.'

'A woman, Mr Stride, can make manners clear,' the exquisite young lady with eyes of shining hazel and a face that was quaint and piquant rather than beautiful responded. 'A woman can make matters clear. But her Self? Mr Stride, you are asking too much.'

'The clarity of the manner and the matter will do well enough, Madam,' Stride replied, slightly taken aback by her first-class statement. He had been to the Connaught before and thought it to be among the finest of restaurants that London could boast. The food had always been exquisite and he particularly relished the excellence of the service. Whenever he put his hand in his pocket to draw out a cigarette and then fumbled for a light, a waiter would appear from nowhere to give fire to his tobacco and as Stride inclined his head to give thanks for this courteous gesture, the waiter was nowhere to be seen. They had started with dressed crab, accompanied by brown bread and butter and the finest mayonnaise that Stride had ever tasted. Now they were enjoying a chateaubriand that had been done to perfection, accompanied by a delectable sauce bearnaise, lightly buttered spinach, fried potatoes sliced into enticing strips and a deliciously dressed green salad. Stride contemplated discreetly the tight black silken gown that Alison was wearing. Beneath it, as his ears informed him, she was wearing petticoats that rustled every time she crossed her legs. The Gewürztraminer they had relished with the crab and the heady and rich Chateau La Tâche they now enjoyed added to this dinner a sensation of intoxication.

'I always think,' Alison mused thoughtfully, 'that good food merely serves as an accompaniment to the juices of the vine. As Rabelais has it in his wondrous *Gargantua & Pantagruel*: "By wine is Man made divine".'

'I see what he means,' Stride said as he savoured the liquor within his glass. 'Even so, and despite the excellence of this establishment, I have information for you that I cannot give until you have answered some troubling and perplexing questions.'

'What a clever man you are!' The girl's peal of laughter did not contribute to Stride's peace of mind. 'Why, Mr Stride,' her face shone with wide-eyed innocence, 'please feel free to ask me anything that you may choose.'

'Thank you.' Stride cut off another piece of rare Aberdeen Angus beef and chewed it thoughtfully, enjoying the sensation of rich, fresh blood flowing down his throat. Every cell of his body told him that this was doing him good. 'I do not care for being threatened. Miss Fanshawe, why *did* you threaten me?'

'Oh, Mr Stride, you did not take that matter seriously, did you? I'm sorry if I upset you but I'm afraid I can't resist the odd joke from time to time. I don't want to cut your balls off and stick them in your mouth. No, by no means. However, I *would* be pleased to receive some results.'

'It would be easier,' Stride returned, 'if you had not suddenly departed without so much as a goodbye and without even leaving me an address and phone number.'

'I'm sorry again, Mr Stride,' Alison answered. 'The fact is

that if *I* am paying *you* my address and telephone number are of no consequence to you. They are none of your business. Don't poke your nose into matters that do not concern you. I want you to poke your nose into matters that *do* concern you, especially,' she laughed lightly, 'since I am paying you to do so.' She bit hungrily into her steak, so much so that blood stained her chiselled, dimpled chin. She wiped the liquid away with a white napkin. 'You can, of course, give me my money back if you have been promising what you cannot deliver...'

'Madam,' Stride replied with a smile, 'this case is far too intriguing for me to give it up.' He proceeded to inform her of the plastic red hand, making her giggle; and of the curious communications involving Septimus Keen, whom he had always assumed to be a creature of his own colourful imagination.

'Well,' said Miss Alison Featherstonehaugh, 'well, well, well. I must say that I thoroughly enjoyed your novel *The Labyrinth of Satan*. It was such a play on Arthur Machen's *The Three Impostors*, wasn't it? What a wonderful read! And when I found out that you were a private detective...'

'How did you find that out?'

'Simple. I hired a private detective. Now, Mr Stride, I think you are the right man for this job; tell me how far you have advanced in the matter. Oh! I see that we have finished with this course and I really do think that we must have pudding, don't you? It's frightfully old-fashioned, I know, and these days out of fashion altogether, but would you care to join me for crêpes Suzette?' Stride nodded in delighted acquiescence since he had not enjoyed this dish since the late 1960s.

'A bottle of Chateau d'Yquem would go rather well with it, don't you think?' he said – and the deed was done. 'Now, Miss Fanshawe...'

'Alison.'

'Adam.' They stared into one another's eyes and when Stride

touched her left toe with his right foot, she did not snatch it away.

'I have many things for you, Alison, and some are in my briefcase in the cloakroom. Allow me to summarize the present position.' Both looked with pleasure upon the waiter who was lighting a spirit lamp and preparing the pancakes. The blue flames licked at the pan as Stride continued. 'The Holy Grail, the details of whose legend I have written down for you, is certainly a noble mythic concept. According to the Christian Mythos, it was a cup containing the blood of Christ which Joseph of Arimathea brought to Great Britain and had buried at the allegedly sacred site of Glastonbury. It is central to the romances involving tales of King Arthur and his Knights of the Round Table, the central motive of which is the Quest for the Holy Grail, also known as the Sangraal. It has featured as well, however, in many pre-Christian cultures. It seems that the Christians have appropriated or misappropriated the idea. We find it in the Celtic legends long before Christianity. We find it in Middle Eastern tales, too. It is sometimes described not as a chalice but as a shield. Or a dish. All agree that the merest flicker of insight into the Grail will transform your life forever, for it is the Holiest of Holies, the Medicine of Metals and the Stone of the Wise. Arthur Machen investigated the matter with his customary honesty and thoroughness and concluded that *the Grail is a stone.*'

'So could the stone I have loaned you be the Grail?' Alison enquired. Our waiter poured cognac, Cointreau and curaçao upon our pancakes and yellow flames erupted joyously.

'I have investigated that too.' By this moment, Stride's trousered knee and Alison's skirted knee were pressed together and Stride had to put a hand in his pocket to adjust his throbbing erection. Stride informed her of the reaction in Hatton Garden. 'I then went to a friend of mine in the Metropolitan Police.' Alison remained impassive. 'He informed me that there was no report of any gem of this nature having been stolen. Indeed, the Metropolitan Police are not aware of any such valuable gem. My next step was to consult an acquaintance at the British Museum. He informed me that the black pearl within this ankh of brass that you have loaned me, Alison, might not in fact be a pearl at all. Professor Dawson thought that it might be obsidian.'

'What is obsidian?' Alison asked as the flaming pancakes were served.

'It is a dark, vitreous lava or volcanic rock like bottle glass, according to *The Concise Oxford Dictionary*.'

'How can dark vitreous lava or volcanic rock be like bottle glass?'

'Glass is made by the action of extreme heat on silica, a naturally occurring mineral: sand is mainly composed of it, for example. "Obsidian", the word, comes from *Obsius*, "name of finder of a similar stone, mentioned by Pliny". According to the *Collins Gem English Dictionary*, obsidian is "dark glassy volcanic rock".'

'So it may not be a pearl.'

'A pearl comes out of an oyster and obsidian comes out of the earth, forged by fire. Now, Professor Dawson professed himself to be no expert in the matter of gemstones. However, he did tell me about the extraordinary "shew-stone" of Dr John Dee, the Elizabethan magus and, for a time, principal adviser to Queen Elizabeth I. Some historians credit this man as having been the founder of the English Renaissance. "All things end in mystery" was a favourite saying of Arthur Machen, and here is one. Dr John Dee, according to his records, used a number of shew-stones. A crystal and his "magic mirror" can be seen in the British Museum. The latter, which is black and made of obsidian, was obtained from the Aztecs by a member of Cortes's Mexican *conquistador* force. We do not know how it came into Dee's possession though it is possible that it may have been through the piratical plundering of Spanish galleons by Sir Francis Drake. Long after Dee's death, it somehow passed into the hands of Horace Walpole, author and the nephew of England's first acknowledged Prime Minister. He glued beneath it the sneer of Samuel Butler in *Hudibras* (1664), referring to E. Kelley, Dee's notorious assistant who used to "scry in the spirit vision".' Adam Stride, quoting Samuel Butler, now proceeded to burst into verse:

' "Kelley did all his Feats upon
The Devil's Looking-glass, a stone
Where playing with him at *Bo-peep*
He solved all problems ne'er so deep." '

'Curiouser and curiouser,' said Alison. 'What happened next?'

'The history of this alleged stone is explored further by Hugh Tait in 'The Devil's Looking-Glass: the Magical Speculum of Dr John Dee', in *Horace Walpole: Writer, Politician and Connoisseur*, edited by one Warren Hunting Smith and published in New Haven, Connecticut, USA and London, UK, in 1967. The British Museum, meanwhile, claimed to have acquired this object in 1966, October being the month. Professor Dawson suggested, though he hastened to add that this was only a suggestion, that "a chip off the old block" might have been taken and forged into this ankh of brass with which you, Alison, presented me.'

'I applaud the thorough nature of your research, Adam,' Alison replied, 'and I hope you have enjoyed your pudding as much as I have. What do you say to the cheeseboard?'

'*Always* have the cheeseboard,' Stride answered, 'and it goes best with half a bottle of fine claret. A Chateau Mouton Rothschild 1966 might not suit us too badly here.' By this time, as he ordered, their knees were firmly interlocked.

'But one thing worries me,' Alison added. 'Is the stone within the brass made of pearl or of obsidian?'

'This is what worries me also, Alison,' Stride replied, meanwhile gloating over the cheeses that had been brought to them. He made a point of gouging the ripest portion of Stilton as she cut eagerly into the Brie and then used a spoon to scoop some Caerphilly. 'Two men initially refused to deal with me on this matter.' He was referring to Mr Cohen and Mr Levi of Hatton Garden. 'Never mind their names. They owed me favours and I needed some truths and I fear I had to put the screws on.'

'Oh, Adam,' the young lady fluttered her eyelids demurely, 'I didn't know that you could be so wicked.'

'Sometimes,' Stride muttered. 'Anyway, both are expert in the matter of gemstones. I saw them separately again after their initial refusals to have anything to do with the device and their respective expertises left me gobsmacked. For one man,' he referred to Moses Cohen, 'pronounced that it was a pearl, *a black pearl*. Yet in the second opinion,' he thought of Mr Levi, 'he had no doubt that the stone was of *obsidian*. This could be said to both confirm and contradict Professor Dawson's opinion that chips might have been taken from the old block. Feeling completely confused, I tried the experiment of taking it to a pawnbroker in Finsbury Park. He told me that a brass ankh with a piece of *rubber* embedded in it was not worth very much. So, you see, Alison, it appears to change all the time.

'The matter becomes more perplexing,' Stride continued. 'And then I met Mr Ron Butcher.' He proceeded to tell Alison all about his peculiar encounter.

'This is all absolutely astonishing!' Alison exclaimed. 'The more so since I met a man answering to your description of Butcher only the other night. A big, bulky, ugly man with a florid face and whose gross facial features were adorned by a ginger moustache which merged into a pair of unpleasant and bulbous chin whiskers . . . do you detect a resemblance?' Stride nodded. 'Adam, have you ever been *stalked*?' Stride shook his head. 'This man was following me wherever I went. I feared for my life! I complained to the police but they told me that they could do nothing unless I were to be mutilated or murdered. Well, that won't do me very much good, will it? And so it came to pass that I was sitting in a wine bar at Parsons Green, which was full of the usual braying yuppies with their ghastly mobile phones – frankly, I think that anyone who pulls out a mobile phone to state: "Hallo – I'm in a Parsons Green wine bar" should be pelted to death with rotten vegetables – but I was waiting for a girlfriend. Unfortunately, Davina is always late. As I drank a glass of the house wine, which tasted like the sweat off the feet of the treaders, this huge man, ghastly in his features and just as you described, entered and strode to my table.

'"Good evening, Madam," he declared in a hoarse, rasping voice that was most inelegant. "I do apologize for troubling you but I would like to discuss a matter which may turn out to be of benefit to both of us. Allow me to explain. My name is Ralph Chicken and I am so pleased to be of service," he lifted his homburg hat, "to so fair a lady. If you think that I have been 'stalking' you recently, you are quite correct. Allow me to explain my reasons."

'"For how long, Mr Chicken," I replied, "must I allow your explanations?" Now I hoped that Davina would be late, since it was hardly a credit to be seen sitting with this most unprepossessing individual.

' "Oh, I can make a long story short," he replied with a sinister smile. I noticed that he was drinking the house red as though it was beer. "I have the honour of being an assistant to Dr Lipsius, the fabled collector of the arts and objects of antiquarian interest." '

'Just a moment,' Stride interrupted. 'Dr Lipsius is the principal villain in *The Three Impostors* by Arthur Machen;

and I also used this fictional creation in my *The Labyrinth of Satan*.'

'That may be so, Adam,' Alison answered as Stride's knee slid her skirt back up along her thighs. 'Mmm. Coffee, brandy and *petits fours*? Let us have armagnac. It is, I find, so much more satisfying than cognac.' Stride ordered the drinks and heard a soft 'Very good, sir.' 'But to continue with my tale, this man informed me that a brass ankh with a black stone residing therein had been robbed from the priceless collection of Dr Lipsius fifteen years ago by a certain Jacob Keen' – Stride instantly sat bolt upright – 'and had passed into the hands of my father.'

'I need more information here,' said Stride.

'Adam, it appears that you are as puzzled as I am.'

'Yes,' Stride returned, 'for sometimes when I have stared at the stone within the ankh I have seen a flickering picture of Arthur Machen.' He coughed and lit a Senior Service. 'Sometimes I see nothing.' He blew out a perfect smoke-ring. 'Pray continue with your story.' The toe of his shoe stroked her slim calf and she appeared to shiver.

'Mr Chicken,' said Alison, 'informed me that according to his employer, Dr Lipsius, I was in possession of a sacred gem . . .'

'Yes, yes,' Stride muttered slightly irritably. 'What was the connection between your father and Jacob Keen?' he demanded as the waiters served them silently.

'I don't know. My father never spoke about it. The only reason I have this gem, if gem it is, is because the contents of my late father's safety deposit box at Coutts were left to me in his will.'

'Then why not sell it to Mr Chicken?'

'I might,' Alison answered. 'But I would be a fool to do so without some sort of proper valuation. That was why I approached you; yet despite what I have paid you and your laudably thorough research, you appear to be no wiser than me.'

'No wiser, perhaps,' Stride returned, 'but possibly better informed. What was the nature of your late father's business?'

'He had an art gallery in Bond Street and also dealt in antiquities. You must have heard of Osprey's?'

'Of course. But I gather that it is no longer with us.'

'Yes,' Alison said. 'My pater was a major shareholder and now it is closed for good.' The waiter offered cigars and she selected a slim panatella, an H. Upmann. Stride selected a Jamaican corona without a label, since he had a preference for Jamaican rather than Cuban cigars. 'But to continue with my story...'

'Of course, Madam...' Stride's knee rubbed between her stockinged thighs.

'Mr Chicken,' Alison resumed her tale, 'asked me to hand it to him. Obviously I could not do that, since I have loaned it to you, though I did not tell him that. I asked him to supply proof of ownership. He asked me if I would prefer to spend the rest of my days looking over my shoulder. I informed him sharply that I was hardly accustomed to being threatened. He made a rather curious reply. He said: "Oh, you haven't gone to Adam Stride, have you?" and then he laughed in a most inelegant fashion: it was rather like dirty water gurgling down a drain.'

'I wonder,' Stride said, 'whether your Mr Ralph Chicken is the same man as the unpleasant Mr Ron Butcher of my brief acquaintanceship; whether this Dr Lipsius for whom Mr Chicken claims to work and whom I had always thought to be a creation of Arthur Machen's imagination, a creation that I used in my own novel, *The Labyrinth of Satan*, really has some actual existence; and what on Earth his motive could be in troubling you? Moreover, how could he know that you were dealing with me?'

THE GOD GAME

'I cannot answer that,' said the young lady, fluttering her blue-shadowed eyelids demurely. 'I find myself to be caught up in matters that are quite inexplicable and that, furthermore, virtually frighten me to death. That is why I came to you ... Adam.' Her shining hazel eyes implored his further assistance as her shoe lifted itself beneath the table to give a light touch to his rampant member and then withdrew. 'I am all confusion at present, especially since Mr Chicken handed me this.' She extracted a manuscript from her crocodile handbag. 'Mr Chicken told me: "Next time you see Adam Stride, just show it to him. He'll know what it means." '

Stride ordered more armagnac as he thoughtfully perused:

BACK TO BASICS

by

Septimus Keen

'The only trouble with Magick is that it doesn't work,' said Nicholas as we took cocktails together at the Savoy. Nicholas was an elegant dandy, an Oxford wit, a rationalist and a sceptic, whose company I always enjoyed and who earned a good living as a journalist for a prominent Sunday broadsheet newspaper. He was obviously enjoying his gin-and-tonic, a drink that I have always found to be ghastly, as much as I was enjoying my Bloody Mary.

'I don't agree with you at all,' I replied. 'I find that the only trouble with Magick is that it *does* work.'

'I admire your faith, Septimus,' he returned, 'since faith is the ability to believe in something one knows inwardly to be untrue. Can you supply me with the slightest bit of proof?'

'Well, I am conducting an experiment later tonight, Nicholas. Before I came out to meet you this evening, which we agreed was just for a drink, I executed a magical spell.'

'Of what nature and to what end?' he chuckled. 'I have always appreciated your delightful eccentricity.'

'Oh, you and your bloody scepticism, Nicholas. How is your love life?'

'Probably pretty much the same as yours, Septimus. I like to fuck women.' That statement was true.

'Have you never wished for something more than just a fuck? Something truly exceptional?'

'Um . . . yes. And are you telling me that you have found it?'

'No. But I intend to do so tonight. Ancient books of Magick contain spells to that end.'

'Do they really? Which books? And what sort of spells?'

'I refer to the great Masters of the Renaissance: Paracelsus,

Cornelius Agrippa and Dr John Dee. I also refer to the great twentieth-century magus, Aleister Crowley.'

'Ah, yes, the Great Beast 666 himself. Did you take your "spell" from him?'

'Do I detect a slight trace of sarcasm in your attitude, Nicholas? No; what I did was to start at the seven-pointed star drawn by Crowley and which is also called the Star of the Great Whore, BABALON. Whilst I was staring at it, focusing my mind on THAT and nothing else, I also ingested sixty psychedelic mushrooms harvested in Cornwall by friends of mine and intoned the Name "BABALON" as I stared at this star.'

'It sounds to me, Septimus,' Nicholas responded, 'as though you are going to get laid tonight, probably by some girl who is swanning around on Ecstasy. Forgive me, my dear chap, but I see nothing remarkable about getting laid. Anyone can do that. I ask you again: where is the Magick?'

'Do you see that girl over there?' I drew his attention to an exquisitely beautiful girl with long dark hair who was sitting quietly in a corner whilst sipping a cocktail which looked to be composed largely of pineapple juice. At that instant, she turned towards me dark eyes that were all aflame with desire. I was very surprised to see her sitting there since I was acquainted with her only as a clerk behind the counter in my local building society where I had a small account; yet I had always fancied her quite desperately without knowing quite how to bring my desire to a satisfactory sexual closure. 'Allow me a moment.'

'Hallo,' I said, 'it's Diana, isn't it?' I knew that from the identification card put up by the window of each clerk. 'Septimus.' We shook hands gently. 'May I join you for a moment?'

'Of course.' She sipped her drink. 'I am a little surprised to see you here.' She would be, knowing the state of my account.

'Are you waiting for someone?' I asked, thinking that only a wealthy boyfriend could bring her here.

'Yes,' she replied. 'You.'

'You surprise me.'

'I surprise many people,' she retorted. 'You see, I rather enjoy coming to the Savoy. Interesting encounters often take place here.' I invited her to dine with me at a Thai restaurant I knew nearby and introduced her to Nicholas, who was his customary charming self. Eventually he announced that he had to take a friend out to a club, probably one of his many charming ladies, and Diana and I went on our way. Our dinner was exquisite and then we took a cab back to my home, which was at that time a bedsit in Kilburn. Diana expressed no surprise at its untidy state. I have the utmost respect for women who do not beat about the bush and so we tumbled into bed together.

It was quite exquisite to hold in my arms a woman whom I had fancied from behind an urban building society counter and then met at the Savoy. O! I shall never forget that night. My body told me that I was making love with a woman. The rest of me was somewhere I had never been before.

There was a light in my head much brighter than the room's single candle illumination. My blood tingled as though its billions of cells all had lives of their own. It felt as though most of me was one long, thick living wand glowing with a white heat inside a golden chalice lined with liquid velvet. It wasn't moving much. The first time it had acted as if it was taming a wild mare. Then there had been a blinding sunburst that had made my body buckle, writhe and scream and something in me had kicked the base of my spine again and again and again. And something of me that was more than just my seed had passed into this woman.

She had wanted more. She had told me that I was great and could be greater. She had sucked a new life into me and drawn it back into her church for a renewed baptism. Her vagina was as strong as it was soft and welcoming. It wetted me, squeezed me, kissed me and came all around me as I seemed to float along a river that was made of milk and honey.

Absolutely everything that I had ever asked for in an experience of sexual congress was there. I fell asleep in a state of bliss.

I awoke later in the night, expecting to embrace a woman who had been all moving flesh and blood. To my horror and astonishment, I did not find this. I felt only bones. This alarmed me greatly and I leapt to the light, turning it on.

There was a skeleton in my bed.

The skull was grinning.

With horror wreaking havoc upon my heart, I put forward tentative fingers to touch the bones of this skeleton. To my terror, it crumpled into dust before my very eyes.

I shrieked out and ran to a corner of the room. Now I could no longer see a skeleton: I could see only dust. Fearfully and tentatively, I approached the bed. There was nothing there except a pile of dust upon the sheets, rather as though I had been suffering recently from a bad case of dandruff.

On the following morning, I received an unexpected cheque through the post and went to my building society in order to cash it. As usual, Diana was sitting behind the counter.

'Pleasure seeing you yesterday,' I said as I banked my cheque.

'Oh, yeah?' she looked at me enquiringly. 'Where?'

'The Savoy,' I said, thinking that she was playing games with me – or else wishing publicly to deny any liaison with a customer.

'Oh, Mr Keen,' she giggled, 'I'd never have any occasion to go there. Now, how would you like your money?'

Having had no desire to reveal myself as a lunatic in a Kilburn building society branch yet feeling quite hopelessly bewildered by all that had transpired, I met Nicholas at the Savoy again the next evening as we had agreed, and proceeded to tell him about everything that had happened. I was only too happy to join him in a glass of Chateau La Tâche, the 1987 vintage.

'My dear Septimus,' he chortled, 'you always delight me with your tales. This one is even more preposterous than usual, though there is a clear and rational explanation. You undertook what you assured me was "a magical operation". You then proceeded to ingest substances that alter consciousness. What happened at your home, therefore, is purely something brought about by your own imagination.'

'Possibly so . . .' I answered hesitantly, 'for that is usually how the Devil speaks to us . . . now, come off it, Nicholas, for you are my witness. Last night, in here, did I not pick up a beautiful young girl with long dark hair?'

'No,' Nicholas answered. 'I shall tell you exactly what I heard and saw. After listening to you regarding your Magick burble, I saw you approach a fat old lady with grey hair and glasses. To my absolute stupefaction, you appeared to find her sexually attractive and I can only assume that you only did that because you knew who she was.'

'Sorry, not quite clear. Who, in your opinion, *was* she?'

'Why, have you not followed the news at all? The woman you spoke with was Sophia Maria, in her time one of the world's more notable singers of opera. Of course, at ninety-three, this lady is rather past her prime and I attributed the intensity of your attentions to your temporary inebriation and love of opera.'

'Just a moment.' I swallowed my own saliva. 'Did you see me leaving this bar with her or didn't you?'

'Yes,' Nicholas answered, 'I saw you leaving arm-in-arm with this elderly lady, mentioning something about the excellence of Thai cuisine and a good place that you knew. I left the hotel shortly afterwards and picked up some bitch I fucked without recourse to Magick and old age pensioners.' He smiled uncomfortably. 'But no, Septimus, you could not possibly have gone home to Kilburn in order to make love to Sophia Maria, even if you do have a fetish about old ladies. You must have left the bar around eight in the evening. Now, the remainder of the evening must consist purely as an adventure of your somewhat extravagant imagination.'

'What are you saying?'

'Have you not read the papers? It's in every Arts section. Sophia Maria died here in her suite last night.'

'What an intriguing tale...' Stride murmured as his bowels endeavoured to fend off a gnawing unease. 'I find it doubly so since the style of this tale by "Septimus Keen" that I did not write is so similar to the tales attributed to "Septimus Keen" that I *did* write.' His knee was locked between Alison's and through his trousers he could feel the magic texture of her skirt. 'Why don't we retire to my place, where we can discuss these matters in the privacy they assuredly require?' Alison nodded a gracious acquiescence. 'Excellent! Allow me to attend to the insignifant trifle of our bill of fare...'

Afterwards, Stride could not have sworn precisely as to what took place and nor could his trusted assistant, Ms Rosa Scarlett, whom he had requested to trail him. Rosa Scarlett later told him that she followed him home as instructed and saw him enter with Miss Alison Featherstonehaugh. She then received instructions from Adam Stride via mobile phone to go home, which she did only too gladly.

Adam Stride recalled going to bed with an exquisitely sexy bitch of a woman, but little else. He remembered that his ribs had ached from the crushing embrace she had given him during one of her orgasms. She had given him something greater than himself in return. His consciousness was reeling from it. She had wiped out his mind and invaded his soul with – what was it? A blessing? A curse? He could recollect just one extraordinary moment.

Two hands were stroking all along and up his spine. He stared into her shining hazel eyes. These were blazing in a face completely calm.

'Now,' said Alison. His buttocks jerked as though struck by

lightning. *It* flared up his spine and struck his brain, stunning his awareness into a crackling white criss-crossed crescendo of starfire that poured down his body like molten lava. As he lost control in a series of spasms, Death appeared to him and opened his eyelids. And at that instant, she quenched the fire that threatened to consume him. She came like a tempest of storm and rain, deluging him in a hot flood of lust.

'O,' was all that he could whisper. He vaguely remembered that she kissed him, licked him, smoothed his shoulders with her hands and laid him gently upon his bed.

'Sleep, lover, sleep.' Her words echoed in his memory.

On the following morning, Adam Stride awoke to an empty bed and curious memories.

One souvenir had been left by the bedside: it was 'Back to Basics' by 'Septimus Keen'.

Stride decided to have a cup of very strong coffee prior to going to his office downstairs and asking Rosa Scarlett for her report on the events of the previous evening.

As he was taking his coffee and fumbling through his possessions for all that he might need today, he came upon the ankh within his trousers. He glanced at it briefly, being somewhat hungover, and then started. The picture was as clear as if he was watching breakfast television. In front of Stride, portrayed clearly within the gem, was a fiercely concentrating Arthur Machen.

There was a flash of astonishment in Machen's keen, bright eyes, then the stone clouded over and the vision was gone, so completely that Stride now felt he was staring at a featureless black India rubber ball.

CHAPTER SEVEN

PECULIARITIES IN PENTONVILLE
(PLAYING DOUBLES)

Way back in 1899, Arthur Machen was finding it rather hard to make sense of the new angles of the world presented to him. Outside it was a cold winter's evening and a dense mist was gathering around Verulam Buildings. At six o'clock, he usually inspected his writing of the day and reckoned up the day's portion. Sometimes he cursed himself for wrecking a fine conception with maladroit execution, since he was a perfectionist in all literary matters. As he was wont to say: 'One dreams in fire and one works in clay.'

He read through his work, the first chapter of *The Secret Glory*. At times his being glowed over some felicitous phrasing. At other instants, his face blushed scarlet with the shame of failure and he made notes and resolved to rewrite. He took extraordinary pains to make his prose fluid, easy to read and also beautiful. Having seen some errors that he had made, he noted them for subsequent correction. He intended this to be the greatest novel he had hitherto written, finer even than his *The Hill of Dreams* that still languished without a publisher. He did not know it then, but *The Hill of Dreams* would not be published until 1907 when it would be condemned by a critic as 'the most decadent book in English Literature'. He did not know it then, but his *The Secret Glory*, a novel about a young man persecuted at a minor public school who unexpectedly comes into possession of the Holy Grail, for which possession he is subsequently murdered in the Middle East, would not be published until 1922 when it would be received by critics with derision.

What he *did* know was that he held an extraordinary object in his hands, the brass ankh inlaid with the black pearl, and that its nature puzzled him intensely, since he had received it in so extraordinary a manner and its reception had been followed by rationally inexplicable encounters. He had even been told that within his hands he held the Holy Grail.

Machen had studied all the tales of the Holy Grail during months of arduous research in the Reading Room of the British Museum. His learned essays on the subject had been published in journals of quality such as *Literature* and *The Pall Mall Gazette*. He firmly believed and had firmly argued that in considering the Holy Grail, there is a matrix deriving from Celtic, Mediterranean, Turanian, Teutonic, Nordic, Middle Eastern and Christian myths and legends, all of which might not be precisely historically accurate but some of which enshrined sacred truths of the spirit.

Although the Grail had been described variously as a Cup, a Chalice, a Dish or a Shield, Machen's profound studies had led him to concur with the *Parzival* of Wolfram von Eschenbach in stating that *the Grail is a stone*. Surely it could not be possible that, here and now, he was holding the Holy Grail in his own hands? He glanced at fragments of a poem he had attempted earlier in the week:

'One day when I was all alone
I found a wondrous little stone . . .'

'No, it's not terribly good, is it?' Machen muttered to himself as he sought after the possibilities of a finer choice of words. What *was* he to make of the gem before him? He had stared at it upon many occasions and the stone had refused to yield unto him its secrets. On other occasions, however, he had glimpsed visions in the stone as if he was watching a series of pictures at an exhibition. He had seen at various times an Egyptian, a Greek, an Israelite, a Roman, a medieval monk, a scholar of the Renaissance, another scholar of the Enlightenment, a French Revolutionary, an American mystic, an English magician ... and then there were weird disruptions of time since he could suddenly see visions of the mid-eighteenth century's so-called Hell-Fire Club under Sir Francis Dashwood. On other occasions there was something else that he saw and that worried him further. This was the picture of a man dressed in futuristic garb who seemed to have access to futuristic machines. All these men appeared to be gazing at the stone with a manic intensity of concentration and seemed to be as astonished to see him as he was at the sight of them.

Now, as he stared at the stone, he saw this man of the future again. His image flickered momentarily within the stone and then it was gone. After ten minutes of fruitless, dull staring, there was nothing more to be seen. Machen sighed and replaced the ankh in a secret drawer of his lacquered Japanese bureau.

Troubled by doubts and perplexities, he clipped a lead around the collar of his beloved bulldog Juggernaut and resolved upon a walk. He had always held that eastward and northward of the Gray's Inn Road still remained all the splendours of the unknown. Here he loved the feeling that he had left the London that he knew far behind. There was something different, something strange, in the whole look of the quarter. It was rare to find any building younger than sixty years. He was sure that they were all secret people who lived to the east of the Gray's Inn Road: secret and severed people who had fallen out of the great noisy march of the high road for one reason or another, and so he saw them as dwelling apart in these misty streets and squares of 1850, wondering when it would be 1851.

Entering into Frederick Street, Machen then climbed the hill of Great Percy Street and felt that he had entered a Silent

Land, a paradise for a poor student whose chief needs would be peace and a dwelling a short distance from the British Museum. There was hardly anybody about; he passed through a short street without meeting a soul. There were no shops here to draw people; there was a deep, leafy silence. For trees grew everywhere in this happy place. They leaned over garden walls, they congregated together in hushed squares, they thrust in profusion from little patches of odd ground, from behind railings, in every unexpected corner, and there were short flights of steps that led to mysterious alleys or passages or byways going to nowhere in particular. Here, too, he found unexpected ash groves and sweet quivering poplars and little houses strangely tucked away. Here there was no jangle of the tram and, in thirty minutes of walking, Machen saw neither cab nor vehicle of any sort, since the storms of his age did not beat about this place.

It was hard for him to leave these quiet backwaters but he struck on boldly through Great Percy Street, by Amwell Street, into Claremont Square, which was built around a great cistern of the New River Company. He had long known Pentonville as a dreary, dusty hill; but on the winter's day that he climbed it, he saw one of its grey, grim housefronts all glowing purple with rich bunches of ripe grapes: Dionysius crowned and triumphant and seen from that sad mount of Pentonville. He reflected that strangeness, which is the essence of beauty, is the essence of truth and the essence of the world. Standing on the summit of an undiscovered height in London, he felt that he looked down on a new land.

He descended the hill slowly and reverentially, to find the grave main highway as quiet, sedate and serious as if London was a hundred miles away – though an advance guard of the new raw redbrick villas had already come within a field of a second-hand bookshop with its bow-windows and small square panes. Seeing a public house, he resolved upon the imbibing of some refreshment. On entering, he was utterly astonished to see a dead ringer for The Young Man with Spectacles whom he had portrayed in his novel *The Three Impostors*, whom he recognized seconds later as an acquaintance from The Hermetic Order of the Golden Dawn that he had recently joined. It was William Butler Yeats. Machen greeted him with his customary courtesy and gladly acceded to Yeats's request for a pint of old and mild. Then he informed him about the recent walk that had led him there.

'And then besides these odd remnants and oddities,' this Irish poet replied, 'there stretches the vast expanse of the modern suburbs, all red and new, shiny and flimsy, climbing the green hill before your eyes, breaking into the heart of the old wood. And the myriads who live in these new houses: who are they?'

'City clerks, very likely,' Machen answered, 'but there will be a sprinkling of high mystics, and here and there an alchemist who watches for the Engendering of the Crow, and hopes yet to see the glory of the Son Blessed of the Fire.'

'I am a Son of the Water,' said Yeats. Machen found this statement to be true enough since he had read some of Yeats's poetry and found it to be rather wet. They had met within the portals of a secret society devoted to Ceremonial Magick and called the outer order of the seventeenth-century Rosicrucians. 'But what is your opinion of the Golden Dawn?'

'I must confess,' Machen replied, drinking deeply of his beer, 'that it is doing me much good for the time being. To stand waiting at a closed door in a breathless expectation, to see it open suddenly and disclose two figures clothed in a habit that I never thought to see worn by the living, to catch for a moment the vision of a cloud of incense smoke and certain dim lights glimmering in it before the bandage is put over the eyes and the arm feels a firm grasp upon it that leads the hesitating footsteps into the unknown darkness . . .' He paused as he recalled the ceremony of his initiation.

'Child of Earth, arise! And enter into the Path of Darkness...'

He recalled being led to the North, South, East and West, each time to be challenged, purified and consecrated. He remembered the chant:

'Holy art Thou, Lord of the Universe!
Holy art Thou Whom Nature has not formed!
Holy art Thou, The Vast and Mighty One!
Lord of the Light – and of the Darkness!'

'All this,' Machen continued to address Yeats, 'was strange and admirable indeed. Strange it was to think that within a foot or two of those closely curtained windows the common life of London moved on the common pavement, as supremely unaware of what was being done within an arm's length, as if our works had been the works of the other side of the moon. All this is very fine . . .' *An addition, and a valuable one*, he thought, *to the phantasmagoria that is being presented to me.*

'Very fine indeed, sir,' the dark young man of quiet and retiring aspect, who wore glasses, answered him. 'But are you not aware of the dangers?'

'Sorry?' Machen looked puzzled and stared momentarily at his bulldog.

'My life,' said William Butler Yeats, 'has been put in daily jeopardy by a fiend in human form. Ah, I see you doubt my words. Mr Machen, are you at all acquainted with Aleister Crowley, otherwise known as Count Vladmir Svareff and our Brother Perdurabo?'

'Only vaguely,' Machen answered truthfully, as he always did. 'He is the one who took the motto: "I shall endure", a graduate of Cambridge University, a wickedly handsome young man who leads, by all accounts, a somewhat reckless sex life;

and he has published some volumes of poetry that I have yet to read. What is his poetry like?'

'It is *abominable*!' Yeats shouted, his eyes growing dark with rage behind his glasses. 'Furthermore, this daemonic reprobate is well known to be an expert in Black Magic.' Yeats foamed at the mouth with indignation and spilled his beer. 'He hangs up naked women in cupboards by hooks which pierce the flesh of their arms!'

'Sorry, not quite with you there, Mr Yeats,' Machen murmured. '*How* does one go about hanging up naked women in this manner? Don't they protest? Don't they go to the police?'

'Crowley is so infernally cunning that the police would never catch him,' Yeats replied. 'And now this monster is going for me! He has hired a gang in Lambeth who are grievously to maim or preferably slaughter me, and he is paying each member of the gang a retaining fee of eight shillings and sixpence a day.'

'This sum,' Machen observed, 'sounds as if it was the face value of some medieval coin long obsolete. How do you know this?' He was listening in wonder for he felt that there are some absurdities so enormous that they seem to have a stunning effect on common sense, paralysing it for the moment and inhibiting its action. It was at that moment that a smooth, smiling, clean-shaven man entered the pub and touched Yeats upon the arm. As if he was indeed the Young Man with Spectacles, Yeats wheeled round as if spun on a pivot, and shrank back with a low, piteous cry.

'I'll get you yet, Mr Crowley, I warrant ye, I'll get ye . . .' And with that, William Butler Yeats ran from the pub.

'Poor fellow,' Aleister Crowley murmured. 'Looks as though he's in need of help. Ah, a very good evening to you, Mr Machen, also known,' he whispered in an undertone, 'as Son of Aquarius in the context of our Order.' His eyes twinkled with mischievous glee. Machen shrugged his shoulders; meanwhile a grip of

Crowley's hand acknowledged that they were both members of the Golden Dawn. 'You don't care for me? No matter. After all, as the philosopher has it, what is matter? Never mind. And what is mind? No matter. No doubt you have been enduring poor Weary Willie's customary abuse of my character? In any event,' he smiled with teeth as white and gleaming as those of a shark, 'allow me to introduce my dear friend, Miss Elizabeth London.' Machen arose to greet a young lady with a face that was quaint and piquant rather than beautiful, with eyes of shining hazel. 'What will you be drinking?'

'A pint of porter, please, Mr Crowley.' Machen regarded the matter with increasing bewilderment whilst preserving his outward composure.

'I wish *I* liked beer,' said Crowley. 'Everyone I know seems to get so much pleasure from drinking the stuff. Elizabeth?' The lady quietly ordered a gin-and-tonic. 'Heigh ho!' said Crowley; 'it will be a lemonade for me.' Machen studied him carefully as he went to the bar. He was quite extravagantly dressed in a black frock coat with silken knee-britches of black, white silken stockings, black leather shoes which had clearly been hand-made, a frilled white shirt of silk and around his neck there was a scarlet Ascot tie of satin. Machen could not recall what Yeats had been wearing since he only noticed the clothes of other men if they were either very good or very bad. Could this be the associate of Dr Black whom he had seen upon a certain fateful night? And could he have been the mysterious Mr O'Malley? Machen decided that this was unlikely.

As Crowley returned with the drinks, Machen was exchanging pleasantries with the girl, who had much charm of manner. His head was whirling, not with physical fright, since he was no coward, but with perturbation of the brain. He recalled the girl whom he had seen at the window on that fateful night in the autumn when he had mysteriously received the stone within an ankh: she had had raven hair. He remembered the lady whom he had visited in the company of the perplexing Mr O'Malley, ostensibly for his bulldog to be admired: she had had flaming red hair. Miss Elizabeth London, sitting here before him, had curly blond hair. Very well: there were three different women who all bore similarities of facial feature to one another; it was just a feeling of unease that when he had last seen Miss London at a meeting of the Golden Dawn, the lady who had looked so very much like her was in possession of a magnificent head of *brown* hair. It struck him that not for nothing had he subtitled his novel *The Three Impostors*, 'The Transformations'.

'A fine dog, sir.' Crowley's words dragged Machen's thoughts from speculation to present reality. Juggernaut was usually wary of strangers but to Machen's stupefaction, Crowley's stroking had led Jug to roll over on his back and wave his paws in the air as Crowley scratched his tummy.

'Be careful, sir,' Machen responded, 'for though he is indeed a fine dog, he can on occasion bite very hard.'

'No doubt,' Crowley returned, 'but he has no cause to bite men like me. Anyhow, I'm jolly pleased to run into you tonight. In some magazine, I forget which, anyway, one of those things of high literary prestige that nobody buys, I read an article of yours about the Holy Grail. I thought that it was extremely good. However, I disagree with you when you state that the Grail is a stone. My own research convinces me that the Grail is a Cup, a Chalice – and that this is but a metaphor for the Mysteries enshrined within a woman's cunt.'

'Mr Crowley, you make the sacred so profane,' Machen retorted acidly.

'No, Mr Machen, *I* make the profane so sacred.'

Machen was just about to fulminate with honest indignation when he was interrupted by the lady, and since he was always a gentleman, he gave way to her speech.

'Mr Machen,' she asked him in a very soft and gentle tone

of voice, 'you are not by any chance the man who goes around pretending to be Arthur Machen the noted author, are you?'

'What do you mean, Madam?' he replied in the icy tones of a polite man who feels himself to have been insulted. 'For better or for worse, I happen to be Arthur Machen, man of letters.'

'That may be so, sir,' she replied, 'but I happen to know Arthur Machen, the published author of *The Great God Pan*, 'The Inmost Light' and *The Three Impostors*. He is a most charming gentleman who has yet to receive his just recognition in the world of letters and although I respect you as a Brother in the Golden Dawn, I cannot see how you can possibly claim the credit for his achievements. This is hardly the behaviour of a gentleman.'

'Madam, you leave me quite flabbergasted . . .' Arthur Machen was upon the point of apoplexy, such was his outrage. It was rare for him to lose his temper but he was coming close to it. '*Who* is this man who claims to be me? I demand to meet him!'

'Meet him here,' said the young lady and passed him a manuscript.

PLAYING DOUBLES

It was, I suppose, something of a dare with myself to make a Pact with the Devil. Even so, my life was so rotten at the time that I felt I had nothing to lose, not even my soul, since I did not believe in an eternal soul and I did not believe in Hell. I had bought *The Book of Black Magic and of Pacts*, edited by one A.E. Waite, at a second-hand bookshop and within my garret, an attic room in Kilburn, I proceeded to carry out all the instructions given. It took me about a week to assemble all the necessary equipment. (I felt that the hand of a hanged murderer was not entirely essential.)

I knew enough about these matters to know that the key to all matters of Magick consists of a combination of Will and Imagination. As far as I was concerned, my choice was between suicide or a Pact with the Devil. Since I had no job, no money and no woman, life as it was going on held no attractions for me whatsoever. I found the society around me to be perfectly disgusting and could see no point in continuing to live: at least, not in this way. Suicide, it has been said, is something done by people who take life too seriously, and that was why I rejected it. It was preferable to try the Devil even though I did not believe in his existence, seeing this creature merely as the God of any religion one chooses to dislike. Nevertheless, since so many people over the ages had believed and still believed in the Devil, it was possible that I might by invoking him attract energy and so achieve greater satisfaction in life.

Details of the arrangement of the incense and the candles were done according to the textbook. My voice resonated throughout the house as I pronounced the names of daemons but I do not suppose that my neighbours worried since my landlady had recently embraced Buddhism and chanted herself.

At the climax of my ritual, I saw shifting shadowy shapes upon the wall and was conscious momentarily of an icy presence. But nothing more.

I advanced towards the altar I had created, slashed my forearm with my shaving razor and let the blood drip on to a piece of parchment upon which I had written my Pact in black India ink. The terms were that the Devil would give me material success in exchange for my soul. As far as I could see, I could not lose by this bargain since I did not believe that there was any such thing as an immortal soul. I suppose I did the thing as a bloody joke.

I went to bed, resolved to make a comic story out of this preposterous folly of mine, something one could tell to close friends on a drunken night. I was not expecting the nightmares that came with the deed; and perhaps the most merciful quality of the human mind is its inability to recollect the precise details of every pain. I recall only that in my fevered dreams a malevolent old lady in a long black coat unloosed upon me a flying reptile that tore at my flesh until I woke up screaming.

No sane man takes a nightmare seriously and so, on the following day, I attended a sociable Sunday luncheon party after which I wanted to go to a pub in Maida Vale. The day had been most enjoyable and I had met a delightful girl with whom I had made a date. It was a pleasure to walk from Marble Arch along the Edgware Road as the sun was setting with a warm orange glow and to reflect upon the pleasures of solitude that lay ahead this evening: I always like things to be quiet at this time.

I was walking on my way and thinking of nothing in particular when I saw a man striding towards me. As he saw me, his jaw fell open and he gasped with astonishment. He made no other sign of recognition and continued on his way towards Marble Arch.

Myself, I was equally astonished. This man was impeccably

dressed in clothes tailored with the utmost discretion. Anyone who saw him would have thought him very wealthy or else pretending to be so. My bemusement was occasioned by the fact that he looked just as I imagined I myself might look in ten years' time. I could not tell the state of his hair, since he was wearing a high hat of silk, but I did discern that his moustache and beard were grey. His face was not attractive but grizzled, as though it had weathered many storms.

It was too late to pursue him. I continued on my way until I found my favourite pub by the canal at Little Venice, where I could sit and enjoy quiet contemplation of the waters as I regarded the gentle progress of the boats. One of the reasons that I enjoyed this pub so much was simply that I knew nobody there and so could contemplate whatever *I* wished in quietude without unwelcome importunities.

'Good evening,' I said softly as I entered. 'A pint of your "Old Devil" ale, please.'

'You're barred.'

'What?' I had never been barred from a pub in my life. 'What have I done?'

'You was rude and insulting to the Guv'nor.'

'That's impossible. I don't even know who the Guv'nor is.'

'Look, mate, I'm just doing me job.'

'All right,' I said, 'I'll go. But you have got the wrong man.' I proceeded in a baffled way to the Warrington Hotel, an excellent pub where I enjoyed a beer with the local poet. As I was leaving, the Guv'nor there followed me out into the street.

'Don't come back,' he said.

'Why?' I demanded. 'What have I done?'

'You're an arrogant bastard.'

This might well be the case but I was not aware that these were grounds for being banned from a public house. I was too astonished to say anything other than: 'Good God!'

I proceeded nervously to a third pub in St John's Wood that

was managed by Spaniards who greeted me warmly, to my immense relief. I was supping my pint quietly when the son of the house emptied my ashtray, wiped my table and said:

'Good evening, sir. And how is your excellent school going?'

'Sorry?'

'Your school, sir, to which my sister goes. Ah, what a wonderful education she receives there, sir! Rarely has there been so estimable a Chairman of the Governors!'

'Thank you,' I muttered bemusedly. Feeling increasingly bewildered and unhappy, I headed for a pub in that curious area where St John's Wood, Maida Vale and Kilburn intersect. Here I took a quiet pint and hoped to high heaven for no disturbing interruptions. But my introverted musings were intruded upon by a pale young man with spectacles who approached my table in a quivering fever of perturbation.

'I am extremely sorry that I was late with it, sir,' he said as he handed me a canvas bag. 'I do appreciate everything that you have done to help me, sir, and I apologize profusely for my lateness in recompensing you for your extraordinary kindness.'

'Thank you . . .' was all I could say as he darted out of the pub. Upon opening the canvas bag, I found a very large brown paper envelope that contained – though I did not count it at the time – ten thousand pounds in cash. I took the Underground Railway and went home to my bedsit.

On the following morning, I banked the money and went to a pub on the Kilburn High Road in order to question the senior citizens of the area, with whom I was on drinking terms. I said nothing about the money. I simply complained indignantly about the unfair treatment I had received in two pubs on the previous evening. The elders of the area informed me that they would look into the matter and let me know the upshot of all the issues involved within forty-eight hours.

'We've discovered it, Arthur,' one of the patriarchs told me two days later in a Kilburn High Road pub of the sort that does not welcome women unless they are with their husbands. In fact, the elders' secret government of the area ensured that no women or children were ever harmed along the Kilburn High Road. 'There's this man who is a dead ringer for you. Some of us have even greeted him, thinking it was you. He really does look just like you but a little bit older. Anyone could mistake him for you and some people have. Unfortunately, he has been behaving very badly in one or two pubs of late, making a right bloody disgrace of himself, and one or two of the less observant people seem to have thought that it was you.'

'Gentlemen, I *don't* misbehave myself in pubs,' I protested. 'You must know by now how I conduct myself. Have you ever seen me make trouble in a public house?'

'Oh, nobody's saying that about *you*, Arthur,' another of the Kilburn elders interpolated. 'All we are saying is that someone who looks very much like you *has* been causing trouble and grief.'

'Well, I'd like you to know that it isn't me, gentlemen,' I replied as I drank up. Although the elders were not accusing me of anything, they nonetheless seemed rather relieved to see me go.

I felt completely confused and gripped by a need to quit the area for an evening. I strode along the Kilburn High Road, once the great Roman road to the North called Watling Street, later the first stage of a cart track transporting goods from the docks in the Middle Ages, and went roving in the side streets, eventually wandering to the Kensal Green area and finding a pub near its fabled cemetery. There I bought myself a pint of old-and-mild and was hoping for a spot of peace and quiet. And then I saw him.

He was sitting at a table supping old-and-mild and looked exactly like me, only a little older. My heart was beating substantially faster as I approached him.

'Hallo,' he said. 'I've been expecting you, Arthur.'

'Hallo,' I said as I sat down opposite him. 'To whom do I have the pleasure of speaking?'

'My name is Arthur too. I am you in a year and a day.'

'A year and a day . . . ?' I echoed, for it looked as though he – or I – had aged ten years. 'What do you mean?'

'You *did* sign a Pact, as I did, did you not?'

'Yes . . . ?'

'This is the result. Look at me.' I did. His suit was from Dover Street, probably Pope & Bradley, and every other item of his apparel was clearly from Jermyn Street or nearby. 'You have ten thousand pounds, don't you?' I nodded. 'This sum was given to me in error by a foolish youth who mistook me for somebody else. Since I had the proverbial luck of the Devil, by a combination of sound investment in property and wildly speculative gambling I took it to half a million within six months. Very enjoyable, too. Now I have millions. I have been enabled to fund my dearest fantasies. Women? I have lost count of the beauties. Travel? I have been everywhere I have ever wanted to go upon this globe. Vengeance upon enemies? Hell, life is cheap. There is not a single desire I have ever entertained that I have not had consummately gratified. As the Devil states: "I am come among you for a short time and having great wrath." I have also done some good things. One of my greatest fantasies – and yours – has always been to found and govern an absolutely excellent school, which matter has been satisfactorily accomplished. Perhaps you have noticed it? Oh, you have nothing to worry about, Arthur. Within a year and a day, you will be as happy as I am.'

'And is there any sort of price to be paid?' I queried.

'Your soul, of course, you fool!' he expostulated. 'But if you don't believe that you have one, then what is the worry? Does Death frighten you?'

'No,' I said. 'But it depends on where you go afterwards.'

'I am going to die today,' he informed me in a manner so cool that it was as though he had declared his intention of going to buy a ham sandwich. 'Still, a condemned man is allowed a last request, and mine was to see myself as I was and to make mischief so as to bring about increased awareness. This request was graciously granted, with results of which you are aware.' As I was endeavouring to comprehend all that he had told me, a wickedly handsome young man entered the pub and, waving aside his offer of a drink, tapped him upon his left shoulder. I shivered without knowing quite why and my strange companion did not introduce the intruder. 'Good luck, Arthur,' he said in friendly fashion, 'it certainly hasn't been a bad ride.'

'Where are you going?' I demanded.

'Kensal Green cemetery,' he replied and his pale friend nodded cold acquiescence. 'And after that, Heaven.'

'Just a moment,' I objected. 'If what you say is true, I shall be here in a year and a day speaking exactly the same words that you have spoken to me and to a younger version of myself. Up until that instant, my luxurious year and a day has been totally scripted and I cannot deviate from it one iota. I have no free will. I shall end up just as you are, and my younger self will end up just as I am, and *his* younger self will end up just as he is and this process will be repeated throughout all eternity...? Sounds like Hell to me.'

'You could say that,' he replied as his pale companion urged him to go with a flick of his left hand. 'Have fun.'

NOTE

This haunting and intriguing tale by Arthur Machen, originally provisionally entitled 'The Fourth Impostor', is presently unpublished.

'Now look here!' Arthur Machen could barely contain his impending explosion of outrage. 'This tale, whatever its merits, was *not* written by me. How dare anybody claim my reputation, slight though it may be, for a work of this nature, totally devoid of my style? I have *not* . . .' He stopped since he suddenly noticed that he was talking to nobody.

During the time that Machen had been engrossed by the story, Aleister Crowley and Elizabeth London had vanished from the tavern. His faithful bulldog Jug was slumbering peacefully at his feet. As his reeling mind endeavoured to contemplate immediate events, his concentration was abruptly interrupted by a man who burst into the inn. He was big and bulky and perspiring profusely and, as he dashed towards Machen's table, the latter noted his pair of bulbous chin-whiskers which merged into an unpleasant and bristly ginger moustache.

'For the love of God, sir!' he demanded of Machen. 'Please! Have you seen here a young man, pale and nervous, who wears spectacles? Pray answer me. My life depends upon it!' This was all and more that Machen needed that night since the man seemed to have walked out of his *The Three Impostors* as the villain Richmond impersonating Mr Wilkins as he encounters Machen's *alter ego*, Mr Dyson.

'No, sir.' Machen remained impassive and concealed his own inner turmoil. 'I have not. Why don't you ask at the bar?'

'You'll regret that,' said this grossly unpleasant man who then barged out of the bar, rather than making further enquiries, and stormed back into the streets outside. Machen drank up uneasily and then walked home with his dog. It was a fine, starry night and, fortunately, there were no further incidents to disturb him along the way. He was fond of saying that 'All things end in Mysteries'. But his head whirled upon perceiving these particular mysteries so flagrantly displayed.

After feeding Jug, he took several glasses of tawny port and gazed at the stone in his present possession. All he saw was himself.

CHAPTER EIGHT

PROGRESSIVE PECULIARITIES IN PENTONVILLE

(THE HERMIT)

Adam Stride detested Tuesdays. This was not because of any awareness on his part that the Black Tuesday Wall Street Crash of 1929 had temporarily plunged the western world into an apparent choice between communism and fascism. Although he *was* aware of that fact, he simply disliked the nature of the day because it seemed to him to lack a positive identity. Since he enjoyed his work, he relished Mondays as a sprinting start to the week, a day to get things done. A good Wednesday made him feel as though he was breaking the back of the week. Thursday was for him a time of consolidation of gains. Friday was the end of the working week, on Saturdays he cast aside all thoughts of work whenever he could and he always richly savoured the prospect of a quiet Sunday. But Tuesday seemed to have no identity at all.

To make matters worse, on this particular Tuesday there was just the sort of weather he loathed. Stride loved the sunshine, the pattering of raindrops, the crunch of freshly fallen snow beneath his boots, the howling of a wild wind. But a dull day of low cloud depressed him. He stared out of his office window at the surrounding gloom and saw miserable people shuffling along the streets, casting down their eyes, their spirits evidently as low as his own.

It depressed him, since he took tremendous pride in his work, that he was making very little progress with the case of Miss Alison Featherstonehaugh. His body ached to encounter her again; his mind itched to know more about her. The matter of the stone in the ankh perplexed him every bit as much, for whatever sense was located therein was not giving up its secret, or secrets, to him. He had shown it both to Rosa Scarlett and to Antonina. 'A black pearl within brass, Mr Stride,' Rosa Scarlett had said. 'Can't understand why she should pay you ten thousand pounds with more to come to investigate this.' 'What *is* her interest?' Antonina had demanded. 'I mean, you say you see funny things in it but I don't. It's just a rather ordinary black pearl set in a brass ankh and it can't be worth *that* much.'

Can I get a witness? Stride sighed inwardly, since it was part of his professionalism always to give value for services rendered. To this end he had compiled for Miss Featherstonehaugh *A Dossier concerning the Holy Grail*. This document traced the history of the Grail according to all recognized historians and all those who had recorded myths and legends. It concluded by praising Arthur Machen's research and his conclusion that *the Grail is a stone*, whilst stating that it was most unlikely that the stone within the ankh, entrusted to his care, was indeed the fabled wholly wonderful object of reverence within so many cultures.

It was possible, Stride supposed, that the ankh with which Alison had entrusted him had indeed some especial significance. After all, he had seen astonishing effects with his own eyes, discerning the face of Arthur Machen. A number of people were clearly so interested in the matter that Miss Alison Featherstonehaugh had chosen to pay him a substantial sum and had promised much more. There had also been the disturbing meeting with Ron Butcher and the confrontation with other characters from his own novel *The Labyrinth of Satan*, as well as further stories by Septimus Keen.

It was all rather hard to make sense of the matter. Stride prided himself upon his own rationalism whenever he was engaged in his work as a private detective. He furthermore prided himself upon his rationalism whenever he was investigating the life of Arthur Machen. Now he was faced, as Machen had been, with a bizarre series of events that totally defied *all* rational explanation.

To what extent could Machen's involvement with that fabled secret society, the Hermetic Order of the Golden Dawn, explain matters? Again Stride stared out of his window in search of inspiration – and momentarily recoiled at what he saw.

He had paid a street artist to chalk the Sign of the Red Hand upon the pavement, experimenting with the method of Machen's character, Mr Dyson. Dyson had argued with his friend, the scientific Mr Phillipps, who worked with probability, that he worked upon a theory of *im*probability. Dyson had stated that if he put a sign significant to someone in a public place, sooner or later, that sign would be seen by the person it was meant to attract. Of course, the chances of the person concerned initially noticing that sign, Dyson had admitted, were perhaps a billion to one. However, as each day passed, the odds against the right person perceiving the right notice decreased. Eventually, Machen's Dyson had argued against the sceptical incredulity of Machen's Phillipps, there would be a coincidence, one that was most fortuitous.

Stride loved the James Bond novels of Ian Fleming much more than he liked the films and he was particularly fond of the old Chicago saying quoted in *Goldfinger*: one is happenstance; twice is coincidence; the third time, it's enemy action. For sitting at a café just across the street and calmly yet pointedly surveying the Sign of the Red Hand was a smooth, smiling, clean-shaven gentleman, well-dressed, a dead ringer for Davies in Machen's 'The Inmost Light' and *The Three Impostors*; and in Stride's own *The Labyrinth of Satan*. Stride seized his blue coat and, instructing Rosa Scarlett to follow him, left his office and crossed the street to accost the man at the café, who continued to look nonchalantly at the Red Hand of the street artist.

'Excuse me,' Stride said, indicating a vacant chair, 'is this seat taken?'

'Please, and by all means,' the man murmured and continued in his study of the Red Hand. Stride ordered a coffee and sat down.

'Amazing, isn't it,' he murmured back, 'what these street artists can do?'

'There should be a gallery for these paving stones,' the gentleman responded. Then, after taking a sip of his coffee, he added: 'Good day, Mr Stride.'

'Good day to you, sir,' Stride replied as his coffee arrived. 'How do you know my name? I don't believe we've met.'

'At least you did not say: "Are you talking to me?" I would have answered: "We will be."'

'"We" being who?'

'You'll see. How's your coffee?'

'Dreadful. How's yours?'

'Abominable, atrocious, awful and appalling. Why is it so impossible to enjoy a good cup of coffee these days in London? Why, sir, only the other day, when I had a fairly decent espresso in Soho, I asked the Sicilian proprietor for the nearest place to his where I could obtain a good cup of coffee. "Turin," he replied, "but if you want the best, you must go to Naples or Palermo." I had to explain that I only had an hour for morning coffee. Mr Stride, I do wish that you had had this artistry chalked on a paving stone outside a place that served better coffee.'

'With whom do I have the pleasure of speaking?' Stride enquired.

'Ah, I was wondering when you might ask me,' the smooth, smiling, clean-shaven gentleman answered him, producing a crocodile-skin wallet virtually bursting at the seams with cash and business and credit cards. He then passed a white card to Stride. 'Keep it,' he added.

Stride stared at the object with growing astonishment for it read:

Owen G. Davies
Director
Lipsius Antiquarium

'Very helpful as a business card,' Stride commented with acid sarcasm, 'since it has neither address nor phone number.'

'Quite so. We are very selective concerning those with whom we deal. We approach them first. They cannot approach us.'

'Mr Davies . . .' The whiff of bad hamburgers and over-fried onions from a nearby street-stall made Stride feel nauseous. Staring at the Sign of the Red Hand, he knew that he had invoked the theory of Improbability and here it was now, sitting opposite him as Davies working for Lipsius, beings out of Machen's novels and his own. 'I am so tired of playing games,' he said.

'Perhaps you are, sir,' Davies retorted evenly, 'but others aren't.'

'Let's get to the point. What do you want?'

'Some hours of your time, Mr Stride.'

'Mr Davies, as a professional man, I charge for my time.'

'Appropriately so. But I think that your time on this matter has been paid for by a Miss Alison Featherstonehaugh.' Stride tried to veil the shock he felt inwardly. 'Come with me on a taxi ride to Pentonville.'

'All right,' Stride said.

They arose from the table and Davies looked out for a cab. He ignored several, easily available, then suddenly hailed one. As he and Stride clambered within and made themselves comfortable, he produced a silver cigarette case and flicked it open, offering it to Stride, who was dying for a cigarette but had noticed the dismal THANK YOU FOR NOT SMOKING sign.

'Virginia on the one side, Turkish on the other,' said Davies. Stride was reminded of the Bulldog Drummond novels as he shrugged and took a Virginia and Davies took a Turkish, both of which were lit by the flame of Davies's golden Dunhill lighter.

'Oi!' the cabbie shouted. 'Can't you fucking read!'

'Can't you fucking see?' Davies retorted coolly. 'Excuse my Oxbridge parlance,' he added to Stride. The cabbie turned his head.

'Oh, I'm sorry, Mr Davies, didn't realize it was you.'

'That's all right,' said Davies, 'just remember for the future.' He blew out three perfect smoke rings in succession. 'London is the greatest city in the World,' he continued as the taxi headed for Holborn. 'Of course, the real Londoners are the Cockneys, who settled long ago upon the Thames Estuary. "Cockneys"? The word, I think, derives from Cockaigne, the central city of the holy island of Albion, a far-flung dominion of the legendary Atlantis.'

'You may well be right, Mr Davies,' Stride returned evenly, 'but could you please give me the derivation of "Antiquarium", which I see on your card is graced by the name of Lipsius?'

'There is actually no such word,' Davies replied with a smile, 'unless I have invented it. I suppose it is a cross between "antiques" and "aquarium". Ever felt like an ageing goldfish in a bowl, Mr Stride? And please don't gulp.'

'Certainly not.' Stride repressed his impulse to do so. 'What is the purpose of this journey?'

'Stop,' Davies commanded the cabbie, who obeyed instantly. 'Allow me to attend to this insignificant trifle,' he added as he politely ushered Stride out of the cab and paid for the fare.

'God bless you, sir!' the cabbie shouted as he drew away.

'I want to show you some things and to ask you some questions,' said Stride's enigmatic companion. 'Let us turn here, sir, eastward and northward of the Gray's Inn Road. Arthur Machen always held it to be the most secret and sacred part of London, a place unknown to most. Walk with me, sir, and I shall explain matters further. Although the bulldozer has unfortunately made its mark, fortunately it is still rare to find a building younger than one hundred and sixty years old, for the most part. Can you deny that there is something different, something strange, in the whole look of the quarter? The London that you think you know is far behind you. Here we encounter secret and severed people who have fallen out of the great noisy march of the high road for one reason or another, and so they dwell apart in these misty streets and squares of 1850. My dear sir, in this land, I sometimes fancy that people here live in 1959, wondering when it might be 1960. Here and there, we encounter wealthy men of the City: how many Porsches, Jaguars and Mercedes vehicles did you count on that street we just passed? But equally, up in that curious attic, hidden in a turret, there may be a young poet dying by inches.'

Entering into Frederick Street, Davies led Stride up the hill of Great Percy Street and the latter felt that he had indeed entered a Silent Land as described by Machen, a paradise for a poor student whose needs would be peace and lodgings a short distance from the British Museum. There was hardly anybody about; they passed through a short street without meeting a soul. There were a few shops here to serve people from the immediate locality but from nowhere else. There was a deep, leafy silence, for trees grew everywhere in this happy place. They leaned over garden walls, they congregated together in hushed squares, they thrust in profusion from little patches of odd ground, from behind railings, in every unexpected corner, and there were short flights of steps that led to mysterious alleys or passageways or byways going to nowhere in particular.

Here, too, Stride saw unexpected ash groves and sweet, quivering poplars and little houses strangely tucked away. Here there was no bellow of the bus and in fifteen minutes of walking, Stride saw many vintage cars of the 1950s but he did not discern a cab. The storms of his age did not come to beat about this place.

Davies led Stride through Great Percy Street, by Amwell Street, into the heart of Pentonville, its Hill. Stride recalled the words of Arthur Machen, reflecting on that strangeness which is the essence of beauty, the essence of truth and the essence of the world. Standing on the summit of an undiscovered height in London, Machen had felt that he was looking down on a new land.

Stride had always resolved, as soon as pressure of work permitted, to go and climb to the top of Pentonville Hill and today promised an ideal opportunity. Unfortunately, this place really had changed since Machen's original description of it. Iron railings had been placed around it and access was now only for local residents who had keys to the gate. Most of them seemed to own a Mercedes or a BMW.

'The perils of privatization,' Davies murmured, then added: 'A drink, Mr Stride?' Stride nodded acquiescence as they proceeded towards a pub. 'Unexpectedly warm for this time of year,' Davies observed and rightly. The air was smelling of damp and fallen leaves over which their leather boots had crunched. 'Let's go and sit in the garden. What's yours, sir?' Stride asked for a pint of the best strong bitter and walked into the courtyard, took a table and stared moodily at another table at which four strong men were sitting.

'Nah, George, yer fucking wrong,' one of them was saying, 'with all respect. Manchester United *will* beat Newcastle United in the Premier League.'

'You don't know what yer fucking talking about, Bill. And I mean that with all respect,' said his companion. 'Two more wins and Newcastle United will draw level, believe me. Then there'll be a play-off and Newcastle plays much better football. *Goals*, you get my point? That's what the game's all about, ennit?'

'Don't agree with you, George,' said the third man. 'It's no good scoring goals if you let too many in.'

'Bollocks, Jim!' the fourth man shouted. 'With all respect, what's soccer all about? I'm talking about men such as Pele and George Best, Di Stefano, Puskas of Hungary and Bobby Charlton.'

'What's your opinion?' Bill asked Stride. 'Since yer look as though you was listening.'

'I was and with interest,' Stride replied, 'and I couldn't help overhearing. Since you asked my opinion, the essence of soccer is *ball control*.' The men nodded in agreement. 'I could be wrong but from what I've seen, Manchester United is better at that.'

'Cheers, mate,' said Bill. 'Like some of this?' He proffered a big, fat spliff that they had all been smoking.

'Many thanks. Very kind of you.' Stride took it, inhaling with an almost obscene greed, and exhaling with a virtually erotic satisfaction. 'Work locally, do you?'

'Dead right, guv'nor,' said Bill. 'We're marble workers!' he declared proudly.

'Splendid,' said Stride, passing back the joint. 'I'm glad to know that your noble craft is still in existence.'

'Oh, it is, mate,' said George. 'Ha! ha! We're specialists in headstones.' Stride felt uneasy as Davies returned with the drinks, bitter for Stride and a gin-and-tonic with ice and lemon for himself.

'Must be going,' Bill said. 'Right, lads. On yer feet and up! All the best to you, guv!' As they departed, Stride was uncertain as to whether 'guv' referred to Davies or himself.

'I have a problem,' said Davies. 'Cheers.' He drank.

'So do I,' said Stride. 'Cheers.' He drank. 'Let's stop beating about the bush and get to the point.'

'By and large,' Davies responded, 'all in all, if we get down to the grass roots of the matter, whereby we put our noses to the grindstone and our shoulders to the wheel, for it would be wrong not to see the wood for the trees, and let's face it, there's always one rotten apple in every barrel . . . it would assist our discourse, Mr Stride, were you not to speak in clichés.'

'So I retire suitably chastized, Mr Davies? What the fuck are you on about?'

'I would like to hire your services as a private detective.' Davies sipped his drink delicately. 'I have reason to believe that your services have recently been engaged by a Miss Alison Featherstonehaugh. How do I know that? She is my half-sister and whenever she drinks too much, which is too often, she tells me everything I need to know. Well, *almost* everything and sometimes not nearly enough. I am very concerned about her welfare. I understand that you have accepted an initial down payment of ten thousand pounds in cash to render her various services.' He lit another cigarette. 'Is that correct?'

'Yes.'

'The notes she gave you are forgeries.'

'No one else seems to think so.'

'That is because they are *perfect* forgeries. Possibly the best yet. The police are presently working upon the case. My dear half-sister is somewhat wayward and wilful. You see, Mr Stride, that money that Alison has given you may well render you liable to criminal prosecution.'

'Then I shall go to the police with my banknotes tomorrow and give them a detailed account,' Stride answered. He had no fear of the police but he suddenly saw a vision of ten thousand pounds fizzing up to the skies in flames. 'Kindly don't threaten me.'

'Oh, I wouldn't dream of it. There are two things I want

from you and I'm prepared to pay for them to the tune of ten thousand *genuine* pounds. One is the ankh of brass within which a black pearl reposes that Alison misguidedly stole from the collection of Dr Lipsius the noted antiquarian and which, I have reason to believe, lies in your possession.'

'Mr Davies, whatever you may know, I have a duty of confidentiality and a further one of obligation to my clients which precludes a conflict of interest. Certainly for a fee, I will investigate the matter of suspected forgery. Now *you* tell *me* about the ankh.'

'Certainly,' Davies answered with a wicked grin, reminding Stride of the Cheshire Cat. 'It is a most mysterious object. Some say that it is the Holy Grail. Others say that it is carved from obsidian stolen by the Spaniards from the Mayans or the Aztecs of Central America and then taken from one of their galleons by that notable English pirate Sir Francis Drake, after which it passed into the hands of the Elizabethan magus Dr John Dee. No one knows for certain. It is very difficult to trace its history precisely, though there are legends stating that it passed through the circle of Sir Francis Dashwood and his so-called Hell-Fire Club. Lord Edward Bulwer-Lytton was said to have had it, which fact, if it is true, might explain the inspiration for his remarkable work *The Haunted and the Haunters: or, The House and the Brain*. Somehow or other, in the 1890s, it passed into the hands of a Dr Black. Another beer, Mr Stride?'

'Definitely, Mr Davies, but I shall be the provider of our continued refreshment. Another gin-and-tonic? Lemon? Plenty of ice?' The matter was accomplished in a trice. 'Please,' said Stride, 'continue with your most intriguing tale.'

'Very well.' Davies sipped his drink and offered and lit more cigarettes. 'Coincidentally, this Dr Black had the same name as the villain in "The Inmost Light" by Arthur Machen, in which a Dr Black performs an experiment whereby the soul of his wife enters into a stone and a demon enters into the body of his wife, whereby she kills herself. This jewel of the inmost light comes into the hands of Machen's hero, Dyson. Curious coincidences occur, wouldn't you say, Mr Stride? Does Life imitate Art or does Art imitate Life? You tell me.'

'I shall tell you the three most honest words in the English language,' said Stride: 'I don't know. But,' he swallowed more beer, 'I think you can give me more data, so enabling me to make a more discerning judgement.'

'Of course, sir. You see, the black pearl within the brass ankh appears to have passed into the hands of Arthur Machen, owing to an accident. Machen was apparently subsequently persecuted by a group of people who wanted it back.'

'They didn't kill him, did they?' said Stride.

'No. But he was somewhat bewildered. Tell me, Mr Stride, do you believe in alien intelligence?'

'I have an open mind on the matter. I await concrete proof.'

'You will never have it. Tell me, Mr Stride, if you were a biologist investigating ants, would you not observe their behaviour?' Stride nodded. 'If you were endeavouring to understand the nature of apes, would you not undertake experiments?' Stride coughed. 'One would be particularly interested in experiments involving the most intelligent of the naked apes.' He smiled. 'After all, your scientists like to put rats in a maze and play games with them.'

'I see.' Stride stared directly at Davies. 'Now it is clear at last. You are an alien from another planet and you are experimenting on me. A likely story, sir.'

'No comment,' Davies replied. 'But to continue, the Stone passed from Arthur Machen into a society entrusted with its safe keeping. There it stayed until Alison took it, probably in a fit of madness. And brought it to you. The interests I represent would like it back.'

'Not without her consent,' Stride answered, adding, 'There

is the possibility of arranging a meeting. Please understand that my first loyalty is to my client.'

'But I am your client now.'

'Not if there is a conflict of interests.'

'I have ten thousand genuine pounds here,' said Davies. 'She has given you fakes.'

'That remains to be seen.'

'Oh, and it will be. Moreover, my payment includes another matter. I want you to find out everything you can about a certain Septimus Keen. I have reason to believe that he may have contributed to the present peculiar behaviour of my sister.'

'Stop,' said Stride, 'just stop a moment . . . Septimus Keen is my own invention as portrayed in my *The Labyrinth of Satan*. He is a fake. I have received documents claiming that he actually existed in the 1890s – and if so, what are these reports about him being around today? – and to this end I met a Mr Ron Butcher in order to discuss the matter at his request. Now, do cut the crap, Mr Davies. You, Mr Butcher and Alison Featherstonehaugh are dead ringers for *The Three Impostors: or, The Transformations* by Arthur Machen and *The Labyrinth of Satan* which I wrote. What now? Are you going to introduce me to Dr Lipsius?'

'Possibly,' Davies returned calmly, 'and in due course.'

'But Dr Lipsius is a creature of fiction, invented by Machen and preserved by me.'

'Is he?' Davies sighed airily, breathing out smoke through both nostrils in two jet-streams. 'No doubt you'll see in due course if you don't return the gem that does not belong to you.'

'And you are offering me money to trace Septimus Keen, a character I invented?'

'Yes,' said Davies, 'for someone has become so obsessed with your fictional character that he or she is claiming to be Septimus Keen. Look.' Stride regarded the package presented to him by Davies before starting to unwrap it. 'I received this through the post only yesterday. See! It is the Pain of the Goat.'

'*Dyson and Phillipps both cried out at the revolting obscenity of the thing*, as is stated, I think, in "The Red Hand" by Arthur Machen. Well, Mr Davies, what I have here before me is a silver statuette, it seems, showing a goat-god fucking a woman up the arse. It is really rather beautiful. Arthur Machen may have been shocked by it but I am not. What I don't understand is: where *is* the Pain of the Goat? He seems to be having a jolly good time.'

'Mr Stride, you have not paid sufficiently close observation to the lady's hands.' Stride looked again and saw that one of the woman's hands was grasping the shaft of the goat's rampaging penis. The other was at the goat's testicles and holding a knife.

'O . . .' said Stride. 'Would you like it back?'

'It is part of the payment,' Davies retorted languidly. 'I think you will find that the silver is valuable. Now look at the other item.'

Stride looked and saw:

THE HERMIT

by

Septimus Keen

I like to learn something new every day. Every now and again, however, events occur that baffle all rational exposition. For instance, my lady has a collection of teddy bears and by it a Ribena box which plays jingles if anyone drops into it a tuppenny piece. This simple mechanism can only function if a tuppenny piece is dropped into it. It was most astonishing, therefore, to be awoken in the middle of the night and to hear it playing 'The Teddy Bears' Picnic' quite relentlessly without any kind of physical explanation.

Contrast this with the occasion when two acquaintances of mine were taken out to dinner by a mutual friend. The latter stated that he had discovered an excellent restaurant in Barnsbury and, requesting that they parked their Jaguar just off Upper Street, Islington, led them through a maze of squares festooned with flowers and quiet streets of houses built in the Regency era that would have elicited the approval of Jane Austen herself. Lionel led George and Lil to a house which displayed a sign: GIORGIO. They entered to be welcomed warmly by the proprietor, a stout man with a thick moustache, and his wife, a slim woman who was elegantly dressed. It turned out to be a superlative evening. Every dish was exquisite and so was every wine, since Lionel spared no expense to entertain his guests royally. Others who were dining in this restaurant seemed to be delightful people and George and Lil informed me that they thought it the finest restaurant they had ever entered in their lives.

'Grace,' Lil said to me, 'grace. I think that's so important in life.' Obviously one agrees: I know that George and Lil have been called vulgar yuppies by some, yet I was very pleased to hear her say that. They enjoyed their evening at the restaurant so much that they wanted to find it again. But they could not find it anywhere!

'How amusing,' said Lionel, when I told him of what I had heard. 'You see,' he smiled gently, 'one of the advantages of having money is that it enables one to play jokes. George and Lil are pleasant yuppies who had, in fact, no *idea* of grace. I therefore hired a private house, the finest chef that money could buy, gracious greeters and pleasant dinner companions. It was a one-off. I wanted excellence, I wanted them to *see* excellence. But unless they look very, *very* hard, they will never realize that vision again. They will look and search time and time again for the Paradise on Earth which they have once seen, but they will never find it.'

My story of the Ribena money box playing 'The Teddy Bears' Picnic' has, to my knowledge, no rational explanation. George and Lil must be equally bemused but there is a rational explanation here in that, unknown to them, it was an elaborate joke orchestrated by Lionel. How is one to explain the following data?

I had met Lionel at The Fantasy Centre in Holloway Road where we had casually fallen into a conversation about Aleister Crowley, for he was enquiring as to whether the shop had a paperback copy of *Moonchild* or alternatively *Diary of a Drug Fiend*. As it fell out, both books were there. He expressed his pleasure at his purchase and, staring at me curiously, invited me to join him for a beer at a local pub, The Wig and Gown. He was a tall, slim man of somewhat dandified dress: perhaps in some circles his black frock coat, tight black trousers, handmade black shoes, satin shirt of pale blue and chiffon scarf of yellow might have aroused smiles, as might also his cigarette holder of ivory and his cigarettes of Russian tobacco, wrapped in black and tipped in gold. Nevertheless, he was excellent company, even if his accent was slightly foreign and his canine teeth appeared to be unusually long.

THE GOD GAME

During the course of our conversation it turned out that we both knew George and Lil. He also asked me if I knew anything about Aleister Crowley. I answered that I knew of him as a poet, mountaineer, chess master, magician and mystic, condemned by the gutter press of his time for being 'the wickedest man in the world', mainly on account of his compulsive womanizing and advocacy of true will that is free. Lionel concurred warmly with my opinion. He asked me my opinion of *The Book of the Law*, dictated in Cairo to Crowley by an allegedly praeter-human intelligence called Aiwass or Aiwaz who gave out truths far beyond Crowley's conscious ken.

'It is beautiful,' I said, 'but I do not entirely understand it.'

'Nor do so many,' Lionel replied with a heavy sigh. 'But let me quote you a verse from memory. I think it is Chapter II, Verse 24:

' "Behold! These be grave mysteries; for there are also of my friends who be hermits. Now think not to find them in the forest or on the mountain; but in beds of purple, caressed by magnificent beasts of women with large limbs, and fire and light in their eyes, and masses of flaming hair about them; there shall ye find them..." '

'Is that the case with you?' I asked.

'Oh, yes,' he replied. 'I am a Hermit. I adore the pleasures of solitude, though I abhor the pains of loneliness from time to time. Occasionally, it is a pleasure to socialize. Tell me, what do you think of Lil?'

'She is a very beautiful woman,' I replied truthfully, 'and that extract from *The Book of the Law* describes her rather well. I suppose she *is* actually a magnificent beast of a woman, with large limbs, and she *does* have fire and light in her eyes and masses of flaming hair about her.' I added: 'And she is charming with it.'

'And what is your opinion of George?'

'Nice chap.' I saw no reason to tell Lionel that I had had an affair with Lil before her marriage to George, whose income was ever so much higher than mine. 'Nice chap.'

'Isn't he?' said Lionel.

From that time onward, I used to meet Lionel roughly once a month and we talked about Science, Art, Literature and Esotericism. I enjoyed his company very much indeed and he had excellent taste in pubs. He informed me that much of his time was spent at home where he liked to contemplate the Universe. Eventually he invited me to his house.

It was in a quiet Regency terrace in Barnsbury. Each room was furnished in a different style. Alexander Pope would have approved of the drawing room, where Lionel initially welcomed me with an exquisite amontillado. Thence he showed me to another reception room which would have given pleasure to Charles Dickens. We enjoyed hot milk punch there, then I followed him up the stairs to a library that would have delighted Oscar Wilde himself. There must have been at least three thousand books there and every framed print had been executed by an artist of the eighteen-nineties. Here we had a glass of bitter absinthe; this is a drink which really does make one feel rather dizzy. I was surprised when we entered the next room to see a place that was clean and spartan and furnished with chrome-framed black leather seats, computers, televisions and fax machines. Here he offered me a line of cocaine and I accepted it. I had always thought that cocaine was somewhat overrated and that nobody would bother to praise it were the substance priced at twenty-five pence a ton. But two portions of the white powder *did* make me feel rather fine.

'Upstairs . . . ?' he suggested. I nodded agreement. 'Look out of this window,' he asked and I complied with his request. I saw the moon and the stars in the sky. It was a full moon.

'Beautiful view,' I said.

'Isn't it?' Lionel replied. 'But look again.'

I looked and saw to my astonishment that now it was a waning moon.

'Different, isn't it?' Lionel anticipated my response. 'Why not look again?'

I looked and saw a waxing moon.

'It's a very odd window, isn't it?' Lionel murmured. 'Visitors tell me – such few as I have – that every time they look out of that window, they see the moon in a differing aspect.'

'They're dead right,' I replied. 'How is it possible?'

'Oh, all things end in Mysteries,' said Lionel. 'How should I know? It's just a very strange window, that's all. But do come upstairs.' I swallowed and accompanied him. We entered a bedroom and the sight made me gasp. The first item to hold one's attention was a four-poster bed, followed by the walls that were festooned with pornographic prints.

Lil was lying in the bed that was provided with silken sheets of purple.

'Hallo,' she said, and smiled wickedly. 'How are you? Good to see you.'

'Hallo,' I said, 'you are looking more beautiful than ever.'

'I hope so, and thank you,' she cooed. 'It must be because I have left George. He was *so* boring. Anyway, it doesn't matter now. He's dead.'

'I killed him,' said Lionel. 'He *was* terribly boring. Anyway, I wanted his woman.'

'I'm so glad,' said Lil, rustling her purple sheets with visible joy. For a moment I was utterly confused.

'I enjoy being a Hermit,' said Lionel.

'Thank you for your hospitality...' My voice emerged as a choked croak. 'Pleasure... must be going... another appointment...'

'*Such* a pleasure seeing you,' Lil laughed.

'Indeed,' I told her insincerely. 'I'll find my own way out,' I added to Lionel.

First I needed a very stiff whisky at the nearest available pub. Then I went to visit George. Even though I did not especially like him I could barely believe that Lionel had calmly admitted to killing the man. His house was just off Islington's Upper Street and the first thing I noticed was a FOR SALE sign. I therefore went to the Compton Arms, a pleasant pub with good beer, where I knew George to be a regular. I made enquiries behind the bar and the barman was helpful, since he had seen my face before, often in the company of George.

'George is dead,' said Bob the barman. 'Heart attack, I hear from his widow, Lil. She's in terrible grief.'

'Oh . . .' I said. There didn't seem to be much more to say. Then I added: 'Always liked the man. Don't know where his funeral is going to be, do you?'

'Nah. Why don't you ask his widow? She should know.'

Now I come to the point of my story, for this is not a joke. I returned to the house where I had been entertained only hours earlier by Lionel and rang the doorbell, intending to demand the truth. The door was opened by a fat old lady with grey hair and glasses, wearing a woolly cardigan and a tweed skirt. She appeared to be utterly astonished by my enquiry and wondered if I had come to the wrong address. No, she had never had tenants in her house answering to my description.

I am usually quite thorough in matters of this nature and so I showed her Lionel's calling card on which the address was clearly given as this house in Islington Park Road. Moreover, when I had left the place in agitation, I had made my own note of the address. The old lady then smilingly invited me into her house for a cup of tea, all the while declaring her bewilderment, which I echoed.

I was kindly invited to sit down in the room where, only

hours earlier, I had taken sherry with Lionel and commended the setting as being the sort of place that Alexander Pope would have loved; but how it had changed! There was now Fifties G-Plan furniture. Upon the walls there were family photographs, including one of a small naked boy by the seaside, touching his penis: it was captioned 'Holding His Own on Brighton Beach'. There was a goldfish in a bowl and another goldfish bowl which contained jelly babies.

'Quite nice here,' said the old lady, who told me that her name was Jane Jones, as she carried a brown farmhouse teapot into the room. 'Got to let it brew a bit,' she added. 'Mind you, the place has never been the same since my husband Stan died. London will never be the same for me without Stan.'

We drank our tea and chatted and then I took my leave. All references to Lionel and Lil did nothing other than puzzle old Mrs Jones. I thanked her warmly for her kindness and hospitality.

The quantum physicists state that we could all be living in many dimensions. Arthur Machen was convinced that all things end in Mystery.

As I departed from the house where I had experienced extraordinary events involving Lionel and Lil and then a pleasant chat and tea with old Mrs Jones, I fancied I saw Lionel and Lil laughing and embracing at the end of the street. But they vanished almost instantly and I cannot swear to it.

'This is a very strange tale,' said Adam Stride, 'although I rather like it.' As he looked at Davies, he reflected that it echoed the bizarre nature of events in his own life here and now.

'Rather good, isn't it?' Davies lit another Turkish cigarette.

'I want to meet this man who claims to be Septimus Keen.'

'So do I,' Davies returned coolly. 'Why do you think I am paying you? Here is ten thousand pounds.' He passed over a brown paper envelope. 'Who pays the piper calls the tune, they say. Ever head the piping of Pan? It is said that *Pan*ic is induced.'

'How did you come into possession of this tale?' Stride noticed that his body was rigid and his knuckles white as he took the envelope.

'It was dropped through my letter box,' Davies sighed wearily. 'I suspect that Alison is involved. Ask her.'

'You're her half-brother. Why don't you?'

'Unfortunately, for reasons I have explained, we are not at present on speaking terms. But I think that you are.'

'The ankh?'

'Yes,' said Davies. 'Oh, and I want it back. I suspect that the fellow purporting to be Septimus Keen out of your *The Labyrinth of Satan* may have exercised a malign influence upon my half-sister. I would like to meet him.'

'So would I,' Stride answered. 'When do *we* meet again?'

'At my convenience,' Davies replied. 'You have the money and the Pain of the Goat. I shall contact you soon enough. Goodnight.'

As if this evening had not been sufficiently perplexing, matters remained to trouble Stride further. Upon examination the next day, the statuette of the Pain of the Goat turned out to be made, not of silver, but of an alloy of copper and nickel.

Although the banknotes of Alison Featherstonehaugh were once again accepted as being of sterling worth, those of Mr Davies, her purported half-brother, proved to be fraudulent.

A phone call from Alison Featherstonehaugh gave Stride the information that she did not, in fact, have a half-brother called Davies.

Stride had seen Davies leave by the front door of the pub. Rosa Scarlett had been, at her employer's request, sitting in a car opposite that pub and usually she was very thorough. She was sure that she had seen no man of Davies's description as given by Stride leaving that pub.

'You must have been nodding,' Stride said.

CHAPTER NINE

THE ESSAYING OF EVIL
(THE BOY FROM BRAZIL)

The man known to some as Gordon Pugh put down the book he was rereading for at least the ninety-third time, *The Three Impostors* by Arthur Machen, and beamed with pleasure. With his left hand he gestured for his deaf-and-dumb Filipino manservant, who had been standing in dutiful attendance behind his chair, to bring him another cup of jasmine tea. The manservant nodded obediently and left the room.

Pugh reflected on how much he enjoyed Machen's novel, finding new truths within at every fresh perusal. Placing it on a revolving coffee table next to his chair, he reflected that the Everyman edition was in fact the finest yet. Then he stared thoughtfully at *The Labyrinth of Satan* by Adam Stride as his servant brought him his tea and was then dismissed by Pugh with a wave of his hand. It was with some satisfaction that Pugh regarded the room in which he had chosen to take his afternoon tea. The room was a shrine to the 1890s and so displayed the works of Beardsley, Whistler, the post-Impressionists and fashion plates and cartoons from *Punch* upon its walls. There were 2,000 books on the firm oaken shelves within the room and all of them were either works written in the 1890s, works that in Pugh's opinion were precursors of the 1890s – including much that was both erotica and ephemera, in addition to the sinister volumes that some might have termed 'Black Magic' – or works that Pugh regarded as deriving from the 1890s.

No one knew quite what to make of Gordon Pugh. To all outward appearances, he was simply a stout, balding man of late middle age who radiated benevolence and serenity from the crown of his shining scalp to the soles of his handmade black leather shoes. Very occasionally, his name appeared in the *Financial Times* and it had been known once to appear in *The Economist*, where it had been stated that he lived a very, indeed a *strictly* private life. It was said that he had made his fortune by speculating in currency. No one knew or ventured to guess where he had derived his initial capital, though there were rumours of a rich father who had married a Brazilian heiress, and certainly Pugh's passport stated him to be of Brazilian nationality. He only spent four months of every year in the UK and there were no criminal charges that had ever been laid against him anywhere. There were no civil lawsuits either. He had, it was true, given large sums of money to the Tory Party, but this was not widely known and the donations concerned could not be traced since the funds had been channelled through an obscure company in Liechtenstein, a company of which Pugh was not one of the official directors.

The log fire that the servants had lit was now blazing animatedly and as Pugh turned his gaze from there to the bow window outside which snow was falling, he congratulated himself upon being filthy, stinking rich. He had been born a multi-millionaire but now he was a billionaire owing mainly to his policy of always hiring the most intelligent staff who could also discern that their own best interests lay in being corruptible. All who served him were paid exceptionally well and were paid too to report upon one another. Pugh's executives were consequently millionaires whom he was able to ruin at any moment.

One of the pleasures of being wealthy, he felt, was being able to indulge in all his whims. Today had been exceptionally good for that. A Member of Parliament who had opposed the interests of one of his companies had today been exposed in a tabloid as an addict of flagellation. An agent of his had found a leading TV broadcaster guilty of homosexual acts in public lavatories, and the dossier was upon his desk, along with photographs taken by another agent of a wealthy commercial rival dressed in women's clothing. A newspaper editor had been surreptitiously photographed in the lavatory at a fashionable nightclub snorting cocaine after penning an article condemning it. Pugh did not actually care morally about any of these actions. He merely smiled at the institutionalized hypocrisy that gave him this kind of power over people.

That was not the only satisfaction of the day: another agent of his had bought a small painting by van Gogh, auctioned in Amsterdam, for one million pounds. This was not in fact the finest work of van Gogh, rather was it a sketch for something more, but Pugh had congratulated his executive and had paid gladly. It had given him a subtle satisfaction to know that a poor sketch that could barely be sold for the price of a glass of wine in its time was now his for a million pounds while men and women of integrity starved to death, just as van Gogh had done.

Pugh experienced an extraordinary ecstasy in the essaying of evil. On one occasion, a publishing company he owned had been ordered to watch out for the work of a man named John Sterling. The editor did indeed receive a manuscript from John Sterling and said that it was brilliant. Pugh asked for it, read it and agreed that it was. His agents subsequently learned that John Sterling was twenty thousand pounds in debt. His agents gave John Sterling, who had a wife and four children to support, one hundred thousand pounds on condition that he wrote nothing like the book concerned ever again and on the further condition that all copies of the manuscript would be burned. John Sterling accepted the deal. Then, a year later, he committed suicide.

There was also the matter of Pugh's obsession with Arthur

Machen's work. His staff had repeatedly noticed the matter and he had even been overheard saying: 'Damn the man! He's got so much bloody integrity.' Now Pugh picked up the phone and made four calls. To each person that he called, he gave the same message:

'Dr Elias Lipsius here. It's about Adam Stride. Be here.' He then added the precise details of the timing.

The man known to Adam Stride as Mr Ron Butcher received on his mobile phone a call from 'Dr Elias Lipsius' to 'Richmond' at 4:30 p.m., though he was in fact highly inconvenienced by the matter. 'Richmond', 'Ron Butcher', a.k.a. Bill Worthing, as his neighbours in Basildon knew him, readily agreed to be there on the instant that 'Lipsius' had demanded and returned to his work, inwardly cursing the shortened schedule of his day. In the basement of one of the many garages he owned, Bill Worthing had a man under torture.

Bill Worthing was known to his neighbours as a pleasant fellow. All the East End had declared, 'It couldn't 'appen to a nicer fella' when Bill had moved to a manor in Basildon, Essex. His neighbours, to whom he was warmly hospitable, praised his house with its golden doorknobs, its swimming pool, its bar by the dining room festooned with strip-lighting and backed by a full-colour reproduction of the coast at Malaga. 'Oh, Bill's a good bloke,' it was usually said in the pubs of Basildon. Presently, Bill was waiting for information extracted from an unwilling source along with their teeth. Pliers were useful persuaders.

This big, burly man with an ugly face adorned with an unpleasant ginger moustache which merged into a pair of insalubrious and bulbous chin-whiskers had arrived to take a flat in Barking ten years before. In the surrounding pubs, he complained loudly that the East End had been gutted and rolled over into 'up-ended concrete boxes of Kleenex tissues'. He had also said that he was interested in doing business. One night, a local tough had challenged him. All who saw it remembered the fistic shots to the heart, liver and kidneys with the final blows that broke a jaw, broke a nose and blacked two eyes. Soon after this, Bill Worthing agreed to go on patrol for a local outfit and upped the protection dues by the simple expedient of hurling a fish-shop cat into the frier when the owner became difficult over the matter of increased protection. Word got around.

Nobody really knew where he came from and after he had made his mark – it was some man who had publicly insulted him and who somehow ended his days in concrete shoes in the Thames, near Wapping – nobody was too keen to raise the matter that openly. Bill Worthing proceeded to build up a prosperous business of garages, used cars and property; and some even said that he ran his own protection rackets and enjoyed ownership of pubs and clubs and casinos, both legal and illegal.

By the time that Bill Worthing moved to Basildon, he was a highly respected citizen who drove a scarlet Jaguar, gave much money to local charities, especially the local boys' boxing club, and was obsessed with screwing glamorous tarts, habits that were not resented by his neighbours. Malicious gossip connected him, no doubt unjustly, with the Brinks-Mat bullion robbery. Certainly the police had raided his home and found nothing: the story that he painted some gold bricks pitch black and used them as doorstops which the police did not notice had to be apocryphal.

The call he was expecting came from a phone box: Bill Worthing had trained his associates not to use mobile phones for any suspicious communications the police could intercept.

'Guv, it's 3-1, 5-3 on and a ten-point accumulator. Doomsday is the tip.' There was a loud cough. 'Or maybe Galleon. It's the 3:30 tomorrow at Newmarket.'

'Galleon.' He rang off. He had taught his men to use a code

and at last they had learned it. Three teeth had been painfully pulled without sufficient information concerning a grass being extracted along with them though much had been gleaned that was useful, even so. More might be done with a shit sandwich force-fed through the mouth. Then they'd release him and have him followed at all times. Meanwhile there was enough data for a leading underworld rival to be terminated along with his gang for the hideous sin of reneging on an agreement.

Now it was time for a rather different kind of code and measure, in going to meet the man who called him 'Richmond' and whom he called 'Dr Lipsius'. 'Richmond' was only too well aware of the man's eccentricities, and knew the value for a humble millionaire in having dealings with a billionaire. Exceedingly wealthy men, who could buy and sell a mere millionaire for a relative pittance, could also afford to indulge themselves in anything else they chose.

'Mr Bill Worthing' was seen by his neighbours to be driving his scarlet Jaguar away at 5:30 p.m. He was wearing a tailored brown suit with a shirt, bought at Harrod's, that was screaming blue murder; a multi-coloured silk tie, purchased in Rome, that could have adorned a peacock; and brown boots that he had purchased from Harvey Nichols. Shortly before he reached London, he stopped at a garage that he owned, rather as if he was in need of a repair, and a few minutes later, continued on his way in a scarlet Jaguar – only it had a different number plate. At another garage, that he also owned, he placed a brown pork-pie hat upon his head and took a minicab, run by a firm that he also owned: this was a white Ford escort.

He was no longer Bill Worthing. He was Richmond and he knew that if you wear a brown pork-pie hat, all that anyone will remember about you is that you wore a brown pork-pie hat: it is an excellent form of disguise. During his ride into town, he wondered about 'Lipsius', who had invested so much money into his business schemes in exchange for favours that hardly seemed onerous. Richmond was also rather drawn to Lipsius's obsession with artistry. He was aware of the latter's obsession with that obscure author Arthur Machen and his *The Three Impostors*. This, he knew, was why Lipsius had purchased a house on Chenies Street, just off Goodge Street, a place warmly welcoming and Victorian – and mentioned as the house of Lipsius in *The Three Impostors*.

'Did you *enjoy* beating him, Richmond, eh? Hm?' were the words with which Lipsius greeted him as the servants showed him into what was called 'The Doctor's Museum' by those who had gazed at its contents. Richmond had never especially relished the sight of penises and testicles in fish tanks. 'I gather that torn-out fingernails followed the teeth, on account of which I have some information for you, rather more up-to-date than yours. Did you *enjoy* having him beaten, Richmond? I did. It is in consequence of this that I have valuable – oh, possibly invaluable – information to the lasting benefit of your business interests. I must say I'm most surprised that you didn't make it a DIY job, my dear Richmond. Why, as the old lady said when Jesus Christ was crucified: "Lord, it was 'is 'obby."

'But Richmond,' Dr Lipsius continued silkily, 'we must never quarrel, eh, Richmond? Hm. Some sherry?'

'Oh, fuck it!' exclaimed the person who sometimes wrote under the pseudonym of Septimus Keen but who was known to his friends, acquaintances and neighbours as Benedictus Catesby, as the phone by his bed rang. There was every reason for him to say that. He had just been in the process of making love to the blond, voluptuous and desirable Venetia Woodruffe, but he had been earlier warned of the possibility of a call. 'Okay, I'll be there,' was all he said before replacing the receiver. Then, after a momentary frown, he returned to making love to Venetia. This encounter was satisfying to both parties, who smiled as they came and thence lay together, warm, silent and still.

Afterwards, Catesby made Venetia a coffee and brought her a brandy as she dressed, for she said that she had to be home for her husband.

Venetia had no regrets as he ushered her out of the door with a parting sweet kiss. Benedictus Catesby had just made very fine, sweet love to her and the memory of his tongue in her mouth was as good as the recollection of his penis in her vagina. She had met him while watching the lions and the lionesses at London Zoo and he had seemed to be such a charming young man, especially since her husband Hubert hadn't fucked her in over a year. It had been quite a pleasure to meet a young, handsome poet whose works had been published only in amateur magazines and to listen to his paeans of praise for her.

It had not mattered to her that his place, which he had boldly advertised to her as being in 'Westminstah – just opposite the Carlton', had turned out to be a grubby bedsit in Maida Vale, just by the Kilburn border, and so technically in the Borough of Westminster, with a charming view of the Carlton Bingo Rooms. There was something romantic about this educated poet without any money but with so much charm and so she had gone to bed with him, thoroughly appreciating the fact that he had fucked her brains out.

She smiled to herself and wished him luck as she returned to her home, which was only two blocks away from Catesby's bedsit. This was most convenient for an extramarital affair. She was actually quite fond of her husband Hubert, and she would have done virtually anything to save his business, which was on the verge of bankruptcy. He said that it wasn't, though from reading the papers she knew that it was – in addition, the language of his body told her all she needed to know.

A friend of hers, a lady aristocrat she had known since her

schooldays and who seemed to be working for British Intelligence, had informed Venetia that provided she was prepared to make the acquaintanceship of Benedictus Catesby and report on his home, every problem of Hubert's business would be satisfactorily settled.

With a smile of self-satisfaction upon her face, Venetia strutted towards a telephone booth, her hips moving in wild satisfaction within a tight black miniskirt as her shining black high heels clicked upon the pavement. She called a certain number and spoke animatedly of lovely design labels that she had seen at the absolutely fabulous shops she had visited today on Oxford Street, even giving the prices and the details of various bargains to her apparent girlfriend. She then went back home, back to a mansion in Maida Vale, and when her drunken, disappointed and dispirited husband arrived, she greeted him with a smile and a kiss and told him that everything would be all right.

Pugh, who had now become Dr Lipsius, was very pleased to learn, via one of his agents, that a small matter had been accomplished neatly by Venetia.

As soon as Benedictus Catesby could heave a sigh of relief without being overheard, he did so. He had enjoyed his time with Venetia but was glad that she had gone. He was somewhat irritated by the man he knew as 'Dr Lipsius', useful as Lipsius was to his purposes.

Venetia would not have been surprised to see Catesby pull off his clothes and throw them on the floor, since he had earlier made it quite clear to her that he was a bachelor: his room resembled a rubbish-tip. However, she might well have been surprised to see him enter a nondescript cupboard, remove a light switch temporarily from the wall, press a few minuscule buttons and then, as some shelves gave way, enter into an entirely new world. Here he preferred to think of himself as 'Septimus Keen', for it was that name he used to grace his writings.

Thank heavens for a mobile, he thought, considering the advantages of multiple numbers and names; then he looked with pleasure upon a completely different flat, one that could have passed muster in *Interiors* magazine as being a masterpiece of reconstructed eighteen-nineties Decadence. It was as though a shrine had been erected to the glory of Beardsley, Wilde, Harris, Dowson, Huysmans and Crowley, not to mention Arthur Machen, whose taste in Japanese lacquered desks of many drawers had clearly been respected. Arthur Machen, however, might have frowned somewhat upon Catesby's subsequent activity as 'Septimus Keen' lovingly selected knickers, a petticoat, seamed stockings, a black suspender belt and high-heeled shoes of gleaming black leather and then sat down before a mirror to make up his face. His hands were swift and expert: within thirty-one minutes 'Benedictus Catesby' and 'Septimus Keen' had become 'Arabella D'Arcy,' ready and willing to visit the man who lived a life as 'Dr Lipsius'.

'Septimus Keen' now slipped on a calf-length, hip-hugging skirt in pink, shocking pink, and a white frilly blouse with a brooch of aquamarine, the tailored jacket that stopped just short of the hips providing a finishing touch of pink. A woman stared back at the person who looked into the mirror. That person murmured: 'Hail, Septimus Keen.'

Septimus Keen had always loved Maida Vale for its contrast of style and sleaze. The best and worst could be found there and so, on receiving an unexpected legacy, Keen had established a double life – or even a triple life – made possible by the purchase of two flats under two different names. Benedictus Catesby was known locally as an eccentric writer who had no car and very little money but who still somehow managed to inveigle attractive women into his bed. From the outside, the flatblock where he lived had been built in the plain brick style of the 1950s. Arabella D'Arcy was known to her neighbours as a woman of independent means who drove a Porsche. She had virtually no visitors other than women friends, and she often went on holiday, sending her immediate neighbours boring postcards from exotic locations. The exterior of her home consisted of a Georgian façade of white stucco with Doric columns and iron-railed balconies. The third identity, of course, was that of Septimus Keen.

Arabella decided to take a taxi tonight so as to arrive punctually at the venue to which Dr Lipsius had summoned her. She also took in her valise, since she knew it would please him and her colleagues, another tale by Septimus Keen.

Davies received Lipsius's call while he was enjoying *tapas* at an allegedly Spanish bar in Islington, though he wondered why London lagged so far behind Madrid in this relatively simple matter of wine and appealing snacks. He thought that a mobile phone was useful for his purposes, which presently included calling a lady friend and rearranging a date for the morrow, though he deplored the bad taste of yuppies walking down Oxford Street with their mobiles, only to say: 'Hallo, I'm in Oxford Street.'

Davies had done many things in his life and presently, as 'Clarence Gardgate', he had an art gallery in one of the more exclusive parts of Islington where he delighted in exploiting the (in his opinion) poor taste of a rich and radical chic clientele. His gallery deliberately took four kinds of painting. First, to give credibility to his operation, he stocked many well-painted pictures from all over the globe that he sold at reasonable prices. Most of his visitors could afford to spend a few hundred pounds. He was a frequent visitor to the Saatchi & Saatchi gallery and, whilst privately he thought their stuff dreadful, he paid a few pounds to starving artists to mock-up work that was similar and charged thousands for the end results. He also slipped in a few paintings that he personally liked and for which he charged, again, a few hundred pounds. It gave him genuine pleasure to sell these. It gave him great sadistic glee to sell work that he regarded as rubbish at much higher prices.

But there was a further artistic endeavour that gave Mr Davies even greater glee. He had in his pay a man of exemplary technical talent who could copy the style of any Old Master immaculately. How Davies smiled when the alleged experts at auctioneers and art galleries authenticated these pictures!

The man often known as 'Davies' thoroughly enjoyed the work he did for the man he called 'Dr Lipsius'. Davies had a very low boredom threshold and required drama to make his life consistently stimulating. Although he was a millionaire, he respected the man for whom he had chosen to work since he further aroused in Davies the power of the daemonic.

Davies had a house in what has been called 'gorgeous, blooming Georgian Barnsbury Square'. He had furnished it perfectly in the style of the era and so many women had been delighted by romps in his four-poster bed. Much to the surprise of his neighbours, he did not have a car.

'What's the point here?' he had demanded languidly of his neighbour, Lord Mandeville, over vintage port on the previous night. 'First I have to buy a car, then I have to tax and insure the bloody thing. Since I don't have a garage, where do I park it? Louts might put bricks through its window and slash the tyres if I leave it out in the street. And then, where do I take this awful car of mine? As far as I'm concerned, the West End is the only place for me – but by car I have to travel there at an average speed of four miles per hour. The next problem consists of parking it, which can be done at some outrageous price provided that you don't mind being accosted by yobs in some frightful multi-storey car park. On top of that, I am not allowed to have a drink in the way I would wish since the police have power to stop one for doing that at any moment. Tell me, Harry, for you've always struck me as being quite sane, why do *you* have a car?'

'To go to the country, of course.'

'Understandable,' Davies had said, 'though the country, I confess, holds no great attractions for me. As Oscar Wilde declared: "Grass is hard and lumpy and damp and full of dreadful black insects." '

'You're such a bloody townie, Gardgate.'

'Yes,' said Davies; and he now ordered a black cab to take him to his rendezvous with Lipsius.

The woman known to Stride as 'Alison Featherstonehaugh' and to others as 'Helen' received the call of 'Dr Lipsius' at her home in Hampstead where she was sipping chilled white port as she awaited a call that she knew would be coming. Her home, up the hill and just off the High Street and with a beautiful view out on to Hampstead Heath, had resounding contrasts in store for any visitor who could penetrate through to the upper floors.

Her downstairs living room had been furnished in mid-Eighties high tech, with chrome, silver, glass and the colours of black and white predominating. Anyone invited to what she termed 'Oh, it's just the drawing room upstairs' saw a set piece of the 1890s that could easily have been displayed within the Victoria and Albert Museum were it not for the overt sadomasochistic features.

Her bookshelves proudly displayed leather bound volumes of classical erotica such as *Gynaecocracy*, *The Petticoat Dominant*, *Mistress & Slave*, *A Guide To The Correction of Young Gentlemen*, and *The Black Pearl*. The framed prints all around this room echoed Aubrey Beardsley's masterpiece of flagellation, his illustration to John Davidson's *The Wonderful Mission of Earl Lavender*. Other anonymous prints were all of men being spanked, caned, whipped and birched by women. There was a flogging block upon the maroon carpet and a cane, a whip and a birch had been proudly positioned upon the white walls.

The woman known here as 'Lady Domina' in her past had thoroughly enjoyed her work. There were women who whipped men in a tired and listless sort of way, that she knew; but she derived genuine enjoyment from the activity. She loved to see a man squirm and pay her for the privilege. Although she admitted the fact only to a few close female friends, 'Lady Domina' used to soak her knickers in love-juices at the sight of scarlet, glowing, well-whipped male bottoms. She had executed her calling so well that she could earn more in an hour than most could in a week – and this was without including the extra income she derived from hidden tapes and cameras that, through the long-established network of shared sexual peculiarities, gave her access to some of the highest in the land.

She had seen the decline of 'Appy 'Ampstead from a delightfully mixed and beautifully bohemian area into a borough of tawdry and tacky triviality, a relentlessly risible yuppie domain. In the ice-cold manner of a true lady of business, she had bought closing-down bookshops, old-fashioned tobacconists, traditional pubs and cosy restaurants, transforming them into over-priced boutiques, health food stores, wine bars and restaurants that changed names rapidly according to the fashion of the time. The fact that she had played a principal part in ruining 'Appy 'Ampstead did not worry her at all.

She had the money to be able to walk a few steps to her private garage, clamber into the driver's seat of her gleaming black 1957 Bentley Continental, the smooth purring car of James Bond in the early novels, and reflect that Bond's enemy, SPECTRE, could not have done as well as she had as she drove to see Dr Lipsius.

THE GOD GAME

*

'Some sherry, eh, hm?' Dr Lipsius regarded his guests. Helen was wearing a tight black suit, Arabella was wearing a tight pink suit, Davies was wearing a loose suit of grey and Richmond was wearing a baggy brown suit. Lipsius himself had chosen to wear clerical black.

'Is the "eh, hm," really necessary, Dr Lipsius?' Davies enquired politely. 'I know that we quite properly enjoy the re-enactment of glorious times past but, much as I enjoy bacon, is it not a little *ham* to overdo the matter?'

'I have always appreciated your wit, Mr Davies. Do I detect a slight trace of sarcasm in your attitude by any chance, eh, hm? Now, for the sherry, do you want fino, or manzanilla that is a little more salty, amontillado that is the *sack* of which Shakespeare spoke, or sweet and creamy oloroso? Ladies first, I always say.' Helen took fino, Arabella asked for amontillado, Davies requested manzanilla and Richmond wanted Bristol Cream. 'Good, good,' said Dr Lipsius as his Filipino servant served them. 'For myself,' he glanced at Arabella, '*I* shall have sack too. With it, we shall enjoy nuts; bring them,' he added in an undertone to his visibly adoring assistant.

'Yessir!' the boy replied. 'Which nuts would you like, sir? There are walnuts, hazelnuts, pecan nuts, cashew nuts, brazil nuts . . .'

'Enough.' Lipsius cut him short. 'Just bring the whole bloody tray.'

'Yessir.' This matter was easily accomplished as Lipsius switched on a screen that showed a picture of Adam Stride. 'I think you have all had dealings with this man. Insofar as I can see, he is *not corruptible*. This matter annoys me.'

'It would,' Helen sighed as she scrunched a brazil nut between her pearly white teeth. 'He is a clever man and therefore it annoys me also . . . although it *is* rather fun to torment him with puzzles that he will never solve.' She giggled.

'He's okay,' said Richmond, 'in his way.' He drank his sherry as though it was beer. 'But I wouldn't mind snapping the neck of that arrogant bastard.'

'It is so enjoyable,' Davies remarked thoughtfully, 'playing with an intelligent human being and completely confusing him, as though he was a rat in a maze. After all, we have to keep up our noble traditions. Remember what our predecessors did to Arthur Machen?' Everybody laughed and raised their glasses.

'And what of Septimus Keen?' Lipsius queried.

'Oh,' said Arabella, 'I have another tale for you that I think you will find to be directly apposite to the subject under discussion.'

She thence proceeded to read them:

THE BOY FROM BRAZIL

by

Septimus Keen

Who knows what is real and what is not? For instance, I have 156,000 Brazilian cruzeiros in cash. In Brazil, these might buy me a decent dinner: in London, they are worthless since not even the sleaziest bureau de change will do anything other than dismiss them with a visible gesture of contempt. This is in spite of the fact that Brazil is essentially a very wealthy country in terms of its productive potential. Never mind what the money might buy in Rio: in London terms, the cruzeiro is indeed zero.

This reflection brings me to my tale of a Brazilian boy at school whom I hated. His academic performance was excellent and he gained a scholarship to Oriel College, Oxford to read Modern Languages. He was Captain of the First Eleven at both cricket and football. He was blond, blue-eyed and exceptionally handsome. All the girls ran after him, amazed that a Brazilian could have blond hair. Nevertheless, some do. Every girl said that he was fantastic in bed. All the boys liked him on account of his affable manner, adherence to common sense and extraordinary sporting achievement. I would have approved of him for that too, had it not been for one thing: the boy was a Nazi.

Heinrich von Stahlein was a ghastly boy. As Head Prefect, he delighted in sadistic punishments such as scrubbing the changing-room floor with a toothbrush or cutting the lawn with nail scissors. Oh, and he was particularly fond of enforced cold baths on freezing winter mornings. Actually, I wasn't a victim of von Stahlein's persecution of the weak and helpless since I was the House Monitor for Music and the Arts and so on the team, as it were. I did all I could to stop the cruelty at what was a purportedly enlightened co-educational establishment but there was no stopping von Stahlein, once he'd got into power. I even remember him berating me one week because I hadn't punished anybody.

There was one thing we did have in common, however, and that was esotericism, the study of the hidden wisdom. We passed many intellectually joyous hours in discussing the merits of Zoroaster, Hermes Trismegistus, Paracelsus, Agrippa, John Dee, Levi, the Golden Dawn and Crowley, all of whose works we had purchased eagerly from our local second-hand bookshop, where in these matters the genial proprietor knew neither the correct price nor the true value of what he was selling us. We both declared that we would set out to find the Sovereign Sanctuary of Adepti and, in the folly of youth, we shook hands and swore that whoever found it first would inform and propose the other.

Von Stahlein went to Oxford and I went to the Adepti. No, that's wrong. You don't 'go to' the Adepti. They come and find you. If you have been putting out signals for many years, that is what will happen, though never in a way you expect. My way of life was fully accepted by my Brothers and Sisters in the Order, and it was through their assistance and their rites and ceremonies that I experienced *ecstasy*, a union combining all within with all without, an experience for which I state a glorious human orgasm is only a poor metaphor. This experience makes you love more. It makes you hate more, too.

Time drew von Stahlein back into my ambit. I had by this time learned from my Brothers and Sisters to lead many lives, just as they did. One of our operations consisted of offering a variety of courses in spiritual enlightenment under the auspices of multifarious organizations. One applicant to The Society of the Swastika, which ostensibly involved itself in matters of Nordic Runes and Teutonic mythology, was Heinrich von Stahlein. Perhaps he was attracted by our slogan: 'The Way is Light'.

Heinrich von Stahlein was always a man for a challenge and, after an exchange of letters, we met at a pub near Centre Point for an 'interview'. He was initially surprised to see me but soon accepted that I had been initiated into some sort of secret society that practised Magick. I asked him questions and listened as he answered. So did certain Brothers and Sisters who were seated at the next table.

The progress of Henry Starlen, as he now styled himself, had been astonishing. At the age of twenty-three he was earning a fortune in commodity broking whilst doing part-time work for the Conservative Central Office. However, he told me, he had never abandoned his old ideals. He still hankered after something *more* . . . yes, he hankered after an initiation that would test him to the very limit.

'Yes,' said my Brothers and Sisters in the Order when we discussed the matter afterwards.

Henry Starlen travelled by the Central Line to Ongar one evening. At the station, a man who looked so dull that one could never recall his face said: 'Need any directions sir?' and, on receiving an affirmative, informed him where to find all the features of the locality. Starlen was braced for the occasion of his initiation. He desired enlightenment and was convinced that he was so tough that absolutely no ordeal could frighten him.

The directions he had been given led him through a forest and proved to be accurate in that, emerging from a copse, he saw a huge oak tree and some familiar faces. These folk had lit a bonfire and were dancing around it. Evidently they had been there for a while, since there were spades by the tree and, in front of it, a large black coffin, just as he had been told there would be.

'Welcome, Candidate!' they cried out joyously to him. He

accepted their standing of him in the centre of a circle as they weaved around and about him.

'Candidate,' I said, knowing that no one sane ventured into this part of the woods after dark, 'do you consent to all?'

'I do.'

'You realize that you will be buried alive for eight hours in symbolic reverence for the life, death and resurrection of Adonis, Attis, Osiris, Dionysus and one known as Jesus?'

'I *do*.' His fists clenched at that point.

'Take cakes and wine with us, Candidate, to sustain you in your noble ordeal: and may Enlightenment dawn upon your brow, O Son of the Swastika!'

In order to expedite his Holy Ordeal, the biscuits had been baked with hashish and the wine he received had been spiked with LSD. He was very relaxed as he lay down in his coffin. The lid was lowered. The coffin was laid reverently in its grave. Earth and turf were thrown upon it. He still had no reason to be worried. There was a tube for speaking, breathing and hearing through that penetrated the lid of the coffin and went up above the surface of the ground. I reflected that he might now be thinking of his mobile phone, the one I had surreptitiously removed from his underpants.

My partners had walked away. I watched the sun set in a blood-red sky. The woods around me were wild and beautiful and it seemed that as the branches swayed in the wild west wind, there was within the noise of the swirling leaves a song of vengeance.

'It's all over,' I said loudly into the speaking tube. 'The coffin lid is nailed down. Heinrich . . . Eat shit, fuckface and have fun.'

'*How can you!?*' he screamed.

'Easily,' I said as I removed the air tube.

The premature burial wasn't discovered until some days

later. It seems that Heinrich had clawed away half of the coffin lid. Well, the Nazis always were highly tenacious.

'O Septimus!' Helen cried out in delighted applause. 'You're such a darling! And you're so divinely *wicked*!'

'Thank you.' Arabella blushed modestly as her companions also indicated their approbation.

'Splendid, Septimus.' Dr Lipsius beamed briefly and then his tongue flicked out to moisten his thin lips. 'I wonder what Adam Stride will think of *that* when he receives it?'

'That is his problem, Doctor,' Arabella returned, 'not mine. But I am *so* looking forward to the next scene.'

'Indeed,' Lipsius returned, now increasingly certain that Arabella D'Arcy/Septimus Keen and Benedictus Catesby were one and the same. 'It is such a pleasure, is it not, to play these games. It is one of the many pleasures that money can buy. We all adore Arthur Machen's *The Three Impostors* and it is such a *joy* to play out these roles. And who better to play with than Adam Stride, author of *The Labyrinth of Satan* in which we feature? I look forward eagerly to hearing in detail of his encounters with Mr Ron Butcher, Mr Owen Davies and Miss Alison Featherstonehaugh.' At that instant, the boy who had served the nuts knocked, entered and knelt at the feet of Lipsius.

'Dinner is served, sir,' he said respectfully.

'Thank you,' Lipsius answered, giving him permission to arise. 'A new recruit,' he added. 'Makes a pleasant change to have a servant capable of speech even if the poor chap is as deaf as a post. Well, I trust that caviar, turtle soup, goose-liver pâté, a selection of smoked fish, roast British beef and pudding and cheese will be to your satisfaction . . . ? Over dinner, we can discuss the eventual fate of Adam Stride after which we shall . . .' They all smiled. 'After which we shall partake of the

Rites of Avaullaunius.' He coughed, and then added: 'Eh, hm?' and smiled thinly at Davies.

'And the Stone within the Ankh?' Helen enquired.

'We require more data,' Lipsius returned silkily. 'I do hope that Stride is having fun with it. So, it is said, did Arthur Machen.'

CHAPTER TEN

BEWILDERMENT IN BARNSBURY

(OUI AND JA)

Over the past few weeks, Arthur Machen had repeatedly stared into the mysterious Stone set within the brass Ankh. There were moments when he saw absolutely nothing. At other moments there was a blur before his eyes and he saw men of Tudor times whom he fancied to be Dr John Dee and Edward Kelley. There were instants when he fancied that he could discern the face of Horace Walpole, moments when he thought he saw the face of Sr Francis Dashwood of the so-called Hell-Fire Club. Still more puzzling than any of these matters was the fact that he kept having glimpses of a time that he could only suppose to be the future.

There was no other way of explaining what he saw. Machen could clearly discern the face of a clean-shaven man staring into what he presumed to be the Stone, his eyes sometimes fixed in a stare of manic intensity. Behind the head and shoulders of this man, whose clothes were clearly of neither times present nor times past, Machen could discern machines executing functions unavailable to the technology of his own day. Although the matter made him fearful, he had tried to communicate with the face in the stone but hitherto without success. One of the problems was that this man bore a disturbing resemblance to the Mr O'Malley who bore such a close likeness to his creation Davies.

That was hardly the only matter that disturbed him acutely. He also caught glimpses of the lady 'with a quaint and piquant, rather than a beautiful face, and with eyes of shining hazel', whom he fancied he had invented as 'Helen' in his books. There were also glimpses of Richmond and Dr Lipsius. To add to his perplexity, he often caught sight of a bearded man staring at him with a perplexity equal to his own.

Although Adam Stride did not know what Arthur Machen was thinking, he was having similar experiences whenever he stared into the stone. He kept on seeing visions of beings he thought he had merely developed further in his own work from Arthur Machen's original concept. Lipsius, Richmond, Davies, Helen; and, too, apparitions of his own creation, the transvestite Septimus Keen. However, within the stone he also saw the face of Arthur Machen.

Arthur Machen replaced the Stone reverently within the hidden drawer of his Japanese desk. For today, he had seen more than enough; yet for the future, he had not seen nearly enough. No doubt, he reflected wryly, that might come in due course. It was enough for now. Taking a broad-brimmed black hat, a long black cloak, his favourite pipe and his dog, Arthur Machen ventured out into the streets.

His winter had been passed in relative solitude and he had relished the state. After the bombardment of irrationalities he had suffered, it was a relief for him to contemplate the Stone and to work on his writing without further disturbance. He had attended a Study Group of the Golden Dawn only once and there he had heard of Black Magic and of Orders that endeavour to ensnare the unwary for their own nefarious ends.

Machen set off for Barnsbury, one of his favourite areas in all of London. It was a fine early spring day, with the crocuses blooming, but it was also the sort of day that Machen mentally labelled 'the February cheat'. He felt that there was always a day in early February that boldly announced spring, after which the weather became worse then ever. The walk of some miles from Holborn was nothing to him and he had his own reasons for approaching the area via the vulgar bustle of the Caledonian Road. He agreed with Thomas Chatterton and William Blake that London is a holy city and that many of its secrets are to be discerned in the valley where once stood the Church of St Pancras.

Although Machen was a keen logician, he was also drawn to the irrational, thus setting up a tension of duality within his own nature. He genuinely had certainty in the experience of ecstasy and had ultimate faith in the purity abiding within the interior of the soul. He was also painfully aware of the demons that lurked therein and of which, having been brought up as a Christian, he was profoundly ashamed; yet by which he was also unduly fascinated. He hoped now that a good walk would enable him to think more clearly and hence to resolve his inner perplexities.

It was certainly a pleasure for Machen to turn right into Richmond Avenue and to notice again how, on the right, each house was guarded by twin plaster sphinxes of a deadly chocolate-red that crouched on either side of the flights of steps leading to the doorways. He had written many letters enquiring after the origins of these statues yet had elicited no information other than that these sphinxes had passed from Egypt to Napoleon and from Napoleon to that sacred, shy part of London that is largely unknown even to the native Londoner. Absolutely nobody seemed to know how or why this had happened.

Passing one of the oldest taverns in London, but resolving to visit it later, Machen came into a square surrounded by houses of the Georgian period, though on one side of it there was a terrace of little Queen Anne houses, with old gardens in front of them and with luxuriant vines upon their walls. Just as he was relishing the sight, he felt a prickling of his scalp and was possessed by the uncomfortable suspicion that somebody might be following him. Upon looking around, however, he could see no one likely to justify his apprehension.

Machen decided to enter the leafy garden of the square and enjoy the sight of early spring flowers and the newly green leaves of the trees fluttering in the wind. He looked for a comfortable bench upon which he could sit and was glad to see one that was empty, which he took. Jug the dog, who had had quite enough of walking for the time being, lay down contentedly at his feet. He might have enjoyed the peaceful idyll he desired had it not been for the sudden appearance of a young lady dressed in the height of fashion in glistening emerald green who walked towards him, switching her hips, and who then proceeded to place her tightly-wrapped rear on the bench at the end furthest from Machen. She wore a hat festooned with ostrich feathers and a black veil of lace and appeared to be possessed by the most abject misery as she sobbed into a white silk handkerchief. After a time, the loudness of her sobbing became virtually intolerable.

'Madam,' said Machen, 'it is sad to witness such sad and evident distress in a lady. May I assist you at all?'

'I do not know, sir,' the lady returned, turning upon him a face which behind the black lace veil looked to be pretty and sweet. 'Is it fair to unburden myself of my troubles?'

'Why not?' Machen answered and lit his pipe, a bulldog, which contained his favourite tobacco, shag. 'I can promise you a sympathetic ear.'

'I feel,' the young lady confided, 'as if I was living in a novel by Arthur Machen. You haven't read him, by any chance?'

'Read him?' Machen exploded indignantly. 'I've *written* him!'

'Are you sure?'

'Of course I'm sure!' Machen shouted. Then he added:

'Pardon my vehemence, Madam, since for better or for worse, I am indeed Arthur Machen, author of *The Great God Pan*, 'The Inmost Light' and *The Three Impostors*.'

'This becomes increasingly strange,' said the young lady. 'Oh, help me, sir, if you can! For one of my dearest friends, for whose life I fear, has told me that *he* is Arthur Machen, author of the very works you mention.'

'He can't be,' Machen protested, feeling as though everyone in the world, including himself, had gone mad. 'Tell me about him.' He smiled gently. 'And tell me about yourself.' His head was whirling on account of his lack of recall. *Was* she the raven-haired girl he had seen fleeing on that fateful night? Was she the mysterious lady who had admired his bulldog but who presently paid it no attention? Did she bear any resemblance to the lady who had come with Crowley?

'I thank you for your patience and understanding,' she sighed. 'Allow me to introduce myself, albeit in my unhappy state. My name is Alison Hyde.'

'A pleasure to meet you, Miss Hyde. My name is Arthur Machen.'

'Do you know,' the attractive young lady regarded him quizzically, 'you are the fourth man who has said that to me within a week.'

'Sorry?'

'I am a great admirer of the work of Arthur Machen,' said Alison Hyde. 'I was under the impression that a dear friend of mine was *the* Arthur Machen. Yet the other day I was sitting in the Café de l'Europe with an old friend. It is a delightful venue and one has good food and good cheer for reasonable prices. Also, it's such a pleasure to look out over Leicester Square. My friend Alan and I were thoroughly enjoying the atmosphere when a young man barged into the place shouting: "Cream tarts! Cream tarts!" and he passed them around freely to anyone who wanted them. When I asked him his name as he brought his tarts to our table, he said: "Arthur Machen."

'"That's ridiculous!" my dinner companion exclaimed. "Since *I* write tales under the pseudonym of 'Arthur Machen'." Don't you now comprehend the nature of my perplexity, sir? I have now encountered four men who all claim to be Arthur Machen, author of literary works that I adore.'

'Madam, I can gladly furnish you with letters from my publisher that will demonstrate beyond all doubt that, for my sins, I am *the* Arthur Machen.'

'That's what they all say,' the young lady replied. Machen had been shaken by her story since it was another incident of Life repeating Art. *The Incident of the Young Man with the Cream Tarts* was the unforgettable opening to *New Arabian Nights* by Robert Louis Stevenson and it was this that had inspired Machen to essay *The Three Impostors* and tell tales within tales as he endeavoured to express the sacred nature of London.

'Why . . .' Machen enquired cautiously, 'does your friend state that he is Arthur Machen, author of my stories?'

'I fear now for the life of the dear friend I know as Arthur Machen,' the young lady stated and shuddered as she did so. 'He is a very strange young man who loves literature and the arts but I do so worry about him. Mind you, his recent behaviour has concerned me even more than usual. He keeps a box of ice in his house, which ice he uses to concoct refreshing drinks, but a few days ago I was somewhat disturbed to lift the lid and to find a dead cat in there.'

'A dead cat . . .' Machen faltered.

'Yes. When I asked him why, he answered that he had developed an interest in taxidermy and would soon be having that cat stuffed.'

'I see,' said Machen. He did not see at all at that moment. 'But how on Earth can he claim to be Arthur Machen?'

'How can *you* claim to be Arthur Machen, sir,' the young

THE GOD GAME

lady replied, 'when this man has handed me this as his latest work?'

Machen looked and read:

OUI AND JA

It all began as a perfectly innocent scientific experiment, arising out of one of those chance meetings so often associated with the Reading Room of the British Museum. I had often seen Pierre there, a tall, rather bird-like individual, who aroused my curiosity by his ability to cover at least twelve sheets of paper with what looked like mathematical calculations within half an hour of his arrival. Afterwards, in the early evening, he did what I did, which was to take a beer in a pleasant tavern in Museum Street and reflect over the day's experiential portion. We fell into conversation and I learned that he was a graduate of the Sorbonne, obsessed with Mathematics, and that the generosity of deceased relatives enabled him to pursue his hunger for numbers in circumstances of modest comfort. I asked after the nature of his research.

'Infinity,' he replied. '*Mon cher monsieur*, your English mathematicians, technically excellent though they are, work on wrong lines altogether in endeavouring to formalize mathematics within a finite system. There *is* no finite system,' he declared as he lit another of the French cigarettes he smoked continuously and drank brandy. 'There is nothing logical about *anything* infinite: the premisses of the professors, based upon finite assumptions, contain internal contradictions.

'*My* mathematics – flawless!' he boasted proudly. 'I have proved that an infinity of rational numbers is smaller than an infinity of decimal numbers. I have demonstrated the impossible properties of infinite sets. My proofs show that a line of zero length – that is to say, nothing – can contain as many points as the entire Universe. I have made it clear beyond all doubt that one divided by infinity equals zero; and that one divided by zero equals infinity. In consequence it follows that in this Universe we inhabit, anything is possible at any moment.'

'Stop,' I said, swallowing copious quantities of beer as I wondered whether I was dealing with a madman. 'I am not a mathematician but I understand from acquaintances who are that you are not allowed to divide by infinity.'

'Why not?' he retorted with exquisite French simplicity. 'What is it that frightens them? The world around us is a very strange place, much stranger than your logicians would allow.'

Our conversation was at this point interrupted by a voluptuous woman who greeted Pierre with effusive joy. He introduced her as Heidi from Munich, a woman who was managing London properties left to her by her late English father. Though she seemed a little bit simple in her grasp of our intellectual conversation, her manner was friendly and charming. The same could be said for Pamela, my lady friend of that time, who arrived as arranged a couple of minutes later. Pamela was a tall, slim blonde whose skills at that curious new invention, the typewriter, had enabled her to take to a clerkly life and independence. I had only known her for three weeks but I was already quite fond of this very ordinary woman.

As soon as the ladies were with us, however, and sipping port-and-lemon, the manner of Pierre became less intellectual. He laughed and he joked and then he demanded of me:

'Have you ever had any experience of the Ouija Board?'

'Yes. But to be candid, Pierre, I am really somewhat surprised that you now descend from the noble intricacies of Higher Mathematics to the parlour tricks of spiritualism.'

'On the contrary, I receive from the Ouija Board and the spirits attracted by it some of my finest inspiration.'

'You astound me, sir!' I exclaimed. 'What? A man of your obvious intelligence gadding about with a glass on a table? Certainly I don't deny that curious phenomena occur on these occasions, but in my experience all the communications we receive from these alleged spirits amount to gibberish or the most hideous banalities.'

'I disagree entirely,' he returned, quite heatedly. 'Do you dare to undertake a scientific experiment?'

'Certainly,' I answered. 'When?'

'Preferably tonight. I live not far from here, just by Baker Street, in fact. We could go there after a nice dinner – *mais non*, that is not such a good idea since an empty stomach is better for the seeing of spirits. Let us have our nice dinner afterwards.'

'I think I have a better idea,' I responded. 'I have a little place just across the road from here. Let's go there and after our experiment, which is presumably with the Ouija Board, we can have a pleasant supper. In fact, why don't we essay that now since I have some wine at home? Here and now for *Ouija*?'

'*Oui*,' said Pierre.

'*Ja*,' said Heidi.

'Pamela . . . this may be new to you but it might be jolly interesting . . .'

'Oh, yes,' said Pamela, 'my aunt was always very interested in this sort of thing.'

At the time, I lived in a very small flat just off Museum Street. There was a bathroom, a tiny kitchen and a living room with a bed, table and chairs. After I had served the wine, the four of us sat down at my round oak table and I obliged Pierre's request to provide him with paper, pencils and a glass tumbler. The ladies watched with fascination as Pierre tore up my pieces of paper and proceeded to label them. Eventually he arranged a circle consisting of the letters of the alphabet, numbers from one to nine and, at the north and south ends of the table, scraps of paper stating YES and NO. At the centre, there was the glass tumbler upturned. At his injunction, the four of us placed our right forefingers upon the tip of its rim with appropriate solemnity.

'Is there anybody there . . . ?' Pierre asked after a time. It seemed as though nobody was. 'Kind spirit, please manifest thyself.' Minutes passed and all I felt was an ache of boredom. Suddenly, and when I was least expecting it, the glass began to move. This was a phenomenon I had seen before, felt before, and so I was not disturbed when the glass slid across the table, seemingly under its own motive power, moving to YES. I did not think that anyone was consciously moving the object since it is difficult to do so with a fingertip; yet I felt that the glass *was* being moved by physical forces, the nature of which is as yet unknown, activated by the four of us.

'Kind spirit, will you answer our questions?' Pierre requested. The glass jerked away and returned to YES. 'Ladies first, I always say. Pamela, you are our hostess. What is your question?'

'Will I get promotion to Supervisor?' Pamela asked, adding quietly to me: 'It's so hard when you're the only woman in the company.' The glass sped over the table to NO.

'Heidi?' Pierre asked.

'Tell me something for my life,' she requested. The glass span around the table, moving to letters at random, before coming to rest at the centre of the table. Both Pierre and I had written down 'gbhkqitrd'.

'Gibberish,' I said.

'But it is your turn,' Pierre insisted gently.

'All right. Spirit, please tell me who killed the Little Princes in the Tower . . .' The glass whirled around the table in a way some might have found alarming before moving to spell out: 'tmdfgh7'. 'More gibberish!' I snorted in disgust.

'Not necessarily,' Pierre countered. '"h7" could mean Henry VII.'

'Possibly. And possibly not. But now it is your turn, Pierre.'

'O kind spirit,' he declaimed, 'please give me *the* number that I am seeking.'

There was no doubt that the glass shot instantly to the number '8' and Pierre gasped.

'Of course!' he exclaimed. 'Why did I not see it before? This is a maxim of Pythagoras, who taught that all phenomena were constructed in octaves. Yes . . . there is the octagonal geometry of Sufism and the Buddha's eight-spoked Wheel of the Law, with its Noble Eightfold Path. Ah! This is also the key to the *I-Ching*, the Chinese *Book of Changes* in which the basic polarity of yin and yang, the female and the male, is developed into the eight trigrams, and they combine into the $64 = 8 \times 8$ hexagrams that map the possible flux of all forces. Just a moment . . . the Qabalistic system is predicated on eight since there are ten Spheres and twenty-two Paths, making $32 = 4 \times 8$ . . .'

'Pierre,' said Heidi, 'I am not entirely comfortable with this spirit. Let us go before you are damaged.'

'No, not yet!' Pierre shouted in a trance of apparent ecstasy. 'Now I see it all! Don't you understand that if you have the figure 8 lying on its side as in ∞ you have the well-known sign of Infinity.'

'Pierre . . .' Heidi whined, 'I want to go.'

'Just a moment,' he responded excitedly. 'Let us suppose that the greatest number that the human mind can imagine is Infinity multiplied by the power of Infinity. I shall call this expression The Aleph. Hah! Small wonder that in the Tarot cards, The Juggler has the sign of Infinity above his brow . . . and the Tarot relates to the Qabalah; and the Tarot has four Suits and twenty-two Trumps, each suit is made up of ten cards so that makes $32 = 4 \times 8$. Now, what happens if we multiply the Aleph, which is Infinity x Infinity, by the Aleph . . . ?'

'Pierre, *please*,' Heidi begged him, 'can we *please* go home?'

'Oh, very well,' Pierre responded, slightly irritably. Ensuring that we all still had our fingers on the glass, he turned his china-blue eyes up to the heavens and said: 'And now, we thank you, O good spirit; depart in peace.'

The glass sped to NO.

'For me, that is it,' Heidi stated, turning to Pamela and myself. 'Thank you for your kind invitation to dine with you but not for me tonight. Pierre, please, you must rest.' She took her finger from the glass.

'I must close it,' he replied and asked Pamela and myself whether we would mind if the glass was moved back to the centre of the table. The sensation of moving it normally was as different as could be from the earlier independent motion that it had manifested. 'And now, O kind spirit, depart in peace.' With a smooth, almost purring motion, the glass sped to NO.

'I really am going,' said Heidi. 'Goodnight, everybody.' With that peremptory goodbye, she stormed out of the flat. Pierre took his finger from the glass.

'I must go too,' he said, in the tone of voice of a man who has received a revelation yet who really does not wish to upset his lady love. 'Thank you so much. You must come and have dinner with us another time . . .'

After the abrupt departure of first Heidi and then Pierre, Pamela and I were still stuck with the latter's home-made Ouija Board.

'What do we do now?' she asked me.

'Put our fingers on it and ask it to go away,' I said. We did so and absolutely nothing happened.

'You don't 'alf 'ave some weird friends,' she remarked.

'I suppose so.' I proceeded to gather all the papers into a bin and used the tumbler to rinse my mouth. 'Anyway, it was an interesting experiment that led nowhere and proved nothing.' I offered to take Pamela out to supper but she demurred, saying that she had noticed a pot of home-made soup bubbling upon my cooker and that she would rather have that. I was flattered, although (even if I say so myself) my home-made soup – carrot and orange on this occasion – *is* good. With it we had a freshly baked cottage loaf with Welsh butter and Cheshire cheese, accompanied by spring onions and pickles and followed by my braised oxtail with hot mustard. Oranges and apples followed that, after which we tumbled into bed, laughing genially about the séance and the genial but mad mathematician.

Around the early hours of the morning I passed into a state that is midway between sleeping, dreaming and waking. It was as though I entered into a waking state from a dream, being aroused by an intensely horrible sound: it was as though a crowd assembled before Buckingham Palace on a Royal occasion was *cheering in whispers*.

I sat up sharply, noticing that Pamela was equally startled.
'Did you hear that sound?' I demanded.
'Yes . . .'
I stared wildly around the room. To the left of the bed there was a window and since the linen curtain was thin, the gas lamps without usually gave sufficient light for me to see my room clearly. Under all circumstances, I could always see, at the end of my living room, a thick drainpipe in the corner, a duct that occasionally disturbed my sleep with its gurgling. Unfortunately, on this occasion, I could not see it and that was because there seemed to be a black cloud before it, impeding my vision.

I stared hard at it, endeavouring to penetrate the fog before me but to no avail. As I stared, I suddenly felt very cold and although I do not consider myself to be psychic, the hairs on the nape of my neck began to prickle and arise.

'Leave it to me,' said Pamela. Springing out of bed, she threw her arms into powerful swinging motions as she softly chanted a verse in a sing-song, the words of which I do not remember. Upon her return to the bed, I noticed that clear visibility of the drainpipe in the corner had been restored. The black cloud had vanished.

'How did you do that?' I murmured.

'West Country witches,' she replied; and then her blue eyes blazed as if set alight by something beyond my ken and I fell asleep in her arms, having no further dreams that I can recall.

There were a number of sequels to this evening of *Ouija*.

In the morning, as I was making coffee for Pamela and myself, I noticed that the silver spoon for which I had been searching in order to stir in the cream and sugar had been bent about the drainpipe, about eight feet up.

'What do you think of that, Pamela?' I demanded. 'There isn't a ladder or a chair that would enable you, me or anyone to twist a silver spoon around a drainpipe at the height of eight feet... or did you do it whilst I was asleep?'

'Don't be stupid,' she replied. 'Do you think I have the agility to get up eight feet and then the strength to wrap a silver spoon, bending it with my own hands, around a drainpipe?'

'Then how did it happen?'

'Must've been the spirits. It's wot 'appens when you try to go for the Infinite. Anyway, thanks for your hospitality. Maybe your friend Pierre will now have greater communion with the Infinite and with the spirits. Right, must make a move and go to work.' I helped her on with her coat. 'Do bear in mind that some entities will go to any lengths to stop vital information getting through to people.'

I never saw Pamela in the flesh again. The company at which she had worked informed me that she had left abruptly and all my endeavours to trace her proved fruitless.

A day later, the daily newspaper informed me that there had been a hideous blaze, a conflagration, at a flat just off Baker Street, consuming both a Pierre Dubois, a student of mathematics with an independent income and, inevitably, all his papers.

Foul play was not suspected. Spontaneous combustion was

the theory suggested in one journal of ill-repute, a theory that would have been laughed out of any court. The Coroner ruled that this was a case of accidental death caused by the deceased's habit of smoking cigarettes in bed. On pursuing my own enquiries further, I found that Pierre Dubois had had his will proved at two hundred thousand pounds and that after bequests of one hundred thousand to his various scattered relatives, he had left the remainder to a Miss Heidi Heinz.

It sometimes strikes me, regarding the nature of women, that the deeper one goes, the more rotten it gets. For some months later and again in a paper, I saw a sketch of a noted Cambridge professor, apparently 'the greatest mathematician of England', landing from a liner in New York. He stated simply that it was his intention to demonstrate that Mathematics is a closed and finite system which can be logically deduced from five axiomatic assumptions. Behind him and portrayed as arm-in-arm, there were two pretty ladies, exquisitely well-dressed, whom he described as being his research assistants, Pamela of France and Heidi of Germany. And, yes, I recognized these ladies, noting especially how the cartoonist had accentuated their long canine teeth as he drew their charming smiles. The reporter from *The New York Times* asked them if they agreed with the learned professor's argument that Mathematics is finite and that consequently there is no mystery in the Universe, since all can be solved by rationality.

'Oui,' said Pamela.

'Ja,' said Heidi.

'Madam,' said Arthur Machen as he handed the tale back to Alison Hyde, 'this is indeed a most singular tale that leaves me quite perplexed. *Did* Pamela and Heidi kill Pierre? Or was it the action of the spirit Pierre conjured through the *Ouija*? Why would any spirit wish to burn a being who was probing the Infinite? And why do the two ladies proceed in apparent support of a man who believes in the finite . . . I refer to the professor?'

'Sir,' Alison Hyde addressed him with equal formality, 'I give you the three most honest words in the English language, which are: *I don't know*. After all, hasn't Arthur Machen himself declared that "all things end in mysteries"?'

'Yes, he has,' Machen expostulated indignantly as his bulldog snorted in sympathy. 'And I *know* that.'

'Oh . . .' the young lady sighed dreamily, 'if only Arthur Machen were with us now . . . where *is* Arthur Machen?'

'He's sitting here, right next to you!' Machen felt like upending the young lady and spanking some sense into her tightly wrapped bottom. 'What *is* all this nonsense? The tale you have shown me, purportedly by "Arthur Machen", is not by me at all.'

'I did not say it was, sir. I said it was by Arthur Machen.'

'It isn't,' said Arthur Machen. 'At least it certainly isn't by *this* Arthur Machen here. For all I know, there may well be some fellow of the same name, or claiming my name, who has written this. But I would never have made the error, no matter what my own faults, of leaving the matter so ambivalent; and furthermore, I would never have used such a stark style of prose. Who is this man who announces himself as "Arthur Machen" and causes me so much concern? I would like to meet him.'

'I hope that you can,' Alison Hyde replied, 'though I fear he may be murdered before that happy event. Have you ever met a Dr Black?'

'Good heavens . . .' Machen murmured very slowly as his brain spun with stupefying rapidity. 'I have met him once.'

'So have I. And I was frightened of him. He has much superficial charm but I do not care for his way of saying: "Eh? Hm," all the time. I think he is exercising a dreadful influence upon the dear young man I know as Arthur Machen. It's all rather frightfully decadent.'

'Just a moment,' said Machen as a cold gust of wind caused a ripple among the budding flowers. Its bite made him shudder inwardly. 'From what you tell me, there are four people claiming to be Arthur Machen, the author. I had no idea that I was so much sought after. One is the young man straight out of *New Arabian Nights* by Robert Louis Stevenson, who came into the restaurant shouting: "Cream tarts!" The second is Alan, your dinner companion, who I think is a cream tart too. The third is your friend, who can at least write. The fourth is me.' The young lady gazed at him with rapt fascination and appeared to relish his loquacity. Although he concealed the fact, he was highly attracted to her physically and, putting his hand in his pocket as if casually to seek matches for his pipe, he had some difficulty in adjusting the bulge in his trousers. Suddenly the young lady burst out laughing. 'I don't quite see the joke, Madam. Perhaps you could explain it to me,' Machen said as his hand came out with a box of matches and he proceeded to give a new flame to his pipe. 'In fact, what I humbly suggest, at shamefully short notice, is that you dine tonight at the Café de l'Europe with me, Arthur Machen; with the author of short stories who uses the name "Arthur Machen"; with your old friend Alan who has also claimed the name; and with luck there shall be a Young Man with Cream Tarts also claiming to be me. Might it not be amusing?'

'You, sir,' Alison Hyde answered him demurely as she fluttered her eyelashes, 'are certainly most amusing.' Machen noticed that she was wearing elbow-length gloves of scarlet silk and thought instantly of his novella 'The Red Hand'. 'Here.' Her scarlet, silken-gloved hand momentarily vanished into her black snakeskin bag and emerged with a white card that simply named her as Alison Hyde at a reputable address in Primrose Hill. 'Your card?' Machen had to inform her with regret that it was not his habit to bear visiting cards though he would gladly receive hers. 'Thank you kindly, sir, the courtliness of your delightfully old-fashioned manners is assuredly too sweet. I would be only too happy to meet you at the establishment you mentioned, doing all I can meanwhile to ensure that all claimants to the noble name of "Arthur Machen" are present; yes, exactly one week from today at eight o'clock. Do you promise me that?'

'Faithfully,' said Machen, who always kept his word, especially to an attractive lady.

'Excellent,' Alison Hyde told him. 'I knew that you were a courageous gentleman the instant I set eyes on you.' Machen was dazed by her look, her eyes freezing his brain into crystals of ice as she arose, swishing her skirts.

'May I accompany you?' he suggested, his ease of social manner hiding his inward shyness. 'I believe you initially requested assistance for your friend who claims my name and who, it must be admitted, does write well, but who according to you, may be under the threat of murder by the sinister Dr Black. I trust that you yourself are not in danger?'

'Oh, sir . . .' The young lady blushed. 'You are too kind and chivalrous for this modern day and age. I fear you can do little for the author of the tale I showed you until you meet him, which you will next week. All I ask, sir – and may I call you "Mr Machen"? – is that you kindly escort me to a road where I may take a hansom cab?'

'Certainly, Madam,' Machen responded, adding: 'Oh, and do call me Arthur.'

'Very well, Arthur. I shall be Miss Hyde.' She burst out laughing at the confusion upon his innocent face. 'Of course it's Alison from now on.'

He walked her past a square festooned with early spring flowers, a riot of yellow, white and purple with an occasional faint flicker of scarlet.

'This is a sacred area,' he said.

'I know,' she replied, 'but how did you?'

'I started to study London both by walking and by reading William Blake. I was especially intrigued by the lines:

"The Fields from Islington to Marylebone
To Primrose Hill and St John's Wood
Were builded over with pillars of gold
And there Jerusalem's pillars stood." '

'Yes, that's Blake's Golden Quatrain,' Alison murmured. 'It's a sacred rectangle with Euston Road to the south forming its base and Marylebone to Primrose Hill would be its western side . . . ah! there's a cab!' she shouted, forestalling all Machen's intended endeavour to make further enquiry. 'Thank you so much for your consideration and courtesy.' The skirts of the young lady were positively trembling. Machen too was trembling – at the knees. She held out her red hand for him to shake and he bowed to kiss it.

Afterwards, although Machen had always held that Barnsbury was in any case a maze, he wandered it in a kind of waking dream. He had forgotten where he lived, in a sense. He was perfectly well aware, of course, of his actual address which was Verulam Buildings, Gray's Inn Road; and of his present location, which a street sign showed him to be Richmond

Avenue. This should not have presented him with any difficulty. He had lost count of the number of times he had walked home from Richmond Avenue without mishap. The problem was that his brain somehow could not coordinate the relationship between Richmond Avenue and Gray's Inn Road.

For some time he wandered in Barnsbury, wondering when he might ever leave the area. He knew that the most obvious way would be a straight walk to Caledonian Road, where there were always plenty of cabs, and that Richmond Avenue was the best way there but by the time he had this realization, he was wandering along Islington Park Street without a clue as to the way back to Richmond Avenue.

As he meandered in the mouldering squares of Barnsbury and inhaled the perfume of the flowers, he passed a number of attractive women, some walking proudly with their men and some walking alone and purposefully. Each time, there was a *swish* and a rustling of petticoats that alerted his attention to the passing female face. Each time he thought he saw the features of Alison, only to be convinced an instant later that this was not so before being befuddled once more by the suspicion that it might, after all, have been her.

Perhaps it was fortunate that he finally saw and hailed a hansom that took him back to Verulam Buildings. Shortly before he dropped, exhausted, into his bed, he stared at the stone within the ankh and once more saw a man who looked as though he came from the future.

Adam Stride saw Arthur Machen in the Stone shortly before he went to bed and slept uneasily, dreaming that there was some sort of formless horror around the corner. The next morning did not bring actual horror but it did bring bewilderment.

The envelope was of brown paper, postmarked 'London N' with a standard form label that led one to expect either junk mail or bogus religiosity. However, it simply contained a short story called 'Oui & Ja' by 'Septimus Keen'. Stride perused it with growing amazement. The paper had a late-Victorian watermark.

He was aware of the fact that Bertrand Russell and Alfred North Whitehead had taken up the thread woven by Cambridge mathematicians in an endeavour to prove that Mathematics was finite and logical. He knew that Frege had spotted the flaw in this system and that Georg Cantor had exploded it with his Mathematics of Infinity. It had come as no surprise to him to learn that Cantor's intensive contemplation of Infinity, with all its irrefutably flawless technique, had resulted in his suffering several nervous breakdowns: he died in a mental hospital. The mathematical theories of 'Pierre' were the same as Cantor's.

'Infinity...' Stride mused as Rosa entered with a much-needed cup of strong black coffee. 'I think I'd rather have the Big Bang, wouldn't you, Ms Scarlett?'

CHAPTER ELEVEN

INCIDENTS OF LIES AND TRUTH
(THE BORE)

'Miss Fanshawe,' Adam Stride said over the phone to Alison Featherstonehaugh, 'I find that you are not assisting me sufficiently towards a successful completion of the case.'

'Oh, and why do you think that, Adam?' *Damn her eyes*, he thought, thinking of shining hazel. Their night in bed together seemed to have mattered little to her; he had not heard from her in three months until the ringing of the phone today.

'I haven't heard from you in a while.'

'I've been on holiday.'

'How nice for you. Where, if I may ask?'

'A cruise, Adam, just a cruise. I was hoping as I went away that you might have everything sorted out by the time I returned. After all, one doesn't pay ten thousand pounds and promise much more if one doesn't expect to receive rather more information than has been forthcoming.'

'That is precisely my problem, Madam,' Stride retorted exasperatedly. 'I have given you everything you could conceivably want to know about the Holy Grail.'

'Yes, but I could have hired a research student to do that for less than a grand.' She laughed sharply. 'You have not given me anything about the Stone within the Ankh.'

'Yes, I have,' Stride retorted indignantly. 'I have reported to you all meetings concerning individuals who want this gem and who could be a threat to you. You have not told me nearly enough about them.'

'You have told me nothing about the Stone itself.'

'I did tell you, Alison, that sometimes this mysterious object appears to change into rubber; yet within it, incredible though it appears, one can at times see visions.'

'I *know* that, Adam,' her high, clear voice informed him. 'But what is its history?'

'Alison, the name of your father, which you gave me, does not appear in Burke or Debrett. If he did own it, the matter is still unclear. The slender data you gave me on your father does not accord with any birth, marriage or death certificate. In fact, there is no hard evidence that he existed at all. I therefore cannot trace the history of the Stone from that source unless you give me further details.'

'There are no further details.'

'That is why I say that you are not assisting me sufficiently.'

'I thought I was paying you ten thousand pounds to assist *me*.'

'I have been unable to discover any information about the history of the Stone within the Ankh,' Stride said, 'other than that when I look into the artefact concerned I sometimes see the face of Arthur Machen, on whose biography I am working. I can send you or give you any details you might require concerning Arthur Machen. Unless you give me further clues, however, it is not possible to discover how this mysterious gem passed from him into your hands and thence into mine.'

'What a clever man you are!' The girl laughed. 'Yes, of course I shall gladly oblige your request. If you can't then take the ball, so to speak, and run with it, well, Adam, I might just want my money back. Meet me this time next week for tea at the Ritz.' She rang off.

Stride sat with his chin in his hands and stared gloomily at a calendar on his wall. Glancing at his watch, he made a note: '4:30. Friday. Alison. Tea at the Ritz.' He might have stared at the calendar for a while longer had it not been for a knock upon his office door.

'Come in,' he murmured; and Rosa Scarlett entered. 'Hallo, Ms Scarlett . . .'

'Mr Stride, sorry to trouble you. It's just that something has happened that might interest you.'

'Tell me about it.'

'Well, Mr Stride,' said Rosa, 'I went out about an hour ago to get myself some sandwiches – prawns with lettuce and mayonnaise, on brown bread – that's my favourite – and since it was a sunny day, I decided to sit and eat my sandwich on a nice bench on Clerkenwell Green. You can sit and contemplate so much history there. It has to be one of the oldest parts of London. I was staring at the variety of buildings and marvelling at the peace and quiet when a man walked up and sat on the bench beside me. He was a somewhat insalubrious individual, bulky in build, with a ginger moustache that merged into a pair of bulbous chin-whiskers.'

'Interesting,' Stride muttered. 'Continue.'

' "Nice day," I remarked: and he agreed with me. Then he said: "Still, it's a hard life as a second-hand bookseller."

' "I don't doubt it," I replied.

' "Farringdon Road," he continued, as he swigged from a plastic bottle that could have contained apple juice but was more likely to hold whisky, judging by his breath. "Best place for second-hand books in the whole of London. But it doesn't help," he sighed, "when people steal books. Allow me to introduce myself. Grimsby's the name, Paul Grimsby. My stall's third on the left." He sighed wearily. "Can I bore you for a moment?" I nodded. "I've just had some of my best books stolen – and by a man I trusted!" He coughed. "I tell you, you can't trust anyone these days. I don't know about you . . . don't you have sympathy for writers?"

' "Yes, as long as they're good."

' "So do I, Madam. It makes me sick to see them homeless and starving whilst those without talent, whose work is anyway written by the editors under a popular brand name, make hundreds of thousands. And that was why I gave a job to Septimus Keen."

' "Septimus Keen . . ." I faltered.

'The sun broke briefly through the clouds at that instant scattering itself upon the Green with lances of dazzling rays.

' "Heard of Septimus Keen?" he demanded.

' "Some of my artistic friends tell me that he writes stories."

' "Exactly! And that's why I gave him a job. Although he is as yet unpublished, I read some of his works and I do believe in supporting literature. In common with many writers, he seemed to be hard up, so I made him my assistant, paid him fair wages and tried to find him a publisher. These things take time. I urged him to be patient. I was looking after him. In fact, he soon mastered the essential technique of the second-hand bookseller, which is to buy cheap and sell expensive. Some of my customers are occultists. Septimus Keen was quite superb at going down the East End or to South London and there buying obscure books at cheap prices since they had no value at those places. Once they were on my stall, I could sell them at a thousand per cent profit. Unfortunately he vanished last week and took with him five of my most valuable books. Can base ingratitude go further? Work round here, do you? Tell me, have you ever seen this man?" He pulled a crumpled photograph out of his jacket pocket and showed it to me. I looked at it and did not initially know quite what to say since it was a photograph of you, Mr Stride.'

'That's impossible!' Stride snapped. 'I have never worked at a second-hand bookstall and Septimus Keen is of my own invention. Moreover, your Paul Grimsby answers to the description of Ron Butcher, whom I met some months earlier.'

'The plot thickens,' said Rosa. 'Naturally I said that I hadn't seen the face before.

' "You will," said Paul Grimsby.

' "How do you mean?"

' "Never mind. You'll understand."

' "Understand *what*?"

' "This." Paul Grimsby placed a manuscript in my hand. "He left that behind him. Anyway, must get back to work. If you see anybody looking like him, do let me know. Third stall on the left. Farringdon Road. Pleasure speaking with you." And with that, he arose, turned his broad back, shrugged his muscular shoulders and walked away in the direction of the Farringdon Road. I finished my prawn sandwich, though my appetite was somewhat diminished, and, after a decent interval, went to the stalls on the Farringdon Road, asking after a Mr Paul Grimsby. All with whom I spoke claimed that they had never heard of him.'

'This is mad,' said Stride. 'Dead ringer for Ron Butcher . . . Septimus Keen . . . photograph of me . . .' he mused. He had ascertained that the Septimus Keen certificates sent to him were clever fakes. Again, a growing sense of unease gnawed at his bowels. 'Have you read this story, purportedly by "Septimus Keen", Rosa?'

'Yes, Mr Stride. It is curious and unusual.'

'Oh, pass it over and make us both a mug of tea.' Stride read:

THE BORE

by

Septimus Keen

A bore is someone who deprives you of solitude without providing you with company

Anon.

What on earth is it that constitutes a bore?

'A bore is someone who talks when you want him to listen,' said one lady friend of mine.

'A bore is a fellow of low taste, much more interested in himself than in me,' a gay friend told me.

'A bore makes one snore,' another lady declared.

'I'll tell you what a bore is, mate,' said a man friend. 'You approach him feeling good and you come away exhausted.'

It was with these words ringing in my head that I took up the challenge of some of my Kilburn drinking cronies to go and meet the individual they described as being 'the most boring man in London'. Perhaps I should explain how this curious matter came about.

An argument with my family had left me virtually destitute and subsisting on Income Support in a Kilburn bedsit. I looked for work in the Job Centre and discovered that 'Production Assistants' could earn £1.50p an hour by stacking shelves at some local supermarket. I informed my Claimant Adviser that I was trying to secure a commission as a writer.

'*That's* not a job!' he snorted disgustedly.

My initial forays into Kilburn life had not been fortunate. On my first day, I walked into a local pub and bought a pint of Guinness, after which I looked for somewhere to sit. The place was crowded, apart from a table in the centre of the saloon. There were nine vacant chairs and at the head of the table sat a stout blond matriarch, reading the *Daily Mail*. I walked up to the table.

'Excuse me,' I said, indicating a vacant seat at the other end, 'is this taken?'

'Not yet,' she replied, her eyelashes flickering with

annoyance. 'If you want to, you can sit there for the time being.' I did so and every now and again she looked up from her newspaper and glowered at me. Finding her behaviour perfectly preposterous, since there were so many vacant seats around the table, I glowered back. Now, how was I to know that she was the local Godmother? I left soon after.

I might have had several teeth knocked out for unintentional insolence were it not for the fact that I have a friendly disposition that leads me to chat with people in pubs. Although I initially felt like a stranger in a strange land, I soon came to be acquainted with many of the locals. One of them, apparently a former sergeant in the Royal Marines during the Second World War, who had lived in Kilburn for over thirty years, explained my error to me one night.

'Now, she's okay, is Moira, as long as you don't upset her,' he told me. 'Looks like it wasn't intentional on your part, more of a misunderstanding, like. New and all that. Well, you wouldn't be expected to know, really. Look, just don't sit at her table for a bit and I reckon I can sort it all out for you. Oh, and get us another pint.'

I continued going to the local whilst taking care not to sit at the table of the Godmother. Her behaviour fascinated me. Every midday she would enter, take her seat with a pint of Guinness at the head of a vacant table, and sit there reading her *Daily Mail* for one hour. Nobody dared to approach her during that time. At one o'clock precisely, she folded and laid down her newspaper. This was a signal for people to approach her. Men and women advanced towards her, greeting her warmly, offering drinks to her and taking seats, always leaving free the chair at her right. This was taken every day at two o'clock by a well-dressed, well-spoken man of middle age who was, I later learned, her third husband, William. During the hour before William arrived, there would be many hurried, whispered conversations punctuating what seemed to be harmless jocularity.

Bob kept his word about introducing me to Moira, doing so at two-thirty on this particular afternoon. He had obviously paved the way for me and it was clear that Moira forgave me once I had apologized for an unintentional misunderstanding. She then turned out to be charming and delightful company, regularly inviting me to her table where I sat with affable rogues and villains. Many of them were surprisingly well read, as was Moira, and their conversation was interesting and had its charm, too, albeit laced with ghoulish humour.

'How come you don't seem to be scared of me?' Moira asked me on one occasion.

'I don't scare easily,' I replied truthfully, 'and anyway, Moira, I don't think that, since our unfortunate misunderstanding of some months ago, I have done anything to offend you.'

'Ha! ha!' she cackled. 'D'you hear him?' she called out to her table. 'Why can't you lot all have manners like him?' They grinned. 'Only my husband and him have got any manners in these parts nowadays. Oh, and Kev, get me and William here another couple of pints. The usual.' I passed quite a number of happy hours at Moira's table until the day when my story really began.

It had started as a very bad day. There were stacks of bills I could not pay. There was a severe probability of becoming not only jobless but also homeless. I tried to fight off depression by going to the pub. My last ten quid was in my pocket. Moira appeared pleased to see me and ensured that a drink was bought for me. William, a former Army Major as I had by now gathered, smiled and nodded affably whenever his wife spoke, as usual.

'You seem a bit worried,' Moira commented.

'No.' I tried to hide my financial anxiety.

'Well, snap out of it if you are. The Devil looks after his own,' she smiled broadly, 'and I should know. But there's still one or two things you have to do, my dear. I want you to go and meet the most boring man in London. He's sitting over there. Look.' I looked and saw an utterly nondescript individual. He was a scrawny old chicken of a man, with straight white hair and National Health glasses. A battered brown trilby hat reposed upon his head, and he wore a baggy brown suit with a crumpled white shirt, a soup-stained green tie and shiny brown brogues.

'That,' said Moira, 'is the most boring man in London. Don't you find so many people in London to be so boring?'

'No,' I answered truthfully. 'James Joyce once said he had never met a boring individual in his life. I can't go quite as far as that but on the whole, I find his saying to be more true than not.'

'Ha! ha! D'you hear him?' Moira's laugh was raucous. 'Well, are you on for a bet? I bet you that you won't be able to endure thirty minutes of his company. If you can, then everybody at this table must buy you a pint.' That meant six. 'If you can't, you must buy all of us here a pint each.'

'Bet taken,' I said. After all, it was only thirty minutes of my time, after which I could get drunk all afternoon. So I approached the man who was sitting on his own and soon fell into conversation with him, if it can be called that. He told me that his name was Martin and after that further discussion increasingly resembled hard labour. He did not appear to like anyone or anything at all. He detested Scots, Welsh, Irish, Jews, Blacks, Asians and Americans. He didn't care for women either and grumbled about his wife. Then he complained about the younger generation and told me how much he disliked his two children, both of whom he had disowned and never saw. He found the area to be unpleasant and the pub was just the least worst of the local hostelries.

I tried various other topics of conversation. Sport? No, he did not care for it in any form. Television? He said that he watched it but it was mostly rubbish. The Arts?

'Read a book once meself,' he told me. 'Didn't think much of it.' I searched through this desert of negativity hoping to find something that he might praise, all the while feeling increasingly tired. It felt as though two hours had gone by yet by my watch and to my despair, I had only endured seven minutes. Eventually we did find the one and only theme for him to enthuse about and that was his barber. His speech here consumed ten minutes. It is not very interesting to hear a man go on just praising his barber but at least one expects to see an enviable hair style.

'Ah,' one might say, simply to pass the time, 'he seems good. Where is he and how much does he charge?' Neasden and fifteen pounds did not seem like an appealing prospect, especially when I looked at his hair. Beneath the hat, it looked as though his barber, having clapped a pudding-basin upon his skull, had then used garden shears to clip around it.

'Hm. Interesting,' I said. An Englishman always says 'Interesting' when he is bored and I was, quite excruciatingly so. I was also starting to feel nauseous and dizzy. I glanced surreptitiously at my watch and discerned to my despair that there were another twelve minutes to go. Suddenly I simply could not stand it any longer. I knew that if I spent one more moment in the company of this monster of tedium I might be tempted to extreme violence, so I thanked him for his company and walked away, back to Moira, feeling decidedly ill. Honour would consume all the money I had but *anything* was preferable to more of Martin. I admitted that I had lost the bet and, feeling sick, bought beer for everybody.

'Couldn't take it, could you?' Moira commented. 'Nobody can. Some people's like that. Some people's evil. Now I may be bad but I'm not evil.' Then she added: 'Want to make a grand?'

'Depends for what . . .' I answered, though that kind of money would certainly sort out my problems.

'You see . . .' Moira said as Irish building workers shouted in the background over their eight pints of lunchtime Guinness, 'I reckon that if you can only feel good by making other people feel bad, then you are evil. And I'd pay to have an evil nuisance abated. You know what I mean?'

'Why me?'

'You interest me, darling. And you have style.' She chuckled. 'Why, we could even do business together. Think about it. And if you're still interested after that, meet Bob here across the road at one.'

'I'll certainly think about it, Moira,' I said. The saloon was starting to spin around me. I took my leave as graciously as I could and then staggered home. Once there, I vomited repeatedly and much time was spent agonizing upon a lavatory seat. Upon going to bed, having wasted a day, I was tormented alternately by hot sweats and cold sweats and recurrent nightmares in which I was trapped in a room by this intractable bore. During this awful night, I grew to hate and resent him quite intensely. I slept fitfully, awaking in the morning with a bitter hatred for the bore and, on seeing more red bills, a desire for a thousand pounds.

At one o'clock, I was at the pub across the road to meet Bob again, just as Moira had suggested. In the Gents, Bob passed me a brown paper envelope, motioning me towards the cubicle. It contained five hundred pounds in cash and a small phial of colourless liquid. He was still pissing when I emerged.

'Rest on delivery,' he said, buttoning up the flies on his grey flannel trousers. 'And mind how you go,' he added as he splashed his hands with cold water.

'Good day to you, sir!' I greeted Martin cheerfully.

'Hallo,' he replied with no enthusiasm.

'Like a drink?'

'Yeah.' He stared grimly at his half-empty pint glass. 'The usual.'

It was really surprisingly easy, facilitated further by the fact that there were kids crowding the bar at that moment and I wondered later if Moira had arranged that in order to deflect suspicion. Anyhow, as I bought Martin his 'usual', which was some ghastly fizzy keg bitter, I don't think anybody saw me as I slipped the contents of the phial into it; I ordered the same revolting drink for myself.

'Pleasant day,' I said to Martin, sitting down with our pints.

'What's pleasant about it?'

'Always looking on the bleak side, Martin, aren't you, eh? Cheers!' We both drank. 'Martin, you strike me as being a very interesting man.'

'I *am* a very interesting man,' he replied dully.

'So tell me, in your honest and considered opinion, what is the meaning of life?' He pondered the question, drank some more and in between (to my gratification) deep draughts of his pint, offered me the following learned disquisition:

'By and large, all in all, getting down to the grass roots of the matter, we've really got to put our noses to the grindstone and our shoulders to the wheel on this one. I mean it's none of this pie-in-the-sky lark for me. Got to be down to earth, though I haven't got one foot in the grave yet. Now, with life, you've got to have an aim. No good otherwise. I mean, some people, they really have to pull up their socks and no jam for them as far as I'm concerned. They just can't see the wood for the trees and they don't realize they're not out of the wood yet, see? Breaks my heart the way some people carry on . . . no decency left in this world . . . some people's like that . . . bloody class system . . . anyone for tennis? . . . see me dead before that . . .'

'Are you all right, Martin?' I asked concernedly.

'No,' he answered grumpily, 'and who the fuck is?' He

drained his pint. 'What's yours?' I accepted his offer, which suited my purposes perfectly. He returned with the drinks, sat down and began to bore for Britain again. 'What's this "street cred" I keep hearing about, then?'

'"Street cred",' I said, 'is a phrase used by public schoolboys from Hampstead to denote going slumming in Belsize Park.' Once more I started to feel nauseous and wondered when the sodium morphate might work. It might sound preposterous but the tedium he inflicted was so enervating and odious that it gladdened my heart when his pale, sickly face flushed, his lips turned blue, his hands clutched at his heart, he sat bolt upright with his unpleasant facial features twisting into agony, and then vomited heavily, slumped across the table and mumbled:

'Not going to die. Be boring, wouldn't it . . . ?' More vomit dribbled out of his slack mouth, escaping through his tight lips and rotten teeth. I wish I could state that a light went out behind his eyes but there was no light there at all. He just expired. 'Dying' wasn't quite the word for it since this would imply some dignity. Naturally I was the first to alert the publican, who promptly called an ambulance, but by that time, it was too late. I wasn't particularly worried about any impending police investigation. The poison of sodium morphate comes out in the vomit, which is not usually analysed.

'Crying shame,' said Moira when I approached her table, sat down with her and told her this tragic story. 'And he used to be such an interesting man.'

There are a few sequels to this tale.

It was from that time on that I received regular employment from Moira to sort out various problems for her and this relieved me of all my financial troubles. Our acquaintanceship deepened into a form of friendship.

The Coroner ruled that Martin had died of a heart attack and the police declared that they had no reason to suspect foul play.

Martin's body was buried at Kensal Green. I have yet to meet anyone who admits to attending the funeral or knowing anyone else who did.

There was some surprise on learning in *The Standard* that Martin's will had been proved at £333,000, though no one seemed to know anything about the beneficiaries. One assumed it had gone to the wife and children he openly disliked.

'Nah, it probably went to the bats at London Zoo,' Moira chortled one drunken afternoon. 'After all, he always was a bit of a vampire.'

'Sorry?' I smiled. 'Surely you don't believe in vampires?'

'Oh, I do,' she replied, 'indeed I do, dear. You see, not all vampires suck blood. Some suck your energies. They just take it all away from people. And one way of doing that is by boring people. Don't bores just make you feel so limp and exhausted? We're best off without them.'

'Quite right, Moira,' William chuckled. 'And is anyone really sorry that Martin won't be coming back?'

Some weeks later, Moira and William were found dead in their flat, just off Christchurch Avenue. The news made the national Press and was headlined in the local Press as word sped from pub to pub along the Kilburn High Road. The police stated that foul play could not be ruled out but made no arrests and brought no charges. The Coroner returned an open verdict. Soon enough, another gang took over the patch Moira had once ruled and soon word spread that they were somewhat more brutal. It seemed that in Moira's case the Devil had not looked after his own.

When the new gang took over, many of the regulars took their custom to a pub across the street and it was there that I met a man who gave me some clues as to what might have transpired. I knew his face from a photograph printed on the jacket flap of a book he had written and which I had enjoyed, *The Labyrinth of Satan*, and his name was Adam Stride.

He was a very easy man to talk with, very frank and engaging in his manner and visibly pleased with my compliments about his novel; and he kept buying me drinks. After a while, he became perfectly open about the fact that he earned his living as a private detective and had been hired by persons he did not name to see if he could shed any light on the mysterious deaths of Moira and William.

'They were found in their flat with blue lips and staring eyes, sitting upright over cups of tea into which they had vomited,' he told me. 'Obviously, I suspected sodium morphate poisoning but unfortunately the vomit had been cleared away and never reached the Forensic Department. *You* don't know anything about that sort of thing, do you?' He had keen, enquiring eyes, blazing into the back of my brain.

'No.'

'I've spoken with the police about how they found the corpses,' he continued. 'One said: "*They looked bored rigid.*" Another said: "*They looked bored to death.*" That doesn't ring a bell, does it?'

'No.'

'Oh . . . because I understand that in business terms Moira had a certain rivalry with one Martin who everyone said was very boring, although apparently you used to like chatting to him.'

'Only on a couple of occasions and, even then, just for a bet.'

'A bet, eh?' Stride flashed his teeth ingratiatingly. 'Tell me, do you ever go to visit the graves at Kensal Green?'

'No. Why should I?'

'It's educational and instructive. Wouldn't you agree that there is perhaps more esoteric knowledge in Kilburn than initially meets the eye?'

'Maybe.' I thought of Moira.

'Curious, isn't it,' said Stride, 'that just a day after the death of Moira and William, the grave of Martin Seymour was desecrated by night and his coffin was found ripped open. Garlic had been stuffed into his mouth, a silver cross had been placed across his face and a stake had been drilled right through his heart.'

'Incredible, Rosa!' Stride cried out. 'There's truth in this story though I'm damned if I know . . . just a moment . . . *yes!* There *is* a method in this madness somewhere. Oh! Tea!' He recovered his composure. 'Thank you, Ms Scarlett. Yes, a couple of years ago, I *was* hired by a Kilburn family to investigate the curious deaths of Moira and William Harding, since the police were doing nothing about it. After one week I had reluctantly to admit that the case was beyond my capacities. All the windows were locked. There were no signs of a break-in. Moira lived in a purpose-built block that had a set of porters who also doubled as her minders. It seems definite that on the night of their deaths no one was seen to enter their flat. I suppose it's possible that they could have had sodium morphate slipped into their drinks earlier when they were at the pub but the action of the poison in question is swift. Moira and William were still alive and well four hours after they left the pub. We know that because they both went to their local Asian newsagent to purchase cigarettes. On coming back they had tea – and then they died. Hm. Good tea! Every time I have tea, I wonder why I don't have it more often. Anyway, the police couldn't solve the case and neither could I. There was also the puzzling matter of the desecrated grave in Kensal Green . . .'

'What about Septimus Keen, Mr Stride?' Rosa Scarlett demanded. 'Here he is, stealing a name you invented for his story. And now it seems you've actually met him. Do you recall what he was like?'

'As I remember, the man I met in a Kilburn pub and with whom I had that conversation was tall, young, slim and handsome, and dressed in a tight T-shirt and even tighter jeans; oh, and he wore a leather jacket. Genuine. The jacket, not the man, I mean. A plausible young rogue; a gentleman down on his luck and prepared therefore to be unscrupulous. I did not trust a word he told me, Ms Scarlett. Now, what was his name? Adrian Simpson, no, Adrian Simon Simpson.'

'As in A.S.S?'

'Hadn't thought of that. Negligent of me.' Stride drained his cup of the Assam on which he always insisted in his office and asked for another; Ms Scarlett gladly obliged his request. 'Face it, Ms Scarlett, as Bernard Shaw states: "You can trust an English gentleman with everything except your money or your women."'

'Oh, Mr Stride . . .' Rosa burst out laughing all over her chubby black features. 'But did you see this man again?'

'No. The next time I came to Kilburn, which was in fact the next day, he wasn't there. Subsequently I gathered from my contacts that he had vanished and nobody knew where he was.'

'Well, he seems to have turned up again in no uncertain manner.' Ms Scarlett swigged her mug of tea and drained it. 'Where're you going tonight, if I may ask?'

'Pleasure, not business. I'll be meeting Antonina in The Albion, Barnsbury. She hasn't been there before. It's one of the oldest and finest pubs in London. Been there, Ms Scarlett?'

'Not that one,' she said. 'Well, I hope you have a nice weekend, Mr Stride, it being Friday. I'll look forward to seeing you on Monday, then. But please,' she looked at him anxiously, 'do be very careful. I think we've got some very dodgy customers here, dangerous even. Don't lose your head.'

CHAPTER TWELVE

THE ADVENTURE OF THE TALKING HEADS

(HEADS OR TAILS)

Adam Stride felt slightly dizzy and sick as he walked away from his office that Friday evening, leaving Rosa Scarlett to tidy things up for the coming Monday. Was he living in a world in which most of the inhabitants were mad? Or was he the sole madman in a sane population? At least he would be able to talk to Antonina: one of her many virtues was that she was always a sympathetic listener. Glancing at his watch, Stride realized that it was five o'clock and so he had three hours to kill before meeting her for drinks and dinner. He set off in a northerly direction, resolved to drink his way to Barnsbury at interesting pubs. He had always had a very strong head for drink; but right now he needed fresh air.

The street was drab around him as he reflected upon his love of London, feeling it to be a sacred place, a place where he belonged and where he had his roots, insofar as he had any. He had no idea who his parents were, since he had been adopted by Mr and Mrs J. Stride of Canonbury: honest, kindly people who had gladly paid for his education at a minor public school followed by Cambridge. They had died in a car crash on their way to witness his graduation. Sometimes Stride wondered who his biological parents might have been. Ah! Here was a pub, just before the Angel, which looked quite interesting. Stride entered to order a pint of bitter, found a table and sat down. He was just heaving a sigh of relief from the cares of the week when he noticed that this pub had plastic heads hanging on streamers from the ceiling.

This made him feel slightly uncomfortable in view of the parting words of Ms Rosa Scarlett: 'Don't lose your head.' Just how dangerous could these people be? He suspected that he might be the victim of an extortionately expensive practical joke, yet his instincts informed him that it could be more serious than that. He noticed that he had spilled cigarette ash on his navy blue Austin Reed suit, and then his right hand shook slightly, causing him to spill a little beer upon his Burberry raincoat. Instructing himself to calm down, he drank up and left the pub.

His tie was silk and he had purchased it in Paris whilst working on a boring but lucrative divorce case. It was maroon with a pattern of green stars and it fluttered in the wind, annoying him. *No ties*, he thought, taking it off and undoing the top button of his pale blue shirt from Turnbull & Asser that he had purchased with some of the money received from the enigmatic Miss Alison Featherstonehaugh. *No ties*. That was virtually the story of his life. He needed another beer in peace and quiet with nothing to disturb him and he noticed a pub in an alley just before The Angel. Here he took a bottle of Newcastle Brown and was relishing the prospect when an ugly crew-cropped young man approached him and sat down opposite. Cruiserweight.

He must have been the most ugly individual that Stride had seen since his encounter with Ron Butcher. Stars had been tattooed upon each knuckle. His neck was festooned with a spider's web.

'You were screwing me just then,' he said in a harsh rasp. 'And I don't like people screwing me.'

'Yes,' Stride sighed as his joy in his beer vanished abruptly, 'I can quite understand that. Only I wasn't screwing you.'

'Yes, you were. And you were screwing my bird. I don't like that.'

'Who would?' Stride asked as he stared into the manic blue eyes of the other. 'Anyway, I have no idea who she is. I'm just drinking my beer.'

'She's over there.' Stride looked to see a girl with long blond hair and wearing a black leather miniskirt standing by the bar.

'Ah.' He nodded slightly. 'I wasn't looking at her.'

'Why not?'

'I was looking at my beer.'

'You insulting her, then?'

'Certainly not. Why don't you go back to her?'

'I don't like your attitude,' this uniquely unpleasant man said. 'Carry on like that? Means you're going to get your *head kicked in*.' He spat a gob of phlegm into Stride's beer.

'I don't like *your* attitude,' Stride replied coolly, though he had gone quite white from inner fury. 'Disgusting wanker.' He threw his beer into his antagonist's face as his foot thudded into his balls beneath the table, having noticed that the idiot was sitting proudly with his legs apart. 'Eat shit and die, fuckface,' he added quietly as the thug vomited all over the table; and it looked as though he had shat himself too. Stride certainly knew how to kick in all the right places. 'Don't know what this place is coming to,' he said loudly as he left the pub.

Stride crossed on to Upper Street, feeling disturbed by the encounter and by the horrible suspicion that he was being followed, though he could not make out whoever might be tracking him. He simply wanted to have a pint of beer in peace and quiet. Ah! Now here was a pub he knew to be largely gay, but that at least promised some civilized repose. There was some nonsense about paying in shillings and pence but it was quite enjoyable and preserved the old traditions of Islington. He sat idly at his table and picked up a gay newspaper. The headline stated: HEADS WILL ROLL.

Apparently it was about anti-gay discrimination in Westminster but it made Stride drink up hurriedly and leave. His plan, he decided, would now be to go straight to The Albion, arrive well before Antonina, and enjoy a couple of quiet pints there before she came. It was assuredly best to leave the busy high road here and head into Barnsbury. Stride had always adored Barnsbury as a secluded part of London unknown to the tourist and graced with gardens of exquisite flowers within squares erected during the times of Queen Anne and the Four Georges. Arthur Machen had loved it, he recalled. Damn! He had forgotten to bring his A-to-Z but that shouldn't matter since he had often explored the area just for pleasure. Although in his novel *The Labyrinth of Satan* he had described it as being an area in which anyone could become lost, he felt he knew its ways well enough.

'Heads! Heads! Off with their heads!' His ears were assaulted by a stentorian cry. He looked abruptly at the square on his right: the children were playing some game out of *Alice in Wonderland* and an especially bossy-looking girl had taken the part of the Queen of Hearts. Stride walked on, looking for a familiar turning. No, this could not possibly be the right way. For here he was in Richmond Avenue, staring at the sphinxes before the doorways.

Arthur Machen had described them as being chocolate-brown. Arnold Bennett had mentioned them. Stride now stared at two white sphinxes. Absolutely nobody knew where they had come from, though it was said that Napoleon had obtained them during his Egyptian campaign and, somehow or other, they had come to Richmond Avenue to grace doorsteps. Stride had read esoteric literature stating that the Four Powers of the Sphinx were: To Know; To Dare; To Will; and To Be Silent. Stride was silent now as he wondered where on Earth he was.

He knew, of course, that he was standing in Richmond Avenue but his mind could not make any connection with The Albion and how to get there. A Daimler stopped by where he was standing and two couples climbed out, laughing and giggling.

They were obviously American. 'I told you it's an interesting and unusual area,' said the driver of the car as he ushered his guests towards his town mansion, extracting his keys as he did so and looking askance at the loitering Stride.

'Gee, Dick,' one of the women giggled, 'those sphinxes you have . . . aren't they just so *cute*!' The four vanished into the house.

Of course! The thought struck Stride. How could he have been so stupid as to lose his way altogether? The Albion was simply at the end of Richmond Avenue. He checked his watch: eight o'clock. Where had all the time gone? In wandering around the maze that was Barnsbury, he supposed. Even so, he was annoyed with himself. He hated to be late for anybody, especially a woman, for to leave a lady sitting and waiting in a public house is an act of singular discourtesy. He walked very swiftly to The Albion and then stopped dead.

One of the oldest pubs of London had been gutted. A sign read: 'CLOSED UNTIL JUNE 13th'. The pleasant decor that had once graced the building now lay in skips upon the road. Barely able to believe this ghastly vision, he peered into the panes of the pub's bow windows and saw a sight that froze the streams of his blood more swiftly than a Siberian wind.

Within the rubble of the interior, there was a long stick of bamboo and, impaled on one end of it, there was the head of Antonina.

Stride seized a brick. His guts lurching, his head whirling, he was going to smash his way into the place and then go straight to the police and tell them everything. All that stopped him was a soft but strong female voice.

'Don't make a fool out of yourself, Adam.' He turned and, to his indescribable relief, he saw Antonina coolly smoking a cigarette behind him. Instantly he ran to her and embraced her, tears pouring out of his eyes as he hugged her close to him. 'Oh, you darling,' she sighed. 'Calm down and come with me. They're so crude, aren't they? Look, I know a nice little pub just up the road . . .'

Five minutes later, they were sitting in a very pleasant Barnsbury Street pub, with which Stride was perfectly familiar, though he wondered when he would ever find a solitary, quiet and contemplative pint of beer.

'They're wicked, aren't they?' said Antonina.

'They?' Stride gulped his beer.

'Yes, the people with whom you're dealing.' She sipped her Campari and soda. 'You see, I came along to meet you at The Albion. I saw that it had been gutted and, looking more closely, I discerned my head on a stick. I concluded that somebody on your case, of which you have told me, was trying to freak you out. The head is obviously plastic.'

'Aren't you freaked out by that?'

'No. Who would be freaked out by a plastic head when it is so obvious that it has been done solely to startle you?' She sipped at her drink as Stride lit a Rothman's. 'They are very peculiar people with whom you are dealing. Very peculiar indeed. Did any odd things happen to you on the way here? Other things, I mean?'

'Yes.' Stride told her about everything that had happened to him today, then bought another round of drinks in a pub which seemed to be devoted to photographs of Battle of Britain Spitfires. 'Doesn't this worry you?'

'No. These days a modern girl has to be prepared to handle anything and everything. Tails down! Ha ha! Heads up!'

An hour later they were sitting in an Islington Korean restaurant. Antonina confessed that she knew little about Korean food, leaving the matter to Stride who ordered a platter of varied raw fish; the traditional accompaniment of clear soup, boiled rice and *kimchee*, delicious, sun-dried pickled cabbage; raw beef with raw egg and sliced pears; and then a mixed grill, barbecued with spices.

'Absolutely delicious!' Antonina exclaimed, after a long conversation about trivialities, laced with minor endearments. 'Oh, I didn't tell you. I *hate* to be late, you see, and that was why... yes, I will have some more *saké*, please... I arrived at The Albion an hour early, only to see the tragi-comedy that confronted you. For the time being, I pissed orf to the pub where we've just been, determined meanwhile to be there in good time so as to save you, Adam, a wasted journey. As I was sitting there at a solitary table, sipping my Campari, a smooth, smiling, clean-shaven man sat down opposite me, cradling a gin-and-tonic with ice and lemon.'

'He didn't tell you that his name was Davies, did he?'

'Yes, he did, as a matter of fact. He was quite open about that, even as he deplored the temporary closure of The Albion. I asked him if he had peered into the interior there and seen anything odd but he stated that he hadn't. He informed me that he was "a connoisseur of the curious and unusual" and that "an artistic lady such as yourself" might assist him in tracking down Septimus Keen,' she looked sharply at Stride, 'of whom we have both heard. I thought it best to say that I had only heard of him vaguely in some rock fanzine.' Antonina adjusted her exceedingly tight black skirt. 'He was cordial company and apparently keen on this Septimus Keen, since he regarded him as being "a master of writing" and wanted to publish a book of Keen's short tales.'

'Don't tell me,' said Stride. 'He gave you a tale by Septimus Keen.'

'Yes, well, he did, actually.'

'I'm not in the mood for reading it now,' Stride growled.

'Perhaps you should, Adam. It's relevant...'

'... and meaningful and committed to all the issues

involved,' Stride sighed as he took the typescript Antonina had proffered from her handbag and proceeded to read:

HEADS OR TAILS

by

Septimus Keen

'When I first saw Yusef,' my grandmother told me, 'he was playing football in the street. How do I put it? He was dribbling the ball with a nonchalant lack of grave concern.'

My grandmother always did have a way with words. She lived in a quiet side street just off the Old Kent Road and I used to go and stay with her as a child whenever my mother was away.

'It was then, as I looked harder, that I saw something strange,' she went on. 'That ball he was kicking, it weren't no ball at all. It was a skull. Now I'd heard that some sort of a graveyard had been uncovered nearby by the archaeologists. I suppose that the kids had been pinching things. Still, it made me sick to see a young boy casually kicking a skull around the street and so I went right out of the door with my rolling pin. "Here!" I yelled. "You can't do that! That's some mother's son there!" The little devil responded by flipping it up into the air and heading it in my direction. Well, I caught it and found that it was made of plastic.

'"Ha! ha!" he laughed, oh, how he did laugh. "That is just something my father has bought me from a joke shop." It was, 'n' all. Cheeky blighter!'

I had no occasion to think of Yusef again until my dearly beloved grandmother died of natural causes in the same area where she had contentedly lived. It was my job simply to sort out the belongings of her two-room flat and deal with the paperwork. I had always quite liked this particular patch of South London. Although further up the road, at the Elephant and Castle, a crippled blind man could be mugged and robbed for sixty pence, here there remained some decency. I liked the Thomas A Becket across the road, since it was a shrine to my favourite sport, boxing. There was an exquisite bakery way beyond anything you could find in the West End. There was also a men's clothes shop which sold garments exemplifying cheap gangster chic and which was called 'Al Capone'. Drugs could be purchased easily and readily. No one cared what you did as long as you did not harm a local for no reason. An incident of squealing tyres in a street caused local citizens to rush to their windows and open them fast, though they often shut them quietly and slowly. There were pubs that stayed open very late indeed.

Shortly before her death, I had taken tea with my grandmother, which she had followed with mince pies and generous quantities of brandy.

'Remember my stories about the young devil Yusef?' she had chuckled. 'Oh, I remember him when he was knee-high. These days he's quite a power in business in this area. Oh, and he always looks after the old folks. Sends people to bring them money and meals. Booze too, sometimes. I know he's got his faults but at heart he's a good lad. Pity there are some business rivalries. I don't care for that Mr Brighton, I can tell you. Eat you as soon as look at you, he would. Pretends to be English but he isn't. Does nothing about the mugging, which young Mr Yusef does. Bit of a rogue, Yusef, but he's sweet underneath it all. And he likes to encourage the kids.'

As I was packing up my grandmother's few remaining possessions, I looked out of the window. The kids were playing football in the street as they shouted. There were cries of glee as a strong young man hailed them.

'I have a much better ball for you!' he cried out. Then he threw a skull down on the pavement and the children cheered as they rushed to kick it.

I turned away from the window with an amiable smile as I sorted out the last of my grandmother's things. A van would be coming shortly. She had always taken a great deal of interest in local news and so, as I was waiting, I picked up her latest edition of the local paper.

This informed me that a notorious London gangster, a Mr Dick Brighton, had been quite hideously slain. His head had been severed from his body with one stroke of an axe. The body had been found in the River Thames, near Wapping, but the wallet inside the suit and the tattoos provided the police with full identification.

I turned from that to my own Sunday paper, which contained a feature about gangsterism. Apparently, parts of South London were being taken over by Turkish Cypriots.

The doorbell rang. The van and the removal men had arrived. I picked up and looked at a photograph of my grandmother standing in a local pub with Yusef as her things were taken out. There was no doubt that this man stood outside in the street, teaching the urchins how to play football. It was obvious that they respected him as he lined them up into teams, appointed captains and span a coin.

'Heads or tails?' he demanded.

'Heads!' both captains shouted.

'Shut up!' Yusef laughed. 'You can't have both at the same time. Give me any cheek and, why, I'll have your tail!' The multi-racial mix all laughed. 'But since you both have chosen heads, why, *I* shall kick off.'

As I left the flat with the removal men, I knew that my grandmother had been right about Yusef. This time a real skull was the ball, and he was dribbling it with a nonchalant lack of grave concern.

'I wish I'd written that,' Stride murmured as he handed it back to Antonina.

'No, no,' she replied, declining it, 'it is surely a piece for your files.'

'I see. And it comes from the Davies who pretends all the while to be Davies ... ?'

'Well, yes,' Antonina responded. 'It's hardly my fault if this strange individual suddenly approached me. But frankly, Adam, I fear that you are dealing with a bunch of practical jokers.'

'So do I,' Stride muttered as he paid the bill. 'Let's go back to my place.'

'I'd love that,' she said. 'Thank you, Adam, that was delicious.'

In the taxi back to his place, they kissed tenderly just as they had upon their very first date.

'I'll make some coffee,' Stride said as they ascended the steps from his front door. 'And I think that some brandy would go well with it. 'Fraid I've only got Martell, but I think that's the best three-star cognac. Just want to check the office,' he murmured. 'Some tedious fax may have come in. You go straight on upstairs. I'll bring up the refreshments.' He recalled that he had some dope there too and cursed himself for not buying cocaine to spark off what promised to be, despite his difficulties, a delightful weekend.

'Oh, shit,' he said as he entered his office and heard Antonina's feet pattering up the stairs. 'Looks like more bloody practical jokers.'

Stride was tempted to laugh as he entered his office to see, upon his leather armchair and behind his desk, a wooden pole that appeared to be dripping with blood and upon which some clown had placed the head of Rosa Scarlett. He grinned wearily as he approached it.

Then he screamed aloud as he touched it. *This* head was for real.

CHAPTER THIRTEEN

A VIXEN IN VERULAM

Arthur Machen awoke shrieking from a nightmare. Wiping the cold sweat from his brow, he lay alone and awake, trying to recall the details. It was as though he had been projected into the future and found himself in London one hundred years hence as an invisible and intangible observer. In the dream, he was horrified by the architectural damage that had been done to the city; and then the scene changed and he was standing in the office of a man he recognized, the one he had seen within the Stone. This man was shaking in horror as he regarded the severed head of a black woman placed upon a sharpened pole.

Somebody clubbed the man from behind and he collapsed. Machen heard a voice ring out:

'Two portions of the white powder!' The voice sounded as though it was that of the sinister Dr Black.

Machen arose from his bed and poured himself a stiff brandy.

'I shall never give anyone a white powder ever again,' he murmured as he downed his drink, poured himself another and gazed momentarily at his slumbering dog. He took the Stone from his Japanese bureau and gazed at it once again. After a time he saw mists in the Stone and then visions of his beloved Wales. The Little People, elves, fairies and dwarves of whom he had written, erupted from caves to cavort with one another and to tease human beings with their changelings. Now the scene faded and he saw a pond. Fairies and elves hopped upon the water lilies like children of the pool, yet somehow reminded him painfully of all he had sworn to himself to do and had not yet accomplished.

Now the scene shifted to the rooftops of London in a blazing sunset and beneath this blood-red sky he saw windows and behind every window there was a life or lives. Every window was just as a theatre, giving glimpses into drama that went on within. There was a blur and then a scene of the man he had seen before, chained to a bed and, it seemed, staring in agony at the Stone held up before him as he mouthed the word: 'Help . . .'

'Help . . .' Machen echoed as he endeavoured to make sense of all he had seen. He stared at his diary, regarding the words that he had written before and would write again:

'I believe that there is a perichoresis, an interpenetration. It is possible, indeed, that we are now sitting among desolate rocks, by bitter streams . . . And with what companions?'

The sky was emblazoned with a dull red glow as Machen left the British Museum Reading Room much later on that day. He had spent a lot of time in the Dome of the Reading Room, researching both the Holy Grail and Dr John Dee, all of which had left him no wiser but certainly better informed. It had been a day in which he had withdrawn into a state that he termed 'sacred solitude', for at times he saw himself as being a Robinson Crusoe of the soul. He felt tired as he trod the Charing Cross Road towards Leicester Square: then he recalled the prospect of this evening and energy returned as his step quickened. He was starting to take delight once more in the hustle and bustle upon the street and relishing the prospect of dining with the delectably pretty Miss Alison Hyde, not to mention four people claiming to be Arthur Machen, one of whom was himself. The evening held endless possibilities and it was a delight to contemplate this prospect beneath the flickering gas lamps which illuminated the bookshops. Then he felt once again that he was being followed.

Machen used an old trick he had read about in sensational detective stories. He stopped to look in a shop window and scrutinized the reflections of passers-by. The man he suspected, and whom he had never seen before, passed him by with every air of innocence, bearing a covered tray in his hands. The last fact did not perturb Machen: but the appearance of the personage did shock him. For an instant he thought that this man might be William Butler Yeats, since he was thin, pale, twitchingly nervous in his manner and wore spectacles. Then what was Yeats doing bearing a covered tray? Or was it the Young Man With Spectacles appearing from his own novel *The Three Impostors*?

Machen proceeded to follow him. The Young Man With Spectacles glanced behind him once but did not appear to be in the least bit perturbed that Machen was stalking the stalker. The trail ended at the Café de l'Europe, where trade was as busy as ever.

'Cream tarts! Cream tarts!' the Young Man With Spectacles shouted at a nod from the manager and, whipping the cloth from the tray he was carrying, proceeded to sell cream tarts to anyone who wanted them. Machen meanwhile ordered a table for five and was duly ushered towards it, handing his black cloak to an attendant. He ordered a dry white port and was perusing the menu when the cry of 'Cream tarts!' rang in his ears again and a tray with one left was proffered to him. 'The last cream tart, sir!'

'Why don't you sit down and have a drink with me?' Machen suggested to him. 'And, yes, I shall buy your last cream tart and have it with my coffee. I understand you claim to be Arthur Machen. Is that right? But what are you drinking?' The man wanted a glass of dry white house wine, which was duly brought.

'Forgive me, sir,' he said, 'since I fear I may have troubled you for no reason other than the perversity of others.'

'Do you or do you not claim to be Arthur Machen?'

'I have been known to do that on some occasions,' the young man replied, 'but allow me, sir, to introduce myself, since I have also been known to call myself Robert Louis Stevenson on other occasions. My name is, in fact, Guy Strangeways and I apologize if I have caused you any distress. I am a poor student of the University of London who, in order to support his studies, has to take on evening work. Several months ago, I saw an advertisement in the paper that guaranteed an income, of which I was sorely in need. I was given the job, which was simply to sell cream tarts, picked up each evening from a Holborn bakery – very good too, as I think you'll find – and I also had to inform people either that I was Robert Louis Stevenson, author of *New Arabian Nights*, or Arthur Machen, author of *The Three Impostors*. I was happy enough to do that. Tonight I was instructed to follow you and to endeavour to sell you a cream tart, which I have done. May I also add, sir, that I am a great admirer of both *New Arabian Nights* – oh, and of Stevenson's *The Dynamiter* – and of *The Three Impostors*. Will you take it ill if I ask you your name, sir?'

'Arthur Machen,' said Arthur Machen.

'Ah – so you are *the* Arthur Machen. Congratulations on your book, sir. Very fine literature.'

'Just who are these people who employed you?' Machen queried.

'The Sirius Employment Agency, Hampstead. They always pay me a cash commission for all cream tarts I sell. In fact, I must go and get some more. I do apologize if my activities have troubled you at all.' He drained his glass. 'Thank you. Now if you were pleased to excuse me . . .' Machen had rarely seen a man depart so swiftly: any endeavour to detain him would be hopeless. His head whirled as he now ordered a glass of gin and quinine water and wondered when other companions might be joining him. It was embarrassing to sit alone at a table for five when there were people queuing at the door. He was rather relieved when a smooth, smiling, clean-shaven gentleman joined him at the table, saying: 'Excuse me, sir, but is this seat taken?'

'Mr O'Malley, I think,' he said.

'No, sir. You must be thinking of my half-brother, Mr Charles O'Malley, to whom I bear a certain resemblance. Are you by any chance Mr Arthur Machen the author?'

'Yes.'

'Well, splendid. I believe that you will be dining tonight with my dear friend, Miss Alison Hyde . . . ?'

'So I am led to believe.'

'Well, Mr Machen, I owe you an apology. May I buy you a bottle of champagne and explain before Miss Hyde comes, as I assure you she will?' Machen nodded, feeling utterly bemused. The man sitting down before him and ordering champagne looked very much like Mr Charles O'Malley with a castle in Ireland, yet he could not be sure. He could no longer be sure of anything at all. 'Cigarette, Mr Machen?'

'Thank you, but perhaps later,' Machen responded as he pulled out his pipe. He packed it thoughtfully with shag, his favourite tobacco, as the champagne came and was opened with an unduly vulgar *pop!*

'Allow me to introduce myself, sir. My name is Alan Hopper. Perhaps Alison has told you much about me? Cheers!' He raised his glass. 'With champagne I always say that the first glass is the best! Now, what was I saying? Ah, yes, I have pretended to be Arthur Machen.'

'Why . . . ?' Machen faltered helplessly, whilst endeavouring to maintain his composure.

'I happen to be quite a wealthy man, sir. In consequence, I find my life to be somewhat dull. I have no worries and no cares and I am bored.' He lit a cigarette and sipped some champagne. 'In consequence I read books and one of the best books I have ever read is *The Three Impostors* by you, sir, Arthur Machen.'

'Too kind, sir, too kind,' Machen muttered.

'That remains to be seen, sir. Then a friend drew my attention to an agency that undertakes to bring excitement into one's life. Basically you go there and tell them a story of themes you would like to have happen to you. You pay them money and they set it up, catapulting you into a series of interesting adventures whereby you know, however thrilling it may be, that you cannot come to any harm. It is a benevolent Dr Black who runs the agency.'

'I see . . .'

'You *will* see. You must excuse some perversity among those with the wealth. I informed Dr Black that my name was Arthur Machen and that I wanted to experience, in Life, the Art of my *The Three Impostors*. The Sirius Agency—' Machen sat up rigidly as he recalled the cry of 'Cream Tarts!' '. . . oh, heard of it? Well, they set up a series of tales of the unexpected for me. Unfortunately, *you* blundered into it and have become involved in a story that concerns *me*.'

'Well, that explains much.' Machen drank a generous quantity of champagne. 'Correct me if I'm wrong but I seem by honest error to have wandered into a script designed for you.'

'Precisely. *I* was meant to pick up the pearl, the black pearl within the ankh of brass. Did you, by accident?'

'No,' said Machen.

'You were not a part of this piece of theatre?'

'It seems that I have become a part of a piece of theatre,' Machen responded thoughtfully. He hated to lie but he did not trust the man before him at all. 'However, I have no knowledge concerning the object of which you speak.'

'Think about it, Mr Machen. Mistakes occur, after all.'

'Yes,' Machen said. 'I think they do, sir.' He was not quite sure what impelled him to keep the object away from his interlocutor.

'Alan!' A high, clear, female voice interrupted his thoughts and Alison Hyde, swishing her skirts and petticoats, burst upon their table, kissed Alan effusively and politely pecked Arthur Machen upon each cheek. 'What a pleasure to see you both!' she trilled. 'Alan, I trust that you will be joining us for supper? On, yes, and I *shall* have some champagne.'

'Must be going, actually,' said Alan. 'Urgent business. Put the dinner on my account here. Oh, and everything else. Mr Machen, *do* have second thoughts about all we have discussed.'

'I shall,' Machen answered. 'Are you or some person at the Sirius Agency, Hampstead, which you have mentioned, by any chance the author of strange tales by Arthur Machen that I did not write?'

'Sorry?' For an instant, Alan Hopper looked utterly bewildered.

'Miss Alison Hyde here, on our first acquaintanceship, kindly showed me a story entitled 'Oui and Ja' that she said was by "Arthur Machen"; and which you, she informed me, claimed to have written.'

'Ah!' Now Mr Hopper smiled as he suddenly poured himself another glass of champagne. 'I applaud your keen powers of observation, sir. I did indeed show Miss Alison Hyde here the tale to which you refer. I did indeed claim to have written it as "Arthur Machen". That was because I thought that she was an actress from the Sirius Agency. Since she seemed to be playing along with her part, I felt that I should play along with mine.'

'Oh, Alan!' Alison Hyde exclaimed. 'You are simply too priceless!'

'That's as may be, Madam,' he returned.

'But . . .' Machen was struggling in an endeavour to hold fast to the matter and wished that he had the jaws of his bulldog, 'then who *did* write the tale?'

'Your guess,' Mr Alan Hopper replied, 'is as good as mine, sir. I received it through the post one day and decided to impersonate the author.'

'I thought you said that he would be coming tonight.' Machen looked at Alison.

'Oh, he will be,' she simpered.

'I wish you joy of the meeting,' said Mr Hopper, 'but kindly excuse me.' He shook hands with Machen and kissed Alison affectionately as he took his swift leave.

'*Such* a dear, sweet man,' Alison Hyde commented.

'Yes . . . well, this is a pretty picture, isn't it, Alison? We have a table for five and there are now just you and me plus the possibility of one more arrival with two suspects eliminated. Let us just move to a table for two and we can always take a chair if he eventually comes.' He knocked the dottle of his pipe into an ashtray as Alison smiled acquiescence. Since he was a regular customer, the matter was accomplished in a trice and they were soon dining on *antipasta*, onion soup, breaded veal in a rich wine sauce with buttered spinach and fried potatoes accompanied by the mixture of mustards requested by Machen, a blend of English and French which, before his time, he called *Entente Cordiale*; then *crème caramel* and a generous cheese board, all accompanied by the good house wines and followed by coffee and brandy.

Machen was too old-fashioned in his manners to raise any matters of potential tension once a meal had been started. In any event, he would have found it difficult to do so, owing to the charms of Miss Alison Hyde. They enjoyed light conversation concerning matters of culture, about which she proved to be both fluent and witty, and he found his sexual desire to be rising. Although initially he had been a shy youth, losing his virginity at a surprisingly late age even for his time, he had had a number of affairs prior to his marriage to the wife he had truly loved and to whom he had stayed faithful.

Now he thought that his period of mourning might well be over.

'Arthur,' the young lady tantalized him as she enjoyed coffee and a yellow Chartreuse, 'you write so well – if it is truly you – about *West* Country witches. Have you ever heard of the *East* Country witches? East Anglia?'

'Enlighten me, Alison. I am all ears.'

'Walls have ears,' she responded with a charming smile that was all dainty white teeth. 'I have certain things to tell you *which* – or should I say *witch*? – require privacy.'

'Alison,' Machen smiled back. 'I know just the place.'

Machen certainly felt that he had no cause for regret as the delectable Alison reclined in his chambers at Verulam Buildings, Gray's Inn Road . . . apart from one matter. He had gone out in a state of confusion. He had always been a little absent-minded. *Had* he remembered to put the Stone, previously upon the table, in its safe hiding-place within his Japanese bureau? He did not dare to check whilst Alison was there.

'You're so logical, aren't you?' Alison was saying as he served her his finest port. Certainly her mysterious friend Alan had been true to his word in having an account at the Café de l'Europe and their excellent meal had cost him nothing.

'Logical?' He paused. 'I like to think so. I'm a keen student of scholastic logic and that really is the only logic.'

'Is it?' Alison fluttered her eyelashes, swished her skirts and raised an eyebrow archly. 'Then solve this problem for me. How do you take one from nineteen so as to equal twenty?'

'Does "from" have an ambiguous meaning?'

'Sorry. I should have said: "subtract".'

'Then it is not possible,' said Machen. 'Sorry, Alison, you cannot subtract one from nineteen and make it twenty. Furthermore, I do not believe in the existence of four-sided triangles.'

'Then all the more fool you,' the young lady replied. 'Give

me a piece of paper and a pencil. Ah, thank you; you see, you should be aware of other dimensions. Look.' Upon the paper she wrote: 'XIX', then sighed as though she were dealing with a rather dense student. 'That is nineteen in Roman numerals, is it not? Subtract the I and you have XX – twenty. Really, Arthur, for a man of your intelligence, you are sometimes surprisingly slow.'

'Ingenious,' Machen sighed. 'Whatever next?'

'Kiss me,' she implored him.

Machen needed no further encouragement. Springing to his feet, he seized the enchanting young lady within his arms, his lips met hers and his tongue essayed an enchanting voyage within her lascivious mouth. He fondled her small young breasts and she yielded to his every caress. He stroked her neat young bottom, then his left hand lifted her skirts and petticoats, his fingers caressed her thighs and slid towards her sex – only to discover a rampant penis.

With a cry of disgust he flung himself away, only to fall fainting upon the floor.

CHAPTER FOURTEEN

THE DANGERS OF DISORIENTATION
(THE PURSUIT OF POWER)

Adam Stride awoke with a throbbing headache to wonder where on Earth, or in Heaven or in Hell, he might be. He slowly recalled that the last sight he remembered, one quite sickening, had been the head of his personal assistant Rosa Scarlett impaled upon a stick. Then there had been a blow and everything had gone black.

Slowly he became conscious of the fact that he was in dire circumstances. He was lying upon a bed and there were manacles upon his wrists with chains leading to iron posts drilled into the floor. His throat was parched and he noticed that there was a plastic glass of water by the bed. He lifted it, grateful that there was sufficient slack in his restraints to let him do so, and drank greedily as his chains clanked.

Slowly, very slowly, he became conscious of his surroundings, commencing with his own physical state. It was obvious that somebody had knocked him unconscious and then given him quite a hiding. Possibly he had a cracked rib or two, there seemed to be grazing on the back of his aching skull, and his heart, liver and kidneys were throbbing with pain. He was lying upon a bed of black iron, naked and covered by a black satin duvet. His head whirled with terror and bewilderment as he recalled once more the head of Rosa Scarlett; and he agonized over the fate of Antonina.

He had never been in a room that was anything like this before. The walls were all mirrors; so was the ceiling and so was the floor. Wherever he looked he could see himself reflected unto infinity. There was nothing but Adam Stride reflected forever whichever way he looked.

The only other items of furniture in the room were a lavatory and a bath.

Gritting his teeth against his pain, Stride discovered that his chains permitted him to use the lavatory. There was paper by it, though he took no pleasure in seeing himself excreting wherever he cast his eyes. His chains also allowed him to take a bath; there was soap, shampoo and towels. Since there was precious little else to do, Stride took a hot bath in the hope that it might ease his bruises. As he washed himself, he noticed that there was a machine, a spy-hole in the top right hand corner of the cell, that was probably recording his every movement.

The sight of himself going on to infinity was making him feel slightly sick. Stride clambered back on to the bed, placed the duvet over his eyes and thought about what he could do next. After a time, the door opened and two men who looked like Filipinos entered with food and water.

'Who the fuck are you?' Stride screamed. 'What is this?!' They might as well have been deaf and dumb for all the attention they paid him and their features remained impassive. Stride leapt from his bed, reasoning that he could wind his chains around the throat of one of them and threaten to strangle him, holding him as a hostage, but the servants had obviously been given clear instructions. They looked at him with scorn as his chains restrained him from his intended assault, bowed impassively and left the room, having placed water and bowls with food and plastic spoons before him. Stride found that he could reach out to take these, just. One bowl contained a very tasty stew of pork and vegetables and the other contained well-cooked rice. He was now very hungry, so he ate the food, which was delicious, and wondered what would happen next.

It was impossible to tell how time was passing since he had been stripped of his watch. Stride judged it best to put the duvet over his head once more and await further developments as he chanted arithmetic tables to himself and then tried to recall his favourite quotations from Shakespeare. These ran out after a time so Stride played within his head his favourite songs by the Beatles, the Rolling Stones, the Doors, Bob Dylan and Jimi Hendrix. When nothing had happened after this, he started to sing 'Frigging in the Rigging' by the Sex Pistols for, once more, there was fuck-all else to do.

Suddenly a door opened and he heard a voice:

'Did you *enjoy* beating him, Richmond, eh? Hm? *Did* you enjoy beating him? I don't quite hear you.'

'Yes, I did, Dr Lipsius.'

'Oh, *good*. Richmond, we must never quarrel, must we, eh? Hm? Now go and see him.'

'All right, Doctor.'

Moments later a bulky man stormed through the door and slammed it behind him. He was wearing a very expensive suit in pepper-and-salt tweed with a lime-green shirt and a scarlet tie. His empurpled face sported a pair of insalubrious ginger chin-whiskers into which his thick moustache merged. He brought a chair into the room, a straight-backed chair of stout oak. Reversing it, he placed it at the back of the mirrored room before sitting down and wrapping his thick thighs about it.

'Good day, Mr Stride,' said the man whom Stride had last seen as Ron Butcher. 'My name is Richmond.'

'Good day, Mr Richmond,' Stride responded wearily. 'Or is it good morning, good afternoon, good evening or good night? Hard to tell, what with your hospitality. And am I addressing Mr Richmond, Mr Butcher or Mr Grimsby whom my valued assistant Rosa Scarlett had the misfortune to meet?'

'Shut yer mouth, Stride, unless you want another hiding.'

'Oh, do come along, you sweet little coward,' Stride taunted him. 'And you are *such* a coward, aren't you?' Stride blew him a kiss of contempt, hoping to enrage the man so as to bring him within range. The man responded by walking up to Stride and unlocking his manacles. Instantly Stride lashed out at his groin and throat, only to have both moves blocked. Heavy fists thudded into his heart, liver and kidneys and he puked and shat simultaneously as Richmond clicked on the manacles once more.

'What was that you were saying about my being a coward, Mr Stride?' he heard Richmond's voice say out in the cold distance. 'I did tell you to keep yer mouth shut. Well, you might as well lie in your own mess.' Stride gasped as Richmond regarded him calmly. Five minutes passed in total silence as Stride groaned. 'You see, it's all very well giving lip and having a good time as long as you pay the bill. When d'you pay the bill, Mr Stride? When *do* you pay the bill?'

'Looks like now . . . ugh! Ugh!' Stride coughed. 'But why're you doing this to me?'

'Oh, you'll see.' Richmond sat back contentedly, extracted a silver cigarette case from his pocket and lit an untipped cigarette with a chunky golden Dunhill lighter. 'Like a fag?'

'Yes.'

'Well, you can't have one. You smoke too much. Better for your health that you don't.' He inhaled and exhaled with visible satisfaction, blowing out three perfect smoke rings. 'See those? They're nice, aren't they?'

'All right,' said Stride, 'you've got me. To what end?'

'I'll see what I can do to answer your questions. Depends what they are.'

'Why am I here?'

'You'll find out. Next.'

'Where am I?'

'Nowhere.'

'What're you going to do to me?'

'That depends upon what you say.'

'How did I get here?'

'Light tap on the noggin. Afterwards a man dressed in the uniform of a local security guard carried you out in a sack.'

'What was the point of that?'

'You'll see.'

'Why was Rosa killed?'

'Oh, you mean your black assistant? Well, it was nothing personal, but she was in the way, wasn't she? Couldn't have her tracing us back here or anything like that. Nice clean stroke with an axe.'

'You fucking bastard!' Stride yelled. 'That was a decent, innocent woman. And you just went and killed her . . .'

'For our amusement?' Richmond returned. 'Yes. You haven't been reading enough Shakespeare lately, Mr Stride. "As flies to wanton boys, are we to the gods. They kill us for their sport." The whole atrocity, incidentally, has been pinned on you. As far as the police are concerned, you took too many drugs, the evidence of which is there, went crazy and slaughtered your assistant in a rather ghoulish kind of way. The police are looking for you but don't worry; they'll never find you. Oh, being pale and silent, are you?'

'Antonina . . .' Stride whispered hoarsely.

'You have no need to worry about her. We could torture you mentally with that if we chose but in our mercy, we've decided not to do so. She is alive and well and safe. We had no reason to harm her.'

'Kind,' Stride muttered as he inwardly thanked heaven for the news and hoped that Richmond might here be telling the truth.

'Recognize this?' Richmond held up the black stone within the brass ankh.

'Yes. How did you get hold of it?'

'Easy. I'm an expert safe-cracker. Here.' He tossed it on to the bed. 'Look into that eye now and tell me what you see.'

Stride, his chains clinking, picked up the ankh and stared into the stone. At first he saw nothing, then he stated:

'Right now I can see a man who looks like Arthur Machen. There is distress and concern upon his facial features.'

'Yes, I like reading Arthur Machen,' Richmond reflected thoughtfully. 'Always liked his saying: "The World is a much stranger place than is commonly supposed." See anything else?'

'Glimpses of other faces . . . almost as though I was viewing the visages of many who have previously looked at this . . .'

'Keep it for the time being,' said Richmond, 'since a man of your obvious education might be able to see more. Anyway, it's been a pleasure talking to you and I hope that we can continue the conversation at some future date. Oh, ever had a shit sandwich? You know, one made with dog turd for its filling, the same kind veteran gangsters of the Fifties used to feed to people who annoyed them? No? Then mind yer manners.' He left.

Time passed and Stride had no means by which to measure it. He had little to do other than stare at the stone that appeared to have occasioned his present grief. Faces flickered within it, including that of Arthur Machen, but there was little more. After a while, Stride was interrupted in his deliberations by a quiet opening and closing of the door and the man he knew as Davies stepped into the mirrored prison cell, taking the same chair as Richmond, only turning it around so that he could rest his back.

'Good day once again, Mr Stride,' said the smooth, smiling, clean-shaven Mr Davies. 'Davies is still the name,' he added. 'I hope that my dear colleague Richmond has not been too hard on you. He can sometimes be overly crude and barbaric.'

'Bloodied but unbowed,' Stride returned. 'What *is* this all about?'

'Perfectly understandable behaviour, coming as it does from a naked ape,' Davies murmured. 'See anything interesting in the Black Pearl?'

'Faces from the past.'

'Quite so. Any Arthur Machen at all?'

'Yes.'

'Appropriate. I am told that he held it in his hands for a time. Mind you, sir, so many have. So many. I suppose that in your moments of leisure you are seeing them.'

'What is this all about?' Stride sighed. 'And have you harmed my client, Miss Alison Featherstonehaugh who pronounces her name "Fanshawe"?'

'You will slowly learn what it is all about and, no, we have not yet harmed the lady to whom you refer. Cigarette?' Stride nodded, inwardly aching for one. Davies picked up the plate from which Stride had eaten his dinner and, taking out a crocodile cigarette case from an inner pocket, dropped a cigarette into it. He added a box of matches and casually tossed the plate over to Stride. 'There's one match in there. Please don't use it to set fire to your bed or I shall simply let you burn to death, which is an unpleasant way to go.' Stride saw there was no alternative other than to light his cigarette, then an idea occurred to him which Davies promptly forestalled. 'Don't bother using the plate as a discus, Mr Stride. Whatever you may imagine, you are not within reach of me. Now just spin the plate back after you have used it as an ashtray, would you? Thank you. Tell me, since you seem to be such a clever individual, how can Christmas Day follow New Year's Day in the same year?'

'They can't,' Stride responded. 'Christmas Day always comes before New Year's Day.'

'They can,' Davies retorted. 'In any calendar year, New Year's *Day* comes before Christmas Day: it's New Year's Eve that follows Christmas, you fool.'

'What do you want of me?'

'You've been studying Arthur Machen, haven't you?' Stride nodded. 'What do you feel was the nature of his mysterious "Process"?'

'Oh?' Stride sought a way out. 'You want to know that, do you?' Now it was Davies's turn to nod. 'I'll tell you if you tell me what this nightmare is all about.'

'No,' said Davies, 'I can't do that. What I can do is promise and guarantee that you will neither be killed nor tortured; that your client, Alison Featherstonehaugh—' he pronounced it 'Fanshawe' '—will not be harmed; and moreover that no harm will come to your dearly beloved girlfriend Antonina. That is the easy way. If you wanted it the hard way, we could, of course, torture you and torture them. Which way, sir?' He smiled ingratiatingly, flicking an imaginary speck of dust from his immaculately tailored dark grey suit.

'And do I go free?'

'Oh, free as a bird, as long as you spend another night here and speak with other of my colleagues.'

'I presume that all this is being surreptitiously taped?'

'You presume rightly, Mr Stride. What, in your opinion, was Machen's "Process"?'

'Are you at all familiar with the work of Austin Osman Spare?'

'Yes,' said Davies. 'He was a brilliant visual artist, yet to give him his full due he also wrote books about Magick. His *The Book of Pleasure: the Psychology of Ecstasy* – I think it's called that – is particularly notable. If I remember correctly, he advocates a method of Self-Love for attaining this state of ecstasy and also the productive use of obsessions. Something to do with "riding the shark of his Desire . . ." as I recall.'

'Absolutely,' Stride answered as he rattled his chains.

'There's only one problem, Mr Stride. If I understand Spare's life correctly, he was not published until the early years of this century. Yes, it is probably true that as a child he was initiated into these Mysteries by an hereditary witch; a Mrs Paterson, if I recall it correctly. Yes, he did join a magical order run by Aleister Crowley, who admired his talent and expected great things from him, and this order derived from the Golden Dawn, of which both Machen and Crowley had been members. Yes, you have probably found that subsequently Crowley, having been repudiated by both Machen and Spare, though for distinctly separate reasons, became Head of the Ordo Templi Orientis, which purported to teach Sex Magick, ways to attain enlightenment through a combined concentration through workings of autosexual, heterosexual and even homosexual practices. My question is simply: how could Machen have been aware of these matters since they were not available prior to 1900 or later?'

'Intuition,' Stride answered. 'He used his imagination. He had also spent much time studying the work of the Alchemists, the Hermeticists and the Renaissance Magi. Like all true artists, he discerned the truth.'

'A sorcery that consisted of magical masturbation?'

'Yes.'

'Have you ever tried it?'

'No.'

'Do you think that it works?'

'Maybe so.'

'What leads you to think that Machen may have done this?'

'Dr Penzoldt's analysis of Machen's superb tale of horror, "The Novel of the White Powder" in his *The Three Impostors*, which uses Freudian analysis to reveal a masturbation complex: and Machen's all too obvious "The Red Hand". Poor Dr Penzoldt was so horrified in his otherwise excellent *The Supernatural in Fiction* that he declared the matter to be an unfitting subject for Literature.'

'So Machen indulged in magical masturbation . . .' Davies

mused aloud, 'and refused to admit to it afterwards?'

'I think so.'

'How did Machen's characters in *The Three Impostors* come to life around him?'

'How do I know?' Stride burst out exasperatedly. 'They certainly seem to have come to life in *mine*. Now would you kindly let me go?'

'Why should we?' Davies replied with an infuriatingly bland smile. 'You're really rather interesting. Anyway, we can't have you running to the police, can we? Tell me, do you think that a magical act might attract all sorts of attention?'

'I don't know.'

'Though your novel *The Labyrinth of Satan* implies that it might . . .'

'Sometimes we fictionists write things beyond our ken.'

'Quite so, Mr Stride. Oh, yes. Quite so.' Once again there was that infuriating smirk from Davies. 'I shall keep my word and you will be well looked after here, I can assure you. How shall I take my leave? "Pip! Pip!" perhaps? "Tickety-boo"? Hell's teeth! Sometimes even I am no longer sure of anything. Good day, Mr Stride.'

'Am I the victim,' Stride moaned aloud, 'of some elaborate, resourceful and sadistically cruel practical joke?' He hoped to high heaven that it might be no more than that. Then the door opened to admit Miss Alison Featherstonehaugh, who was wearing a fussy white blouse and a tight, calf-length navy blue skirt. She placed what could have passed as 'rear of the year' upon the seat Davies had vacated.

'Good evening, Mr Stride,' she said. Then she produced a little bell from her snakeskin bag and tinkled it. Instantly the two Filipino servants Stride had seen before entered to take the plate that Davies had given him. Stride realized that it would be quite useless to resist for the time being. At least they had also brought him a paper cup of whisky and a cigarette that one of them lit for him with a Zippo lighter. 'Please do not essay any foolish action. These men may be deaf and dumb but they are also expert in the martial arts, watching for your every possible offensive move as if you were a dangerous animal, which I suppose you are.' Stride saw that his intention of whipping his chains around their throats would end in disaster. They *were* observing his every movement.

'So you paid ten thousand pounds for *this*?' he asked as the servants withdrew. 'How could you do that, Alison?'

'It's Helen, actually. Call me that now. Tell me, do you like seeing yourself reflected to Infinity by mirrors throughout the room?'

'No. Do you?'

'Yes, actually.' She smiled prettily. 'Let me ask you a question. A man once had a brilliant hand at cards. He had three Aces and two Kings: a Full House. Why didn't he win?'

'Perhaps his opponent had four of a kind or a Straight Flush . . . ?'

'Good, but no. The game was Blackjack. And I gather that Richmond used his blackjack on you. You're not hurting too badly are you?'

'I am feeling as well,' Stride said, 'as any man who has been blackjacked, kidnapped and chained in a room, God knows where, whilst being mentally tormented could possibly feel. Was it worth paying ten thousand pounds for this?'

'You do so amuse me,' Helen replied, exploding into a high-pitched squeal of laughter.

'*You* don't amuse *me*, I'm afraid,' Stride retorted. 'My loyal assistant Rosa has been brutally butchered for no purpose, it seems, other than your amusement. What are you going to do to me? Kill me?'

'Remember what I said when I first met you?'

'No . . .' Stride said, although he did.

'No?' She raised her eyebrows, delicately pencilled.

'Oh, then do it!' Stride yelled, feeling driven to the verge of insanity. 'Go on. Cut my balls off and stick them in my mouth! There doesn't seem to be much I can do about it. Just tell me *why*? What harm have I ever done to you?'

'You wrote a book.'

'Yes, *The Labyrinth of Satan*. So?'

'It gave away too many secrets.'

'Then why play through this charade?'

'You're not a particularly sympathetic character, you know, Adam. In fact you're just a selfish bastard.'

'That's as may be. But I wasn't aware that one could be killed or tortured for that.'

'Then you are in for a surprise.' Helen/Alison took the little silver bell from her bag again and tinkled it. A woman wearing a nightmarish rubber mask promptly entered the room, bearing a sharp knife in her right hand. 'Yes,' said Helen.

The woman in the vampire mask approached Stride, whipped off the duvet and stared smilingly at his limp and shrinking genitals as the knife twitched in her hand. Stride, quite horrified, regarded her every movement and as she made a stab towards his testicles, he seized her wrist with his left hand and wrapped the chain attached to his right hand around her throat. The knife fell from her hand on to the bed and Stride picked it up. The girl gurgled as he tightened the pressure on the chain.

'Release me!' Stride roared. 'Or I'll strangle the bitch!' To his stupefaction, Helen remained wholly unperturbed, calmly producing a camera from her bag and taking several photographs.

'Oh, go ahead and kill her, Adam,' she smiled. 'I shall simply call the police, we shall leave this house and go to another: given the evidence left behind, where will that leave you?'

Stride ripped away the rubber mask to disclose the male face of one of the silent Filipino servants he had seen earlier.

THE GOD GAME

'The breasts are falsies,' Helen laughed, 'and the knife, you'll find, is made of rubber. This servant is both deaf and dumb. You can strangle him to death if you like and if it affords you any satisfaction. It is a matter of complete indifference to us. If it gives you pleasure to strangle an innocent man to death, go ahead: I shall watch and photograph the matter with considerable interest.'

'You bitch,' he snarled.

'Oh, I *am* a bitch. What a compliment coming from a man of your calibre! Go on, kill him! The poor chap thinks that he's merely playing a bondage game with some pervert. Well, do make up your mind!'

'I see.' Stride released the wretch. Helen dismissed him from the room with a gesture as she neatly placed an untipped cigarette in her long black holder and lit it with a Ronson petrol table lighter, again produced from her bag. 'What's your game, Helen, Alison or whoever you are? I have just released an innocent dupe I could have killed. I freely admit that *I* am an innocent dupe. So why are you holding me here?'

'Ever heard of experimentation?'

'Why experiment on me?'

'I suppose that's what animals think when they come under the knife of the vivisectionist,' Helen responded in a cold tone that chilled him. 'You are a convenient subject.'

'For heaven's sake let me go!'

'Why?' Helen's look was pitiless.

'Why not?'

'You're much too interesting.'

'Oh,' said Stride. 'You are mistaken. I am dull, tedious and quite exceptionally boring.'

'That,' the young lady replied, 'remains to be seen. However, let us proceed to the next matter. I would like to read you a bedtime story.'

'Thank you, but I am hardly in the mood for bedtime stories.'

'Oh, but you *must* listen to this one.' In her high, clear, slightly lisping voice, she proceeded to read Stride:

THE PURSUIT OF POWER

by

Septimus Keen

Have you ever wanted to play God by manipulating men and women whilst luxuriating in the life of the utmost Decadence? I have: moreover, I have done so.

I was lucky to inherit a vast fortune that enabled me to do whatever I wanted. As it happens, my passions are for the Arts, most notably the Arts of the Theatre. Don't get me wrong: I venerate Science as well, particularly the work of the quantum physicists who demonstrate that the impossible – the impossible according to common sense, that is – is actually the true case.

Everything that occurs within the atom is impossible according to common sense. Only recently scientific experimentation has demonstrated that an atom can be in two places at the same time. I think, of course, of the Black Pearl, but more of that anon.

Absolutely nothing is fixed; everything is relative; and beyond that there are quantum jumps. Einstein stated: 'God does not play dice with the Universe.' I say that she does.

Money gives one power and I am fascinated by its use and abuse. It enables one to indulge in obsessions. I remain unclear as to what brings about an obsession, though I suspect it is to do with sexual imprints implanted unconsciously in infancy. In any event, I am obsessed with the London of the 1890s and I want it to flourish in the 1990s. In the 1890s, many thought that civilization as it was known in Europe was fast coming to an end. Indeed, that particular conception of Western civilization *was* wiped out by two World Wars.

Presently, we are enjoying the decadence of a capitalist system upon its last legs, a system utterly unable to cope with a breakthrough to a new and revolutionary form of consciousness. I hope that there are intelligent idealists out there who know that the temporary American lead in world affairs is rooted in a pathetic insistence upon global conformity that is wholly doomed to failure: such idealists may be able to make a better world. Myself, I couldn't care less. I find our so-called leaders to be so stupid that I care only for my own pleasure.

My own pleasure comprises sexual perversity, excellent food and drink and the creation of theatre upon the streets of London that alters fixed perceptions of 'reality'. It was an absolute pleasure, too, for me to join with a troupe who shared my views in some measure and who warmly welcomed the fact that I like gender bending. They love the Decadence of the 1890s as much as I do, and wish to update it and recreate it in the 1990s. Their rituals are also quite extraordinary.

The Golden Dawn of the 1890s indeed generated excellent Magick, and attracted many of the finest people of its time. But a century later, its achievement resembled a beautiful Rolls-Royce that travels at five miles per hour. *Our* work brings Magick directly into life.

Doctor Lipsius appears to relish the exploration of evil for its own sake. He relishes the part that he has taken. He has an exquisite taste in gems and statues and other objects of religious and magical significance: he is also a very fine chemist and I have witnessed his concoctions of mind-altering substances being given to his witless dupes. One of them wipes out all memory.

Yet it would be a mistake to see Lipsius as being merely an evil villain, rubbing his hands with joy and going: 'Heh! heh!' His interest in human behaviour and animal experimentation is genuine. Lipsius is not, of course, his real name. He delights in taking it because he feels that in *The Three Impostors*, written in the 1890s, Arthur Machen discerned truths beyond his conscious ken.

Myself, I delight in the fellowship of Lipsius's associates.

Richmond is crude but useful, and his ghoulish humour makes me laugh. Davies is subtle and wicked. Helen can be quite exquisitely cruel and of all of us, I think it is she who has the finest thespian ability. We enjoy using our skills to bring some fatuous fool into another dimension. We don't do it for the money, since we don't need that. We do it for our own pleasure and in the interests of Art and Science.

This august troupe chooses its victims carefully. There was a Tory MP who died wearing ladies' underwear and with a polythene bag over his head. The Coroner ruled it an accidental death – but we had certainly enjoyed ourselves setting up this 'accident'. We drove him insane by pandering to his every whim and then destroying all his preconceptions. 'The Three Impostors'? Or is it 'The Three Imps'? One is reminded of Bat-Mite in the *Batman* comic books: Bat-Mite, the elf, is actually much more powerful than his hero.

Most of all, I love to disturb authors by making their books come to life all around them. You wouldn't believe how the poor little dears freak out. There was a woman who earned a fortune writing books, all of which might have been called *My Nervous Breakdown over Relationships in Hampstead*. We gave her a nervous breakdown all right by simulating relationships based upon the characters in her wretched books. So at last she suffered a total mental collapse in Hampstead and killed herself into the bargain. About time, too: her books were awful. Good riddance to bad rubbish, I say.

Edgar Allan Poe once wrote a good tale called *The Imp of the Perverse*. A man called Adam Stride wrote a novel called *The Labyrinth of Satan*. This was based upon Arthur Machen's novel *The Three Impostors* and it was surprisingly imaginative and accurate, thus arousing the imp of the perverse within us. Actually, we have no patience with the childish nonsense of satanism: it isn't real and we are.

There was a period of research, revealing the fact that he

was a private detective, very good at his job, a man priding himself upon the scepticism of his intelligence. Purr-fect! It seemed even better when we learned that he was endeavouring to write a biography of Arthur Machen, details of whom are kept in the archives of our Black Lodge. Whirling Adam Stride into our maze proved to be a relatively easy matter: and it was fascinating to see his confusion.

Presently Stride is our prisoner and will be our unwilling victim in another experiment.

Stride is very manly. I am somewhat feminine.

I wonder how he will respond to our latest venture in gender bending. While I remain very fond of him, nonetheless the creation of a false reality for him proved to be an exceedingly enjoyable operation.

Next!

'What did you think of that?' asked Helen

'What am I supposed to say?' Stride demanded.

'You know, Septimus Keen is really your greatest fan.'

'Really? Then may heaven preserve me from fans.'

'Oh? Objecting to your fantasies becoming a reality? Does Life imitate Art or does Art imitate Life?'

'I've heard that before.'

'Heard it, yes,' said Helen. 'But have you *seen* it?' She chuckled. 'In this infernal imbroglio, there is a twist in the tail like a scorpion's sting.' She rang her little bell again. 'Meet Septimus Keen.'

It appeared to Stride's tired eyes that a slim young man with blond hair walked into the room, kissed Helen full upon the lips and stared at him with bold blue eyes.

It was Antonina.

CHAPTER FIFTEEN

A WOLVERINE OF THE WORLD
(THE WICKED WOOD)

When Arthur Machen finally recovered his senses, he found himself to be lying on the floor in his own home with a man dressed in female clothing looking down upon him.

'You are such a dear, sweet man, aren't you, Arthur?' the voice cooed. 'Now, do you want to know what has been happening to you or not?' Machen nodded dumbly. 'Well, *do* stop crawling about on the floor. Have another drink. You don't have any need to say anything. You see, you were quite right in suspecting that there are many secret societies, many occult sodalities. You were quite wrong in thinking that your book *The Three Impostors* made no impact because of its atrocious reviews. There are those who discern quality, especially when a book reveals truths far beyond its author's conscious ken. Yes, of course we have been playing with you. It was too tempting a prospect to resist. I have no fear in telling this to you. Whoever you try to tell, no one will believe you. Would anyone believe the events of tonight? And so you *will* keep quiet, won't you, Arthur, as is your wont? I know that you are still asking: who wrote the stories by "Arthur Machen"? Well, I did, you fool! I just wanted to show you that the things of which you write have an objective reality.

'I see you shrink from me in horror. Come, come, sir, have you not yourself invoked these horrors? Allow me to read you my latest tale. You will not object? Very well.'

And with these words, Machen's domineering guest proceeded to extract a manuscript from a bag and to read him:

THE WICKED WOOD

by

Alison Hyde

Poor Alan! That is perhaps the least I can say since I was well acquainted with the woman who brought about his present condition. I know the story from both sides.

Alan was at that time having difficulties in seducing women. His features were initially unprepossessing, he was shy and, for the time being, although his talent was undeniable, he had no money, causing him to lead a somewhat celibate life.

He thought he had finally struck lucky on the day that he met Artemis in a second-hand bookshop in Hampstead. Typically, it was Artemis who approached him, asking for help in locating a book, which help he gave gladly. She was living in the area at the time – a rather delicately furnished flat, as I recall – and she invited him to tea there. And then she seduced him.

Now I have been to bed with Artemis myself and, speaking from a woman's point of view, it was a weird and wonderful experience. I wondered what it might be like for a man.

'Incredible!' he told me. 'It was not like making love to one woman: it was like making love to *all* women, all at once!'

'He's not bad,' she told me, 'but he is somewhat inexperienced and also frustrated.'

'She has an extraordinary flat,' he said. 'Upon the mantelpiece there are, for example, little mannequins. I asked after them and she told me they were models of her previous lovers. And there were whips upon the bedroom walls which she said were for certain of her previous lovers.'

'He's quite interesting to begin with' she said, 'but after a while one tires of him. He is always doing the same things. I shall take this dog for a walk.'

'She took me to Hampstead Heath,' he told me. 'Just by

Jack Straw's Castle, as you go from Hampstead to Highgate, on the left there is a wood. She called it: "The Wicked Wood".'

'I love to take my lovers there,' she told me. Artemis was in fact one of the most stunning women I have ever embraced, with a shock of long blond hair, a slender waist, pert breasts and a neatly shaped bottom that women would die to have and men would die to kiss.

'O!' Alan exclaimed to me. 'What a beauty! What a strange, wild and lascivious woman! She told me that the wood was enchanted and I could well believe it, once you are away from the main road. We lay down on the moss by an oaken tree stump and we made love. She whispered words of tender endearment as we lay upon the leaves and it was as though I had been vouchsafed a vision of the Universe as a union between the infinitely great and the infinitely small.'

'Another,' she said to me.

'She told me that once I had made love to her in this enchanted forest, my life would never be the same again,' Alan said. 'And, yes, it can't be. She was so beautiful and yet disturbing, shaking up my every perception of reality. We arose and continued with our walk. Suddenly, I saw a man standing on a mound and watching us. He appeared to be a turbaned Sikh dressed in a blue raincoat but Artemis informed me that all she saw was a man dressed in Tudor costume. "Then who is he?" I asked. "One of the many," she replied.'

'There are many ghosts in the Wicked Wood,' she told me.

'It was at that point,' he said, 'that things became very strange. She said something about going to pick chestnuts whilst I gazed at the rising moon, yellow, like overripe cheese, and slightly sickly. I looked around to see where she had gone – and she had vanished. I ran everywhere, shouting out her name but no answer came at all. Thinking that the only thing to do would be to get out of the wood by Jack Straw's Castle, I set off in the direction we had come. It was a nightmare. By night, nothing looked the same as it had done at sunset. Creeping plants appeared to entwine their tendrils about me as thistles tore at my clothes and every time my hands reached out to steady myself I was stung by nettles. I fancied that I heard wolves baying in the distance, though of course that's impossible. Though how do *you* explain the appearances before my eyes of the Sikh in a blue raincoat, an arrogant Tudor gentleman, a contemporary dandy, a swaggering youth in outlandish garb that I did not recognize, all of them standing on mounds and looking at me? I know you'll think I'm crazy, but I saw that in the wood.'

'He would've,' she said. 'It's why I take them there.'

I was very sorry to hear that Alan was eventually found wandering in the wood and talking loudly to himself by a man who alerted the police. It was obvious that he required medical care.

He really hasn't been the same man since that experience. He remains obsessed with Artemis, who has since moved to another address, and he roams the streets in a futile search for her. Indeed, he appears to have no interest in his life other than Artemis. Since I feel sorry for him, the other day I took him out to lunch in Covent Garden. This was not a success since he kept looking at every woman who passed by in the hope that it might be Artemis.

I went to see Artemis the other day for tea. She is now living in another part of Hampstead, yet, as always, her flat is delicately furnished. There seemed to be a few more mannequins upon the mantelpiece and as I passed the bedroom on the way to the bathroom, I noticed another whip upon the wall.

Later, sitting by her front room bow window, I noticed that there were a number of men roaming the streets with vacancy in their eyes. Initially I thought that the circus was in town and that it all might be geared towards the engendering of publicity.

I saw a man dressed like King Henry VIII, a Sikh in a blue raincoat, a contemporary dandy, more than one young man dressed in clothes from no era I could identify and – could it be? – Alan in his Norfolk jacket and sensible trousers? I drew Artemis's attention to the matter and suggested that she might like to invite him in to tea. How she laughed!

'The Wicked Wood has worked its Magick,' she declared. 'Wood, as you know, gives one power if properly employed. I've never really liked men. They're so crude, rude and lewd. I just want these dogs to spend all their lives sniffing the scent and never finding their prey. Women are beautiful,' Artemis said to me. 'Darling, would you like to come to bed?'

'That's all very well . . . well, well, well, well,' Machen muttered.

'That's you wandering in the Wicked Wood. And you carelessly left the Black Pearl here.' The Ankh was tantalizingly held up before Machen's eyes. 'Now, would you like to know the truth?'

'Yes,' said Machen, murmuring: '"What is truth?" said Pontius Pilate.'

'All right. Call me Septimus Keen. That is the name I assume. What I require is your word of honour, sworn upon your soul, that you will never tell anyone of the events that have been inflicted upon you; you can hint and be vague, of course, but you can never fully describe this. Agreed?'

'Yes.'

'Well, then,' said Septimus Keen, swishing his skirts with glee, 'where do I start? There has always been a hidden wisdom within humanity deriving from unknown sources. For instance, your scientists are saying now that if we multiply the height of Egypt's Great Pyramid by some formula, we get the distance from the Earth to the Sun correct to three decimal places. There have always been forces that seek to impede human evolution, most notably the Christian Church. During the centuries of persecution inflicted on all who sought to advance human knowledge, there were secret societies. Some of them were corrupt or became so. Some of them were simply useless. Some strove earnestly to advance the evolution of humanity. Some were simply cynical. I belong to one of these last. We like to experiment upon human beings in the same way that scientists like to experiment on rats.

'We take names,' Septimus Keen continued, 'and we act out our parts in life, taking, incidentally, much joy in the matter. We collect curious and unusual objects. Very few people have the slightest notion concerning the work upon which we are engaged. Its faintest intimations have only been indicated via Art and Literature. You, Arthur Machen, kept writing the truth without really knowing that you were doing so. Take your *The Great God Pan*: here an evil doctor attempts an experiment whereby Pan takes over the body of a girl who proceeds to destroy the lives of men in London. Did you know that it is perfectly possible to drive a soul out of the body and replace it with another being? Take your "The Inmost Light" wherein another evil doctor, Dr Black, drives the soul of his wife out of her body and into a gem, her body becoming possessed by a daemon . . . that is perfectly possible too, but not many people know that.

'You really did excel yourself, Arthur, when it came to your *The Three Impostors: or, The Transformations*. You didn't know what you were actually writing about, yet somehow you, as a creative artist, managed to get as close to the truth as anyone has done hitherto. Well, there *was* a grouping of us and we wanted to show you just how true your works are and also to observe your reaction, amazed as we were by your powers of perception. Yes, there is what one could call an acting troupe that creates sport and art and I suppose that, by conventional standards, we are decadent, awful and evil. In any event, we decided to stage some theatre for you. Remember the night when the Stone fell into your lap?'

'Yes . . .' Machen sighed. 'But how on Earth did you know that I would be walking in the direction that would allow you to play out this drama?'

'Simple, Mr Machen. You seem to take a similar evening route every day. Also, there's the concentrated mental energy to which you opened yourself and that can draw an individual towards a particular point. Plays were played out for your benefit so that we could study the reactions of an intelligent and creative human being.'

'What was the point of the short stories allegedly written by me?'

'You were writing in many dimensions, sweetheart. We wanted to show you more dimensions still. We hope that on account of your experience you will write many more tales of truth and beauty, that may enlighten and delight those sufficiently intelligent to read them.'

'And the Ankh?'

'Oh, the Black Pearl. Ah! You were mistaken in thinking that it is the Holy Grail. That is something else altogether. I wish you luck in your Quest for it. Meanwhile the stone in the brass is simply something chipped from a meteorite that landed in Central America many hundreds of years ago and was brought to England, robbed, I believe, from a Spanish treasure ship.'

'I find difficulty,' said Machen, 'in believing a single word that you say.'

'Quite right too, and I wouldn't if I were you. One can always make up a story to cover anything. Define a lie, Arthur.'

'A declared and purported statement that is knowingly not the true case.'

'Very good. Tell me, have you ever heard of atoms?' Machen snorted disgustedly in response. 'Of course you have. What goes on within the atom?'

'Who knows?'

'Oh, more will certainly be known. Suppose I were to tell you that within the atom, there are yet smaller particles – let's call them *electrons* – and that *one* electron can go through *two* points simultaneously?'

'Impossible!' Machen snorted indignantly again.

'It's already been proved in terms of mathematics. It is only a matter of time and improved technology before the scientists find this paradox to be a fact. But enough of this since I see that you are not up to it. Here, take a look at this stone and tell me what you see.'

Machen seized the ankh, stared into the black, opaque surface and saw his own face. Then there was a bewildering rapid succession of faces from all times in the past and, insofar as he could tell, the future. One man in particular struck his attention since his facial features were contorted in agony. True to his word, as always, he described exactly what he saw.

'Very well.' Septimus Keen took back the ankh and Machen found himself powerless to resist. 'I hope that this has helped you. You will die about half a century in the future and whatever happens to anyone after that is hardly your concern. Thank you for your kind co-operation in the course of our experiment. I hope that it has assisted your creative insights and I wish you every possible success for the future. Don't forget the vow of silence you swore to me. Goodnight.' The strange, skirted visitor departed, leaving Machen feeling both numb and dumb.

In the days that followed, absolutely nothing of the slightest interest happened. In later years and in his *Things Near and Far*, Machen would write:

'And soon Miss Lally, another character from the book, appeared, and like her prototype discoursed most amazing tales, was the heroine of incredible adventures, would appear and disappear in a quite inexplicable manner, relating always histories before unheard of, a personage wholly diverting, enigmatic and enchanting . . . till the prompter's bell sounded and the curtain fell and the lights went out.'

Machen never would comprehend precisely what had happened to him and in addition there was the oath he had sworn upon his honour as a gentleman, the oath not to reveal the incredible facts. He openly confessed that he could make nothing of the bizarre events of 1899–1900. He prided himself on being able to tell the truth but he could make no sense of this. He called himself a Silly Fool, for whereas previously his every encounter had been pregnant with significance, now there was nothing except the mundane.

He revised the final chapter of his *The Hill of Dreams*, generally considered to be his masterpiece, in which the hero's book is finally revealed to be a mass of illegible scribblings. He wrote two tales that many consider to be among his finest: 'A Fragment of Life' and 'The White People': these exquisite works could not find a publisher for some years, and even when they did, they were excoriated by the critics and sold badly.

Even so, his loneliness was alleviated, for he remarried happily and had children, after which he went on the stage where he won much praise for his acting ability. In later years, he became a star columnist for the London *Evening News*, a job that paid well but which he detested. He found national fame when the worst tale he ever wrote, a patriotic story penned to oblige the *Evening News* called 'The Bowmen' – the knights of St George come to the rescue of the British Army at Mons in 1914 – was confirmed as true when officers and men wrote from the Western Front to state that they *had* witnessed the events described and that Machen had invented nothing. Time and time again, Machen insisted that he had written fiction. Nobody believed him.

The *Evening News* sold 100,000 copies of 'The Bowmen'. Unfortunately, Machen had assigned all rights to the company for a small fee.

Appearance and reality were similarly confused when the Editor of the *Evening News* asked Machen to write an obituary for Lord Alfred Douglas, who had brought about the ruin of Oscar Wilde and who had always expressed in print his detestation of Machen. Machen wrote some scathing words. Unfortunately, Lord Alfred Douglas was still alive and sued for libel. Machen was sacked.

He was saved from penury only by the sudden rediscovery of his works by American aesthetes who applauded him as being 'the flower-tunicked priest of nightmare' and so for a time, and much to his surprise, he lived quite well in St John's Wood. When the Wall Street Crash of 1929 wiped out aestheticism and frivolity, he had to make endless shifts to make ends meet, though many hold that during this period he wrote some of his finest and most subtle works. He was astounded when, during the 1940s, a committee headed by T.S. Eliot, George Bernard Shaw and Max Beerbohm raised thousands of pounds to ensure that he could have comfort in his old age. He died in 1947, shortly after his beloved wife Purefoy, and under the belief that he was in a monastery where the Abbess was kind to monks who had visions.

Throughout his life he kept his oath to the person called 'Septimus Keen', declining to discuss in detail the events of 1899–1900. Privately he had continued to wander the streets of London, little knowing how much his tales would inspire future generations, wondering what might become of the man of the future whom he had seen in the Stone, whose name he did not know was Adam Stride.

CHAPTER SIXTEEN

VISIONS OF VENGEANCE
(BEYOND THE GRAVE)

'Antonina, how could you?'

'It was easy,' she said.

'Why?'

'Have you read any Mickey Spillane?'

'Yes.' Stride was trying frantically to determine the sex of the being before him, formerly a woman he had known and loved.

'Have you read Mickey Spillane's *I, The Jury*?'

'Yes.'

'Then you'll know its ending. The woman with whom Mike Hammer is infatuated takes off her clothes in the sexiest possible way as he explains to her just how he knows she killed his best buddy with a dum-dum bullet and made him crawl. She approaches him with open loving arms. He notices that there is a pistol in the flowerpot behind him and realizes as she puts her arms around him that her intention is to blow his brains out. He pulls the trigger of his .45 first and blasts her belly away. "How could you?"'

'Yes,' Stride sighed, 'I know the closing line: "*It was easy,*' I said." What has this to do with me?'

'You're a private detective. Have you read *Vengeance Is Mine* by Mickey Spillane?'

'Yes . . .' Stride noticed that Helen had quietly slipped out of the room.

'Do you recall the closing lines?'

'As it happens, yes.' He shivered.

'Mike Hammer is infatuated with Juno the murderess, isn't he?'

'Yes . . .'

'Can you recall the closing line?'

'Yes. "Juno was a queen, all right. *Juno was a man!*"'

'So am I, Adam, so am I; or so I was. I did not like being a man and so I became a woman. You have been fucking a transsexual.'

'I like to learn something new every day,' Stride responded.

'I think it was H.G. Wells who said in his *The History of Mr Polly*: "If you don't like your life, then you can change it." Well, I did not like my sex, so I changed it. Any objections?'

'Yes, plenty,' Stride retorted, feeling as if he was becoming utterly insane. 'Why on Earth did you become involved with me?'

'The answers are all in the story that Helen read you.'

'So you manipulated me all along. Congratulations, Antonina.'

'Kindly call me Septimus.'

'What was the point of pretending to be Septimus Keen, a character I invented?'

'You mean, you *thought* you invented.' The transsexual lit a cigarette and blew a cloud of grey smoke at him. 'There *was*, actually, in the London of the 1890s a legendary character called Septimus Keen.'

'Why,' Stride gasped, 'isn't Septimus Keen mentioned in any of the documents of the time?'

'Keen chose to remain anonymous or pseudonymous. Only a few knew, and they were sworn to secrecy. Would you like to talk about the matter further?'

'Yes. I'd also like a bath, fresh sheets, release from these chains, a stiff drink and a pipe and slippers, but I fear I'm asking for the moon.'

'Oh, well, you can give yourself a bath. And yes, I shall have the sheets changed. All rather messy with your puke, piss and shit aren't they?' Keen giggled. 'Have a bath. I've seen a naked man before.'

The change of sheets was done by the silent Filipino servants as Stride took the bath he once more needed so badly while Keen smoked and regarded the scene with insouciance.

'You'll be seeing Dr Lipsius later so you'll have to be on cracking form, Adam. Meanwhile, allow me to read to my latest masterpiece.' With those words, the reading commenced:

BEYOND THE GRAVE

by

Septimus Keen

Many have asked me for my views on Edward Exmond, the celebrated artist and one of my dearest friends, since our friendship goes back to our schooldays. I am inclined to think that I am among the two who know the truth. There is a third but she is no longer with us.

At school and at Goldsmith's, Edward was renowned for his technical versatility and he went on to become, for a time, ranked among the most fashionable of contemporary artists. A high point in his career came when a Cork Street gallery presented an exhibition of his *Satires on Contemporary Life*, and I went to see the Private View. There were five pieces.

Breakfast consisted of a table with chairs, a packet of cornflakes, a carton of milk, cups of tea and coffee, plastic eggs, bacon, toast, tomato, sausage, mushroom and baked beans plus a television screen on which some idiot twittered.

Lunch consisted of two mannequins sitting opposite one another at a table replete with plastic smoked salmon, tiger prawns, rare lamb, *mange-touts*, and wild strawberries accompanied by bottles of mineral water. There were also two mobile phones which beeped continuously.

Tea consisted of a table and two chairs upon which two Victorian female cardboard dummies had been placed. These dummies regarded a teapot, cups, milk, sugar (with tongs) and cucumber sandwiches. Upon the table there was a white card and the letters, which had been scrawled upon it with a red felt-tip pen, read 'FUCK THE RICH'.

Dinner consisted of a table with two chairs and an elaborate arrangement of knives and forks and cutlery and glasses, with a menu announcing twenty-two exotic courses, written in French with exquisite calligraphy. There was music by Oasis and the chairs were vacant.

Supper, which won high praise in certain quarters for its minimalism, consisted of a table upon which reposed a cup of cocoa, a tumbler and an empty bottle of whisky and had a naked mannequin slumped in one chair.

A few conservative critics deplored the exhibition but many praised Edward's excellence in language that I found to be virtually incomprehensible. He was hailed as the coming master of deconstructionism, post-modernism and even semiotics. A multimillionaire from Los Angeles proceeded to purchase the entire collection for two hundred thousand pounds.

After the party, Edward invited me back to his somewhat surprisingly spartan flat in Kensington, and over the finest armagnac he asked me what I had thought of it.

'Edward,' I said, 'I am delighted by your success. Good luck to you! But given your talent, this is shit.'

'I know,' he replied complacently, 'but it's what they want. These days you can sell a fart in a jam jar provided that the public are convinced that it's Art. I cottoned on to that racket years ago. You see, I couldn't possibly hope to sell my *real* Art, that which I paint with my heart and soul, that into which I put my blood. So I slept with the right people, whored my arse and sucked cock in all the right places, made all the right connections with all the right art critics and gallery owners . . . you see, these days people are so insecure, they have no confidence in their own judgement and they need to be *told* what is Art. A good friend of mine doesn't do too badly from nail clippings in ashtrays, though a cleaner threw away one of his latest masterpieces recently, thus losing him five thousand pounds. No problem. It only took him a couple of hours to buy another ashtray, cut his toenails and smoke some more cigarettes.'

'How can you betray your principles?'

'Oh, it's quite easy, really.' Edward yawned. 'As a pander to the tastes of these useless fools, I make enough money and enjoy fame as I get on with what really matters to me. Do you know David Henderson at all?' I shook my head. 'His *Fart in a Jam Jar* was recently thrown out by the cleaners and the assistant manager went into a right bloody panic. Eventually it was rescued and there were the initials "DH". It was thought that this might well be the work of Damien Hirst, giving it a value of £30,000. However, it was eventually ascertained that it was by David Henderson, dropping the value of a fart in a jam jar to a mere £2,000. I have no idea why people buy dated Dada. It might have had some validity in 1919 but it has none now. Even so, I take advantage of this ludicrous situation. I couldn't possibly make any kind of living otherwise,' said this slim, handsome young man. 'For my next exhibit, I am seriously thinking of putting out a black bin-bag of garbage with the label *The Garbage of Edward Exmond: Look Through It*. Some critics will praise it and some sucker will buy it. Five thousand, perhaps?'

'Do you do *any* good work these days?'

'Oh, yes,' he answered calmly. 'Would you like to come and take a look?'

And it is here that my story really begins.

At school, Edward had astounded both his teachers and his contemporaries by his astonishing ability to render accurately in pencil, ink, charcoal, water colours, egg tempura, pastels, engraving, etching, clay, bronze and oils, any object or subject set before him. There was no need for a camera whilst Edward was around. They say that the camera cannot lie but Edward portrayed truths. Even the soccer thugs were awed by his skills and would have regarded bothering him as a crime equivalent to spitting into the face of one's mother. In fact, they took his sketches of them home for proud display to their mothers.

Unsurprisingly, Edward was very popular with the girls. He treated them with a gentlemanly courtesy, fucked them and left them whilst managing to stay friends subsequently. One of these girls was Pauline Naseby who came from a neighbouring school. She was a rather attractive tall blond girl whom I quite liked, although she was conventional, destined for marriage, I thought, to some doctor, lawyer or chartered accountant. Edward lost no time in seducing her: and one day he suggested, since I was short of a girlfriend that weekend, that I came to dinner at the Naseby household with him to meet a friend of Pauline's called Janine. I agreed. A blind date was better than no date at all and if I did not like her, I could always make my excuses and leave.

The Naseby household was in Chiswick.

'Fortunately,' I said, 'I still have my Himalayan outfit and shall start out early tomorrow, providing I can obtain mules,' quoting Aleister Crowley, whose works I was (unofficially) studying at the time.

Chiswick can be divided into three parts, as Caesar divided Gaul. There is the gracious eighteenth-century Chiswick by the Thames, a haven at the time it was built for wealthy city dwellers who required a weekend retreat. There is the twentieth-century Chiswick High Road, which is pleasant, ordinary and undistinguished. Then there is nineteenth-century Chiswick, a suburb of Victorian villas built on account of the expansion of the District Line railway; the Nasebys lived just a five-minute walk from Turnham Green Underground station.

I had no difficulty in finding the house, which was in a Victorian terrace built for the middle classes. A Rover stood in the paved space before it. I was welcomed warmly by Mr Naseby and shown into what he termed 'the drawing room', where Mrs Naseby was having medium dry sherry with her husband, her daughter Pauline, Edward and Janine. Conversation was pleasant and superficial. After a time, we proceeded into 'our dining room', where the crockery and cutlery had been laid out with the utmost ceremonial formalities. There is little to say about the decor. All over Middle England there are millions of rooms exactly like it, though I could have done without the gilt-framed reproductions of Impressionist paintings.

Janine, a buxom brunette, was pleasant, cheerful and quite sexy company. I took her to a rock gig a few days later, fucked her on the grass and then lost interest since she was not particularly bright. Pauline was her usual charming self as she uttered pleasant banalities such as: 'Mummy always knows how to serve soup at exactly the right temperature.' I was glad that I had chosen to wear a suit, shirt and tie since the Nasebys appeared to dress for dinner. Edward had chosen to turn up in a leather jacket, a torn T-shirt and ripped, tight jeans, clearly annoying Mrs Gillian Naseby, who has to be one of the most annoying and pretentious bitches I have ever met in my life. It was clear that she could not bear Edward.

The dinner was reasonably good, though it was clear that one was expected to express compliments even if it hadn't been. I quite like tinned tomato soup with a dash of Worcester and freshly squeezed orange. There's nothing wrong with a casserole of chicken with tomatoes named Chicken Marengo, accompanied by Mrs Naseby's story about a victory of Napoleon's. Who could object to a good Summer Pudding? Supermarket Cheddar with cream crackers and margarine is acceptable. I have nothing against a decent Spanish burgundy: though was it really necessary for Mr Naseby to go through the ceremony of uncorking the wine, sniffing it, tasting it and then pouring it for us as Mrs Naseby praised the sophistication of Burgundy and her husband turned the label away? As the coffee came in dainty little cups, accompanied by dainty little glasses of Grand Marnier, Mr Naseby offered cigars, which were taken by Edward and myself.

'Excuse me, Mr Naseby,' Edward said. 'Could I possibly have a cigar cutter?'

This seemed to me like an eminently sensible proposition. The cigars required a cutter, unless we were expected to cut them in half with a knife and stick the other half behind our ears. Should we chew off the ends and spit them out on to the Wilton carpet? I suppose one could have screwed through them with a match but that would have been somewhat naff behaviour.

'It seems,' said Edward as Pauline paled, 'that, as one wag has it, I am provoking a silence so pregnant it is virtually in labour.' Mrs Naseby's hate-filled glare at Edward was a fury-fuelled spray of psychic venom that I shall never forget. Her eyes went as cold as dry ice.

'A c-cigar c-cutter?' Mr Naseby stammered.

'Yes, I assume you have one somewhere.' Given the preposterous formality of this provincial dinner, his was an eminently reasonable assumption. It was also clear that, despite its pretensions, this house did not have a cigar cutter.

'Oh . . .' Edward murmured in all apparent innocence. 'Mrs Naseby, am I up the metaphorical shit creek without the proverbial paddle?'

'What an absolute fucking disaster of a dinner!' Edward exclaimed when I saw him next day at his father's house in Parsons Green. His parents were divorced and his father was presently away on business. 'Here, have another slug of Dad's whisky! Poor girl, Pauline. What parents! She should be over here in a couple of hours. What did you think of her parents?'

I gazed at the genuine Impressionist paintings upon his father's walls.

'Not much,' I said. 'Fairly typical of their class. Mr Paul Naseby is obviously a moderately prosperous man of business . . .'

'Oil. But I wish he wouldn't wear a brown suit. He's the

sort of wanker who picks up the phone and says: "*Mr* Naseby speaking."' I laughed. 'And what did you think of Mrs Gillian Naseby?'

'Quite an attractive and witty middle-aged woman...'

'Yes, she is, God damn her. Go on.'

'Twinset and pearls brigade. Has her husband round her little finger and under her thumb with a lock on his cock.'

'Exactly. And she wants her daughter Pauline to be her clone. Go to the tennis club and marry some chinless wonder like Paul Naseby. Well, it won't happen! Not as long as I have anything to do with it. Gillian Naseby is *evil*!' he exclaimed vehemently. 'Look at this photograph! Tell me what you see. *Exactly* what you see...'

'Well, Edward, I see a sofa of mauve velvet and there are two women sitting upon it. Judging by their facial features, it is a mother with her daughter. Mrs Gillian Naseby is wearing a navy blue twinset and pearls, the skirt being pleated at knee-length, pulled up slightly so as to expose her neatly turned calves and ankles which taper into a pair of shining black leather shoes with high heels. Her blond hair has been crimped into a permanent wave and above her blue eyes there are lids with cobalt-blue shadow. As for her daughter... bloody hell! Her daughter Pauline looks pretty much the same, only twenty years younger.'

'Quite,' said Edward. 'Wasn't it Oscar Wilde who said: "All women become like their mothers. That is their tragedy"?'

'Yes,' I replied, 'and he added: "No man becomes like his. That is his tragedy." '

Shortly after that meeting, we left school to pursue our varied destinies, University in my case and Art College for Edward, though we continued to meet for a drink occasionally. On one such occasion, at the Princess Louise in Holborn, he startled me with his news, producing a photograph of a young girl with spiky purple hair, dressed entirely in black leather.

'Guess who!' he demanded, drinking from a bottle of Mexican beer with a slice of lime at the top.

'I have no idea.'

'That's Pauline, you idiot!'

'What?!' She was unrecognizable.

'Yes, of course.'

'She has a tattoo on each arm.'

'Yeah; you see the nature of my benevolent influence? Instead of going to the tennis club and marrying some suburban dimwitted chinless wonder, she is now at the University of North London and fucking some leading rock star.'

'Not you?'

'No.' He looked perfectly contented. 'I'm fucking other people and so is she. We're just good friends these days: and she is grateful for the fact that I opened her eyes, got her to see something more in life.'

'Mrs Gillian Naseby must just love you for that.'

'Oh,' he laughed, 'she loves me to death. Recently I happened to bump into her in Liberty's. It was wonderful seeing her lipsticked mouth so tightly screwed up and her eyes blazing sheer hatred at me . . . ha! ha! "I will *never* forgive you!" She *spat* the words. "You will *never* forget me." Doesn't matter at all any more. I heard from Pauline that the stupid bitch is dead now. Heart attack.'

This brings me forward to the occasion after Edward's commercial triumph when he admitted me to his studio and showed me what he called his *real* Art. Canvas after canvas was stacked against the walls of a bare room that stank of paint, linseed oil and turpentine. He showed me the first painting.

This was done in the earlier style that I recalled, painted with a degree of photorealism and quite exquisitely well-crafted.

It showed a suburban street that I recognized as being in Victorian Chiswick at sunset with a light sprinkling of rain. There were lights in some of the windows. The only human figure was a silhouette of a woman with a fine figure laying down cutlery for what appeared to be an impending dinner party.

The second painting displayed a dinner party, the window giving one a view of a Chiswick side street at night and I recalled the scene well. A mild Paul Naseby was pouring out Spanish Burgundy into the guests' glasses as he turned the label of the bottle away from the viewer. Janine and I were looking at one another with eyes of lust. Pauline was looking longingly at Edward who was regarding Gillian Naseby with disdain as he held up a cigar cutter and she was quite white with icy fury as she glared at him.

The third painting showed Paul Naseby kneeling at his wife's feet to kiss her high-heeled shoes. His credit cards lay spilled over the floor. She reclined upon a mauve couch and on the wall behind it there was a painting of Edward fucking Pauline. Gillian Naseby's eyes were red with anger.

The fourth picture showed these same eyes as Mrs Gillian Naseby stood glaring in a department store, wearing, as in every previous painting, a navy blue twinset and pearls, with a pleated skirt. Behind her, there was a painting of her purple-haired, leather-clad daughter.

The fifth painting displayed a gravestone with the legend: MRS GILLIAN NASEBY: 1934–1994. R.I.P. There was a pale yellow waxing moon in the ultramarine sky and above the grave there was a delicate outline of Gillian Naseby.

She was the theme of every subsequent painting. I saw Impressionistic versions of Gillian Naseby, Cubist versions of Gillian Naseby and abstract versions of Gillian Naseby. In a Dada version of Gillian Naseby a bottle of Coca-Cola had been shoved through her smirking mouth. A Fifties-style photorealist painting had her standing on a railway station platform with a steam engine in the distance, with her husband on all fours and secured by a dog collar and lead. A picture in the Pop Art style had her saying: 'Where are you now, Superman?' as the costumed hero grovelled at her feet.

'Edward . . .' I said, 'ah, yes, thank you, I could do with another brandy . . . don't you think that, exquisitely well-crafted though this is, you might perhaps be allowing yourself to indulge in a slightly unhealthy obsession?' I coughed helplessly. 'I mean, I think I get the picture.'

'You're dead right,' he answered. 'Ever since that wretched bitch died, I haven't been able to escape her. She visits me in my dreams, she visits me in my fantasies, I can't paint without her. I mean, I'm just an artist and you know these matters better than I do. Is she a ghost? Then what is a ghost? Is she a vampire? Then what is a vampire? I just don't seem able to paint any other figure. I recall that she used to read books about Alchemy and Vampirism, which is unusual for a suburban housewife, even a bored one. I am no coward but, actually, I *am* scared. You wouldn't like to spend the night here, would you? I have a spare bedroom.'

'I'd be quite happy to do that, Edward. Remind me. You told me one time. When did your mother die?'

'Coffee?'

'Please.' He vanished into the kitchen.

'Damn! I forgot to buy milk. Never mind,' he sighed wearily. 'I'll go and get some. It's only five minutes walk up the road . . .'

'Edward, you're tired,' I said. 'But it's been a good day for you. Leave it to me.'

'Oh, thanks awfully. That's jolly kind. Just leave the door on the latch.'

Edward had never been especially adroit when it came to practicalities and so his directions to the nearest late-night grocery store proved to be quite hopeless. Everyone I asked pointed me in the wrong direction. The fact that I kept thinking about his paintings hardly assisted my endeavours at navigation. Here was a man earning a fortune for his trivial tosh whilst applying his extraordinary craftsmanship to portray a private obsession; and one which evidently frightened him. Eventually I found a store where I bought cream as well as milk and navigated my way back to his flat, determined to discover more.

There was nobody in the living room when I re-entered. Perhaps he was in the loo.

'Edward!' I called out. There was no reply. *'Edward!!'* No, he wasn't in the loo. The door to his bedroom was closed and so I knocked three times before entering. Then I froze.

Mrs Gillian Naseby was sitting in a straight-backed chair and staring into the mirror that adorned her walk-in wardrobe, and she appeared to be in a state of bliss. She was wearing a navy blue twinset with black pearls and the pleats of her skirt were fluttering lightly as the wind wafted in from an open window. A camera positioned in the left-hand corner of the bedroom had taken a polaroid photograph, controlled by the mechanism she held in her right hand. She sat still.

I gasped in horror as I discerned that someone had scratched her eyes out and that there were teeth marks upon her throat.

No, on further fearful inspection, it wasn't Mrs Gillian Naseby who had died of a heart attack, for I researched the matter.

As the certificates concerning illegitimate children and abandoned orphans later showed me, Edward Exmond had gone to meet his mother.

'Very interesting,' Stride said as he soaped himself. 'I admire your literary talent. If you want me to admit that your tales as Septimus Keen are better than mine, I'm quite contented to do so. I just wish you'd take these bloody chains away!' They clanked against the sides of the bathtub.

'I may be able to assist you . . .' The one whom Stride had known as 'Antonina' and whom he now knew as 'Septimus Keen' approached his naked body in the bath and grasped the manacle upon his right wrist. 'I'll see what I can do.' By the time the hypodermic needle had been slid into his vein, it was really too late to do anything.

CHAPTER SEVENTEEN

IMPS IN INFINITY

Adam Stride awoke with a throbbing headache to find himself in a new environment. He was now chained by his wrists and ankles to the stout oaken limbs of a four-poster bed, and although a sheet and blankets covered him he was naked beneath these coverings. There was a pint glass of water on the bedside table beside him and from it protruded a tube that reached his mouth. He sucked in some water greedily and gratefully, then considered his surroundings.

The wall directly before him was lined with leather-bound books. Among them were volumes by William Butler Yeats, Oscar Wilde, Ernest Dowson, Arthur Machen, Aleister Crowley, Bram Stoker and other notable figures of the 1890s Decadence movement. A paperback book had been carelessly – or carefully – dumped in front of this collection. It was *The Labyrinth of Satan* by Adam Stride.

The wall to his left was decorated by paintings, etchings and engravings. The wallpaper had evidently been designed either by William Morris or by some competent imitator. He could see works by Doré, Aubrey Beardsley, Austin Osman Spare, Alistair and others unknown to him. All stressed the same theme: the interchangeability of gender.

Stride looked to his right. There was an octagonal granite altar upon which reposed a statuette of the twin-sexed Baphomet, the goat god. Stride was familiar with the figure. The Knights Templar had been accused of worshipping this idol during the Middle Ages. In the nineteenth century, when writing his *Ritual and Dogma of High Magic*, the fabled French occultist Eliphas Levi had stated that all occultists adore the wisdom that is contained in this 'frightful' symbol. In the twentieth century Aleister Crowley, excoriated as 'the wickedest man in the world', had taken Baphomet as his name when he became Head of the Ordo Templi Orientis, a group that practised Sex Magick. In front of the idol, eight black candles blazed, all placed in candelabra fashioned in the form of writhing serpents. There was a window behind Baphomet – no, there wasn't. It was a looking glass.

Stride remained grateful that he was no longer being tormented by continuous reflections of himself. After an indeterminate time, a door opened and a man entered, radiating benevolence and serenity from the crown of his bald head to the soles of his immaculately polished black leather shoes. His left hand carried a glass of port and he smiled pleasantly as he sat down in an armchair opposite his captive.

'How are you, Mr Stride?' he enquired.

'Don't tell me . . .' Stride sighed wearily. 'It's Dr Lipsius.'

'How perceptive you are. Yes, that is one of the many names I use.'

'What is the point of all this?'

'My dear fellow,' Lipsius shrugged, 'what is the point of anything? Hedonism, perhaps, eh? Hm? Or possibly the pursuit of knowledge? Anyway, I do feel,' the thin, dry voice continued, 'that I owe you some form of explanation and apology.'

'I am always grateful for small mercies.'

'Come, come, sir. Don't be unduly cynical. I don't intend to have you killed. Just one more – ah – operation and you will be free as a bird. Forget about going to the police. They will only arrest you for the murder of Rosa Scarlett; and it won't be any use blabbering on about us since they will never believe you. And in any case, we shall by that time have vanished, remaining as elusive and intangible as an early morning mist upon the moors, having assumed new identities. Curious matter, isn't it, identity? Eh? Hm?'

'It appears,' said Stride, 'that I am your captive audience.'

'Oh, indeed, my dear sir. You are one of the most endearing zoological specimens that I have ever captured. You are a dedicated rationalist, fascinated by the lure of the unknown. Of course there is a factor infinite and unknown in every equation. Why, sir, only recently, scientists demonstrated that *one* atom can be in *two* spaces simultaneously. Does that not remind you of the Black Pearl within the Ankh, of your glimpses of Arthur Machen one hundred years before? And both of you wrote truths way beyond your conscious ken. Yes, there *is* a Black Lodge dedicated to pleasure, our own ecstasy and often the agony of other human beings.'

'What are you?' Stride demanded. 'Aliens?'

'Oh, that's irrelevant.' Lipsius dismissed the question with an airy wave of his pudgy hand. 'Let's not go into questions of whether we have the elixir of Life or not. It is perfectly possible that when one of us goes, another carefully chosen candidate takes his or her place. In our ways we love to live out many identities. Perhaps our leading expert, our leading star, you might almost say, is Septimus Keen. It is certainly curious that you somehow discerned his presence in your *The Labyrinth of Satan* and then came to know her under the name of Antonina.

'We engage in all manner of activities,' Lipsius continued easily. 'No one knows who we really are. We observe the behaviour of humanity and relish the human comedy – and tragedy – whilst so doing. One of our activities consists of collecting curious and unusual objects such as the Ankh of the Black Pearl. Now tell me, Mr Stride, you held that object in your hands. Roughly one hundred years ago, Arthur Machen held the same object in his hands. By your account, you saw him. By his account, he saw you. What does this phenomenon make of conventional notions of Time? You were both in London, albeit in slightly different spaces, yet connecting at particular times. Certain objects contain within themselves the power to bring about a confluence, a perichoresis, an interpenetration, eh? Hm?'

'Is this the customary lecture you give to a man before you kill him?' Stride enquired.

'Mr Stride, how many times do I have to tell you that we are *not* going to kill you? I merely wish to make matters more clear for you. You see, in our group, we adore Theatre. Yes, Theatre Arts. Is there a greater stage for Theatre Arts than London? We gain great satisfaction from creating a drama and playing it out within this wondrous, great city, in which we become what we are not, realize our own fantasies, make the fantasies of our victims come true and view a finer play than anything that could ever be presented in the limited space of a theatre.' Lipsius finished his port and drew the curtains on Stride's four-poster bed.

'Now the curtain comes down on this little drama, Adam,' he said. 'The "hero" will not be rescued at the last minute.' He produced a syringe from his pocket with indecent glee. 'I have worked for over twenty years to develop this serum. I have every confidence that it will work.' A door opened behind him. 'Don't worry, Mr Stride, you're not going to die. It will merely be a form of reincarnation. Scalpel, nurse,' he added.

CHAPTER EIGHTEEN

CARE IN THE COMMUNITY

P earl Black, who was blond, pretty, petite and aged twenty-four, was very pleased to have landed a job after six months of unemployment. She had qualified as a State Registered Nurse and had originally had great expectations. But a year with the NHS had left her so grossly disillusioned that she had been unable to bear it any longer. She had disliked being on the dole, though at least she had not had to work an eighty-hour week and in financial terms, given her rent, she had only been twenty pounds a week worse off. Finally, though, the agency with which she had registered had found her a job that was the answer to all her prayers.

It would be her job to live and work with a middle-aged woman in Vauxhall. Pearl Black knew nothing about Vauxhall other than that it was just south of the river, with a Victoria Line Underground station and a big supermarket. It was one of those anonymous areas of London that seem to have neither history nor reputation.

At two hundred and fifty pounds a week plus free accommodation and no utility bills, the deal was better than anything she could have expected. Although she was not a qualified psychiatric nurse, mental health had always been one of her interests. She had no objection to a condition of the job that required her to write a weekly report on the condition of the patient, who was apparently sustained by a modest private income from a family trust, and deliver this to the agency.

The problem, it appeared, was amnesia, brought on by a severe overdose of drugs that had led to a car crash. Fortunately, the patient had not been in any way physically impaired. She just had absolutely no idea who she was.

Pearl found her to be quite an attractive middle-aged woman with a pleasant manner, although very disorientated.

'Where am I? Who am I?' she kept repeating as she wandered about her comfortable modern flat with its two bedrooms in a redbrick box-like 1950s building. Her family appeared to have abandoned her altogether save for the payment of bills. No friends visited.

Pearl had occasionally dealt with mental patients before and had been given all the relevant data. The lady came from a moderately prosperous family although both her parents had died some years ago. She had attended the City of London School for Girls, achieving five O levels and one A level. She had never married. Such work as she had done consisted of assisting in second-hand bookshops, rather as though she had preferred a solitary and scholarly life, an assessment confirmed by the wall of bookshelves housing leather-bound volumes with a particular emphasis upon the literature of the 1890s.

On her second day at work, Pearl noticed that her patient was reading a paperback entitled *The Labyrinth of Satan* by one Adam Stride. This startled her somewhat since she had been reading a sensational story in *The Sun* about Adam Stride the author. Apparently he had also been a private detective, one who had enjoyed excellent relations with the police. Then one day, for no apparent reason, he had taken an axe and chopped off the head of his assistant of seven years, Ms Rosa Scarlett, in a particularly grisly act of murder, since he had then stuck her head on a sharpened pole and vanished off the face of the Earth. The Nurse decided to draw this story to the patient's attention, noticing that the photograph of Adam Stride bore an uncanny resemblance to the woman in her care, then dismissing the thought as ludicrous, a mere coincidence such as occurs all the time in Life.

'Oh . . .' said the woman, with *some* gleam of remembrance flickering in her eyes. 'I used to know Adam Stride. Pleasant fellow. And he did *this*? Who would have thought it?'

Pearl Black felt that she was making some progress with her patient, Septima Keen.